escapology

also by ren warom
and available from titan books

Virology (June 2017)

escapology

ren warom

TITAN BOOKS

escapology
Mass market edition ISBN: 9781785650932
Print edition ISBN: 9781785650918
E-book edition ISBN: 9781785650925

Published by Titan Books
A division of Titan Publishing Group Ltd
144 Southwark Street, London SE1 0UP

First mass market edition: May 2017
1 3 5 7 9 10 8 6 4 2

A CIP catalogue record for this title is available
from the British Library.

Printed and bound in the United States

For Jacqui—who drank with the Blue Monkey God
and laughed and loved life.

part one

the story of a shocking boy

Curled up against the window like a squashed bug, Shock squints down at the tops of rain-swollen clouds, the plunging cliff-side drops of the 'scrapers, and half imagines he might be dying.

The mono speeds up, merging clouds and 'scrapers to silvery grey smears. It looks like the world is melting, an ugly dream swilling like full-body nausea just under his uncertain flesh. He's never been in Slip as long as that before and never will again. It's made him unsure of everything, thinned reality out to an untrustworthy husk.

He can't find his focus, his physicality. Keeps wondering why the fuck he has legs and can't swim. What this meat sack is with its tight skin and ever-present grind of hunger in the goddamn fuel tank. Can barely think, his brain swilling like half-liquefied tofu in a bone box.

Can't work out, in fact, what he's doing in this sardine-crush mono on the way to Plaza of all places. He has a bed calling him, probably musty by now but still warmer than this, dryer at the very least. A baggie with two bumps left hidden under the pillow he's pretty much been jonesing for.

So what the fuck is this?

The mono slows, approaching lower Plaza. He thinks he'll stay on for the round trip, back to where he started, but then he gets up, driven by impulses he's not yet making sense of. Too scared to take the shoot in case it pulverizes what's left of his brain, he careens down flights of stairs, fingers gripping the rails spasmodically, convinced the ground will disappear, or he will, or both.

Drops off the last into the usual Plaza crowd and allows himself to be carried, bound by a straitjacket of bodies streaming toward the high end. Tries again to riddle out why he's come here of all places, but only two thoughts wriggle through the tofu mass toward comprehension.

First, the commitment to hunting down and bitch-slapping the little POS in Risi who fed him this giant cosmic shafting. Ten neurone-frying days jacked into Slip writing virads for fuck's sake. Outrageous. Frankly uncalled for. What was that punk's name? Reg? Ralph? Rudy? *Arsehole*.

Second, coming off the back of this road-kill feeling and the lack of those pillow-hidden bumps, is the cell-deep need to find a little chemical relief for his ills. He's going to hate himself for this in a week's time, but only because he'll need more and he won't have enough flim to eat, let alone calm his head.

Tracking into a line of liver-whore salarymen half-cut on synth-saki, he manoeuvres by degrees over to a grubby little coffee stall with dimly lit back seating known as Ducky's. Ducky Took runs the joint; a sleazy, skinny little Euro, claims to be Irish but talks like wharf-jocks, all dropped aitches and hard consonants, ready to punch your tongue out. If he's anything near Irish, Shock's a fucking Scandawhoov.

"Yo, Duckster," he croaks out as he swings in, clinging to the cracked plastic of the counter like grim death. "Got any bumps? I'm screwed from ten days in the swim."

Ducky struts out from in back, pipe-cleaner legs shucked in skin-tight denim, old school, and sweat-soaked wife-beater hugging his bird-bone chest. He's got swagger all right, but no meat to back it up. He sniffs, wiping snot off on the back of one thin, hairy forearm; it glistens in the lights, snail-trailed next to several the same.

Ducky whistles. "You in the swim? How the mighty 'ave fallen, aye? Fought you was a gonner, I did. Like them other Haunts."

"What other Haunts?"

"Ones gone AWOL."

Shock tries to parse what the hell Ducky might be saying. Fails miserably.

"What?"

"Yeah, got some Haunts gone bye-bye. Signal dead an' all that."

"Ducky, Haunts don't *have* a fucking signal, that's why we're Haunts."

Shrugging, Ducky picks his nose. Grumbles, "Jus' what I 'eard, innit. No need to split 'airs."

"Whatever. Have you got bumps or fucking not?"

"Might 'ave. Yuh got flim?"

"Just got off ten days, Ducks. I have flim."

Ducky nods. "Then I've got me some scrams and a few baggies of skippers. Wot's yuh poison?"

Shock screws up his face. He doesn't like the S-series. Whoever synthed that shit got their quantities cracked. S high starts ugly, like drowning in syrup, and thins out to something too close to normal. But the nearest dealer to Ducky's is about a mile further down the Plaza and Shock won't make it, can already feel withdrawal seeping into the matter of his cells like rot. He leaves it any longer he's gonna be scooped out hollow and fold to the floor like an empty suit, carrion for the crows of Plaza to pick clean. In other words, choice is a city hub in high orbit, way beyond his reach.

"Gimmie a dozen scrams."

Ducky goes out back, returns dangling a baggy in filthy fingers. Handing over a stack of flim, Shock tries not to think about those fingers bagging up his S; it'll make him hurl whatever poor-excuse-for-food synth he was tube-fed for the last ten days, and keeping things down is a priority of his.

It takes forever to open the baggy, the meat jacket still refusing signals from the tofu brain, but he finally peels the plastic lips apart and shakes out two. Presses them hard into the skin of his neck until they pop, leaving as always a gross taste in the back of the throat.

Totally worth it.

Veins of cold steal in on the back of that foul taste, carrying relief to tired matter, beginning the inexorable slide from dead cells to cellular fireworks. Saluting Ducky he pushes off from the counter and stumbles out onto Plaza, tucking the baggie next to his flim.

As the buzz hits, Plaza lights become stars bleeding to mildew stains on a rotten canvas. The street stretches, sags, melting into heavy folds. Muting sound. Diffusing movement to a glutinous crawl. Shops ooze around him, droning out noise that only a moment ago was the frantic beat of dub-tech, the chitinous whir of machinery, the jabber of voices ramped to eleven.

And he's swimming again, legs treading water, arms fanned like fins. He grins, some sort of sloppy bastard brother to a smile, and rolls off down to wherever it was he was headed. Should check his IMs, but can't figure out where his brain is any more at all. Bliss.

The crowd trickles past as he floats through, unable to

strike the lunatic smile from his face. It's stuck on with S—sticky psych glue. He waits it out, jaw aching, like it's a shuttle on the mono, until the glutinous drag fades from his bones, his brain, and leaves him clearer, a little awake, verging on aware.

The trickle transfers from crowd to cheeks, a physical/perception shift inexplicable without experience of S, and allows his smile to drool away. He lifts hands heavy as orbiting moons and scrubs at his face, anticipating the ticklish needles that follow the numb and trying to rub them away before they set in. It's useless, but he does it every time.

His IM blips at him, loud as a thunderclap in the skull. Too loud, like his brain's achieved self-awareness and rebelled by throwing the vol-switch on his drive to max. Halfway through seriously considering this as a possible version of reality he finally clicks to the fact that it's been doing the same damn thing for about two minutes, gradually getting louder. Something he programmed in to make sure he got calls about work even when he's so borked on bumps his head might as well be a meat popsicle.

"Oh screw you, past me," he mutters, accessing his neural drive.

Where the fuck are you, Shocking boy? Mimic, tart as a pickle. Her voice provokes instant intestinal distress.

"Shit."

He'd forgotten all about Mim. She hit him up the second he broke surface for air, so to speak, with a job offer he could have done with ten days ago, before being forced to resort to trusting Ronnie. Rick? Or was it Rita? He *will* remember.

He'd love to tell Mim no, interacting with her in any way being so much like oil choosing to co-mingle with water it's ridiculous, but she's his only remaining decent meal ticket; a fact that makes him want to smash his face into the sidewalk or something.

He cannot believe this is his life. It can't be.

Six months ago, he was sure it would go differently. He Failed his Psych Eval, smiling the whole time. Walked out of that room without a backward glance, practically waving both middle fingers. Didn't want the life of a Pass, no thank you, he had a whole different career progression in mind; a way back to Sendai District, his holy fucking grail.

He jumped straight into high-level, mui, mui illegal jobs with payoffs that make the wad in his jacket look a goddamn joke. Had every reason to believe himself a shoe-in for the top echelons of Fail society, the kind of flim that makes Sendai a given. Only it's all gone horribly pear-shaped. Or rather Mim-shaped.

They used to be a thing. Or at least he thought they were, until she put him into a situation that helped him understand how mistaken he'd been. Thanks to her, his career took a swan dive, and he currently holds the dubious honour of being a walking corpse in the eyes of three of the Gung's significant players. Only one of those hanging death sentences is directly her fault, but as a beginning of the end goes it was a doozy, setting the scene for all the rest, and he feels entitled to a certain visceral dislike. So why does he still work with her? Simple mathematics. Before Mim, Shock was alone.

She's all he's got.

Having zero friends is fine when you're coasting on glory, not so fine when all that goes away and you need help. These past months, chasing basic survival, he's slid right down the Fail food chain to the slime at the bottom of the pond. Been dicked on flim, moved from shitty apartment, to shittier, to cage in an attempt to stay off the streets, and escaped brain-locked servitude by the skin of his teeth at one particularly dodgy job—bad luck following bad.

Basically put, he's experienced the steep learning curve he initially avoided, the curve most other Fails walk after those red letters flash up, condemning them to self-subsistence in a world that does its level best to make such magic as difficult as possible. You have to be special, a J-Hack, or affiliated to a crime lord, and if you're not one of those then you're meat. That's what Shock is now. Meat. And he's a Haunt. Top 0.5 % too. In other words, very fucking special.

He stumbles headlong into a tight-knit group of salarymen, who jeer and shout him away, reeling down rain-smeared concrete. Yeah. Look at how special he is, still so screwed from the virad job he can hardly put one foot in front of the other.

His drive blips again.

Do I numb my arse for a no-show or what?

Shock groans, the truly repugnant gut-warping anxiety of hearing Mim's voice is worse than waking in a Slip-sling, naked and bristling with grubby tubes too wide for the orifices they're crammed in to. He wants to do anything except turn up, but there's that thing about choice and city hubs in orbit. Pulling his jacket tight, Shock turns unsteadily toward the top end of Plaza, the world spinning around his queasy skull like cartoon bluebirds.

There are many places to party on Foon Gung's claustrophobic sprawl but Plaza's the only one bright enough to be seen from the hubs, the cities smugly orbiting the boundary to endless space. Plaza's high-end is a migraine-provoking frenzy; a gaudy parade of VIP clubs, Slip joints, art houses and karaoke bars. Despite the money practically oozing from the cracks in the sidewalk these multifarious amusements look cheap stacked side by side and swaddled in neon and fairy lights spangled as a K-rock star's thong.

This scene is as far from Shock's idea of a good time as it's possible to get, but he's not surprised Mim's blipped to meet him here. She's a freaking magpie, and always out for maximum flim expenditure. Doubtless she's not numbing her arse much, probably got a gaggle of lanky Biz-Cad creeps orbiting her horizons, dazzled by the glare of her headlights.

Reluctantly jacking her IM, Shock hooks her signal, tracing it to one of the cheesiest karaoke joints on Plaza: Keen Machine.

"Fucking jim goddamn dandy," he sneers, shielding his eyes from the high-intensity blast of illumination that comprizes the entrance.

Concentrating hard to remain steady on his feet, he rolls in past the muscle, a gaggle of uber-pumped gorks in suits, their necks so thick they look like truncated thighs, and heads for the bar. There's a skinny little short-arse with neon fangs serving the whole thirty meters of polished copper by herself, clacking to and fro on knife-blade heels and snarling at everyone as she juggles glasses and snatches flim.

All out of sympathy, his head still basically tofu beneath the straggly S bump-sheen and Mim-xiety, he orders an apple juice, no ice, with two shots of pure green caffeine for himself and a voddie lime slim for Mim and skulks off to hunt her down in the shadowy recesses.

Predictably, he finds her holding court amongst a gaggle of wide-eyed Frat boys from the Biz-Cad, a different shade of learning than the academies, for hI-Qs and the wealthy. These are the latter, all spending daddy's money and trying to look smart in clothes so new they still smell of the print factory; a clean, sharp scent not unlike bleach.

Mim's in her usual uniform, a bodysuit fitted close as second skin in holographic material, blending her into the corner like a mirage; the only signs of her existence an inky mass of iridescent black hair and those crazy mirrored eyes. Mim's a chameleon—you can't see her, only her surroundings and yourself, reflected back at you into infinity.

That's Mim's problem. She lives her role. 24/7 365 in Imp-mode. Consequently she's only ever been any use as a reflection. Expecting to find a person somewhere in those vague distorted echoes is a sure-fire route to ending up disappointed. At least he did. Disappointed and sick to the core, his heart aching, just like it is now. He only has to look at her to feel wrecked. She's a wall he keeps crashing into.

He still remembers the first time he saw her. In Tech. She'd transferred in from Cad after a Tech-skills test, was perched like a crow in the window of his lecture hall on the seventeenth floor, smoking a long, purple cigarette. Psy. Illegal as hell. She wore a flimsy, red-plastic playsuit and shades, had her feet rammed into matching bladers, stack-heel shoes with a mag-strip for speeding along mono lines, and he fell for her catastrophically.

Her distant grin and cold mirror eyes gave him shivers he mistook for attraction, and that off-hand way she has drove him out of his mind, full-on crazy as a primo high. He took to following her like a shadow, hanging in her wake, nebulous as a cloud of smoke and half as noticeable. Sometimes he thinks she only noticed him by accident, out of the corner of her eye, like seeing a ghost. Appropriate. It makes him laugh nowadays. But only now and then.

It took him a year to persuade her to fuck him, another for her to scheme a way to get rid of him. By that time they'd moved in together and everyone spoke their name in one long breathless mouthful, like they were conjoined twins in a freak show. What a fucking waste of two years, and he doesn't plead the stupidity of youth about any of it. He's forgotten how to be that kind to himself.

Unable to muster up a shout, Shock stands at her table and stares, waiting until she notices him, trying to ignore how much like the old days it is. This is his choice, not hers—and it's all business. There's nothing personal in it. When she clocks him, her headlights flare, and she throws down a serious grin, like a challenge.

"Shocking boy, long time no spy." She makes shooing gestures with tiny hands tipped with nails like talons. She-bird. Bird of prey. "Skeddadle, dickheads, my boy is here. We have business."

"I'm not your boy," he says with infinitely more calm than he feels, sliding in beside her and slamming her drink down next to a half-empty flute of what looks like liquid purple glitter and smells bad as candy-coated burnt rubber. "What's the job?"

"What, no time to reminisce?"

She tries for a hurt tone, but it falls light years short. Sounds like she's asking a bug she's got under a magnifying glass if the sun burns yet. The fact she still gets to him as easily as when he thought they were a going concern makes him despise her even more. Or maybe he just despises himself?

He should quit the habit of her. Quit this vicious cycle, a viscous cycle, clinging to him like she still does, out of convenience, and he lets her. More fool him. He takes a deep breath, feeling like he's sucking the whole club down into his lungs.

"Job, Mim, or I'm out."

Her teeth flash, blinding, making him dizzy.

"Tetchy," she drawls, and he knows that she's feeling his discomfort and loving it. Fuck but he hates her. "I need a bullseye, close as dammit to my stats as you can hit. Two K flim."

Mim is an ID sniper, an info clone, an Imp. She hunts, copies, and temporarily replaces for the purposes of theft. Pretty good at hacking bullseyes on a basic level, Mim's proficiency dive-bombs to below useless with any kind of VA, Virtual Armament.

Her current fuck, Johnny Sez, an L-plates hack, can only crack up to level 6. For anything above that, she has Shock, her reluctant hacker on call. It's a crap job, and far too intermittent, but it's flim and really he's in no position to be picky. He wishes he were. Whenever he works for Mim, she always wants delivery in person. Maximising his discomfort is one of her favourite pastimes.

"I need the company you expect me to phish in before I Y or N."

"Olbax Corp."

Olbax. Great. Could be worse though. Could be Paraderm.

"That's a pretty mean amount of VA for Two K. Two K barely even covers my fucking rent."

"Take it or leave it, sport. Not running a charity here. Or maybe you don't think you need it?" She gives him the sly look, up and down. "I'm guessing that's why you're looking so swell. Corpse-chic suits you."

Shock tries not to react, it costs him way too much dignity and temporary control of an eyelid.

"Fine."

She reaches out and pats his hand.

"Good Shocking Boy. Info in your IM as we speak."

Sliding out of the booth, the back of his hand tingling like it's been stung, he makes for the Risi District and enough alcohol to drown a land ship the size of the Gung. Maybe this time it'll be enough to drown out the ugly mix of hate and need he gets from too close proximity to her.

He makes a concerted effort to forget about the job before he's even halfway there. At some point his IM will blip and Mim will squeak a reminder. Until then, fuck her, fuck everything. All he wants to do is drown.

ask me why i do
this again

Cleaners should never have to run, they stalk and sneak and snatch their prey when least expected; anything else constitutes a heinous insult to their skills. Ducking under the corner of a brightly striped awning, Amiga slams through the crowd in pursuit of the wiry, wired-up Streek who until about thirty seconds ago had no clue about her presence at his back.

Goddamn kimchi merchant chose literally the worst moment ever to howl in her ear: "*Beautiful Kimchi, just like halmeoni makes it—super cheap!*" Before she had time to put a dart through that loudmouth's neck, her target had turned, spotted her and was away like a streak—haha—of piss.

If she didn't fucking adore kimchi she'd boycott it from her diet to make a point. Maybe she'll go back to the market and buy from the seller three stalls down. Yeah. That'll feel *good*. Probably a better option than killing the guy who busted her, and definitely less harmful to her karma. Although if it's karma she's got to be worried about then she's already royally screwed.

Bursting out from between the last row of stalls in the market place, she finds herself in the middle of a tight-knit group of Hindi ladies in jewel-bright saris. They shriek, slap at her like she's a bug. With their multitudes of rings, it's like being pelted with tiny, stinging stones. No, this is not at all humiliating.

"Ow, come *on*!"

Charging out of their reach and down the street, she spots the skinny little shitbag clambering up a fire escape along another alley to her left.

"Fast," she murmurs, half impressed, and sets off after him, sweating like a five-hundred-pound rikishi in a sauna. This jumpsuit works for blading, especially way up on the mono where it gets super cold, but it does not work for a frantic pursuit down tiny, stinking over-crowded alleys, and up ramshackle fire escapes. At least she changed out of her bladers. Small mercies.

Amiga reaches the top in time to witness his wild leap to the next roof. As he lands, the skinny little shitbag looks back and has the audacity to laugh. Unsurprising. Streeks are fucking crazy, and usually fucked up. They're Cad students, socially engineered within a stifling constriction of class schedules, minimal flim, and claustrophobic Pod hotels for maximum lunacy in order to thin the herd before graduation.

Around seventy percent of these fuckers don't live to sit their Psych Eval—all the better to keep the competition for Corp roles to a manageable minimum. Doesn't mean she's not going to beat that smile off his idiotic rat face when she catches him, but it adds a certain pathos to the situation.

He laughs again as he takes off sprinting across the roof, that crazed Streek cackle, and an aggressive need to pop a dart in his idiotic skull wrestles its way into her fingers. Growling, she backs up and takes a running leap, digging for self control. Popping his head like a pus-filled cyst would be satisfying in the short term, but she's on strict instructions. Her delightfully violent and unforgiving boss, Twist, wants this little fucker alive. Failure to meet this condition would mean a very swift change of conditions for her. The Cleaner would be Cleaned. Thoroughly. Twist always makes a particular example of favourites.

And there's a thought she very much wishes not to be having.

She follows her irritating target around the corner of a cooling unit and runs headlong into an unexpected reason for his reckless amusement. Streeks. About a dozen of them. She slides to a halt, considering. They smile at her. Like vultures with mouths and teeth. Thing is, she's not carrion. She is in fact the very furthest thing from that, and this is the single advantage of being Twist's favourite. Amiga smiles back.

"I don't want to spoil your fun," she says gently. "All I'm here for is that little rat." She points at said rat. "No one else has to get hurt today."

Giggling, the Streeks fan out. Of course they're not going to listen. Of course they want to play. Why wouldn't they? This is what they're made to do. So be it. They can see what she's made to do. Amiga relaxes. Taking that as a cue, they come at her hooting and cackling, switchblades and shoge flicking into their hands, into the air.

Amiga breathes in deep as the first one nears, spinning his shoge a trifle wide but with definite skill. Stepping under the chain, she slams her palm into his face, full force. His head flies back, a high spray of blood rising above it, bright as a mohican.

Snatching the front of his jacket to hold him steady, she scoops his arm into hers and spins him, applying pressure until the joint pops out. He screams, cut off to gurgles as she plucks the shoge from limp fingers and slits his throat.

Stunned by her speed, too stoned to react with anything like the same, the others howl at her. But she's calm, ready, spinning the shoge in skilful arcs and already moving. Sends it whipping out into their flesh before they can find a response beyond rage, cutting gaping holes in arms and thighs, in the taut flesh of their bellies.

She's a quiet storm scything through them, blood spiralling around her like red snow. Bodies fall in swift succession until there are only two left standing: Amiga and the rat.

Market sounds drift up from below. Somewhere a pigeon coos softly. The rat's face is a study. Rage and terror. He keeps looking down, as if eyes alone can undo the wreckage of his crew. They look so vulnerable now, these walking statistics, no more than the sad fact of their numbers in a graph. The first lesson Amiga learnt when she started to kill was how easy it is, and how utterly horrifying that can be.

She tosses the shoge aside, feeling tired. She really wants to punch something hard, something that will hurt. Anything to shake the sensation of not quite being human.

"Are you going to come quietly now?" she asks.

He screeches, thrusts his face forward and laughs high and loud. Then legs it.

"Bollocks."

Lifting her arm, Amiga sends a dart from her wrist-bow through the back of his knee. Watches impassively as he collapses to the rooftop, clawing and screeching.

"Should have done that first and saved some energy," she says to herself, walking over to snatch him up by the scruff of the neck. She zip-ties his hands to his belt to stop him flailing at her like an angry toddler. "Man, I need a drink."

*

Hauling the rat down from the roof turns the puddles of sweat forming under her jumpsuit to a small lake. Comfy. Halfway down she IMs Twist, and he tells her to wait for a car. What choice does she have? It's not like she can drag this fucker through the streets.

Her mood falls from not amused to downright pissy. Back in the alley, which is both stenchy and freezing, they wait. Terrific. Her boss is being a pain in the arse lately, this business with Haunts stealing all his attention. Whatever it is he wants, he's ploughed through three of them already—literally, since they died in Slip—and he's still not satisfied. Other crime lords are beginning to notice, and it's making Twist act pretty damn weird.

Take that Haunt he'd sent her after, Shock Pao, idiot extraordinaire. Pao screwed him over and Twist wanted him creatively filleted. She was doing her level best to make that dream come true, despite catching a Haunt being hella high on the difficulty scale, then *bang*, Twist pulls the contract. Twist *never* pulls a contract. Out of character much.

The car takes an age to arrive, by which time Amiga's lost the feeling in her toes. Once inside the vehicle, the Streek starts up a horrible racket, so she knocks him out and settles back into the cool leather of the seat. Real leather, of course.

Traffic's terrible and in the endless void of time, the quiet broken only by the soft snoring of the rat and the purr of the engine, Amiga starts to think. Inevitable really, and always a mistake. By slow degrees thought becomes a mire, sucking her in until she's struggling to find air.

Those Streeks were so young. Younger than her, and she's not yet twenty-three. Now they're just empty bags of flesh and bone, leaking blood. Wasted potential. How does *she* justify being their ending?

It should be simple. Do your job. Killed or be killed. If she hadn't then sure, she would have died. But to her the equation is incomprehensible. Her or them? What kind of a trade-off is that? Her life is worthless. By extension, so is she. Or perhaps she was worthless to begin with and life had to run to catch up?

"Shit!" Amiga punches the seat, furious with herself, with the day, with that stupid kimchi merchant. This is not a good place to be. If she goes to Twist carrying all this fucking weak bullshit in her head, she might as well hand him a knife and expose her throat. Only she can't stop. Can't breathe. Can't shake this feeling she always gets, that it wasn't fair, wasn't honest—that the blood on her hands is beyond cleaning. That she's the sum of the stains and nothing more.

Reaching out with a shaking hand, she runs a finger down the glass of the car window. The screen reacts: fading the black through pale grey to clear glass, so she can see light, colour. They're on a main arterial road to the centre of the Gung, surrounded by other cars. Choked in.

Either side of the road 'scrapers rear their endless backs like giants, their shoulders swathed in cloud. Some of these are residential, their myriad tiny windows and slim, useless balconies draped with clotheslines and trailing plants, all tied into chicken wire. She remembers with a bitter twist of the stomach how as a child she'd fold back the wire and lean out, trying to find air.

Her baa-baa, Michiko, might be making maki, or perhaps steaming nikuman on their tiny two-ring stove, the warmth of the steam a familiar comfort. Above her head, on the sleeping platforms of their ten-foot-square family cage, her mother, Indira, and her aunties would be arguing over their sewing machines.

In the sound of their voices, in the steam, in her tiny crack of open window, counting ant-sized cars as they funnelled past below, Amiga could breathe. She'd wish those moments could last forever, because when they stopped, when Michiko took whatever she was cooking in a box to Amiga's father on the dock, Indira and the aunties would turn their vitriol on her. They wouldn't dare be cruel in front of her baa-baa.

Born eighteen years before the world broke, Michiko died at the grand age of 233, when Amiga was six. A hard woman, sharp of tongue and wit, any softness was reserved for her little Amiga-chan, her little dopperugengā. And she is. Amiga has a photo in her drive of Michiko as a young woman, back when Japan still existed. She's sat on a wall, dressed in torn jeans, loosely tied boots, a Mickey Mouse zombie tee and a baseball cap, sticking her tongue out.

They are mirror twins: piercing amber eyes, a pointed face, knife-straight black hair, too many sharp lines for beauty. A hard face to hide. Harder yet to live with. It reminds Amiga of how her mother never forgave her for being Michiko's favourite. But you can't choose who loves you. Or who doesn't.

The car turns, taking a ramp up into a huge 'scraper, to the car parks on the lower floors, their light made cold by reflection through narrow windows onto stark, white stone. Nothing built on this last scrap of solid land goes underground; everyone's too scared of what might happen.

Most who could recall the breaking of the world and its subsequent drowning are dead now, like Michiko, but the horror is a kind of race memory and there's not one soul on the Gung who'd dig into the earth for any reason. Not even to plant a flower. Look at the base of any building in the Gung erected after the breaking and you'll find them laid on plascrete, bound in to the earth. All the better to hold it together.

Shaking her rat awake, Amiga hustles him into the nearest shoot. She knows this building, knows exactly where Twist will be: the revolving restaurant near the top. It's his favourite place to eat. Amiga couldn't even afford the garnish on an entrée. Oh well. Probably tastes like crap anyway. In the shoot the rat starts giggling compulsively, so she gives him a slap. Shuts him up for maybe five seconds, then he starts again. Louder.

She leans toward him and says sweetly, "Shut up or I'll plug your mouth with your eyeballs."

The rest of the journey upward is silent.

They're met by the maître d', who's clearly unhappy about a bloodied Streek in her restaurant but escorts them to Twist's table nonetheless, her hands clasped, white-knuckled, in front of her belly. Twist lounges in his chair, waiting. He's a small, slender man; oriental grace in a Scots package. His cool brown eyes don't look through you, but into you. All the way in. Sometimes Amiga is terrified she can't hide anything from him at all.

He dismisses the maître d' by ignoring her and offers Amiga a smile. It doesn't reach his eyes. This man holds his cards so close to his chest they've fused into the flesh.

The rat starts to struggle, making a very annoying whimpering noise. Pinching the soft flesh between nose and lip, Amiga forces him to his knees, making a pretty mess of the polished stone floor. Twist raises his brow.

"Amiga," he tuts, "you're not usually so clumsy." In his soft Scottish drawl every lilting note can harbour a false sense of security but Amiga is reassured. He's feeling magnanimous, she can tell by the playful tone behind his words, the slight crinkle at the corner of his right eye. Amiga's learnt to read Twist like land ship

Captains read the sea. Basic survival 101.

She sighs. "Kimchi seller outed me. Long story."

He flicks a finger at her. "And that's all from one little knee?"

Amiga looks down at herself and pretty much dies of embarrassment. She's in a top-class restaurant in a pea-green jumpsuit absolutely drenched with blood. Her life: for real awkward at all times.

"No. Well. I may have encountered some of his friends too."

"I see."

Twist turns his gaze on the rat, who's giggling compulsively again and shaking, his bloodied leg jerking against the floor like he's being electrocuted.

"We're going to have a little talk, you and I," he says gently. "About your friend Nero." He flicks a look up at Amiga. "Go get cleaned up."

She nods and heads for the back, where a discreet granite-lined corridor leads to the bathrooms. Their opulence offends her, but she makes extravagant use of the soap and towels, scrubbing her face clean and removing the blood from her bodysuit as best she can. The attendant gives her the filthiest look ever. Normally that would make Amiga feel guilty, but today she's pretty much at tilt.

When she goes back, the Streek's where she left him, and although Twist hasn't so much as moved, the rat's pissed himself and he's been crying.

Twist looks up as she approaches.

"According to our mutual friend here, you wiped out half of Nero's crew today. Who's getting a bonus?"

"This bitch," she pokes a thumb at her chest, hoping she looks way more casual than she feels.

He smiles, and this time it reaches his eyes. Her violence

always delights him. She used to be proud of that.

"I'm done with this now. You Clean the rest ASAP. This little shit gave up the whole op. It's in your IMs."

She nods. "What do you want me to do with him?"

"Toss him. And leave the others where they can be found. Be creative. I want Nero to understand the full import of his mistake."

"You want Nero for your collection?"

"Of course. He wants some notoriety, he can reside amongst others who shared the same delusion."

"Understood."

Back in the shoot, Amiga calls for the top floor. The Streek's pretty much given up fighting. He's slumped in her grasp, whimpering away to himself. He fucking stinks. Probably he's shat himself as well. Being on the unpleasant side of her boss will do wonders for your digestion first, and then your mortality.

Amiga is as afraid of Twist Calhoun as everyone else is. She's a Cleaner; her job is all about swift, discreet violence, but he's not one of those crime lords who employ Cleaners because they themselves can't clean house. She's seen him commit violence with brutal, cold efficiency. Needless cruelty. He's something else, her boss. He gets his hands good and dirty when he wants to, and these days working for him fills her with a blank, all-consuming loathing. But a girl's got to eat, and once you work for someone like Twist, you don't just walk away.

At the top floor she hustles the rat up a flight of stairs and out onto the roof. Over to the edge. He gains some fight back here, struggling and wailing. She yanks him close enough to speak right into his ear.

"I do not enjoy this. It's my fucking job. We all do our jobs, don't we? Sometimes there're consequences for that. This is yours."

And she throws him over the edge, listening impassively as that final scream fades away. Somewhere down there, over a mile away, he'll hit the ground and shatter into a wet heap. That's what bodies do from this height.

Maybe someone will witness it and start screaming. Maybe he'll hit a passer by, crushing them as he splatters. Fuck but she hopes not. This is her job, and she does what she's paid to, and this is what Twist means when he requires someone tossed. That's the rat's consequence. Hers never seem to end.

The price you pay for doing a job like this is just about everything.

dock of the bay

Petrie doesn't trust calm seas. In these vast waters, calm is a face without expression, hiding its true intent. A mirror for pirates to catch you unawares, for sea creatures grown monstrous large without the limit of land to contain them to sneak up and drag your ship to impossible depths. He's seen it happen, even to land ships bigger than the one he calls home. No, a calm sea fills him with nothing but dread.

Hollering instructions to his crews via IM, he makes his way to the pinnacle of the central crow to keep a better look out. Just ahead, the Tri-Asian ranges breach the serenity of the surface in snaggle-toothed clusters. Beyond them lies the Gung, so close now he can almost smell it on the air: heat, dust and sweat.

The people of Foon Gung like to call it the last land on earth. Plain ignorance. They imagine the great ocean mountain ranges as nothing but underbelly; exposed innards of earth and rock. In truth the earth broke ugly and whilst some lands shattered or drowned, others were lifted to precipitous heights, and if you look, you can find land everywhere.

Tiny islands of green clinging to the bottoms of harsh ranges. Continental shelves tilted at unnatural angles, carrying the remains of cities, their buildings collapsed to a mass and broken but still usable. Ripe for looting and for the occasional group of desperate folk, home. They share their craggy dwellings with huge colonies of raucous seabirds, herds of sea lions and seals, all under the shadow of great albatrosses with wingspans so wide they resemble dragons in the fire of dawn.

And then, of course, there is the land that sails. Land ships. Great chunks that floated away in the first quakes 200 years ago and did not immediately crumble into the sea, held up by a fortuitous grasp on oxygen, stowed away in great pockets in their depths. Miracles of the ocean, some people call them. From the tip of the crow, Petrie looks down to survey his home, Resurrection City.

She's so massive from prow to stern that, from up here and on a day as calm as this, it might be possible to believe yourself on dry land if you didn't know any better. Before the breaking of the world, Resurrection City was a corner of Eastern Africa, Somalia to be exact, and her crew and citizens comprise an ethnic mix of Africans, Afrikaans, and émigrés from other land ships all living and working together. An extended family of once-strangers.

Shaped like a Palaeolithic spearhead, she scythes through the waves on twelve sets of massive jerry-rigged wheels much like an old steam-boat's, but larger, leaner and forged from steel. They gleam darkly in the sun, the sound of their churning a thunderous roar like the approach of giant waves. Her sides like cliffs, she supports upon her extraordinary back a tri-level haphazard city of freakish driftwood and metal towers, dazzling in sunlight and twisted to wind-defying complexity, all strung with a cat's cradle of ropes upon which crawl the thousands of citizens and crew whose daily toil keeps her afloat.

It's a sight that never fails to move him. This immense lady, this ship formed of land, is home. He wouldn't want to live anywhere else. No other ship would be adequate, no city hub grazing the edge of space, no bedraggled commune eeking out an existence on the tiny green spars of land or half-intact cities clinging to the ranges, and certainly not the Gung, whose claustrophobic streets he tried and failed to survive as a teen, running from one horror it seemed right into the jaws of another.

Through the Tri-Asian ranges the sun plays hide-and-seek with Resurrection's haphazard towers until they emerge out the other side, threading between jagged rocks to sea like glass, a mirror for the sky. If you could see to the bottom of the ocean here you'd find the tsunami defence wall. In an emergency the wall rises from the water high enough to blot out the view of the sea for the highest-living citizens in the Gung.

Sailing as long as he has, Petrie's witnessed them testing it more than once; all that steel against the might of the ocean. One day there'll be a wave too high to hold back. Everything down here is on borrowed time, hanging on by sheer dumb luck.

The harbour at Foon Gung is dead ahead now, rearing from the water like a metal-capped grin. Only ten minutes away at full speed, but they daren't come in that fast.

Steady! he yells to the wheel crews. Half power. Don't wanna scrape anything off those harbour arms.

Carved out of the Gung's south-east corner during the breaking, the harbour is only twenty miles wide, with two long arms reaching plaintively into the ocean, and, like the rest of the Gung, every inch of it groans with architecture. Foon-Gung being the last solid land, every one of its seven hundred miles, including the mountains to the rear, bristles with steel and glass and stone, reaching up into the clouds in audacious rebellion against nature.

The Resurrection's come close to nudging one of the 'rises teetering on the edges of the arms before now. His chest shrinks thinking how many people they might kill if they inadvertently topple one—those 'rises are cage apartments, hundreds of families crammed into tight spaces like barnacles on a rock. Not life at all, at least not one he wants.

Bosun Petrie, slow your boat. You're set to break my arms there. Harbour Master Sigmund lacks basic IM manners, always slamming in without so much as a warning chime.

Petrie takes a breath, thankful that Sigmund can't see his face.

We're slowing. I Ialf speed already. We'll dock safe just like we always do. We're a ways out yet.

Sigmund snorts. Sure son, and these folk from Fulcrum love to be kept waiting. Don't spin me any of that bullshit you try with the deputies, I can see your wake from here, and you're coming in too fast. Make 'em wait. You're paying aren't you?

Irritated, Petrie snaps, We are, through the nose as ever, but we're not going to crash in like pirates trying to please them.

Silence.

Petrie curses his tongue. He shouldn't have said that, it was damned foolish. But Sigmund merely comes back with a warning.

Careful, son, a loose tongue is a dangerous thing. Now get that speed down for crap's sake. I've got crews out; don't need 'em ploughed under your wheels.

Aye, aye.

A cantankerous, mannerless old bastard Sigmund might be, but he feels the same about Fulcrum as everyone does. Fulcrum's the Corp that runs the Gung, that owns and runs the Slip that keeps the world together. That's some goddamn power right there. Too much. Four times a year they send Techs to check your server equipment. It's mandatory and costs a bloody fortune. Resurrection isn't alone in sometimes being unable to pay when it's due and Fulcrum always charges more for delays.

When they're close enough for dammit, Petrie clips on to a line and slides down to the central crow deck to stand by his Captain, Cassius Angel, as they negotiate the south-east arm. Folks hang out the windows on the edge 'rises to wave and holler. Used to be they might throw confetti but though a land ship berthing is still an event, it's not the wonder it used to be. Familiarity breeds complacence.

Once they're in the harbour proper, the berthing klaxon begins to sound. Resurrection responds with three of her horns and they have an ear-splitting exchange as the harbour crews and Resurrection wheel crews coordinate her toward her berth, 800 metres out from the docks. The splash of great wheels, louder by far in the enclosure of the harbour churn her to a gentle halt, waves slapping at her sides, loosing small clods of earth they'll have to stop and patch at the Tri-Asian ranges on their way out.

Petrie roars the order to anchor via IM. Feels rather than hears them drop, a deep dragging and grind, a vibration like a shudder, as if the Resurrection dislikes her sudden immobility.

He pats the ropes, grinning. "Easy, old girl. We're not here long."

For the next ten minutes he supervises the wheel crews with lashing and clearing, organizes the Tech teams into groups to make sure the server checks run smoothly.

Hoi, Bosun! Petrie! The head of their medical team, Lane, barely reining in her impatience. We off? I've got four of my staff by the schooners ready to go. Going to need all the time we can squeeze out of this server check.

"Shit!" he mutters, remembering.

Several vicious attacks in the two months since they last berthed to drop off trade goods have left their hospital supplies dangerously low and he promised Lane time to stock up whilst the servers are being checked. Reaching the bays he vaults onto the lower ropes, clips on his zip and sails down the line to unclip and land beside her. A large man and packed with muscle, he towers over her. Petrie towers over most everyone and it never feels normal. He's never become used to the body good nutrition gave him.

"Let's go then," he says.

"Impressive timing there," she says, smiling.

"Hey, you call, I come running. Let's go wangle some inland time."

She places a hand on his arm as her staff scramble down the ropes to the schooner.

"I know you hate handling Sigmund, Petrie. This is much appreciated."

He pats her hand. "Just do me a favour and sneak me some brandy, will you? Chances are I'm going to need it."

"Done."

"You're an angel."

Their schooners are thirty feet long, solar powered and nippy as hell, and the journey from shipside to dockside takes less than ten minutes. The negotiation for an inland trip on the other hand takes over fifty; despite Sigmund knowing he's keeping Petrie from dealing with Fulcrum's Techs.

Maintaining calm by willpower alone, Petrie manages to wangle Lane a whole hour and hire her a truck at half charge so she can bulk buy. He sees her and her team off safely before heading back to oversee the transfer of Fulcrum's Techs to Resurrection. They're none too pleased. They can't leave until they've done their job and they think he's stalled on purpose. Yet another irritation in his day.

Once they're soothed and on their way, Petrie ventures over to the dock to vet the waiting refugees, a bedraggled bunch who've likely checked the berthing schedules and made certain to be here on the right day for a good ship. His head aches at the sight of them. It seems cruel, especially when people are desperate, but a land ship is a working community and they've learnt not to be indiscriminate, as much as they might want to be.

For Petrie, this process is especially tough. He knows what it's like to be willing to do anything to escape a bad situation and yet terrified of somehow walking into something worse. And there's plenty of something worse to go round. Of the hundreds of land ships sailing the ocean, maybe three quarters could be described as friendly. The rest, not so much.

Some are scavengers, taking what's already been remade useful, their grotesque visages built to terrify smaller ships into submission. Others are pirates out for trash, flesh and treasure, preying on any ship caught in their sights and occasionally hitting the harbour district for whatever can be snatched before the sec-drones attack. The worst of all are totalitarian states, with flags and laws and dire punishments for transgression—and the most notorious of these is the Saskatoon Ark, captained by Daly Pentecost.

Petrie was born on the Ark, amongst all that filth and horror, under the iron hand of Pentecost. He ran away when he was fifteen during a short dock for supplies at the Gung. Jumped clean over the side. Pretended to drown so no one would think to follow, swimming through icy

waters to hide under the dock, shivering and terrified of
being found.

He thought then that he could survive anything, but
two years living rough on the streets of the Gung left him
so desperate to get back to the ocean he took the first ship
that came in. Lucky for him, that was Resurrection City.

Today there are thirty refugees hoping for the same
luck, and only he stands in their way. From the info they
shoot to his IM, he has to turn down six straight away. The
rest are a mix of skilled WAMOS—Passes, the so-called
well-adjusted members of society—done with living
inside the system, and Fails wanting to try out life on the
seas—all of whom are easy to accept. Except one.

Her records seem perfect: a high-level Tech WAMOS
fresh out of Corp life and wanting freedom, but her timing
is interesting. Questionable. He beckons her forward.

"Name?"

It's on her info, but sometimes they forget their own
cover stories, the names on fake records bought in haste.

"Volk," she replies in a soft voice with a burr of accent
he can't place. Perhaps Nordic. Unusual if so. Close up, he
can see she's packed with augments, her gaze remote, but
he can feel the life in her. She's angular and fair-skinned,
with untameable red hair to match the energy he can sense
leashed within. She'll make a good sailor if she's fit for it.

Volk. Just like her records. That's a good start maybe.

"No other names?"

"None I like to give. I'm not close to my family."

"Any reason for that?"

"The usual. Confliction of life goals, gradual estrange-
ment none of us particularly tried to prevent."

"I see. You realize we're an extended family aboard
the Resurrection? We're pretty much obliged to get along
even if we don't agree with one other. Not many places

to get away from someone you dislike on a land ship, not even one of her grand size."

She forces a smile, clearly struggling hard to make a good impression.

"I said I'm not close to my family, that doesn't mean I'm incapable of getting along with other people. You can't choose the family you're born to. It's not like you get a free pass from being the offspring of absolute arseholes."

Her dry humour is such a surprise he finds himself laughing.

"True enough. How are you with teamwork?"

"I'm ex-Corp, Bosun. Teamwork was my life."

"Why the Resurrection? I see you've been waiting on a ship for over two weeks. Rest of this bunch have only been here ten days—missed the Hepzibar. You didn't though. Good ship, that. Not good enough for you?"

She regards him steadily, her remote eyes giving away nothing.

"It has a good reputation, yes. But it isn't Resurrection City."

"Afford to be choosy, can you?"

She raises her brows, as if it's obvious.

"With my stats? Of course."

Petrie considers her carefully for a moment. His instincts tell him she's in some deep trouble. Frightened. Is she trouble for the Resurrection though? He thinks not. Not only is her record clean but he's finely attuned to hidden malice and he gets no sense of it from her. He has no concern about anyone who might be after her. Resurrection is a titan, well armed and battle hardened. Coming after her once she's on board would be foolhardy.

"Well, okay," he says to Volk, "I can see you're in some kind of trouble, but you aren't trouble yourself, so welcome to the family."

She nods, but her relief is like a tidal wave, it almost knocks him over.

"Thank you."

"Don't prove me wrong."

"I'll do my very best."

"Do better."

"Aye, aye Bosun."

Aye, aye, indeed. He watches her go, clutching her bag so tightly he knows for a fact her hands are going to hurt for a week, and hopes he hasn't just made a very big mistake.

fed to a joon bug

a neural drive is like a mind, there's no switching it off, no running from it. You can mute it, sure. You can even do as Shock does and fry your brain on bumps, wiping as many clear seconds as possible from the clock. But much like a persistent thought a drive will let you know by hook or by crook when you've a million and one messages backed up and pounding on their horns like angry drivers in a ten-mile tail-back.

Shock's had his on mute since speaking to Mim, which was dumb knowing her pro-stance on harassment. Now his drive's buzzing away with angry message wasps, sending ripples like the after-effects of ECT to bug up his beleaguered brain meats. Cutting straight through the messy high of cheap bumps. He'd delete them all without reading if he hadn't once taught Mim a way to circumvent that. Why did he do that?

"Because you're an idiot," he says to himself, sucking up coffee in desperate gulps and trying to ignore the clamour in his head, drown it with anger and caffeine.

Shock has zero inclination to listen to Mim haranguing him about this freaking Olbax job ad infinitum, but he does want the buzzing to stop already, before his head does an impression of a melon on the receiving end of a baseball bat. Can't have one without the other, and the resulting rebellion paradox is giving him more of a headache than Mim's messages, or a baseball bat. Maybe.

"Not enough coffee in the world," he snarls, giving up rebellion as a bad job. She'll only keep on sending them. Mim's tenacious. Like herpes.

The first message, from thirty-six hours ago, is fairly calm, more of a query. He's not fooled. Calm before the storm, that shit is. And here's the storm, from message four onward, ear-bending as feedback, full-on rant-mode and he's cringing, trying to whip through them all without really listening.

If only Mim's voice when she's annoyed weren't drill-like in its ability to put holes in his skull. By the time he comes to the last, sent roughly two hours ago, he's ready to tear his drive out with his bare hands and stamp it to dust, but the last is a surprise.

Hey, Shocking boy, there's a party tonight. You need to get out and about before you turn into a pumpkin. See you there.

He listens to it twice in swift succession, wondering who's taken over Mim and what it is they want from him. She sounds almost nice. He shudders, full body.

"Gotta be a reason," he mutters, staring furiously at his coffee cup. The dregs are grinning at him. What in the hell is so funny? "You're empty. Bastard."

Wallowing in suspicion, he plays the IM again. Nope, that's her all right. Saccharine mode. He can tell by the level of rot in his brainpan. On the back of the IM rides an info-shot, holding all the party deets. Shock wants to delete it on principle. Mim's never been anywhere near as pleasant as this, even when things were sort of good, but she always dragged him to parties, to people, especially when he was most disinclined, which was most of the time.

He's not averse, or allergic, nor even introverted, he's just reluctant. He's tried and failed so many times to explain that. Truth is, he hasn't got a clue. It's like the part of him that makes him a Haunt leaked out and infected everything else, stole his links to the world at large and the people in it. His idea of heaven would be to nest up in some garden flat in Sendai and never leave, just lie there listening to the birds, tripping out in the green light diffusing through the leaves.

Shock rubs hard at his eyes. Goddamit but he's so tired. If only no were as simple as a single syllable. Mim's sure to send an IM flood if he doesn't turn up. No thought required for that, just a preset on her drive, and it'll drive him crazy on demand. Besides, she probably only wants to grab him for a face-to-face over his reluctance to sort this Olbax shit. Job's probably important to whichever scumbag she's doing it for. Either way, no is a sure-fire route to more mental pain, which means he's got to go for his own peace of mind if nothing else. He checks the time. Five hours to kill.

"I could sleep. But fuck that..."

Chucking his insultingly empty cup into the nearest trash-comp, Shock makes a beeline for the park. If he goes home—if the shitty little cage he's currently holed up in can be called anything so friendly—he'll end up lying in bed, eyes pinned wide, listening to the oldsters he calls room-mates banging on about their dicky bladders and bunions, their boils and haemorrhoids, and likely end up face-planting the concrete. When he does that, if he does it, he wants it to be because he's honestly finished, and he's nowhere near finished. He's still desperate to find a way out of the trap he's built for himself, a way to make everything right—a way to get back to Sendai.

He hangs out at the park till the sun is nothing but a memory and he's shivering in his shoes. He'd stay on for the hypothermia, but makes his way to the party instead, before his lateness threatens to provoke Mim's provocation. This party is located at some J-Hack's safe house in the arse-end of Sakkura.

The place is a real find, covered in black mould and so sparsely furnished it looks long since abandoned, though all five of its tiny rooms swell with bodies, slicked together close as sweat-soaked hair to a cheek. They spill in to the corridor, lining the walls in a tangle of limbs and noise.

Shock squeezes through with his eyes closed, skin shrink-wrapped to cringing bones, and heads direct to booze central, a table in the kitchen so overloaded the plastic creaks in protest. Three bottles of cheap Chinese beer in swift succession give him the strength to turn and face the crush, in time to see Mim catch him in her headlights and fire herself at him like he's a bullseye.

She's wearing a flimsy bodysuit, and those old red bladers. Warning lights. Seeing them arouses a potent mixture of unease and desire. Shock ran those red lights without thinking when they met, and despite the pain of the resulting crash, he still hasn't the sense to stop.

"Shocking boy. You showed."

"I had a choice?"

She beams, all those tiny teeth too dangerous for words, and snags a beer, twisting off the top with one precise hand movement. He imagines it's his dick, and goes lightheaded. Has to dig his nails into his palm to snap out of it, before meeting her eyes, wary as a cornered fox. In his drunken, unmedicated state Mim's gaze is vivisection in a glance, excising the cool he had at Keen Machine and exposing his barely hidden continued attraction to her, soft and vulnerable as a torso full of viscera. He sneers at her—an old defence mechanism and quite useless. All but kicks the wall when he sees the gleam in her eye, that magpie-spotting-a-helpless-chick look.

She takes a long, slow drink from her beer. He can't take his eyes off her throat, he wants to bite it, throttle it, and she fucking knows it. Amazing how much you can hate a person and still want them so hard. He should have run from her, shouldn't have left himself this wide open. But how the hell could he not?

"Care to share your reluctance to open my IMs?" she asks softly.

"I'm busy," he says.

First thing out of his mouth and it's the sort of lie she doesn't need evidence to laugh at. Shit. He steps back, trying to steal some space, some air to breathe. Trying to find minimal distance, to see her for what she is rather than the image he wants to see.

Trouble is, Mim's not only a master at camouflage, she's also a drug, and it's no secret how he feels about those. If she crooked a finger she could have him, and they both know it. After all, he only broke up with her because she made herself a cliff and pushed him off. If she hadn't...

She looks amused. "Busy? Getting high?"

"Yup."

He necks his beer, grabs another two, earning a filthy look from some a-hole behind Mim. He ignores it, feeling hunted, cornered, and wanting to run away from her, back to her. Anywhere but here. Shock's been running forever, and he's so goddamn tired. He lost himself in Mim because it gave him an excuse to stop, because she's a vacuum he can drown in. That's partly why he finds her so difficult to resist. He's pretty sure she's wise to that. Mim's got a killer instinct for weak spots. Hence the red bladers. She hasn't worn them for years. This is all show, all manipulation. He's so fucking stupid.

"I'll get round to it," he says to her, and there's a resounding "fuck the hell off" wound through it. Being belligerent is as close as he gets to protecting his heart.

"Thought you'd say that," she says, almost sweetly. "That's why I invited you."

"Huh?"

Mim gives him a calculating smile.

"This party, you do know whose it is, don't you?"

The first mild stirrings of panic hit. Oh hell no.

"Whose?" he asks warily.

"Mine."

Shock closes his eyes. When he opens them, Mim is gone. He doesn't bother turning around, just sighs and says, "Joon Bug. Been a while."

She wanders around him as if he's a bike she's considering dropping flim on and he cranks his head up to aim a nervous smile toward where her head might be. Joon's a human skyscraper, outstripping him by well over a foot, but then he makes for an unusually short Korean man, barely topping five foot three.

She's dressed in her usual uniform of scabby grey jeans and band tee, this one a black number so washed-out it looks dark grey in places, with the Rorschach pattern of some Doom or Deth band emblazoned across the front. He tries not to stare at her tits, though they're staring him in the face. Joon's not fond of folk engaging with her assets.

"You look rough," she says.

"Being in my situation will kinda do that."

She bends down to eyeball him. She's got incurious brown eyes, deceptively sleepy, though she had her epicanthic fold taken out years ago for perfect, wide, delineated almond eyes.

"You chose your situation, dumbass. Zero sympathy. Mim says you have flim." She quirks a brow. "I do believe you owe me."

Stamping down rage and dismay, Shock stares purposefully at her tits, trying for the wind-up, even though he's fully aware Joon's big enough and mean enough to pound his face in for it. Shit though, being irritating is all he's got now Mim's screwed him the fuck over to get her way.

No surprises there.

"Yeah, I have flim. It kinda has to go a long way."

Joon's finger presses hard beneath his chin.

"Eyes up, bitch. And I don't care how long of a way you have to stretch that shit. You owe me. Cough up, or I'll turn you upside-down and shake it out of you. I know it's on you, it always is."

Ah, Joon Bug, always so altruistic. Long story bite-size? Shock basically got lazy on a job so boring it was giving him brain bleed a while back and hired in help, AKA JB, to handle it for him. Delegation, you understand. Anyway, fact is, he hired Joon, and then failed to spot her her share of the flim. Not paying wasn't exactly intentional, but it happened to look that way to the untrained eye, and Joon's been hungry for a bite of his flim balance, and possibly his flesh, ever since.

"C'mon, Mim's little blue-eyed boy. Cough up."

"I'm not Mim's anything."

"Keep telling yourself that, cupcake. Now gimmie my money."

Shock digs in his jacket pocket. As she said, his flim's always there, it's the only place he trusts; stashes get stolen, cred gets zeroed out. He's got just enough to cover what he owes and have a pittance left over for hitting a Slip shop to do the Olbax job. Which of course he now needs to light a fire under if he wants to get by and keep his lame excuse for a bed for the next month.

He's going to be living on ramen and shitty bumps again.

Mim 1, Shock 0.

Right now his hatred for Mim could burn through every level of this godforsaken shit heap of a 'scraper and sink a hole in the earth deep enough to damn them all. He half wishes that would happen. At least then all this ridiculous shit would be over.

He slams flim into Joon's hand. She contemplates it with great satisfaction, taking time to count every last one, and then stuffs it in her back pocket, where any fucker could steal it. He half considers trying, but he's a Haunt, not a pickpocket.

Joon nods.

"Nice doing business with you," she says. "Help yourself to nibbles." And she's gone, pogoing through the crush, her close-cut dusky-pink hair damn near sweeping the ceiling with every crazy leap.

For lack of anything better to do, Shock stays, ostensibly to eat, but the nibbles such as they are don't appeal. He ends up drinking until his head pounds and reels, hugging the walls, avoiding eye contact with the few people he knows. Most of them ignore him back, used to his reticence.

People don't try with him any more and that suits him just fine. How reluctance becomes a complete inability to communicate even his desire to not communicate is beyond him. There are the odd few, however, whose urge to know what's going on with him now he's become so thoroughly persona non grata with all the wrong people compels them to try to breach his barriers.

Eventually, buoyed by booze, two guys he knew at

Tech, Fails like him, corner him to find out where he's been, what he's been up to.

He excavates himself out from under their questions as rapidly as possible, secretes several bottles of that Chinese beer in his jacket, and hightails it away. It's not only discomfort that makes him want to duck their curiosity, nor embarrassment, it's that he simply doesn't know what to say to them: "I fucked up", as a response, strikes him as wholly inadequate.

nice work if you can get it

Amiga wiggles a finger in her ear and squints up, watching the midday shuttle shoot toward the dark mass of a hub looming way above. At close range the sound of a transport launching would deafen, so they launch from pads sequestered away behind thick glass barriers, swallowing all but a faint burr that tingles the ears. Sleek and grey, they're space-safe; able to reach hubs wherever they might be, in low or high orbit.

Many of the hubs fly over at least once a fortnight, taking in the Gung to allow for direct connections. Others pass more frequently in general orbit. Tokyo is their most frequent and most familiar. During low flyovers, on clear mornings before sunrise, you can see the city enclosed within in miniature, its lights glistening like multicoloured stars.

This shuttle is a direct connection to the Hong Kong Hub, no diversions, no skimming the atmosphere to rendezvous with say London, Chicago, Paris or MidWestern, and Amiga's target missed it by a minute. She's been stalking this woman not so discretely for about an hour. Perhaps to give her an opportunity to get away, she's not sure. The parts of her that she doesn't think work quite right are treating this as a game, like a cat playing with a mouse. The rest of her feels sick.

The woman is in a full-on panic, scrambling for a way out of the bay, still clutching her ticket.

There's only one exit.

Sighing, Amiga shoves down the sick feeling and strolls after her. As she draws alongside, she takes the woman's arm as if they're close friends. The woman jumps, violently, and Amiga hugs her in to conceal it as best she can, carefully steering her away from curious eyes.

"Can't blame you for trying to buy a seat on a transport," she says, trying to be kind. "But your boss made the mistake of crossing my boss. That's not something you run away from. You can't shake Twist Calhoun."

"A minute earlier and I would've," the woman replies, her voice steady despite the pallor of her skin.

"Twist would still send me up to finish the job. He likes all his loose ends neatly tied. Better that you just let it be over and done with instead of always looking over your shoulder."

"You wouldn't say that if it was you."

"No. But it isn't, is it? And there's nowhere someone like you can hide from something like me."

Amiga's IM chimes softly.

It's not Twist, he wouldn't chime, he'd just start talking. Whoever it is can bloody well wait. This woman was just a liaison, innocent really, and she's minutes away from having to kill her gruesomely enough to satisfy her boss's particular tastes. She doesn't want to talk to anyone.

Her IM chimes again.

Does she imagine the insistent note? She opens the link, feeling super impatient.

Busy, she snaps.

Amiga, you're always busy. Look, I need to talk to you about that job. You promised you'd at least hear me out.

Shit. It's Deuce, her ex. Her choice not his and, oh boy, is there a whole fucking novel of unspoken words between them about that. He's also one of the leaders of the Hornets, a J-Hack crew of Fails and dropouts who let her live among them.

Despite making her home with them, Amiga will never be a Hornet. Because if she wants to work with them, she has to stop working for Twist. No negotiation. But there's no fucking chance of that. They think hating a job makes it easy to walk away. Amateurs.

Given all that, Deuce wanting to talk about a job is super suspicious. Means their job must have something to do with Twist, and that makes her pissy. How is it fine for them to judge what she does, but okay to take advantage of what she does if it's useful to them?

Fuck. That. Shit.

Yeah, yeah. Later. Working. Bye.

Cutting him off, she pops in a quick temporary block—he'll only call back if she doesn't. The woman seems to have taken Amiga's silence as a reason to relax. Why are people so stupid?

"You could let me go if you wanted to. Please," she says now, low and urgent.

Amiga can't stand it when they start bargaining; it always ends with her hunting down a bar and getting categorically wasted. And doesn't that go down well with her adopted family? Not like the Hornets never get drunk is it? But no, when she gets drunk, that is one hell of a subject for endless discussion. She'd rather eat her own face than discuss any of this with anyone, including her target.

"Your boss would never have to know. I'd just disappear. Board a land ship," the woman continues, pleading.

Oh hell. Amiga closes her eyes briefly, they're gritty, all sting and itch and feeling far too big for the sockets. Tired or sad? Either. Both. Enough. She has so had enough. Dragging the woman into an alley, she takes a small blunt metal bar out of her jacket and simultaneously rams the woman into the wall and the bar into her temple. It's a precise way of killing, quick and clean—but you've got to do it with enough force to hear that crunch of bone shattering, driving deep into delicate brain matter.

The woman jerks, begins to twitch. Amiga holds tight until her body falls still. Slotting the bar back into her pocket, Amiga pushes two fingers into the pulse point at the woman's neck. Irregular flutters. She closes her eyes again. Hugs the woman's limp body against her chest and holds one hand firm over mouth and nose.

Counts to a hundred.

At thirty she feels the extra weight drop into the bones and viscera. Tension is all gone. Life is gone. But she holds on, counting, more for herself than anything else. When her stomach's settled, and it will, she'll take out her knife and do what needs doing.

Her IM opens.

You're blocking me now?

Fuck! I'm working, Deuce. Why does her life keep doing this?

I'm sorry, but this is important.

This is hella awkward is what it is.

The dead woman is a dead weight, haha. Her arms are already aching. Whatever. She should hurt. She should feel something.

Amiga.

She leans against the wall, giving in. What the hell. It's not like she's got anything she'd rather do and this alley is not a short cut, it's a filthy, stagnant dumping ground. No

one will accidentally stray down here to catch her holding
a corpse. She has time.

Fine. Talk.

Thank you. I think you know why we need you on this
job.

Yup.

I think you also know we wouldn't ask unless it was
important.

She sighs. I do.

It's for Da Fellows.

Slip activist numero uno? I thought he'd gone signal
dark?

So did we.

So now she's intrigued. The Hornets know all kinds
of stuff they don't tell her. For safety—theirs, not hers.
As if she'd ever dream of breathing a word about them
to Twist.

He's been involved in some deep shit and he needs our
help.

Hornets specifically?

Yeah.

Because of me?

Mostly. Also because we're damn good and he can
trust us.

Right. So what does he need from me? Or rather, what
does he need from my boss?

We have to catch a drone and re-program it. You can
help with that.

Um... Why is he stalling? That's not like Deuce at all.
He's a straight-talker, not a dissembler. What does Fellows
need me to do, Deuce?

Deuce makes this sound like a throat clearing.

He needs you to break into Twist's vault and retrieve a
data packet.

She bursts out laughing.

What?

The laughter carries on until it suddenly clicks that she's for real standing here, leaning on the wall, busting a gut, with a dead body drooping in her arms. Disrespectful much. That sobers her up good and quick, which puts the right emphasis on the only logical response.

No. Categorical. You can absolutely fuck off, Deuce. Fellows can fuck off. Twist caught me doing something like that I'd end up in the vault myself, in the display tanks.

I get that it's a lot to ask, but…

No, you really don't, she interrupts because, wow, he hasn't a clue what he's asking because if he did, she cannot believe he would. I won't do it. Do not ask me again. Now I have work to do, so do me the courtesy of leaving me the hell alone.

There's a hurt silence, she knows he's hurt because she knows Deuce. She hates that she knows him so well, that implies investment, and admitting how she was once invested in 'Amiga and Deuce' as a thing aches like cold in the bones high on the mono. He doesn't bother to reply, he's just gone, which also lets her know he's deeply disappointed in her too.

She's surprised to find how much that upsets her, but the weight in her arms gives her a convenient patsy for unwanted emotions. Of course she's upset. Why wouldn't she be? Amiga hefts the dead woman, wondering if she can still do what she needs to. She was ready, but now she's edgy, emotional, she'll make a damn mess of everything. Surely she could just leave this poor bitch here instead of carving her up?

"Twist won't know," she whispers to the woman, who can't hear, of course she can't. "Will he?"

She's never been brave enough to test the theory

of Twist's power to see through her. Maybe she could, sure, some day, but today is not that day. Today she has no energy for any more, and testing Twist's patience is way beyond more. It's too much. So she's going to get this over and done with instead, like a good little Cleaner. Then she's going to go the hell home, cry a lot, get drunk on that shitty beer slowly going lukewarm in her dodgy fridge and sleep for about a thousand hours.

And she's definitely not going to talk to Deuce.

Fine as a rice noodle from a distance, the Mono writhes its way around the towering pinnacles of the city in what looks to the uninitiated like an incoherent tangle. Mono trains are slender and efficient. Operated by computers overseen from the Hive, the central nervous system of Slip, where the Hive Queens have absolute authority.

Amiga likes ants in general, but she hates the Queens. Theoretically they're locked in Hive by Emblem, the key holding Hive to Slip to RL, but they're clever and determined and every now and then they manage to find a way around Emblem into Slip. It's never pretty. Before she saw for herself what they can do, she used to think it was some kind of cliché—the mad AIs. Now she knows better. A cliché is not so trite when it's right there in the distance, huge enough to give you a nosebleed just looking at it, and trashing everything in its path.

Exhausted, she waits for an empty shoot and changes as it carries her up to the platform. Slipping into a streamlined, double-thickness orange jumpsuit and a pair of peacock-blue Bladers. Her work gear she stuffs into her empty backpack. She'll have to chuck the damn thing like always. You can wash blood out in cold water but you still know it was there.

At the platform she waits under sputtering lights in the evening chill for the .351 to arrive. She'd have been on the track already given the chance, but with only minutes before this mono hits platform that's asking to be catapulted off and thrown to the ground several hundred feet below. Not exactly how she wants to spend her evening, smearing her innards all over the pavement. She's fucked up, not fucking suicidal.

The mono's approaching whine fills the station, setting off a scramble for readiness that's guaranteed full-on entertainment. Monos are sardine cans from five forty-five P.M. to eleven P.M. at night and this mass of straining idiots might as well be clamouring for mummification as the .351 comes haring into the station in a whirl of wind and leaves.

There are no trees this high up. The mono brought them all the way from Sendai, where trees are everywhere, and almost all of them real. Amiga loves how wind has a mind of its own, how it seems to pull the leaves along purely for fun. There's a stampede for the doors, a scuffling and thumping as passengers fight for a place to sit or stand before the whine builds, accelerates, and the mono explodes out of the station in a burst of stunning speed.

Amiga's ready.

She leaps, catches the back draft and, as her blades touch down on the track and the magnets activate, she's crouched, her legs moving fast, keeping her within sight of the mono's red-and-white striped backside as it practically flies to the next station. Between the faceless visages of bright 'scrapers and dull 'rises, too fast to see her reflection in the glass as anything more than a blur, she holds steady in the mono's wake through Hangoon and Norii, neither station on the .351's stop schedule.

Next stop is Ginzo, but Amiga's not going that far. The track runs through Sakkura, right through the middle of several 'scrapers, disappearing with hollow pops of sound into long, dimly lit and treacherously narrow tunnels lined with the grimy windows of cramped apartments. The mono does this all over Foon Gung, where it couldn't go around or between, it goes through; and some tunnels hide secrets. Her 'rise, Jong-phu, is one of them.

Under the rails, in the secret space between mono and building, are a series of squats cobbled together by the Hornets. Home. Reaching out, her hand encased in a thick, plastic cast with a catchlock set into the wrist, Amiga hooks onto a zip wire as she flies past, whipping off the track and spinning down into the waiting arms of a webbed sling, curling her body to minimize impact.

Unhooking herself, she grabs the bottom of the sling and vaults out, heading through cramped walkways to the hovel she calls her own. On the way she yanks at the velcro fastenings of the glove, dying to get it off. It's like welding steel around your arm, but it's the only safe way to get off the track.

All the homes here are assembled from huge 3D-printed parts and brightly coloured, though it's hard to see in the meagre lighting. The brainchild of a design genie called Liberty, printed homes have become ubiquitous amongst under-mono communities, transforming them from shantytowns to neat, albeit crowded plastic villages. Everything modernizes eventually.

Amiga's cabin is bright yellow. Neon in fact, to match her personality—a joke she regrets every time she sees it practically glowing in the dark. Sometimes she's too full-on snark even for herself. She hops up on to the side ladder, scrambles to the roof and opens the hatch she never remembers to lock, throwing her backpack and then herself down into darkness. Terrific.

"Oi, on. I'm home."

Her lights are supposed to be movement activated but her sensors are on the fritz and she hasn't the flim for new ones just yet, nor has she quite gotten round to twisting the arm of a fellow Hornet to fix them for free.

Turning to lean on her kitchen and take her bladers off, because she might need to cry and get drunk right now but there's no way that's happening with these clunky-arse things still on her feet, she finally looks at her meagre half lounge, and groans before she can stop herself. Sat on her sofa, a thinly padded ugly old green thing she can't quite believe cost as much as it did, is Deuce, his arms crossed and his least impressed face welded on.

Tall and broad for an Asian thanks to some Nordic blood on his mother's side, he's got his father's poker face, with eyes like a hundred flim chips, and his mother's blonde hair. When they were together she called him her Viking Samurai.

"So," he says, "wanna tell me about your day?"

Stellar. She's so not up to dealing with this shit right now.

"It was work. That's it."

"Uh-huh."

He doesn't look convinced and Amiga has this unbearable urge to rifle through her pack and chuck the jacket she was wearing earlier in his face. Blood would probably make her point, but that would be petty. Beyond petty in fact. Especially as she's fully aware that's not what he means.

This is part of that whole novel between them, the one she put an abrupt The End to, imagining having all this fall apart and go away would make it easier to breathe. Why it hasn't is a mystery she's yet to begin trying to figure out. People give up on you when you fuck up, don't they? They give up on you when you push them away. Why hasn't he? Why haven't the Hornets?

"Look, I don't want to talk shop, it only gives you an excuse to bug me about my job, and all that's going to do is piss me off, so can I get a rain check on the heart to fucking heart?" He opens his mouth but she holds up a hand, unnerved by how hard it's shaking. "No more about Fellows either. It's no. That's it."

"Amiga. It's important."

"Oh for fuck's sake, Deuce. Why? Why is it important that I put my life on the line for some fucking hack I don't know?"

"Fellows needs this thing in Twist's vault. Twist doesn't even know it's there. He needs us to send it to someone, and if they don't get it... Bad shit, Amiga. Bad shit."

"Is that what he told you?"

"Yes."

"And you believed him?"

"Yes."

"Idiot."

He leans forward, holding her with those black eyes. So fucking sincere.

"You know I'm not. Fellows is legit. If he says bad things, he means bad, Amiga. He's been signal dark. Someone of his calibre does not go SD for nothing."

"But he won't tell you the nature of the bad shit?"

"No."

"Then I won't do it."

"Then we will."

Amiga gapes at him, utterly aghast.

"Are you kidding me? You wouldn't stand a fucking chance. You'd all die!"

He sits back and ugh, he's looking at her like she's gone and been an arsehole again.

"So you do it then. Either way it's happening. He

needs this and we're going to get it for him."

Amiga turns around and punches the wall, which is a dumb idea. Turns out 3D-printed walls really fucking hurt.

"Fuck's sake. Amiga!"

Deuce leaps up and grabs her hand and holy smoke coming out of her ears that's too much up close and personal for her to handle right now. She yanks her hand away and backs up into the kitchen, but that dumb as a stump ex of hers just keeps on following. Starts rifling over her head for any kind of first-aid kit, which he finds in seconds despite her looking for two whole hours the other week and finding sweet FA.

Slamming the kit down on the counter, his mouth set in a grim line, he sets to cleaning up the gash across her knuckles and gluing it shut. She's pretty sure she doesn't breathe the whole time.

"Could you, just for once, not be you?" he asks when he's done.

She folds her arms, closing off.

"No. And you're not doing the job."

He folds his arms, mirroring. Bastard.

"I am."

"No. I am." And she only says it because he can't, they can't. "You," she pokes the air viciously, "are going to make sure I come out of it alive."

He says nothing at first, just holds her in that black gaze, suspended. Space would probably be kinder to her lungs.

"If you're sure," he says finally, quietly.

"I'm sure." She's only sure that they're not doing it, but that's sure enough.

Deuce nods. "Thank you."

He heads for the table, no doubt eager to go and get the Hornets et al up to speed on her involvement. She better get free meals after this shit. Lots of them. Never mind that she already does. They all make sure she's looked after when she lets them. Especially Deuce, who has a new fucking girlfriend and probably shouldn't be so considerate. And there she is, all pissy again.

"Don't thank me," she snaps as he leaps for the hatch and starts to climb out. "I'm only doing it because I think you'd fuck it up."

He looks down at her, his face half in shadow, but there's that disappointment again, blazing away. The bridge smoldering behind her.

"I know."

down the rabbit hole

Stuck on a sidewalk swarming with meat suits, Shock stalks the edge for a safe place to cross a freeway locked into insanity mode. He's about ready to commit genocide. Mothball pockets require austerity measures, cheap-ass Slip shops whose only option to jack the Slip is manual and likely to fry half his workable neurones. Unlucky for him, the cheapest Slip shops are in Hanju, his home district, a place he expends considerable energy avoiding. To top it all off, he has to run this one unmedicated. Too risky otherwise. Dandy, just freaking dandy.

He sneers into the traffic, earning a particularly rigid middle finger from some ugly-freak-looking taxi driver. Shock flips the finger back, because the bastard likely deserves it, then throws himself across the freeway, frantically dodging bumpers and praying he can dodge anyone he shares DNA with.

In Hanju proper, he's surrounded by familiar narrow streets and dwarfed beneath calamitously high warrens of apartments. Built too close for comfort, the Hanju apartment blocks have been knocked together over the years, street by street, transforming their innards to some sort of over-populated rabbit warren. Even where they span the road, makeshift—and often residential—bridges have been constructed, joining the blocks together into one gigantic habitation maze; home leading into home with almost no privacy whatsoever.

Shock grew up cheek to jowl with neighbours as far as his eye could see. He still recalls the postmaster walking through his bedroom at six A.M. on the dot, yelling "annyeong-haseyo" to his mother in the kitchen and tossing her the morning paper and mail. Remembers struggling to survive in neighbourhoods of corridors crawling with other Korean brats who hated the very fact of his existence. Made it their business to corner him at every opportunity and pound their disapproval into his flesh.

He went to school with those selfsame brats in a school-house created from thirteen apartments knocked together on the seventeenth floor, under the iron rule of their form teacher, Eun-ji, a forty-something mother of seven who was perpetually furious with the world and the most unnatural mother he ever met bar his own.

Pulling shaking hands through messy bi-coloured hair, he aims for the strands of memory beneath, attached by sinewy strings of scar tissue too tender to sever, too raw to bear. Growing up in the warren was the nine circles of hell and then some. If he could, if the future were populated by wonders the past promised and never fulfilled, he'd wipe the whole memory of his childhood clean away.

Back then he was considered some sort of demon-child. A pariah. As if centuries of once-forgotten superstition found a new home on his shoulders. A Min-seo who wanted to be a Min-jun, refusing to wear the sprigged cotton dresses her mother, Ha-eun, sewed from fabric bought from Cheongparo blockstreet market, and wondering what the hell her body was doing growing all the wrong goddamn parts. No one else understood the parts were wrong, they thought it was the mind.

Ha-eun spent a frightening portion of the meager wages she made washing floors and sewing clothes on quacks and crooks all over Korea-town and beyond, none of them Korean, all of them liars who promised to sweat, bleed, chant or coax by whatever means the demons from Min-seo's mind. A good deal of the memories between three and twelve are coated in the sticky stench of incense and shot through with pain sharp as the scalpels used to carve egress for bad spirits.

It's not hate he feels for Ha-eun precisely—the drugs deal with that—more a low-grade, seething sense of abandonment. Of having had the right to expect more and never getting it. His father, Hoon, was never more than background noise, a disappointed shadow haunting the corners of their rooms. Not a talkative man, he stopped trying to communicate altogether when his daughter insisted she was his son.

In the end, Min-seo was left to deal with the problem alone. That's where luck, that arbitrary twister of chance, came in. Blessed with ability above the top 0.5% in Tech, little Min-seo was hired at nine by Fulcrum's Outreach Programme, a sure-fire highway, barring any Psych-Fail issues, into Corp work. Such an achievement would have earned the forgiveness of her family if she hadn't spent her wages on a gender reassignment.

Thing is, you learn a lot in the city; you learn that drugs can hide the worst hurts and exchanging wrong parts for right is only a matter of flim or cred. So that's what little Min-seo did. At a mere twelve years of age, after two years of secret hormone treatment, and earlier than most surgeons would allow, Min-seo became the boy he always knew he was, re-christening himself Shock in an ironic nod to the reaction of the entire community at Hanju's Songpa blockstreet.

Ha-eun refused to speak to her daughter-son ever again. Shock didn't care; like father, like mother. It made no difference, just removed an aggravating frequency of motherly white noise corrupting his head. Having the right parts, being able to bear living inside himself, was more important. Even suffering to live in Korea-town after the change was a walk in the goddamn park by comparison to the alternative, but that didn't stop him saving to get out.

Paid less than a tenth of the salary full-time adult employees could boast, and flat broke after the surgery, it took him another three years to escape the maze. He relocated to Sendai District, amongst the trees and towers, when he was fifteen and five months. He ended up there by sheer chance, a Slip search, but it was revelatory. Not only in the obvious ways: a room to himself, no postmaster, no beatings, no incense-triggered bad memories or accusatory silences. It was the sense of finally being at peace.

Sendai is where Shock discovered happiness, and even though he could only afford to be there two years in total, they were the best of his life. At seventeen, too old for the programme any more, he was transferred from Outreach plus PT Tech to FT Tech. His savings kept him in Sendai for six months, but then he was forced into student digs.

He's been trying to get back to Sendai ever since.

Being back in Korea-town, too close for comfort to Songpa, not only unleashes feral pain locked deep inside his bones, it makes him feel a failure. And he is, in more ways than one. Sighing, Shock speeds up. He's a long walk from his destination and doesn't have flim to spare for a bus.

"Why in fuck did I have to go to that party? I fucking

hate parties," he mutters, huddling further into his jacket and pulling the tangled wreckage of his hair over his eyes, too recognizable by half. He often wanted to ask Ha-eun what the hell he's doing with bright-blue eyes despite his oh-so-K parentage, but she'd have cried, and he's never been able to stomach his mother's tears.

Naebu blockstreet is where the good Slip shops can be found, deep within the maze of housing. It's a little cold outside, enough for Shock to be shivering after such a long walk, and he's almost relieved to be able to step into the muggy confines of the block. Almost.

Two seconds after pushing in through the crooked blue entrance, the shrieking objection of rusty hinges barely discernible over the varied noise of living within, and he's suffocating, wishing he had enough flim to walk right back out, take the mono back to Henzu District and one of his usual shops. Walking into Naebu's complicated labyrinth of corridors, staircases and home warrens is a lucid nightmare.

He expects to see his mother gazing at him from one of these slender staircases, ripe with all her simmering recrimination, never spoken but always present. It tainted the air around her, a miasma of bitterness like sweat, souring as it dried on her skin. He shudders and hurries forward into the maze.

Clueless as to where the Slip shops might be, he solicits the help of the first elder he encounters. An old man, too old to gauge, narrow eyes sunken into layers of deeply wrinkled fat, sat outside his door on a chair whose red plastic protests the weight of wide buttocks. Shock asks directions in Korean, the old Uncle responds in Engrish.

"Third floor, punk. Take blue stair, go right, first left, follow arrows. Whole row of Slip shops there."

"Many thanks, old uncle." Shock bows, on his manners,

not wanting to invite undue attention.

The old uncle sticks out a trembling hand.

"Two flim for information."

"Everyone's on the make," Shock mutters as he races up the blue stairs, already missing those two flim he really can't afford. Fuck Mim, fuck Joon and fuck his idiotic goddamn self.

Shock finds the arrows as promised. Gaudy neon, they point to a row of Slip shops lit so bright he has to fumble out his shades to look at them. He chooses the shop whose name amuses him most: Na-ho's Slip-porium.

"Help you?" Comes from a skinny little Gothster at the desk, chewing on a strand of green liquorice and maintaining the most outrageously complete air of disinterested cool.

"Need a cell."

"Huh, obv. How long?"

"Five standards."

"That'll be eighteen cff." Dangerously cool Gothster holds out a slim hand, fingers jointed in steel, the mesh under the skin of his palm clear in the strip lighting of the shop. Slip-gamer. Not a Master, his gear is nothing special, but Shock's less interested in that than what Gothster just said. He's not sure his ears are quite working.

"Eighteen? You're shitting me, right?"

Cool Gothster stares.

"Where you been, down a hole or something? Fulcrum upped the price again the other week."

"Ah."

The other week Shock was still in a sling with tubes in every orifice. Might explain why this is news to him, and why his flim packet was so much slimmer than he'd thought. Fuck Fulcrum. Always and forever. Kamilla Lakatos created Fulcrum after the world broke, amidst the chaos of a vast population split between hubs, land ships and this last miserable piece of dry land.

With the old Internet gone, its servers drowned, its satellite connections lost, she saw an opportunity to make something new. What she came up with was the Slip, immersive and inclusive, an ocean of information with avatars to swim through it. Seems good right? Wrong. Within two decades, Fulcrum's control of Slip gave it a monopoly, handing Kamilla control of Foon Gung and she made this hell hole everything it is.

Five months ago she corpsed at the grand old age of 235, allowing her son Josef to finally inherit after about a hundred years of waiting around. It was his bright idea to monetize the Slip, crippling everyone who needs to hustle money from Slipping: Games Masters, Pirateers, Patient Zeros, Archaeologists, Imps, Code Jockeys—and Haunts.

He keeps raising premiums like this, he's going to price Fails right out of the market, which to be fair is probably his ultimate aim. His mother created Fails, now he's going to destroy them.

Suppressing a groan, Shock peels off two tens, almost all the ready flim he's got left. He better find what he's looking for first time, or he'll be digging in trashcans for his supper. Gothster assigns him cell #26. It's grubby and stinks of BO but the link-up is clean, the hardware near enough brand new. Whatever happens in the next five standards it won't be his lobes frying up, and for that Shock is immeasurably grateful.

Settling in as comfy as he can on thin, cheap-looking mem-foam long since gone senile and locking himself in, he raises the jack to his nape and sighs as the nano-wires snake inside. There's the usual bright spark of pain followed by a low vibration in the brainpan, so good it's almost sexual. Fuck it, it is sex. Brain sex.

He falls into unconsciousness with a smile on his face

as the wires throw his signal at breakneck speed, plunging his consciousness into a warm avi-pod, the virtual twin of cell #26, filled with what feels like warm, heavy, slightly glutinous water. Odd to think there's no water, yet he feels it anyway. Body and mind are totally fooled in here, makes him wonder sometimes how dangerous that could be.

Liquid pins and needles flood his senses next, unbearable. It builds to a crescendo he always imagines his unconscious self gritting teeth against and begins to spin his information into golden form. Eight fluid limbs uncoil into the virtual waters, just as he knew they would. He has to be Octopus today; it's an Octopus sort of job. As ever, Puss welcomes him in with a swirl of movement that definitely is not his doing. Weird.

Puss is no more than a skin, an elaborate wetsuit he wears in order to work down here. Sometimes though, he swears it has a mind of its own, that it communicates with him; leading him out of danger, down swifter paths, and warning him of trouble he'd have no way of sensing. Probably it's just some connection matrix it has with Slip, acting as a sort of precog, but it doesn't feel that way, and it taps into his smarts in ways he never does IRL. Allows him full use of a brain fried by too many bumps and the forgetfulness of trauma.

Out of literally billions of people who access the Slip, Shock is one of a tiny percentage who can boast dual avatars. That percentage consists of the stinking rich and the rich in Tech-talent. He is, naturally, the latter. You'd think the latter would be numerous with all the Techs dropped from the Cads after Pysch-Fails, but not so. Avi-creation is dangerous and complex, requiring more than mere Tech knowledge. Octopus is from when he was Min-seo, obtained when her hard drive, thus her connection to the Slip, was installed.

Everyone gets a hard drive and therefore an avi as a toddler, free of charge from Fulcrum. His other avi he designed for the stuff he had to do for his less than salubrious contractors. It's a shark—a Great White. A vicious, predatory son of a bitch. He's not fond of it: it's a tool, a means to an end, and that pre-cog he feels with Puss is missing, as is the ability to access his whole brain. Maybe it's because he built it after all the damage, or maybe it's because he's not as hotshot with avis as he is with everything else. Either way, he sees Shark as imperfect work and it frustrates him.

Shock stretches each tentacle, testing reaction times and data-access speeds. Perfect. Could it be this Slip shop hides some seriously state-of-the-art servers behind its cheesy neon glow? Shock pulses his tentacles and exits the avi-pod into the seething waters of the Slip. Noisy and balls-out insane as the Risi party district, the ocean of the Slip is fathomless as the horizon and filled with golden avis; great whales, eels, little swarms of fish, sea lions, dugongs... If you can name a fish or some form of sea-creature you'll find its golden likeness swimming here amongst these sea-life submarine consciousnesses, hunting and sharing information at the millions of skyscraper-like corals riddling the waters.

Each coral rises from profound depths to dizzying heights, where fake sunbeams lay veils of diffused light within which the golden bodies of countless avi glide with balletic grace. Gaudy as Plaza on a Friday night, these intricately constructed conjunctions of network link-ups and nexuses bristle with avis at all times of the day, as though no citizen in the Gung, sea or sky were ever away for more than a second at a time.

Wearing Octopus, Shock spins fathoms deep, to the bottom of the Slip, to where no one but Haunts and system avi-bots ever go, the hidden data troughs and gullies. There are billions of them, a circulatory arrangement of sub-superhighways for all that information the system needs to keep moving from place to place.

Some, like this, are almost empty. Others are like water slides—raging torrents of information, commands and communications, rife with avi-bots. Riding the gushers is an out and out buzz, full-on tripping, drowning and weaving in data. He lives for those moments as much as he lives for the moment the nugget of data, or morsel of code he's after, is locked tight in his flash and being slunk out of the cells right under system's eyes.

Hidden in the sub-network, he heads for the business nodes, another place only avi-bots come, because beyond the nodes, behind layers of VA only a select few could crack, lies the central nervous system of Slip: Hive. Home of the Queens, massive AIs who oversee all info. The Queens are dangerous and clever, and the only thing between them and the Slip is Emblem, a code-lock kept in the Core at the centre of Hive which the Queens cannot see or enter, although they probably know it's there. And for good reason. Emblem is the key to everything virtual.

Though Emblem's a lock and a good one at that, the Queens are past masters at picking the Queen-targeted VA it places between Hive and Slip and escaping for short periods of time. Fulcrum hides their escapes and the devastation they frequently wreak from the Passes, the WAMOS, but Fails see everything. Working in the nodes, this close to Hive, is about as dumb as it gets, but Shock doesn't care. If the Queens escape whilst he's here, there are plenty of nodes to hide in.

Reaching the nodes reserved for Olbax, he makes nano-wires and sends them spiralling out to connect. The node is like all representational objects in the Slip, a slightly hallucinogenic take on reality. Looks like an aquatic puffball mushroom studded with connection inlets. He has enough nano-wires for each, can have as many as he wants down here, it's all a matter of extracting data from around him and reshaping it.

It's not magic, though some of what he does down here feels magical. This whole place is code, and only various applications of Virtual Armament can keep any of that code hidden from him or locked to his use. A newcomer to Tech is always shocked by the level of VA in the system, but old hands like Shock know why it's there. If it weren't, he'd be a god down here. Fucking Superman.

Working at the hub it takes sixteen sweat-soaked minutes to get past mid-level VA to office personnel files. Not exactly a personal record, but not too shabby either, considering the gently over-toasted wreckage he's been of late. Now to find a suitable candidate. Her shadow for years, he can quote Mim's vital stats chapter and verse; all he has to do is cook up a fit from these office fauna non-entities.

That takes another thirty-three minutes exactly, by which time he's a gibbering wreck. Considering he took four minutes to get here in the first place he's got exactly seven minutes before the plug's pulled whether he's ready or not. Suppressing an odd pang in his stomach, he DL's the details to his flash, retracts his nano-wires, and pulses back to the gully.

He gets out with two minutes to spare and, weaving between the cells, exits the shop with a jaunty wave at the Gothster who, quite rightly, blanks him flat. Foot to street takes half the time street to Slip shop took now he knows the way, and he's shivering at the mono station before long, feeling unusually dirty.

He's done this a dozen and more times before, even for a job of this extent where Mim is essentially going to become this poor, hapless office drone for several days, thereby replacing her, this... who is it again? Realizing he didn't have time to clock her name, he accesses the stats he stole. Unity Jo-Charbonneau. Interesting name.

There's that pang again. Is it guilt? Shock pushes trembling hands into his gut, feeling the slippery material of his jacket slide away under questing fingers.

"Hungry," he decides. Because guilt is too scary by half.

A bowl of noodles later, the pang remains, sat uncomfortable as gas behind a full belly, and the name Unity Jo-Charbonneau spins in his head like a fairground ride, fast and nausea-inducing. He tells himself she'll only feel invisible for a few days, only a few days of wondering what the hell's happened to her life and who that stranger everyone thinks is her might be. Then she'll have it all back. Office mediocrity, small apartment somewhere cheap, all the bland trappings she's thus far taken for granted. And all she'll feel, whoever she is, is relief that everyone once again knows she's herself, and whoever was pretending to be her is long gone and won't be back.

Or she won't. Because she won't make three days. Maybe she'll drown herself at Port, or swan-dive from a mono platform to become a small, spread-out stain on the ground below. Or run into Streeks and end up a crumpled rag of skin in an alley or a dumpster, nothing left to identify the person she isn't any more. But he can't think about that.

Can't think either about the possibility that she's brighter than office material and crowbarred into a less than interesting life through the whim of her Pyschs. Can't entertain anything like that, even if he knows it could be true. Shock survives like this: focus on Sendai; forget everything else.

If he tries hard enough, he can make anything fade to background noise.

amiga and the shit mountain

emper held in a death grip, Amiga pounds stairs three at a time, cursing out of order shoot shafts, the heady apex of a vertigo-inducing shit mountain of a day. Normally she'd plant a flag and own that shit, but her stress-management skills have gone AWOL, sending her from bad to worse, to turning an important Cleaning job into a major clusterfuck, provoking an unnerving response.

Amiga dislikes herself today more than she does most days, and she's holding her bag away from her body as if it smells rotten. In a couple of hours it probably will, but she'll be rid of the contents by then. Getting rid of the sneaking self-doubt and bone-deep dislike won't be anywhere near as easy.

Rounding the corner at high speed, she attacks the next flight with equal ferocity, aware that time has no intention of waiting for her. Three flights more and she's out onto the roof of the 'rise, one of about fifty cluttering up the block. Breath coming in hard gusts, she powers across to the edge and crouches out of sight, checking her watch, counting the seconds and her blessings with them. Four minutes. Perfect.

She accesses her flash, cracking onto the secure frequency cooked up for this little shindig.

Here.

Flesh flashes to her right. Deuce, hiding just a little higher on the next 'rise.

About time, Amiga. What in hell kept you?

None of your damn business.

Faux-hurt ripples down the feed back at her—that's new, clever bastard.

Harsh much.

She rolls her eyes. Neat trick. Asshole.

Isn't it just? he replies judiciously. Adds with extra snark on the side, You're fucking late be tee double-ya, and this is our only chance, so you'll permit me a little grievance.

Get off my case. You know I have other business to attend.

You went on a job first? Did you deliver yet?

Nope.

It's still with you? A great wave of disbelief roars down the feed, rattling her skull.

She hisses, cat-like.

Cut that out, Deuce, or I will carve you up. I had to have reason to get into the vault today.

That's plain nasty.

No, it's my job, asswad! Pissed beyond measure, she slams off the frequency.

It's not his fault he irritates her so much, he never used to until she dumped him. Work that one out. She can't. Taking a deep breath she opens her bag. Next to a black cloth sack she avoids with a fastidious wrinkle of her nose, is a portable bolt-thrower. Deuce's design. A pretty little lightweight contraption one fuck-load tougher than it looks. Over on the other 'rise, Deuce is packing its twin. The wires on these babies have semi-robotic ovoid weights at the end rather than points, equipped with weapon-system immobilizers. They're aiming to catch a drone, not destroy it.

Catch a drone.

Therein lies her whole ish with this shit. Deuce didn't furnish her with all the facts, big surprise. Turns out they're not the only J-Hack collective catching a drone. This thing she's going to thieve from her boss will be going out on five drones in total to hell alone knows where. One drone would be bad enough, but five? Stupid.

Drones are a collective, controlled by the Hive Queens. The collective will notice these ones missing; it's just a matter of time. They won't find them, but that doesn't mean they can't triangulate final positions and use abstracted data to map the probabilities behind the loss. This could, eventually, lead them back to the Hornets. It's an outside chance, but it exists, and the Hornets are too cool about the whole thing. Why? Because the contract is for Da Fellows.

Amiga doesn't dig it. Her danger-dar is on red alert and her continued involvement is down to one single thing: if she doesn't do this they will. And letting them wander happily to their deaths is not an option. But their naive trust in this Fellows type pisses her off. Especially Deuce's. He's got smarts to spare, yet he's wasting none of them on analysing what the hell might be going on here. It galls her no end.

She's halfway through assembling the bolt-thrower when Twist pops into her IM. She jumps for reals, almost putting the bolt through her own goddamn leg.

Amiga. You need to explain why you aren't here, reporting in.

Mouthing a litany of the foulest words she can conjure, she scoots in further to try to hide her signal with the wall—which is so beyond futile she plans to give herself a slap for it later—and replies.

I had some quick business to attend first.

Unpleasant silence.

He speaks, and the displeasure in his flat Scots brogue makes her wince. See that when this business is done, you get your arse over to me double time. I want Nero where I can see his weasel face, and I don't want to wait any longer. Understood?

Crystal.

He cuts her off as cold as she cut Deuce and she bangs her head against the wall a couple of times.

"Fuck, fuck, fuck, fuckity, fuck."

The whir of the drone, almost zen-like, cuts into her thoughts and she's up, completed bolt thrower poised on her shoulder. She sees it down at the end of Zhōngshānlù Block moving fast, a speck of glitter in the pale glow of 'rise spotlights and dimly lit windows.

A nauseating mix of excitement and fear hits her solar plexus. Zhōngshānlù is on the edge of China-town, where it bleeds seamlessly into Korea-town, a little area known as Cho-ree, a fair trek away from Sakkura and Jong-phu. If this doesn't go by the numbers, their numbers are basically up right here and now. If Amiga was religious she'd have gone and burnt a whole stack of incense over this and murmured a prayer or three. Something Michiko taught her perhaps.

High above on the mono line, the .788 zips past, right on time. Behind it should be two other Hornets: KJ and Vivid. They've got the unenviable task of getting the drone back to Sakkura along the mono without being seen. They're bringing a scrambler to block the collective, but if they don't stick to schedule they'll get totalled by the .783, the next mono due, or clocked by drones on patrol. The amount that could go wrong makes Amiga's head hurt. She opens her frequency.

KJ, Vee?

Hey babe. Vivid. Amiga can just about see her, a speck on the line. KJ the lanky speck next to her.

Ready?

As we'll ever be.

Deuce?

Ready for his new parlour trick now and in no mood for it, she blocks the fury wave, but he still yells loud enough to deafen.

What in hell did you cut me off for? Again!

No time for argument. You ready?

Yeah, Yeah, I'm ready.

Amiga checks the time.

Thirty seconds. No one moves until the signal. We've got a three-second window when it's in our sights.

I said I'm ready.

Ignoring his snark, Amiga focuses on the space between the dull gleam of the ovoid bolt and the place the drone will be when she pulls the trigger. The drone whirs along almost silently, until it's close enough that she can see it. Drones are quite beautiful, like Slip avis. She lines up her shot, breathes out, and fires. In the corner of her eye she sees Deuce's line zip out at the exact same moment.

Above them, another line drops at speed from the sky. On the end is a tiny, hellaciously powerful magnet, with the scrambler attached. As the lines strike, spinning the bolts around to hold the drone in position for that valuable window, the magnet hits. She raises a fist to pump it, then realizes something's wrong. The drone, immobilized, should have begun to rise as Vivid and KJ's line reels in. Instead, it's still falling, the lines whirring away along with it.

Dismay fills Amiga's frequency.

What's the deal, Deuce?

Old drone specs are hard to come by, I had to extrapolate weight from rough comparison calcs. Looks like I was off.

He sounds furious. Deuce hates making mistakes.

What do we do?

The magnet needs ramping up before the lines run out and tear it apart.

You got a remote on that thing?

Hell no. Remotes give off signals. We're noisy enough.

She takes a second to analyse the situation. Cut and run, or try to salvage this?

"No such thing as quitting," she mutters, silently cursing the day and her own stupidity.

Hold it steady, she says to Deuce, already regretting her decision.

What?

Hold. It. Steady. I'm going to reel in my line and jump over.

Are you insane?

Amiga chokes out a laugh.

Well obviously. Just hold it.

Securing her thrower, she sets the line to reverse at double speed and stop halfway. As Deuce's line goes taut, she backtracks across the roof and sprints, striking off the edge as hard as she can to launch herself at the line. No gloves, no safety net, no fucking brains. Amiga decides that if she lives she's going to give herself hell.

Her stomach cramps as the world drops away. Cold air whips her hair into her face where it clings like stringy black spider webs, stinging her eyes and catching at her lips, and nausea chases terror from her stomach. The line looms in her face. She grabs it with both hands, holding in the scream as her palms slice open. Slides down the wire in an out-of-control descent that threatens to eject her intestines out through her nostrils.

The drone comes up fast beneath her, a giant, angry robotic beast, thrashing on the rapidly unspooling line. Amiga clamps her boots on the wire to slow herself and comes to an unsteady halt about a foot above its writhing back. Still hundreds of feet away as yet, the ground rushes toward her as the drone's weight drags the line down. She's got to move fast. There's only so much spare line in Vivid and KJ's rig and their throwers.

The air is freezing, dulling the pain in her hands, numbing her frazzled nerves. The drone's struggling hard, trying to get loose of the bolts and the lines, and there's the magnet, dead centre on the thorax, perfect for the distribution of force. How the hell does Vivid do that shit? Eyes like a goddamn hawk.

"Nice shot, Vee," she murmurs, whilst IMing Deuce. What do I do?

Link to it with your flash. Here's the code. Ramp it up to three times the strength, just to be on the safe side.

Got it, she says, breathing quiet as she can to still the thump of her heart. If she panics, it's over. The connection is a tiny jolt, a burr in the brain, and then she's communicating with the magnet. She doesn't know how Tech heads like Deuce can do it all the time: talking to machines with their odd, alien not-consciousnesses. It's like sticking your brain in a bucket of cement. She feels when it works though, and the magnet takes firmer hold. The sudden stop sends a bolt of pure white agony through her hands.

"Mother goddamn...!" She breathes out slow, trying to find her centre, her cool.

Okay, Vee. Reel it in. Quick. You're six minutes to the next mono and almost totally off sched.

Fully compos of that, shug. On it.

The drone begins to reel up fast, forcing her to hang on tight. Deuce yells victory through the frequency. His bolt activates, untangling its line from the drone and shooting back to his thrower at a low-octave whine. She needs to do the same, or her line will snap tight and rip a chunk of the drone out. Reaching down to grasp the bolt, she untangles the line and winds it securely around her torso. Holding on for grim death, she jumps, bracing in anticipation of face-planting into concrete and dreading the climb to the roof with her palms sliced and gushing blood. Fun.

By the time she's pulling her battered body back over the edge and onto the 'rise, KJ and Vivid have reported in from the Hornet's nest. Whole business done and dusted exactly to schedule even with their two-minute delay, and the drone collective none the wiser. Funny how Amiga doesn't give a shit.

Deuce reaches over and helps her up by the wrists.

"You're an idiot," he says. "A brilliant, amazing fucking idiot." He doesn't let go of her wrists either as she sets feet to roof, sliding his hands up to turn hers over and examine her palms and oh this is way too familiar and way too much. Why does it keep happening? She needs to stop giving him reasons to touch her.

"Tell me about it another time," she says, snatching her hands out of his and grabbing some close-fitting gloves from her bag. They're her work gloves and have all manner of interesting things woven on the inside. Should stem the bleeding and keep them secure long enough for Ravi, the Hornet's sawbones, to fix them up. "I'm late to Twist. Deal with my thrower will you?"

Deuce's smile falls apart.

"Sure thing. You'll be okay?"

She nods. "Don't worry about me. Just be ready to haul arse by the time I get back. I want that drone gone from

Jong-phu. This shit is making me hella twitchy."

"Count on it."

She grabs her things and runs off to the staircase door, throwing over her shoulder, "I am."

Twist lives in Sendai, in Denenchofu Plaza; five two-mile high 'scrapers grouped around an enormous glass-enclosed courtyard. Ex-clu-sive. Amiga strides in, ducking as Waxwings and Flycatchers whir over her head, the metal in their wings making tiny musical clicks. They're supposed to be inside but some get trapped out here in the foyer like real birds, butting mindlessly against the glass.

In the courtyard proper the roar of a plunging waterfall assaults her ears. The massive centre of Denenchofu is a full-size real-life reproduction of "Oban Yoko-E" by Hiroshige. Wind-warped trees hang perilously from sheer multi-coloured rock cliffs. Grasses and woodland sway in manufactured breezes, and the cries of golden eagles echo over the bellow of the falls. The only false note in the reproduction, the falls were added to freshen the air and stir the almost lake-sized koi and catfish pond on the other side.

Amiga takes the tunnel carved through the centre of the mountain. Her footsteps tap in the air, a tinny beat beneath the holler of water and the scream of eagles, and she exits into the Temple Gardens beneath a canopy of weeping willows. At this late hour, the silver sides of the Plaza's towers scintillate in the blue glow of biome trees, and she heads for the top of the courtyard, for Central Gardens.

The entrance is chipped to keep out undesirables, but she's a Cleaner and therefore cleared, so as she approaches Amiga lifts her right hand, feeling the tingle as it's scanned. Tries not to smile as the glass doors peel apart, welcoming her into luxury. Never show your pleasure, or it will be crushed.

Central Gardens is designed to mimic an old mountain village. Perfectly elegant wooden houses, painted in delicate shell or cream shades, sit along steep, old stone lanes, their shutters closed to prying eyes. The soft yellow glow of lanterns replaces the brighter blue of biome trees, but trees are everywhere, scenting the air with a soft mixture of jasmine and cherry blossom that never seems to fade. Money it seems can buy anything, including perpetual summer.

There's a discreet selection of shoots for the physically challenged but Amiga—ignoring her bone-deep tired and multifarious nerve-pain noise—chooses to walk as usual, enjoying the fresh air, the gentle swish of heavily laden branches in the artificial breeze and the murmuring of waterfalls in private ponds—storing the quiet as a counterweight to the stress of dealing with Twist. If she doesn't look up or out to the sheer glass walls, she can imagine the world was never broken here, and re-invent her place in it. Pretend she has another kind of life; neither the one she was born with nor the one that allows her to pass into this shrine to riches.

For Amiga, family has always been part of the problem. Growing up in poverty, in that matriarchal tornado of an indifferent mother and bitter aunts and slamming against the immovable walls of her father's disappointment, she learnt to disappear. When Michiko died it was the only way she could cope.

Unsurprising then that she ended up working for Twist, drawn to the sort of family she wants to run away from. She can't explain the Hornets by the same theory. They're an anomaly. Decent kids, with good hearts and good intentions; she can't understand how she deserves them. They're like a precipice she's destined to lose her grip on.

Twist's home is on the fifth level from the top. She waves her hand at the gate. It cranks open and Geo, the Muscle, a great big German with a square head like the butt-end of an anvil, emerges flanked on either side by the Guns, Twist's personal guards. Slender girls with flat amber eyes and neat black ponytails, they're Puerto Rican, deaf mute, communicating when the occasion calls for it in rapid, graceful hand movements. Geo understands them but can't make the signs—his hands are too damn big and clumsy—so they read his lips just like they read hers.

"Here to see Twist."

Geo sniffs. "'Course you are. He sent an escort." He gestures at the Guns, who nod.

Amiga nods back, her stomach loosing from its moorings, dropping into the bowl of her pelvis. Still, she hangs on to her cool.

"For me? Thoughtful, but unnecessary."

A shit-eating grin devours Geo's outcrop of a chin.

"Just for you, babe. You been a bad girl? Not cleaning up after yourself?"

Amiga hefts her bag.

"Cleaning just fine, thanks. Maybe you wanna look?"

Geo swallows, steps back. He's a squeamish one, that's why he's Gate Muscle. Easy, bloodless shit. No one would, or could, threaten Twist on his home turf.

"You keep that for Twist," he mutters.

Amiga shoulders her bag again and walks, Guns on either side of her, up the elaborate stones of the path and in through a front screen painted with a perfect copy of Hokusai's "Amida Waterfall on the Kiso Road". Usually Amiga takes time to admire it and the many other

Hokusai repros painted on the inner screens, but she's too distracted. Acquainted as she is with Twist's techniques, she knows the Guns are merely intimidation; if he wanted her dead, she would be. It still stings though, and she's still afraid. He's never used intimidation on her before. Perhaps she's no longer a favourite? Twist can be fickle.

The Guns lead her through the house into the Solarium at the back, a fragile pod of glass and metal. Twist's twist as he likes to call it, its Neo-Gothic ornamental spikes and lancet arches so at odds with the ancient Japanese elegance of the rest of the house. Twist waits there on a spindly Louis chair.

He doesn't offer her a seat, though the Solarium's full of more of the same, which Amiga takes as a bad sign. As they approach, he raises a finger and the Guns move away. Amiga tries to pretend the loosening in her back is unrelated. Yeah, right. And she's not on the verge of puking either.

"So. Better late than never," he says, and this time there's nothing in his demeanour to reassure.

She restrains her tongue from going into overdrive on apologies and nods, keeping up that pretence of who he thinks she is.

"Yeah."

"You look a bit worse for wear. Everything okay?"

"Dandy."

Twist looks at her gloved hands.

"Injury? Again?"

"Misjudged my exit. No one saw and zero evidence left."

He tuts. "You've a habit for clumsiness these days, Amiga. Lucky you're one of my best. Get it seen to, eh? Wouldn't like anyone thinking I don't take care of my family."

"I will."

"See that you do." He tilts his head in the direction of her shoulder. "Something of mine in there?"

"There is indeed."

Amiga hooks the black sack out of her bag, trying to conceal the overwhelming relief she feels at finally being rid of it. Placing it on the table, she loosens the ties, revealing a half squashed human head, neatly drained of blood and missing eyes, ears and nose. The resulting holes are sewn up with coarse black thread. In life, this head belonged to a lowdown piece of drug-running shit called Nero. Delusions of grandeur. His real name was apparently Terence. And now it's mud.

Twist's mouth twitches. "Nice touch with the thread."

"I like to improvise."

The twitch briefly widens to a smile. He reaches out, flicks the sack back over Terence's remains.

"Okay. Okay, Amiga. You pass this time. But..." He leans toward her, those excavating eyes of his drilling for black gold in her brain. "Look, you're an asset to me, but I'm not blind. I know there's shit going down and you're up to your pretty little neck in it, you and that J-Hack rabble you call friends. All I ask is that you don't drag me into it. Don't make me have to Clean a favourite. Understand?"

She nods, her heart slamming into her ribcage, hard enough to crack bone.

"Understood."

"Good. Now get that in my vault."

Summarily dismissed, Amiga grabs her bag and leaves the Solarium, heading toward the living areas and the vault. Twist's money has bought the kind of vault some of the wealthiest oligarchs in Foon Gung would give their eyeteeth for: a set of rooms armoured like tanks and armed to the teeth.

And she's got to steal from it.

"This had better be worth it," she mutters, moving into the maze of storage as it allows her egress.

First things first, she places the head in the show case, standing clear as it plops gently into its glass aquarium full of preservative and using the glass rod to nudge it until it rests neck down. It's a pretty gallery of the dead this, everyone who ever crossed Twist, or thought about trying.

"I'll be here soon," she says to Terence. "Probably look even prettier than you. Won't that be a treat?" He doesn't reply, not even in her imagination, but then his mouth is sewn shut, and she's a pragmatist all the way through.

Activating surveillance interference supplied by Deuce, she throws her physical signal so it looks like she's still at the tanks and races to the data-storage facility. Deuce also gave her means to access it without detection, a piece of Hunt/Collect software cluttering her neural drive she can't wait to purge. Jacking in, she lets the H/C do its work, rooting out the package Fellows insists is here.

Amiga can hack to a degree. She was on track for Corp and has a fair working knowledge of Slip, Tech and code, but Deuce's shit is way beyond her knowledge, so she's doing this on trust. Not her strong point. It makes for uneasy waiting. But just as Fellows said, the package in question is there, and Amiga works quickly to DL a copy of it, hearing the ticking of the clock loud as death knells.

It takes literally seconds, which does precisely nothing to make Amiga feel less likely to puke up the entire wet contents of her ribcage, and two minutes later she's walking out through the gates, waving her usual flippant middle finger at Geo and resisting taking the shoot. Twist may not immediately grasp his storage has been accessed. He may even take weeks to notice, as Deuce insisted would be the case, but he'll click in a light second to unusual behaviour. So she'll walk back down and all the way to the mono, no matter how exhausted and frightened she is right now, because that's what she always does.

Anything to keep breathing, that's her motto, and it's precisely how she's lasted long enough to be risking her stupid life all over again.

trouble on the high seas

her wheels ploughing up sixty-foot sprays of brine and foam, Resurrection sweeps across open water like a cyclone. She's sailing what used to be the East China Sea, triangulating in on a distress signal, some unfortunate perhaps worked over by pirates or come a cropper on the spikes hidden beneath the ocean around the East China Ranges. Serrated masses of solid rock that, due to a lack of basic sonar equipment, take two or three ships per year.

Once upon a time there were almost one and a half thousand land ships on the ocean, now there are only a few hundred. Give it another century, maybe less, and this way of life will be nothing but a memory. So much of the old world has been lost; it seems a shame that the new might follow it into history so soon.

This signal is loud and will have been heard by others. Resurrection's aiming to be first on the scene. If the ship they find is a total loss, they'll grab whatever they can before it's claimed by the sea and rescue any survivors. If it's not, they'll help it regain sea-worthiness and fend off anyone who might have followed the signal with less honourable intentions.

Perched on his crow at the prow, doused in errant spray and sweeping the horizon through his 'scope for signs of their ship in distress, Petrie spots a glinting in the sky on their port side. Now what in hell is that?

Incoming sou'west, he roars at the port crows. Who's got eyes out there. C'mon!

He looks back through his 'scope. The glinting is larger now, bright as lens flare, and trailing an unmistakable smoking tail. Monkey-agile, he leaps to the ropes, clipping on to spin down, and as he heads for the port side sentry shouts arouse the attention of Cassius Angel, his captain, perched atop the crow at the centre today instead of his customary position on the crow base beneath.

A tall, rawboned man of Nigerian descent, covered in patterns of tribal scars like the flowering chaos of migrating birds, Cassius jumps from his perch and slides to the nearest walkway on frayed ropes. He reaches port side at a flat run just as Petrie does.

"What gives?" he shouts to Petrie over the churn of the wheels.

"Looks like a sec-drone," Petrie yells back, struggling to see the thing through the bright halo of sunlight refracting from its shell as it plummets toward the ocean.

Cassius raises a brow. "All this way out?"

"Can't be anything else. Only birds, cities and drones fly these days."

Acknowledging that with an incline of the head, Cassius says, "Unusual to be sure."

"More'n that. Drone from the land being this far out in the drink. You for taking a look or taking it out?"

"It's not firing," Cassius replies thoughtfully, his more reasoned approach being why he's captain and Petrie's second in command. "Looks like it's damaged, coming in smoking like that. I want a look at it. A careful look. Just to be sure we aren't in for some kind of trouble."

"Aye."

Spinning his clip clamp to max, Petrie clips on to a thick side rope and leaps over the edge, spinning down to join the men and women on the gantries below. The whole of Resurrection is encased on her upper level in a steel framework, within which rest her wheels, her schooner bays and her loading gear, including rank upon rank of grappling hooks ready to use in all their retrieval and rescue operations.

Unravelling the hooks ready to pull in the drone, they're soaked by the impact wave. The drone hits with a sucking roar of sound as whatever's on fire in its tail is deprived of oxygen. Gasping through freezing water as the hooks splash in, snagging purchase, Petrie begins to haul.

He's only ever seen drones in the distance under lights and sun and when it finally breaks clear of the water, he's stunned by its beauty and surprising elegance. Shaped like a ray and see-through, the shell and innards something like glass but tougher and reactive to touch; intricately sectioned wings writhing helplessly within their grasp as they pull it up the City's rearing side onto the flat.

"Unexpected," Cassius murmurs in his deep drawl, running a curious hand the length of the body section and watching as the segments roll together smoothly, rearing away from his touch. "Looks like it belongs in sea, not sky."

"I don't like it being here," Petrie mutters.

His captain looks at him. "You in favour of blowing it sky high, Bosun?"

"Depends. Drones don't allow themselves to get taken like this, not even damaged. Their weapons systems are designed to self-heal. It being out here, and helpless to boot, is probably no coincidence."

"Agreed. But I want it examined to see what's going on."

Swaddled in a sling and attached to the winch, the drone's hauled to the workshops by crews of men and women, all shouting out the count, their muscles gleaming under sunlight and water drops. Inch by inch they lower it in through the access hatch where the workshop crews work swiftly to fasten it safe to two heavy machine benches.

Cassius and Petrie arrive in the workshops as the last straps are being secured. Scratch, Chief Tech of the Resurrection, bounds over enthusiastically, his dog, Samson, trotting at his heels, panting clouds of foul breath into the hot confines of the 'shop. Petrie moves downwind, waving a not so discreet hand. In his opinion Scratch smells as bad as the mangy mutt attached to his shadow and has about as little shame.

"Opinions, Scratch," Cassius demands, before the Tech's even had a moment to lay hands on the vast machine taking up two of his benches. "Petrie here says this thing can self-heal its weapons systems, so why aren't we taking fire?"

"Bosun ain't wrong."

"So...?" Cassius moves back a pace, his hand falling to the spike-gun at his hip.

Scratch flips down his visor. A soft whirring comes from within as he accesses schematics, checks general safety. He sniffs. Shrugs.

"It's not broken, just mostly offline. Stripped to bare functions and disconnected from the collective. Helpless."

Petrie and Cassius exchange deeply interested glances.

"How's it here? Coincidence?" Cassius asks.

"Not a bit of it. It's been tasked to find us. I'm seeing specs for a ship that has to be this one, and a package, locked up with quite the crypt payload. Uh... and it's got Volk's name on it."

"Volk?" Cassius frowns.

Petrie's stomach clenches, a shot of acid firing up into his throat.

"Refugee. I er... took her on at the Gung when we docked for our server check. She's been working between Tech crews. Very knowledgeable. Very useful. I knew she was on the run from something, but this..." He swallows. Shakes his head. "I'm sorry, Captain. I made a mistake."

Cassius reaches out a large hand to grasp Petrie's shoulder.

"Hold hard there, Bosun. We have no idea if this is trouble or not yet. Let's gather the facts before we leap." He turns back to Scratch. "Anything you can see right now to suggest why a new crew member's name might be there?"

"Beats me," he says. "For what it's worth, Cap, I like the woman. Knows her stuff, like Petrie said. Bit remote like and weird eyes from all her implant tech, but she fits. Does more'n her fair share. Smart as a freakin' whip. Can't say as I look at her and think trouble, knoworramean?"

"I hear you, Scratch. Duly noted. What about the damage?"

"Low-range EMP knocked out some of its propulsion systems. Reckon we got pirates." Scratch flips up the visor. "I figure since their first shots failed, they'll not be far behind."

And, as if he's conjured them by speaking, the attack sirens out on the lookout crows begin to howl.

"Anything against saying that right off?" Petrie yells, furious, and receives one of Scratch's eloquent shrugs in response.

Side by side, he and Cassius sprint from the workshops as the ship responds to the threat with a well-oiled, much-practiced routine proven in many a previous battle. Citizens drain downward back onto the living deck via specially designated free routes, hurrying to safety, calling in children too young for school and bolting their doors.

Whilst they disappear, the ship's crew comes from every level and hits the sides to work the big fifty-cal guns and the harpoons, or take up smaller arms. There are thousands of active crew members but this takes place in mere minutes, the guns clanking and rising to aim before the first round of attack sirens has run through.

Approaching on the port side are three pirate schooners. Sixty-footers, riddled with guns and armour. By the time they're within range, the Resurrection's heavy artillery is locked in and loaded and begins a smooth, relentless barrage of ammo made from alloys smelted and moulded in Scratch's workshop. The sea around the schooners churns wildly with heavy impacts punctuated by cataclysmic explosions of wood and steel.

Given no time to properly respond, the schooners manage only a few rough return shots that barely make it to within fifty metres of Resurrection's sides and then they're panicking, trying to turn. They won't make it. These are advance ships and they're too small to have any chance whatsoever against the might of a land ship of Resurrection's size.

Petrie and Cassius stand atop the captain's crow, watching through the 'scope as they collapse into the sea, flaring distress. Petrie's heart sinks with them. He knows these schooners, their colours are only too recognizable.

"They're from the Ark," he says.

Cassius leans in for a look on another 'scope, spits furiously on the deck.

"Shit."

"Pentecost likes to keep his crew close. Our window is tiny. They'll be no more than a day ahead, thirty-six hours at the most," Petrie says, trying to keep the fear from his voice. Usually they avoid ships like the Ark. It's the safest way to get on and there's a whole ocean, plenty of opportunity to steer clear.

They've arrived at smoking wrecks the Ark's just left behind or seen them way out in the distance, but thus far they've managed to avoid contact and therefore conflict. There's no way to avoid it now. The Ark will come for its schooners. It will come for whatever sent them down. And it will keep coming until it catches them. What if Pentecost remembers him? What if this ship, his home, is taken?

"Ark's fast," agrees Cassius. Leaning back from the 'scope as the second schooner disappears beneath the waves with a drawn out groan of metals, he says, "No way we're going to outrun it, not even with two days' head start, and they've got what... fifty, maybe sixty plus schooners?"

"Shoulda let the drone sink."

"Would it have made a difference?"

The question gives Petrie pause for thought.

"Reckon not. They followed it here because they wanted it. They'd assume we had it and attack anyway. We were screwed from the get-go."

"That we were. Bad day. We'll head out, find a hub to hide beneath." Cassius looks out to the ocean, already working out which is closest. "Figure out what to do with that drone once we're secure. Bring Volk in on it."

"Is that a good idea?"

"Her damn name's on it," Cassius says. "I want to know why."

"I don't know about trusting her to tell the truth." Petrie's talking more about his own gullibility here. He desperately wants to have been right about her, because if he was wrong...

"I don't intend to give her license to lie," his Captain tells him, with a look grim enough to convince. Cassius is rarely angry, even more rarely violent, but when his crew are endangered you wouldn't want to be on the wrong side of him. "Now what say we get this ship to safety? Nearest hub is sou'east and five hours at full knot."

"Cape Town Hub. Aye, Captain."

Petrie jumps from the lookout, yelling before he's even hit the ropes, calling the orders for the course adjust and full speed ahead. They don't have a lot of time. The schooners successfully sent their distress flares, small robotic units designed to shoot high and transmit location, condition, and a call for back up.

Doubtless Pentecost has the Ark turned in their direction even as the Resurrection turns to run. Petrie tries not to think about what'll happen if they're not signal dark and out of scope-view quick smart. He knows Pentecost well, and he's never stopped being afraid of him.

mim bearing gifts

f he weren't wearing his Bengs, Shock would be dragging his feet like a six-year-old on the way to the dentist right now. This bit right here, this whole delivery in person, face-to-face, in the physical dimension as it were, is the reason why he sits up later than usual some nights in the redolent fart stench of old men sleeping, the snores like land ships scraping rock from the crust, and contemplates the positive values of starving. The general pros of homelessness. The benefits of possible mutilation and/or horrific death versus the warmth and safety of his cage. And often finds the margin of cons temptingly thin.

This time Mim wants to meet at a detox juice bar. Beyond bizarre. On a par with those nutbag conspiracy theorists hollering on street corners about the breaking of the world being aliens, or illuminati, or Japanese schoolgirls or some shit. Mim would never go on a detox in a million years, unless they changed the definition of the word entirely to somehow mean "filling your body with crap". He used to marvel at Mim's appetite for bad things. That was before he realized that those appetites were a litmus test for the acidic rot sloshing about on her insides.

The bar she's chosen is one of those godawful kawaii-themed fishbowl places, so much pop-eyed, cutesy, frilled-and pastel-coloured crap plastered in every direction it's like a giant amuse plushie walked in and exploded. Mim's waiting outside, leant up against the glass, her suit reflecting garish bubblegum-coloured lettering in eye-watering kaleidoscope. Shock groans and covers his eyes.

"Fuck's sake, Mim, turn it off. Going blind."

"Hell no, wear these." She hands him her sunnies.

He plonks them on. Normally he wouldn't, but this is life-and-death shit. Points at the shop, unable to wipe a sneer from his face.

"You wanna actually go in there? For real?"

"Sure. I'm thirsty."

"I was hoping this was an elaborate joke at my expense."

She grins. "How you know it's not, Shocking boy?" And she struts on in, a tiny, shapely mirror ball of kawaii cute.

Being Mim, she goes for the most obnoxious drink on the menu, a pink-and-yellow confection packed with edible glitter and sugar. If there's any actual fruit in it, he'll eat her sunglasses. He goes for the safe option: more of his favourite bitter green tea whizzed together with sharp apples and biting lime, tart enough to wake the dead. They take a quiet corner, padded with sheepskin and hidden by drooping silver nets. Soon as his arse hits fluff, Shock's ready to shoot stats to her IM, but Mim's IM is on lock. What?

"Unlock and let me dump this shit."

She blinks at him, all innocence.

"This is not just a drop off. When have I ever had you drop off anywhere as tasteful as this?"

And here it is. There had to be something. Mim can never just be straightforward.

"What's the job, Mim?"

"How do you know I have a job for you, Shocking boy?

Could be I want to say hi, catch up, see how you're doing. You still look frankly cadavarish. Could be I'm worried."

He gulps down his drink, wishing the shots of caffeine were liquid bumps.

"Not you, Mim. You only ever want one of three things: flim, a fuck, or my help on a job. Considering how much you paid for the horror you're currently ingesting and how broke you know I am, this is probably not about flim. I hear you've been hanging off Johnny Sez and he's a man-whore, so that's your fuck sorted. Only thing left's a job."

She hisses between neat little teeth hiding too well behind plump lips. So untrustworthy, the bite hidden behind the bark like that. Why didn't he see it? Why does he still want the bite?

"Ooooh, harsh. But you happen to be a-one. I have need of a Haunt. And damn me if you ain't the spookiest spook I know."

"And?"

"This Olbax gig. Ostensibly I'm rumour milling. Spreading dissent. Call me Chinese Whisper etcetera etcetera, buuuuut, I might also be causing mayhem as a diversion. Gotta hunt down a little inside info some Olbax Corp is hogging to themselves and really shouldn't be. It's nice to share. I'll need you to snag that info out. Eaaasy flim."

"So. Olbax again."

Mim's eyes flick away, reflecting everything.

"Not exactly."

"Where then?"

"Paraderm."

She's spoken so quietly it takes a moment to burrow through ear holes and hit brainmeat.

"You can go fuck yourself."

Which is rude enough to piss her right off, but he's

too fucked off to care. Paraderm are major Corp. Make big cheese look like crumbs. Guarantee she's working for someone who wants him dead. Probably why she called. Mim loves nothing more than to poke a wounded animal. Needing her is such bullshit, his kingdom for another option.

Mim stirs the jaunty plastic spoon left in the nauseating crap in her glass and smiles.

"Douse your panties, Shocking boy; calm any thoughts of imminent death. This is Office Fauna only. Level seven, eight at a push."

He's not convinced. "Really? Sure now?"

She shrugs. "As much as I can be. Going on good intel."

Fauna levels in Paraderm are nothing; Shock could do it in his sleep. Doesn't necessarily mean he should. Sleepwalking can be dangerous. So it comes down to what it always does. And here's him pretending he has a choice, just to avoid showing his desperation.

"How much?"

"Five K."

Shock chokes. "Are you kidding me? For hitting Paraderm? What percent is that?" Knowing her it's likely to be far less than fifty, which is another gyp, way worse than the last, considering she can't do shit without his in.

She looks defensive. The only time you ever see anything like convincing emotion on Mim's face is when money is involved. Rather, the unpleasant task of her giving money to someone else, even for a job well done. He imagines it pains her, which makes him want to smile.

"Thirty," she says eventually, unwilling.

He bets himself fifty flim she was thinking about lying. Why didn't she? Maybe she's realized that he's getting tired of this. Tired of her. Or maybe she just really needs this job done. Who the fuck is she working for? Ah well, not his problem. All he has to do is snag the info, hand it over, take his flim and go. And he can afford to push a little too, because no way anyone else will take so little, they'll want 60/40 minimum for a Paraderm job.

"If thirty's it, you can look elsewhere."

They lock gazes, and if he's not mistaken Mim wants to argue, but he can smell the ball in his court already. Sure enough she rips the spoon out of her drink, snaps it in two, and chucks it on the table.

"Fine. Have it your way. Fifty/fifty. Eight K. You're killing me here. Fucking homicide."

"You want those stats now?"

"Give. Your flim's in the usual box. I do wish you'd be sensible and get a cred account."

Refusing to dignify that with a response, he flings the stats into her drive and tries not to laugh as it snaps locked behind them. Rare that he ever gets one up on Mim. He should be suspicious, instead he's hoping with all his heart she's tit-deep in the same shit she forced him to drown in. Black hearted that might be, but that's all he's got left after loving her—a torso full of necrotic meat.

Besides, she's long overdue on collection of all the bad karma she's accrued. Gotta be a mountain of that somewhere with her name torn deep into the core, ragged and bleeding foul waters. So casual, his Mim, in her malice. "Crime's where the money is," she'd said, trailing her nail down his cock. "You want to get enough to get back to Sendai, Shocking boy, you're going to need to commit to crime."

Translated from Mim-speak this meant taking a job from one crime lord and undercutting. Easy, right? Well, yeah. Unless said crime lord happens to be Li Harmony, who's not just a raving psychopath but an Archaeologist. You can't cheat an Archaeologist; their speciality is forensic exploration of info. If there's an info needle someone needs to find, there's not a haystack large enough to hide it from an Archie.

He's a Haunt though, right? Figured he could use his own ghosty skills to hide shit from her. Piece of piss. So yeah, he did the job, liberating the San Sebastian locked data-nodes the Grey Cartel were planning to smuggle up to Chicago Hub. Weeded out a few odd-numbered stacks Mim said he could sell on for, quote "a fucking fortune"— and got caught.

Woke up one morning to a knock on the door of his apartment-share with Mim, the bed empty and cold beside him. And why didn't he wonder about that right away? Because he's a fool. Opened the door to find Li Harmony standing there, picking her nails with a stiletto knife, those black, empty eyes incurious. She started quoting serial numbers and asking dead polite, more dead than polite to be honest, where they might be. Thing is, he'd already sold them on, had the flim hidden in the apartment behind him. Cue major panic. When she stopped picking her nails and made to step over the threshold he lost it; every last iota of common sense.

Slammed the door in her face and started grabbing everything he could to shove in his bag, the door making these hideous fucking grinding noises with every pound of her boot. Last thing he did before splitting was to go fetch the flim from its hiding place—but it was gone. Stupidest thing right there is that, at the time, he thought nothing of it. Supposed Mim had taken it to put in a cred account, aggravated as ever with his obsession for physical flim. He still trusted her then.

He escaped out the back window just as the door slammed open, and hit the streets. Home free, because even Archies can't hack a Haunt's location when they don't have a Mim to spot them by. He searched for Mim for days. Even snuck back to the apartment, hoping to catch her there. Finally found out she'd taken a two-week job on a hub the day before Li came for him. Could've been a coincidence, of course it could. Except it wasn't.

He saw her in one of her favourite clubs when she came back, decked out in brand-new Imp gear, doubtless bought with the flim he'd made from those stolen nodes and laughing it up with one of her Imping cronies. Went over to talk and found her blithely unconcerned. Yeah she knew about Li, bad luck right? Had he seen their apartment? What a mess. She knew he'd get away though; she had faith in her baby's survival instincts.

That's when he clocked the reason for the cold bed. That's when he got it. You can't describe hurt like that, it has no boundaries. He finished with her then and there. The only bit of dignity he managed to scrape out of the whole thing.

He's lost it since though, having to work with her, aware the only reason she doesn't go to someone else is because she won't have to pay him as much. And all Mim's ever said about almost getting him killed, when he IM'd the question, too fucked on Bumps and alcohol to do the sensible thing and leave it all alone? You're alive, aren't you?

No point trying to explain to her the mere seconds between that statement being true and being false. It's not that she doesn't care. She can't. Mim is all about Mim, and though he's made several of his own unbelievable mistakes since, stuff so stupid he can't even begin to parse how he came to do it, his dearest Mimic, Mim the Merciless, has had both hands deep in the cards he's been dealt. Maybe one day he'll stop letting her deal them, maybe one day he'll get smart, care enough about himself to say enough.

But today is not that day.

"So what about the deets for Paraderm?"

Mim shrugs. "Lucky for you I'll be in Olbax. Sez'll be in touch when I have the location. All you have to do is wait until he chimes you."

"Fine."

It's not fine. Of course it's not. Last thing he wants in the world is to have that lanky no good streak of piss Sez in his IMs, but he holds his tongue. Leaves the juice bar without a backward glance and heads for anywhere else. Just walking and walking, because it beats standing there and screaming until his throat explodes.

He walks until his legs ache, until he's so hungry his spine feels like it's being throttled, until he can't think in coherent sentences, until his skin is cold and numb, his face hurts, his feet burn. Only then does he go home. Slams a handful of bumps into his neck, ignoring the clamour for something more substantial and dives into sleep.

And this time as the darkness hits, he wonders if he'll even try to wake up.

the problem with evac

dropping to the floor between the multi-coloured jumble of her kitchen and the living area, Amiga kicks off her blades and shrugs out of her jumpsuit, sweaty skin gasping for air. Out for hours tracking some new J-Hack brat Twist wants done over for trying to jack his home servers, she's bad tempered, too hot, and starved half to death. In just her underwear she sinks cross-legged to the floor and reaches across to the cool box, snagging out a surprisingly luke-warm beer. She offers the uncaring walls of her hovel a heartfelt groan.

"Don't tell me, half power."

Being vagabonds and pirates, the Hornets of Jong-phu steal their electricity from the building's generators. On the one hand this means they never pay for that shit; on the other it means that when the 'rise power level bottoms out, as it often does, they end up with little or no power themselves.

She slams the cap off her beer and necks it, her head pressed back into the plastic edge of her sink unit, trying to ignore how synth-beer when warm tastes exactly like spit. Thanks to zero food in twelve hours, the paltry two percent alcohol hits her starved bloodstream like an over-excited jackhammer and, her bones buzzing pleasantly, she begins to think about the positive. Well she would, if there were any.

Half power means that for sure her cool box has defrosted, so there's a damn good chance the piece of fish she got for tonight's dinner has curled up necrotic toes and gone to food heaven. She sighs, chucking the empty across the room in a perfect arc to her overflowing bin. It bounces off two take-away boxes stuffed onto the top and hits the floor with a bang. Amiga throws up her arms.

"Score!"

Head craned to peer at sparsely populated shelves she contemplates her food options, dismissing them with a snort.

"Dandy. Just mother-frackin' dandy. Guess that's noodles for me tonight. Again."

She has a hate/hate relationship with noodles, but they're cheap, nutritious, and she's a beggar who can't afford to choose. Well, okay, that's not entirely true. She had plenty of flim. Fact is she's stuck with noodles because she spent a spit-load of it on a customized crossbow, but a girl's got to have her toys and oh my she can go a lot of days sucking up noodles to play with that puppy once her weapons guy, Janosz, delivers.

Her wall rattles with the syncopation of knuckles dancing in all too familiar patterns.

Deuce.

"Amiga?" Muffled, and with a distinct flavour of neediness that makes her wince. All she wants to do is eat, chuck her cringing skin under a chem shower and sleep. "You in? We have a problem."

Amiga groans again, grinding the heels of her palms into tired eyes.

"Please don't tell me it's the drone coming back to bite us in the arse."

"No, that went like clockwork. I'm a fucking pro, Amiga. You know this."

Amiga knows. She relaxes, her back slumping against plastic and sticking slightly.

"What is it then?"

"It's EVaC."

Of all the Hornets hidden in Jong-Phu, EVaC is perhaps the least normal and most insular, meaning he's the one Amiga has somehow managed to become firmest friends with. Friendship's easy when there's no pressure to do anything but sit and be in each other's presence. Her other Hornet friendships are more fraught and complicated and often make her feel aggravated.

As fond as she is of them, there's so much she wants to live up to and simply can't, and it doesn't help that they seem to think she's better than she is whilst berating her for being an idiot. What do you do with that level of fuckery?

If Deuce is calling her over for EVaC, she assumes the daft bastard's been buying home-made bumps again to try to restrain the clamour in his skull and needs talking down from wherever it is he's ended up. Boy's not good on medication. None of his type is, and yet they're forever taking it. Genuinely annoying. Her rage rises again, a swarm of angry wasps boiling behind her rib cage. Deuce is interrupting her me-time for this?

"What's with him this time? More bump drama?" She can't quite nix the aggro from her tone—it fairly sizzles.

"Please. You need to come see this." He sounds quietly desperate. Okay, that does not sound like a trip gone bad.

She sighs. "Fine. I'll come."

"Thanks, Amiga." Way too relieved. "And put blades on it, yeah? It's urgent. For reals."

"Okay, okay, Deuce. Shit's sake. Gimme a sec, I'm indecent."

Deuce chuckles through the wall.

"I like you indecent."

The silence that follows is epic, full of acute embarrassment, unspoken half-excuses and inarticulate dissembling. He's probably kicking himself in the nuts that he couldn't quite catch that one fast enough. She can't catch her smile either. Lucky he's not here to see it. Maybe he can sense it though, fairly snapping through the wall.

"Just hurry the fuck up, Amiga."

"Cold, Deuce. Real cold."

Somehow, despite her calling time on what was a super good thing, they're still mates, but they suffer from occasional, often excruciating, lapses into old familiarity. Lately he's getting real uptight about those. Been seeing a fairly antagonistic Chinese chick, Fen Maa, from Hangoon's Miso District, home of the soup. The girl's a Tech-Grad, bound for big things, and Amiga thinks he's making a huge mistake. As far as she sees it, the only way this ends is with Deuce's heart in smithereens. Having dismantled it herself only a year ago, she finds she's unwilling to watch some other girl do the same.

Snagging a slippery green mini-dress from the pile of laundry on the table she swears she'll do tonight, or maybe tomorrow night, Amiga yanks it over her head. Sneaks out the hatch good and quiet, booting Deuce with a bare foot, hoping to scare him, or maybe scare up some of that oh-so-amusing shit he was holding back after his little Freudian skid there. But he's either too preoccupied with whatever's up with EVaC, or too accustomed to her shit, because he only offers her a relieved smile, peeling his lanky frame away from her wall.

"Lead on, compadre," she snaps, even more irritated

with him now, just because. "And hurry it up, will you. I'm hungry. Haven't eaten in twelve. Got to nuke me some noodles before I start chewing on the furniture."

"Thought you had a fish supper waiting tonight?" he asks, walking off through lights dimming under the obvious power fail.

"Cool box defrosted, dumbass. If I eat there's a possibility I end up seeing the contents of my stomach up close and personal until Sunday. Not chancing it."

He grins over his shoulder, casual-like.

"We have some gyudon spare. KJ's been cooking."

"Is that a lame invitation?" she asks, thawing slightly. "Because you know I never turn down free food. Consider me following with chop sticks in hand."

"Metaphorical chop sticks," he says. "Messy."

"Like your attempt at jokes. I think Fen Maa stole your funny bone." It comes out loaded with a little more spice than she intended.

"Don't start, Amiga. Please. Or you can put your metaphorical chop sticks in the actual fucking bin."

Amiga rolls her eyes. He's getting sensitive. He never used to be. Or perhaps he was and she didn't notice before now, the possibility of which irritates her, because the last thing she needs is actual evidence of her inability to act like a real human being. She chooses to back off, maybe for the first time ever. Shit, is that maturity? Where the hell did that come from?

"Fair enough. So what's up with EVaC I have to see so fucking urgently?"

He stops outside the hovel he shares with EVaC and Wi Ji Lin, and turns to stare at her. She can't read his face in the darkness but feels the waft of uncertainty clear as the wind before a hurricane, like he used that annoying little trick of his and sent it whipping down through his IM link to hers.

"I really can't explain. You have to see for yourself."

Inside, Wi Ji, or Knee Jerk, KJ as he's more generally known, stands by the door to EVaC's room looking crazy worried. Considering he's forever this worried about something that's not saying much, so she wends her way around piles of junk to push past him into EVaC's dump. He's curled up on the bed, his long tangle of anemic red hair obscuring his face. That's not unusual at all. But he's silent, which absolutely is. And that's when she starts worrying too.

EVaC's a Patient Zero. A freak. A kyōjin. He downloads virads into his neural flash and jacks into the Slip to distribute them amongst unsuspecting and unwilling punters. It's a dangerous job. Virads are catchy for a reason. Designed to hunt out and infect avis in the Slip to spread the good news about some shit avi users wouldn't otherwise want, they're even stickier at the source, the Zero. Outcome is Patient Zero's suffer permanent infection from all the virads they're paid to spread.

Logos leak into their speech patterns, and their buying habits become littered with the often pointless products they've promoted, hence the piles of junk in the boys' house. Zeros like EVaC, who've been in the business for a good while, never fucking shut up. It's like Tourette's; portions of jingles, catchphrases and sound bites leaping from overstuffed neurones to their lips like coins from a keno machine jackpot. They get seriously twitchy if they hold them in for too long, so they tend not to. In other words, silence in a Zero like EVaC is unheard of.

"EVaC? Buddy? You okay there?"

He curls up harder, and she sits on the bed, pushing aside his hair, her worry escalating when he doesn't fight to stay hidden. He's the only gaijin in the whole Hornet crew and shy about his complexion, even with her. Every

memory she has of chilling with him involves his endless
jabbering coming out almost disembodied from within a
cave of hair.

Amiga sucks in a harsh breath as she cops a load of
his face. It's a frickin' pane of glass, veins standing out in
stark relief, bright blue and red. The capillaries branching
between are oddly shaped, almost logical in their curves
and lines, as if attempting to form letters or numbers.

He feels too moist, not sweaty exactly, more
waterlogged from the inside somehow, and his irises,
whilst still that astonishing shade of light blue, reminding
her of sky reflected in windows, are almost as see-through
as his skin. She swears she can see the meat of his optic
nerve behind them—that complicated umbilicus of
wetware connecting back to the brain.

"Shiiiiiiit." She traces the shapes on his cheek
wonderingly. "How long has he been like this?"

"A few days. Since his last big job," Knee Jerk says
quietly, guilty. He should be. Frankly she is too, because
she's EVaC's best bud and she's not seen him in over two
weeks. Fail. Major, stinking friend fail.

"Seriously?" And all her anger at them and herself
comes out in it.

KJ shrugs. "He wanted to keep working. We're not his
caretakers for fuck's sake."

Holy middle of the conversation, Batman. Amiga feels
like she's just missed out on a chunk of explanation.

"From the beginning, asswad," she snaps.

Deuce takes this as his cue.

"Zero's have been avoiding work," he says quietly.
"We got wind of the why: something going down in Slip,
but no deets, so none of us particularly bothered."

"Explanation, because ignoring trouble in Slip is
downright dumb and you know that even if these two

screwballs don't. Aren't you supposed to be their Jiminy Cricket or some shit?"

He shrugs it off. "Look, Zero business has gotten mad organized in the last two years. You know what BS such structural rejigs create. EVaC's not Guild, he hates the whole re-org, wants no part of it. Doesn't want to answer to Mother Zero, despite proper respect for her, and digs not the notion of being affiliated. Being strictly freelance, and therefore in a position to ignore BS, he started taking the jobs other Zeros were refusing. He was making a bundle."

"So when did he get sick?"

"Round about two weeks ago. We didn't think much of it then. It was just a virus. Y'know, sneezing, runny nose, all that good shit. Then it changed..."

"To this?"

"Not straight away," KJ says. He's beside the door, arms crossed hard against his chest. "He's only been this bad since that last job coupla days ago."

Amiga rounds on them, too furious to feel bad when they retreat as far as they can, blank and guarded. Knee Jerk in a karate stance he couldn't possibly hope to defend himself from.

"And you only just thought to call for help?"

"He told us he was okay." Knee Jerk again, in a tone as pathetic as the excuse. Fitting.

"Riiiight. So you thought you'd what... just wait and see until his shit got serious? Because I think it's serious guys. I think it's definitely fucking serious now."

"What do we do?" asks Deuce.

He hasn't argued with her on the stupidity of leaving it this late, she can see by his face that he knows. Obviously KJ's been kicking up a stink. He's not really an asshole, is KJ, but he's got a pure talent for making a jackass of himself when he gets The Fear, and he gets it a lot. He's a jumpy son of a gun, for good reason. Before joining the Hornets, KJ ran drugs for the Harmonys.

Upshot is he wanted out and they were disagreeable. Consequently, he's sporting the kinds of scars visible even under clothes, and only has the one good ear. Because of that, the Hornets let his habit for panicking and being a jackass slide. But this is a bit beyond the pale. A life's in jeopardy. A Hornet for fuck's sake. She'd happily divest KJ of that one remaining ear if EVaC's current state wasn't a more pressing concern.

She strokes EVaC's forehead again, disliking the cold, greasy feel of it, the way those re-forming capillaries pulse beneath her fingers. It's out of step with his heartbeat, the pulse at his throat. Has this aura of purpose: some manner of animated, active, coherence behind it, like something's inside of him, attempting to communicate with whatever it has to hand. Whatever it is, he won't last long enough for the message to come clear unless they find him some help.

And who can help him? Only one logical answer. She doesn't like it, because it's not going to be easy. In fact it's likely to be veering into the hellaciously difficult, especially with his decision to freelance, but it's all they've got. Whatever's up with EVaC, it's way above their pay grades. They need an expert. They need the expert.

Mother Zero.

"We contact Agen-Z," she says. "She'll know what to do."

"You know she's gone signal dark, don't you?" Deuce says, as if she doesn't know shit, which is true.

"Of course," she says, lying through her teeth. "But it's my job to scare up death truants all the damn time. I'll find her."

She has to find her, because this is her fault too. If she weren't a walking friend fail something would have been done about this shit sooner.

"You won't," KJ mutters. "Mother Zero's no lowlife on the run."

Amiga's about one millisecond away from doing something she'll regret when she catches the expression on Deuce's face. What now? He agrees with KJ?

"You doubt my skills? You? Of all people?" she says.

"No. I just don't think you understand how deep someone like Mother Zero can go." He licks his lips. "But I can give you a name. Someone close enough to get you a face-to-face, if you handle it right."

Amiga pokes at his words, trying to find something to get pissy over. Anything. Anything at all. Trouble with Deuce is, he's smart and knows her too damn well, knows how she'll be feeling right now about failing EVaC, though he'd likely have some pithy argument to counter her "I am basically shit" conclusion. Fuck! Why does he have to be so goddamn reasonable? Why does he have to understand her so fucking well? If he was an arsehole, all of this would be so much easier.

"Fine," she snaps. "Shoot."

"Maggie Joust."

"The Maggie Joust? The ex-GarGoil? For real?" Pops out before Amiga can clap a hand over her stupid, over-sharing gob.

KJ gawps, and Deuce gets this grin she literally wants to pound off his face.

"Oh no you don't, you fucker," she says quickly. "This is not collateral."

"It isn't? Amiga Tanaka hung fucking DethRok," Deuce says slowly. "Now there's an image I can't unsee. Not. Ever." And he grins again.

Shit but she hates him.

"Tell me you didn't go full-on back-combed gore-hound emo-core?" KJ says and busts out laughing, forgetting he's not in on this moment. Not if he wants to live. "That's awesome!"

Amiga snarls at him. "I'm hungry and I was promised food. Fix me a box of gyudon, KJ. And do me a favour?"

"What?"

"Shut the fuck up."

volk

O700 hours. A rising sun frames the jagged prow of the Resurrection like a crown, reflecting diamond-white in coronas of sea-spray. Weather's cool but dry. Slight sou-easter. Ripples on a calm sea speak of waves to come later judging by the bruise on the horizon. Shoals of giant tuna, silver glints on the port side, flash patterns like complex codes six feet below the surface. Two feet above, flocks of gulls mimic their movements, razor beaks pointed downward in anticipation.

Top of his crow near the prow, Petrie mans the 'scope, taking in the landscape of the ship, the comings and goings on the ropes, the early morning activities. He scans the ocean too, watching for signs of pursuit, despite their current positioning. The ghost of the moon haunts the sky and the shadow of Cape Town Hub haunts the Resurrection, obscuring light. Seems to hover above them, way up there. Shadowing their every move.

In truth they crouch beneath, wheels at a slow, majestic churn, barely disturbing the waters; hiding in Cape Town's signal by mimicking its flight-path. Seagulls and tuna. Land ship and hub. Ghosts and shadows. To think only yesterday they sailed the high seas, careless and unafraid. Petrie's no stranger to sudden change, but he's reeling. All he cares about is right here. This ship, the safety of her people, is vital to him. Without her, without them, he would not be able to continue.

The last call for breakfast flashes on the crow's nest monitor. It's usually a klaxon, but they're running silent. Signal may be quiet in the shade of Cape Town Hub, but any noise travels miles in this relative calm. He swings out of the nest. Volk's been in custody since last night. Petrie has an appointment with Cassius to talk to her about that drone this morning.

"Bosun!" Cassius strides over. "Walk with me." Petrie does as he's told and as they stride out, Cassius says quietly, "I know you haven't eaten since lunchtime yesterday, Bosun. Can't have that. I need you focused and strong."

He hands Petrie a breakfast roll in greaseproof paper. Petrie stares at it, stomach reeling.

"I can't."

"Nevertheless, you will. Every bite."

"I'm not a child."

Cassius lays his hand on Petrie's shoulder.

"No, you're my second, and I need you fit to serve. A man half-starving himself is not fit for anything."

Longing to disagree, because he can't face food right now, Petrie unwraps the roll. It tastes awful, but he chokes it down. Everything tastes the same at the moment. Bitter. Repugnant. The taste of fear. He thought he'd left that fear behind, but it's right here, in the pit of his belly, the back of his throat. In his mouth. Too close to escape, just like the Ark, and like the Ark he's afraid it will catch him. Lay waste to everything he's managed to build.

*

The Resurrection has no holding cells so Volk's being held under guard in Cassius's office. They find her sitting at the table, clutching a coffee. Petrie thinks she looks wary when they walk in, though it's hard to tell with those eyes of hers, windows to the soul reduced to the blank reflectiveness of screens. Looking into them is a form of cognitive dissonance.

"To what do I owe my incarceration, Captain?" she asks, voice neutral.

Cassius takes a seat. "You may have heard we had a visitor. Somewhat unexpected."

There's that wariness again, unmistakable now in the set of her shoulders, the minute twitching of her fingers.

"I heard. Drone. I thought it was chased here by pirates. Damaged."

"Not chased. Sent."

She blinks. "Sent by pirates?"

"No. By someone on the Gung."

Her chair shifts, the screech of legs on the wooden floor like a shout.

"Who?" she asks, and there's that fear again. What's she afraid of?

"We're not sure. The drone was given clear instructions to come here. To you."

This revelation seems on the surface to have no effect. Petrie's not fooled. He sees the tension in her musculature, the curtailment of that energy. Her body is on pause, held rigid and waiting. Something about it reminds him of being beaten. Knowing it will hurt more to tense, anticipate, but unable to quit the reaction. She's waiting for a blow.

"Can I see it?"

Cassius shakes his head. "Petrie here gave you passage under a week ago, barring any trouble. Now I have a drone on my ship, sent to you, that's brought the Saskatoon Ark down on our heads. That's more than mere trouble, it's a possible death sentence. Not just for crew; families, children. That's your doing. I want to know why someone might send you a drone. I want to know who the fuck you are and what you're bringing down on me and mine."

Volk's hands are shaking, the tiniest tremor.

"I am who I say I am. I'm Corp. No one special. But I'm also a J-Hack, a Pharm," she says, and Petrie believes it. She's too afraid for that to be a lie. "As for the drone. I think I know who sent it. I hope I'm wrong."

Leaning forward, Cassius demands, "Who?"

"Queens," she says, fiddling with the handle of her coffee cup, nails clicking on the china like a mechanical heartbeat. "The Hive Queens."

A vein begins to tick away in Cassius's cheek. If it could be heard, it would be the sound of his control about to snap. He thinks he's being lied to, of course—it's too outrageous a claim to be anything but a lie. Except Petrie thinks not. Even though what she's said verges on the crazy, she believes it. Her fear is real. Either that or she's an extraordinary actor.

"The Queens?" Cassius looks as close to losing it as Petrie's ever seen him. "You're definitely fucking with me now, and that's not wise. Not wise at all. Not with my people, my ship, in this much jeopardy."

"No," she says, her voice shaking. "I am nowhere near fucking with you."

"Is that so? Kindly enlighten me then. Far as I'm aware, Fulcrum's got them under control. Under lock and key. That's part of what Emblem's for, isn't it? To keep them in Hive, where they belong."

Volk pushes her cup away and folds her hands together. It doesn't stop them from shaking.

"Emblem's locking capability has always been tweaked. It was partially bio-ware for a long time, and now fully. It has to be able to adapt to stop the Queens from escaping."

Cassius sits back, uneasy. "They're trying to escape?"

"Not trying, have been on and off for years, but always got locked back in."

"We'd know. We'd see."

"Fulcrum wipes the memory from WAMOS and you count as WAMOS, just like the users on the hubs do. The only people who remember are Fails and double players like me, and we've known for years that escaping on occasion is not enough for them. They want out for good. They want Emblem. After Kamilla died, Josef reached out to my collective, the Movement. Asked for our help to stop them."

"You're working with Fulcrum? With Josef Lakatos? That little shit's not decent, not even half. He's screwing us all over for Slip use."

"He's not screwing you over at all, he's trying to limit access, make some flim on the side. Fulcrum is close to bust. You have no idea how expensive hiding this has become, how much it costs to stay one step ahead of them."

Cassius rubs at his mouth. "Okay. So then, if you've been working with Fulcrum to stop them, why leave the Gung? Tell me why you ran."

"Like I said, the Queens want Emblem, which is in the Core of Hive, hidden right in their midst but of course the Queens can't get to Core, they can't even see it. They've been working with Twist Calhoun. He's been sending in Haunts, trying to find a way to circumvent Core's defences. We thought it was impossible. There's only a single way into Core and even Haunts can't use it. Or at least we thought so. The Queens must have discovered something, because they attacked us without warning, all at once. Tried to eliminate us, because we're the only things standing in their way. We had to scatter. Go signal dark." She blinks back tears. "I don't even know who got away and who didn't."

"So they have Emblem?"

She laughs. "If they had Emblem, everything we know would be gone. You really need to let me see that drone. Did you disconnect it from the collective? Tell me you at least did that."

"No need," Petrie tells her. "It was already disconnected."

This genuinely surprises her. "You're sure?"

"Scratch is no J-Hack but he knows his Tech. It was disconnected. That mean it's not Queens?"

She looks uncertain. "Could be. They're cunning though. I'd need to be sure. You need to be sure." She directs this last to Cassius, who looks distinctly unimpressed.

"Do I now? All I'm sure of is that you came to my ship dragging serious trouble and I am not happy."

Volk snorts. "Captain, if the Queens really have found a way to get Emblem, it won't matter what ship I ran to. None of you can exist for long without the Gung and its connections to the hubs, and they will tear all of that apart."

"I'm aware they're dangerous," he snaps, "I'm just not convinced by your story here. It's a little hard to take, you have to admit."

"So allow me to prove it," she snaps back. "Let me look at the damned drone."

Cassius leans his head back to stare hard at the ceiling, probably looking for his patience. He won't find it there.

"Fine. We'll take you to the drone," he says to Volk. "You can look, but Petrie here will piggyback."

"He may find it uncomfortable. I'm very augmented."

"He'll cope."

They enter the workshop to find that Scratch has been working on the sec-drone all night. Trying to fix it, connect it to the ship's systems so they can use it as a scout and a weapon. Cassius reckons the Ark's schooners had the same sort of plans. Considering the difficulty of bringing this package to such a specific location, he's assuming the existence of other drones—other drones that the Ark may have captured already. They have to be prepared.

On the captain's instructions, Scratch has removed the memory node containing the package so he doesn't accidentally damage it whilst working. Still attached by a fine, see-through wire, it sits on the shelf innocuously, as if it's no trouble at all. Odds are against it though. Trouble doesn't come in threes, it comes in waves. Tsunamis. Hurricanes. Trouble attracts trouble to itself, like a dying wasp attracts other wasps.

Volk offers Petrie a small smile.

"Ready?"

"Not really, but let's go."

Her IM is prickly with static, makes him rub the back of his head to ease a sensation that isn't real. Her drive is worse, heavy with noise and riotous emotion. He's never been in contact with an augment. He was expecting her to feel less human than this, but she's deeply vulnerable, as if every patch and implant she's added has only served to heighten her humanity. Now he understands her concern for his comfort.

The second she connects to the node her relief crashes over him. He has to breathe through it like pain.

She pauses. Sorry.

I'm guessing it's not Queens?

Definitely not. This is J-Hack work. Unfamiliar. I don't understand. If it's not from Queens, it should be from Breaker.

The person you left your contact details with?

Yes.

She pokes at the node. He watches, fascinated: this is the closest he'll ever get to hacking. Volk hums, impressed.

Well, whoever this is, their crypt is excellent work. Bomb proof. Only top five percent could crack this.

Can you?

I can. But it may take a while.

It takes almost an hour before Volk can get to whatever's locked inside. Stuck in her drive, he's all but drowned in her dismay as she reads it through, making him swallow and swallow again to keep that damn breakfast roll down.

What? What is it? he asks.

Volk turns to face him—a strange sensation with him inside her drive. She's a never-ending reflection of herself, of him. A fractal. A paradox.

We were right, she tells him. They found a way. Breaker says Twist will send a Haunt in before the week's out. That gives us seventy-two hours. We have to stop him. The Queens cannot have Emblem.

How the fuck does anyone stop a Haunt?

Emblem's signal will make him visible. He'll be easier to hunt down.

Hunt? Breaker wants to kill the guy?

Volk's reaction is immediate. Visceral.

Kill him? No!

What then?

Breaker's stuck, the Queens have him at Heights. It's taken a lot to get this message to me. He needs my help. Something only I can make.

Explain.

I'm a Pharm, like I said. I developed a drug called Disconnect to help in the battle against the Queens. It severs the link between user and avi, Breaks Fulcrum's control. The intention was for people to see the truth and force Kamilla to accept help.

I don't get why that's a bad thing.

Volk turns away.

Because our avis aren't representations, she says. They're us. Made from us. Sever that connection and you sever sanity.

Immersed in her drive, Petrie can feel the truth of what she's saying. Extraordinary. All this time, he and his avi, one and the same. How is it he's never felt it? He thinks of how it is inside Slip, the freedom of floating, the connection. Tries to imagine that broken. His mind gone. Goes cold from head to toe. He can't fathom how she could allow such a drug to exist.

Why didn't you destroy it?

Breaker insisted we keep it, so I did the next best thing. I destroyed all but my personal notes and had him hide them in Twist's vault.

What? Why in hell would you hide it with him?

Safest vault in the Gung, and he had no idea it was there. Even if he did, he wouldn't know what it was. We're not daft, Bosun.

So Breaker wants you to use it on the Haunt.

Yes. Her reluctance is clear. As is her resolve. Once he's disconnected, they can't touch him. Ergo they can't touch Emblem.

And what if we can't get you to the Gung? We've got the Ark on our tails.

She reaches out and grasps Petrie's arm, her hand surprisingly strong.

You have to try. Trust me, Bosun Petrie, you do not want to live in a world in which the Queens have possession of Emblem.

So either they help her help Breaker or they end up, what? Queen bait? So what now? There are no easy options here. The drone carrying Breaker's cry for help has put them directly in the path of danger and may have erased any chance of them being able to respond. Petrie looks over at his captain, watching them with wary, angry eyes.

I have to talk to Cassius.

Of course. Will he be amenable?

It's not that simple. The Ark's faster, equipped with more schooners, actual soldiers. I'm not saying we'll lose—we're heavily armed, skilled at warfare, and we've defeated many other ships, though none quite so vicious. If we can't beat it, we can likely cripple it. But if the Resurrection is too badly damaged, we're not going anywhere.

Volk's silence is eloquent. She remains silent as he explains the situation to Cassius. Cassius doesn't much like any of it, but he accepts that refusing to help would be insane, considering the stakes. His concern is the same as Petrie's—how the hell do they get to Gung with the Ark on their tail?

All they can do is try, and live with the consequences if they fail.

"So do we hide or do we run?" Petrie asks his captain.

"Considering how far we are from the Gung, and this Breaker's suggested timeline, we don't have time to hide. We've made ready every weapon we have, couldn't be more primed for a strike. I say we set loose at full clip for the Gung. Lure the Ark out."

The last time Petrie ran, it was in terror, an act of self-preservation that felt like cowardice. Looks like he's come full circle, running away to pull the past back toward him.

And what will happen when it comes? Devastation. Isn't that always the way? Especially when the Ark is involved. Sometimes the past really is best left behind. What he wouldn't give for the luxury.

johnny sez has a bad day

Johnny Sez copped a sweet ride when he hooked up with Mimic, that's for sure," murmurs Li Harmony to her brother, Ho. She's got Johnny curved back out of his apartment window like a fishhook, her blade to his neck. "Remember those pigs on our nai nai's farm?"

Ho giggles. "Sure. Piggies."

"They made such a pretty sound when I slit their throats. He's making the exact same sound. Makin' me itchy for the feel of hot blood on my skin. So silky and sticky."

Johnny is afraid that if his eyes get any wider, they'll explode out of their sockets. He tries to silence his throat, but it's too busy vocalizing the panic currently stampeding through his frontal lobes. For a first face-to-face with his bosses, this is not going as well as he'd like. Mind you, these are not the sort of bosses you want to have any kind of face-to-face with. Johnny's only been working for the Harmonys for about six months. He's heard a lot of stories about them and their family history—all of it ludicrous, or so he thought. Rumour, of course, is always exaggerated, but currently Johnny believes every word of it. This family is fucking lunatic.

Ho leans against the side of the window-frame looking down at Johnny. He takes a long pull on his purple psy stick. His eyes are dreamy, which is worrying for poor Johnny, because Ho's generally not very sane, and a paucity of sanity filtered through psy smoke produces worrying results.

"Maybe he forgot who he runs bumps for?" Ho slurs out thoughtfully. He blinks. "That would concern me. Lack of proper respect makes my skin break out. Breakouts distress me in the same way as wearing brown shoes with a black suit distresses me. I tore the face off this stupid salaryman cunt last week for that. Sartorial ignorance, pure and simple, it ruined my day."

"Oh my poor baby," Li whispers, and her glassy eyes sheen with tears. Digging in her blade, she licks her lips as a thin drool of blood slides down Johnny's neck, dripping to the meagre courtyard below. "Hey, look at that," she says conversationally, smiling at Johnny as if they've known each other forever. "That's a long way down, Johnny. Anyone ever tell you how high you're living? I wouldn't like to fall down there." She jerks him a little, smiling at the high-pitched shriek that whistles out through the constriction on his throat. "I'm not bothered by heights. Am I, Ho?"

Ho shrugs, delicate as a flower and slender as a stalk in his bespoke silk suit.

"I'm not fond. You pushed me off a ledge once. That's when I had my face redone. I look so much prettier now."

Li sniffs. "I was asking about me. Idiot. And I apologized for that."

Ho smiles, whisky-brown eyes filling with mischief.

"I know what the fuck you were asking, bitch. And I accepted your apology, surgery only made me prettier."

Li chuckles, a full-throated sound which could almost

pass for normal amusement, and which scares the shit out of Johnny even more than the imminent prospect of a blade slicing across his throat. Her torso is pressed against his thigh, but there's no warmth where her body touches his.

"You're lucky I decided you can be prettier than me," she tells Ho fondly. "So what do we do with Johnny here?"

Johnny cringes away, worsening his already precarious position. Li's eyes are expressionless, an odd see-through amber, and where they alight on him, they burn.

Tilting his head, Ho stares down at the courtyard intently, as though the answer might be spray-painted on the flagstones in ten-foot-high graffiti.

"I get bored of watching you explain what we want. Having suits steam-cleaned is such a chore," he says gently.

She raises a brow, drawn in a perfect arch.

"One does not simply allow one's girlfriend to go and work for a rival gang-lord without informing one's employers. That's impolite." Li's hand tightens on Johnny's t-shirt. His face feels fit to burst. "It's sad," she muses. "Such a waste. But wasting people is so much fun."

His pupils wide as lychee pits, Ho taps the ash from his psy stick into Johnny's face.

"Don't we rather like this one? You were saying only yesterday how much more profit we're making in the West Blocks."

"Yes. And?"

"You know how tiresome it is to find a new middle man who understands the finer points of marketing..." Ho leaves it hanging. More due to the fact he's drifted off into contemplation of the wallpaper than any attempt to be meaningful.

Growling her irritation, Li yanks Johnny right up, until his nose is all but pressed to hers.

"I was going to carve your face off," she says. Her

eyes go as dreamy as Ho's, and the knife slowly pushes deeper into Johnny's neck. He whimpers. "I'm my Baba's daughter; I do enjoy a good joke. Don't you?" She gives him a ravenous grin, and Johnny nearly shits himself. "But I guess my brother here is right, so I'm going to offer you a little chance to save face. Nod if you understand." Johnny nods, barely noticing the rivulets of blood slipping down his chest.

Ho's still staring at the wallpaper. He murmurs to it as intimately as a lover, so it takes a moment for Johnny to clock he's asking a question. "What's the nature of Mim's job? We know it's for Twist, and we know it's her usual bag. What we don't know, which is somewhat aggravating, is the target."

"P... P... Paraderm," Johnny wheezes out.

"Hmmm. Interesting." Ho flicks an acute glance at his sister. Is he stoned or not? Johnny doesn't want to know. "So who's cracking it for her?"

"W... what?"

Li leans over Johnny.

"I don't think this blade can go much deeper without severing something important. I'd enjoy that, but I doubt you would. That was a simple question. Who is cracking Paraderm for Mim? We know it isn't you, lover boy. You haven't the skill."

"Pao," Johnny spits out swiftly, feeling his bladder wanting to give way and fighting it with every last scrap of strength in him. "Shock Pao."

"Shock Pao?" Ho has such a look of bewilderment on his face Johnny catches himself feeling sorry for him. Fucking hell. "Mim managed to hunt Shock down? Jiejie, I thought if you couldn't find him, no one could."

Reaching out to pat his hand, Li says gently, "Don't fret, bao bei. They have history." She rolls the word around on her tongue like it's a particularly delicious piece of steak. "She's sly that one. Sly and sneaky, two of my favourite things. I was going to kill her for encouraging that boy to steal from me, but then I realized how amusing it all was. I like her, and I just know she'll want to play with us. She likes our style. We can work this to our advantage." She purses lush lips and says, "I'd like to fuck Shock, just once, before I kill him."

"Oh?"

"I want to see how well the surgery went."

"What?"

Li offers her brother a wide-eyed stare.

"You know he was a she, right?"

"No!" Ho's plain stunned. "How'd you know that?"

"Hacked his private files when he first worked for us. I got in for long enough to get a good look."

"My dearest jiejie, you never cease to astound me."

"Naturally, you were never the brightest pea in the pod."

"Only the prettiest."

"For the moment."

Li drops Johnny to the carpet, scraping half the skin off his back on the window frame. Wiping her blade on Mim's curtains, she says in a tone that makes Johnny's anus contract, "You be sure that high-strung fuck of yours knows we're interested in dealing with her, there's a good boy, or I'll have to remove some of your more interesting features so you can never see yourself again without remembering to behave. And, next time she does some work for a rival of ours, don't neglect to inform us, and by inform I mean spill your guts, or loss of face will be the least of what I do to you. Okay?"

Holding onto his neck to try to stem the flow of blood, Johnny nods.

"Okay. Done."

Li beams at Ho.

"See, I do like him! We can keep him for a while." The knife disappears into a sheath hidden somewhere in a suit almost identical to Ho's bar the generous amount of cleavage on display. "I'm hungry. I want noodles. Ho, buy me noodles."

Ho pushes away from the wall and steps over Johnny to take his sister's arm.

"Jiejie, I have no flim on me."

She snorts, an elegant little sound, like a tiny elephant.

"You need to be flexible. You know I always get hungry when I cut piggies."

Ho sighs. "I've been smoking too much. It makes me forget. Forgive me?"

She squeezes his arm. "Idiot. I forgive you. Steal me some noodles. You can still steal, can't you?"

"Jiejie, how long have you known me?"

Ho flicks the psy stick behind him. Still lit, it lands in Johnny's lap. He squeals, jerking himself to the side to get it off his leg. A look of horror ground deep into his face, deep enough to become permanent, even if the wind doesn't change, he watches the two of them stroll out of his digs.

"You did not sign up for this shit, Johnny," he mutters, picking up the stub of Ho's psy stick and taking a long toke. "Those two are barkin'. Bad enough you're fucking the world's biggest bitch, you had to go and get yourself tangled up with psychopaths. You shouldn't 'ave left the ocean. Land." He snorts, coughing over a lungful of smoke. "I'd rather pissin' well drown!"

the neon angel

tugging at the tattered, uneven hem of her skin-tight black micro-skirt and thinking she probably looked better in this get-up three years ago, Amiga squeezes through the queue outside the Bauhaus Club, deep inside Shin District. Turns the deadeye on any fucker who dares to moan. She shouldn't be here. She shouldn't have to be here.

"Fuck memory lane," she snarls to herself, slamming through a wall of DethRokers decked in torn fishnet, barbed chokers and scorn. They turn the latter on her, but her scorn is cranked to eleven and they wither beneath it, fading away like hair dye in the wash.

Why in hell did Deuce have to give her a name that ran into history she'd rather leave locked away in vaults deeper than the one Agen-Z currently calls a hide-out? Even worse, now those boys know she used to hang DethRok they'll never quit bugging her about it. She's already found wigs tied to her hovel hatch. Black lipstick scrawled on the walls. Which makes her madder than she could begin to express with a knife and three days alone with their naked bodies. This information feels too personal for them to have, and yet she's aware she's over-reacting. She should find it funny. She should be normal. Why isn't she? Trouble is, all these memories are pain.

DethRok, the beautiful, dark and bold, the Gothic peacocks of the Gung. Amiga was at home here once, until she Failed, and found out what the term "fair-weather friends" really means. Not their fault they're just as enslaved to the system as every fucker else, but it still hurts.

Now here she is again, face full of kohl and red lipstick, hair Frankenstein's monster might lose his heart to, and dressed head to toe in garb that even in her most generous mood she no longer finds remotely wearable. It used to be her favourite outfit, now she feels like an idiot in it—a fake.

Reaching the doors, black with splashes of too-convincing fake blood, and covered in a rusty steel grid, Amiga finds to her complete lack of surprise that ScarCrow is still manning the guest list.

"Well, well, look who blew back in on the west wind," he says, flicking the long black tail of a deathhawk out of eyes alive with malice.

"I'll blow right through your fucking torso if you don't let me in," she says, smiling pleasantly. "Would you like your name to become a descriptive noun?"

He steps back, malice dulling to fear, and she thinks, You should never have thrown me out. I might not have had to be this. I might have had a chance. She pushes past into the club, already scanning for the man she needs.

Old Saint Jimmy.

Spies him in his usual place, clinging to the bar like some detritus-feeding arthropod, surrounded by his gaggle of GarGoil girls. Much like birds, GarGoils migrate every September, replaced by girls in their last year of Tech or Cad. It still stuns Amiga how many girls battle to revolve in Saint Jimmy's orbit for a year, screaming out tracks written so long ago, and repeated in so many different incarnations, they've become parodies of themselves.

"Saint Jim," she calls out, offering him the benefit of all her teeth in a wide, half-angry grin.

There's history between her and Saint Jimmy, none of it entirely pleasant. He tried to rope her into being a GarGoil back in the day. She couldn't sing for shit, but she played a mean guitar. He tried to grease her up with that oil slick pouring off his tongue like a deep-sea spill, but Amiga was not interested. To her the whole GarGoils thing is slightly ghoulish, though she digs the music. He took her rejection personally, leading to some serious nastiness until graduation when Amiga was glad to be free of the ever-loving stench of the man. Which is why she's not so fucking chuffed to be back in it.

She shouts at Jimmy, who's not paying attention.

"Oi, talking here. Do me the courtesy of listening, or I'll rip your ears off."

He makes a big show of just having seen her, making him look like a demented ostrich.

"Well screw me! If it ain't my Amiga, all grown up!" Pogoing off the bar, he comes swaggering over and envelops her in a stinking hug, eau de BO and alcohol.

Amiga levers him away, just like scraping barnacles with a knife.

"You hate me, Jim."

He lights up a smoke.

"There is that. You'd 'ave been a top-class Ratchet Anne. And look atchoo. Fackin' Fail now. Coulda had a glimpse o' the high life, my lovely. Shouldn' 'ave been so darn resistant. Unshackle the chastity belt, an' all that."

"Do I have to maim you? I presume you've heard whispers about what I do for a living?"

Jim sniffs. Disgusted.

"I 'eard. No, you don' havta maim me. Whaddo ya wan'?"

"You recall Maggie Joust, yes? She was Peroxa Bland. The original. I need to find her. Does she still hang DethRok? Where would I look? Is she here? The Batcave? Boris Karloff? BodyHorror?"

"Whoa, whoa, whoa, love," he says, raising hands like she's storming his barricades. "Thas' a lil more'n one question, innit. Can't 'spect a fellah to jus toss it all out there without a lil incentive."

He gives her a meaningful glance. It makes him look about seventeen times seedier, like the ancient, slick-haired weasel he is. Ugh. Amiga hangs on to her instinct to carve his face off by the merest wisp. Same as all things, there are ways of doing this. Good ways and bad. Amiga hasn't time for Cockney fun, she wants a name and location, that's it. When she steps into his space, she devours it. Shrinks him to an insignificant wrinkle of skin on a bollock by her mere presence.

"Incentive? Really? Perhaps you forgot my job already? Perhaps you forgot the intense pleasure I would derive from tearing out your organs through your fuckin' anus?"

Having been busy sucking on his smoke in what he thought was a suggestive manner, Jim chokes on a lungful.

"Jeez. Jeez. Jeez fuck'n shit. Awite, awite," he splutters as he comes up for air. "Maggie Joust. Maggie fuckin' Joust. 'Angs at the BatCave far as I know. At least thas the place ta start." He eyes her up with red-veined peepers watering profusely, still sparky despite his obvious lack of advantage. "You got proper fuckin' nasty, love. I admire that. Can' say I don'. Take it easy, awite."

He smooths back his hair with both hands and backs away to the bar, eyeballing her as he goes. Amiga allows it for one reason only: they both know who'd die if she stepped up to the challenge.

Anxious not to spend too long in this awful get-up tonight, she leaves the club the way she came in, sneering at ScarCrow as she goes. If she never sees this place again it won't be a hardship. Parts of her heart she'd forgotten about are aching. There's that longing she thought she was rid of, to start afresh, to try again. The one she had for weeks after she Failed. Lost inside and out. Lost and yearning to be found.

She'd sat in her micro apartment staring at the walls for the majority of every twenty-four hours in those weeks, hurting from head to toe, but mostly in the heart, and wondering why it's such a fucking crime to have your own mind. She found no answers. But by the end of those weeks she knew the cracks in that wall as intimately as the lines in her palm. They told her future. What was waiting if she didn't get off her arse and hustle. So hustle she did. Turns out hustling's dangerous. Turns out, so is she.

BatCave, as the crow flies, is a couple hundred metres from Bauhaus, or Boris Karloff, or BodyHorror, the quartet of DethRok clubs collectively known as the B-Movies. BatCave was never a regular haunt of hers. She was a Bauhaus devotee, through and through. Of the various clans of DethRokers from the Cads, Techs and office blocks, some congregate in particular establishments, whilst others roam. All depends on your flavour of DethRok.

Her lack of roaming means the doorman at the BatCave, some miserable-looking dude in a full-length duster and sad clown make-up doesn't know her from Eve, and she gets in via eyeballs halfway up her thighs. If she weren't in a hurry, she'd do him a favour and remove them permanently. Thanks to the name of this place, she's expecting bats, or at least something vaguely vampiric and possibly verging on the Gothic. The BatCave is nothing like.

Sleek and sophisticated, it gleams, muted lights casting soft focus on delicately ruined neo-Romantic splendour and enough backcombed black hair to fill a sinkhole. Amiga heads to the bar. Start where the drink is, and therefore the loosest pierced tongues, and work back toward the door. It takes her over two hours of teasing answers and buying a ridiculous array of pastel cocktails with melodramatic names before she stops hitting tats and strikes information.

According to a slender whip of a fop in ripped pants and braces, who goes by the name of Marquis De Hard and drinks some sort of foul-smelling blood-hued synthetic absinthe, Maggie Joust stopped coming to the BatCave over three months ago. These days she hangs at Mollie's, a fancy new Burlesque joint opened by her girlfriend, the eponymous Mollie. Relieved to be able to take her leave—the soft focus is giving her the grandmother of all headaches—Amiga gets directions, steals his drink for curiosity's sake, and skedaddles.

She throws the beverage away halfway to Mollie's. It tastes like violets and sadness. Why the fuck do DethRokers gotta court misery all the goddamn time?

"Life's a blast, don't they know?" she mutters, pulling the tatty edges of a barely-there leather jacket across her chest.

It's early morning, the deep profound black of those nothing hours before dawn, and the Gung is chilly. Knife-like winds arise from the vast, surrounding ocean and hunt the streets for flesh to ripple with goosebumps, mostly hers tonight. Very few other souls about. When the DethRokers leave the clubs, they'll go in murders. Safety in squawking numbers. She stops for a moment in the light of a biome tree, revelling in the emptiness. Tonight, at this moment, there's only her and the city. If she could keep it this way...

"There'd be nothing, you daft bitch. Make yourself an island. Go ahead. Think the ocean will keep you company? It doesn't even know you exist."

She walks on, shivering, a combination of existential unease and barely-there skirt. She finds Mollie's, bright and raucous, exactly where the skinny fop said it would be, in Fountain Square. Named for its rebellious lack of fountains.

Mollie's is a pile of candy dropped on grey concrete, a dolly mixture of gaudy pink lights and jaunty music, lifting her spirits, although she imagined them all but bolted to the floor. She hums as she sails past a tag-team of temptresses in tight dresses and Moll make-up at the door who throw smiles like pick-up lines. She can feel their eyes on her arse all the way to the bar, but resents it less than the duster-wearing clown at the BatCave. It feels less invasive, more genuinely admiring.

"That's right, girls," she says to herself, smiling. "All my own work..."

"You must be a hard worker."

The voice is low, sultry, but with a tightly wound undercurrent of suspicion, which the speaker seems desperate to hide. Amiga turns to find a tall, voluptuous woman in the most extraordinary orange-striped pantaloon and corset set, peering at her through a be-ribboned monocle that is most definitely not just a monocle.

"This a gay club?" Amiga asks curiously, ignoring the woman's obvious mistrust.

The woman lowers her monocle and taps it on the creamy back of a slender wrist. Amiga immediately thinks, It's not working.

"Sadly not," comes the reply, sounding, if anything, even more suspicious than before. The woman is trying to suss Amiga out. Look into her. She's no Club Hostess or mere scene pro—she has history. Amiga can't tell if she's

141

Maggie Joust or not. In the vids she obsessively watched back then Peroxa Bland was a skinny pre-grad with a skinhead and a taste for tramp-chic. If it is her, she's changed one hell of a lot. "If I had my way, then maybe... But this isn't my place."

"So you're not Mollie."

"Bingo." The word is bitten out.

"Do you know her?"

"Intimately."

"Would that make you Maggie Joust?"

The hardening of the eyes tells Amiga yes, and she squashes the fluttery surge of fan-girliness. Maggie's aura of suspicion has warped to wariness, no, beyond that. There's fear there, and anger too, deep and sharp, like the gulp of air before the fight.

"Who wants to know?"

Amiga's instincts are razorblades. They have to be. Right now they're telling her this is not the time to lie. Whatever's going on with Maggie Joust, what she thinks she's seeing in Amiga is making it one hell of a lot worse. She gives Maggie the benefit of her most open and serious face.

"Amiga. My name's Amiga. And I'm looking for Maggie Joust because I need to find a friend of hers. It's important. Melodramatically DethRok as it might sound, a life is infact at stake."

The monocle rises again to frame a kohl-laden eye with a gleaming green iris, bright as a gemstone. Amiga reckons the monocle is a data-scan, a good one by the looks. Top notch. So she lowers her firewalls and allows it in to digitally fillet her, wondering why it couldn't before. Maybe it's not rigged for the sorts of firewalls she uses, but although high spec they're fairly common. Amiga's no Tech—she just buys the best. Best is no good with scans like that though. Funny goings on here. Real funny.

The monocle drops, swinging jauntily on its ribbon. The woman offers a small smile. Amiga sees bewilderment in it. And curiosity. And the real clicker... relief. What's all that about then?

"Okay. I'm Maggie. Who is it you need to find?"

"Agen-Z."

Maggie flinches, so subtly that anyone not skilled in reading body language would miss it, or misinterpret what they saw as no more than a twitch. She knows where Agen-Z is, that much is obvious, but Amiga doesn't hold her breath. There's something deep going on here. She's crashed quite the paranoia party.

"Look," she says, cutting her losses before they become terminal. "My friend's a Patient Zero. And he's ill. Verge of death shit from the look. She'll know what's wrong and how to help him, if he can be helped. I presume you saw he's J-Hack? He's no danger to you. I'm not."

Maggie's unmoved. "There are problems around helping you that you don't fully appreciate."

Amiga tries again, though she's pretty sure she's on a hiding to nothing but EVaC's RIP.

"I see that. So maybe an exchange of help? We're good for it. The crew I'm involved with, the Hornets, we've been doing work for Fellows..."

She trails off as the temperature changes, cold to hot in a flat second. Maggie was stone, now she's engaged. Snared. Involved. Grabbing Amiga's arm, Maggie ferries her through the throngs of sartorial elite to a small, red door at the back of the club. She waves her hand as they approach and the subliminal click of the door unlocking is like an itch in Amiga's drive, unreachable and aggravating. Hefty security here. More than required to be sure. Yeah, Maggie and Mollie are in trouble all right.

Maggie shoves Amiga through and follows her, closing

the door behind them. Then rounds on her.

"You're working for Fellows?"

"Yes."

"That's impossible," Maggie snaps. "You can't be."

Amiga's amused. "Why? Fellows is signal dark and all, but it doesn't mean he's not working with anyone."

"Fellows is dead."

This is not what Amiga was expecting to hear.

"You what now?"

"He went signal dead months ago. Drive dark, you understand?" Maggie grabs Amiga's arm. "What exactly is it that you're doing for Fellows?"

Still a little nonplussed, Amiga replies unsteadily, "We caught a sec-drone, and I stole something from my boss, Twist Calhoun. A package. All I know is that the package went on our drone and several others to a specific location, to 'Volk', whoever the hell that is."

Maggie falls back against the wall.

"Holy hell, he's sent for Volk," she breathes out. "He's alive. And you have means of contact, yes?"

"Of course."

"Then you just got lucky," Maggie says.

Oh now. Amiga's radar goes into overdrive. This is interesting. This is most interesting.

"You need to contact Fellows?"

"Not Fellows. Like I said, he's dead."

"So who is it we're working for?"

"Breaker."

Fucking hell. Amiga's face goes numb. Breaker. Shit. What in hell have the Hornets gotten themselves involved in?

"Are you sure?"

"Positive. He's been missing, presumed dead. We couldn't find his signal or safely travel to old safe houses to look deeper. Now I find he's not just alive, he's still active, still fighting. You have no idea..." Struggling with emotion, Maggie presses a hand against her chest, catches her breath. "Come with me," she tells Amiga.

Maggie leads her to two steel doors. They slide open to reveal an elevator. And all the buttons go down. Maggie enters as if it's nothing at all, no big deal. Refusing to follow, Amiga stares open mouthed.

"You dug into the earth?" she says incredulously. "Are you crazy?"

Maggie pulls Amiga into the lift, ignoring her protests, and presses the basement button. The doors shut soundlessly, trapping them in a tiny, vulnerable box heading deep into the ground. Amiga stands dead centre, legs locked, knees trembling. She can't breathe, there are fragile walls closing in around her, and beyond them... all of the earth, ready to crack apart and fold in on her. When it comes to the breaking, the official story is that the earth's crust became unstable, suffered massive quakes, and broke into pieces.

Logically Amiga knows this isn't entirely true. Rumours of Corp involvement sprung up centuries ago—a much more logical explanation of the devastation of broken continents spiking the ocean than any natural disaster. If the earth broke itself so completely, so catastrophically, why is the Gung still stable? Why the land ships? How did they know when to build hubs? How they'd have enough time? It makes no sense. Her mind knows this, but her body's thrown logic to the wind. Run headlong into panic.

"Breathe, girl," Maggie says softly, without looking round at her. "You're J-Hack, you know what's truth and what isn't. This is truth. It is safe."

"I know," Amiga mutters through teeth clenched so hard her jaw is shaking. "I just don't want to be down here. If this thing triggers an earthquake, I'm going to fucking kill you."

Maggie chuckles. "You have no idea how amusing that is," she says.

Amiga has no response, all she can think of are those jagged continental teeth, and how it was they were hidden before the earth was broken. How the earth might reasonably be considered to be angry. Hungry.

The lift stops with a jolt, shaking them both so hard they struggle to remain on their feet. Amiga shrieks, flailing her arms out to the walls, and then screams as it drops suddenly, more swiftly than before, the whir of whatever machinery drives it letting out an unending high-pitched whine. Amiga finds herself humming along with it, at the end of her control, about ready to flip into major hysterics. Maggie lays a hand on her back, between the shoulder blades.

"Keep breathing, hon. We're not done yet. You want to see Agen-Z, you come this way. No other way to come. This goes deep, real deep. It's old but secure."

Desperately sucking air, Amiga chokes out an incredulous laugh, says, "You gotta be shittin' me."

"Not even. C'mon, take my arm. You wait. You're going to feel a bit weird about all this huffing and puffing in a moment. Then you're probably going to get angry. Hold on to that. Remember it."

The next time the lift stops, the transition is so smooth Amiga only knows it by the cessation of the mechanical shrieking. The doors slide open onto darkness.

"Out you go," says Maggie.

The first step out raises lights. They flicker into life throughout a gigantic, circular chamber. Skinned in metal, it glints with a complex maze of circuitry like an optical illusion, the eye pulled from junction to junction, dizzying.

Rising from the floor to the roof of the chamber is a huge flared central tower bristling with Tech only Deuce would be able to name. She closes her eyes. Maggie's right. She's angry.

"Is this Fulcrum's? Is it older than the Gung?"

"Yes. And no."

"How do you have access?"

"We found it. Searched for it. We knew there must be a way to it from one of these old buildings, so we kept scanning till we found the right one, and then we bought this place. Turned it into Mollie's. Came here to hide when things started to get dodgy."

Amiga turns to stare at Maggie.

"Is this the only server?"

"No. There are dozens."

"Shit."

"Mollie and I needed to hijack a server to monitor the Queens. This one was situated perfectly."

"Hijack?" Amiga's gaping now.

Maggie's matter of fact as if this is all cool shizz, right? As if it's nothing. But Amiga reels, completely off balance. This is not the real world. It's not. You don't just hijack a Slip server and not bring down the wrath of both Fulcrum and the Hive Queens, especially if you're spying on them. Activating their security protocols is bad business. But Maggie's still talking, cool as anything.

"These servers were built to be self-servicing. Left to their own devices. The only overseers they have are the Hive Queens, and they don't concern themselves unless one stops working. We keep this working smoothly and they'll never find us here. Invisible squatter's rights."

Amiga has nothing to say. Nothing. Then she does find something to say, though she's not sure about hearing the answer.

"Fulcrum. Kamilla Lakatos. Was she part of it? I mean

I've heard things. About the breaking."

"Ah." Maggie smiles a little sadly. "You sure you want to know?"

"Not really. Tell me anyway."

"No need." Maggie waves her hand at the steel skin. A section slides aside to reveal a clear glass panel. A window. "Go and look."

Amiga goes to the window. It looks down onto a platform beside a tunnel so huge it defies visual measurement, makes the eyes feel strained and weak. And filling the tunnel beside the platform like some monstrous, incongruous metallic grub, its mouth a collection of saw-toothed, conic grinders, squats a circular device that even to her ignorant eyes can only be one thing.

"Earth engine," she whispers. Horrified. "It's true then. They broke the world. They actually broke the fucking world. Why?"

"Don't think—Why does anyone do anything?—iNk! Sal's Synth Salad! No vegetables here!"

The voice comes from nowhere, everywhere, buzzing with the digital imprint of a thousand and more trips into the Slip to spread virads.

Agen-Z. Has to be.

Zeros normally have a short shelf life, but this one, the very first, has been going for decades. Amiga wonders how long she's been listening. How she's managed to silence the torrent of virad junk spilling from her mouth until now. This connection must be through Slip, with Agen-Z kept quiet by shutting off her end and listening in.

"Conex—Expedience—A lifeline in your hand."

Still at the window, Maggie steps forward, raising her hand upward as if to try to stop something. Amiga turns, and sees... an angel. Floating down from the central tower on thin plastic wires filled with the bright glare of neon.

Her hair is white, and glows like the moon on a cloudless night, carrying its own ghostly aura.

Incurious yellow eyes, pale as shells, regard Amiga from within youthful, doll-like features accentuated with dots, swirls and cryptically rune-like scrawling resembling black-light tattoos, but that's not what they are, glowing brightly even in the lights of the server room. Her naked body is covered with more the same. A rainbow of hues, re-making her a neon angel written in indecipherable code. Around the tattoos wires loop through flesh and bone in bloodless intricacy, moving slow and sinuous as sun-drunken snakes.

"I could—Carrey's Synth Choc—tell you everything. The why. The how," she says to Amiga, her mouth a bright pink bow of light, hypnotic in motion. "I could change your world. But that's done, I imagine, and," her head tips, white hair lolling through bright wires, "—Is it the real thing?—that's not why you're here. Why wait on wheels?"

Amiga's head is spinning. Substrata servers. Earth Engines. Broken worlds. Corp conspiracies. And shining neon angels, suspended on wires.

"EVaC, my friend. He's sick," she croaks out. "He... he's not Guild, nor Affiliate, but he needs help, and only you can help him."

"Septo, Dirt Just—Show me—Met It's Maker!"

Amiga IMs images of EVaC in Agen-Z's general direction, confident she'll catch them. Sure enough she does, in an elegant move that would have Deuce writing sonnets. Agen-Z raises her yellow eyes to Maggie, who speaks for her, and Amiga realizes this is how it usually is. Agen-Z, the Mother Zero, has more control than any she's ever met, but that control prevails only in silence.

"She'll help," says Maggie. "But you have to help us first. You have to get a message to Breaker. Deliver it personally. It's too dangerous for us to try and reach him any other way."

Amiga stares between them.

"But... what if the line we have no longer goes to him? EVaC will die."

Maggie holds Agen-Z's gaze. Nods.

"She won't let it come to that, you have her word. All Patient Zeros are her family. If he worsens, you'll have my IM. Use it. Someone will come for him."

"And what about Breaker?"

"Contact him through the IM you were given. He'll have alerts even for lines left dormant. We'll give you something to send. You mustn't look at it. It has to remain sealed. Any tampering may endanger him. If he's able, he'll contact you. I guarantee it. She guarantees it."

"And I have your word she'll still help EvaC if you're wrong?"

"Yes."

"Whatever that's worth." Amiga looks between the two of them, slow and measuring, and not a little threatening. "I don't trust you yet."

"But you'll do this?" Maggie asks her.

"For EVaC. Yes."

This is the sealed package for Breaker. Is that Maggie or Mollie? Only now, with the voice directly in her IM, does Amiga realize how similar they sound. When he replies, he'll have something for us in return. When you have it, IM me, and I'll tell you where to meet me. Maggie then.

"Now go," Maggie says. "We'll be closing soon."

"I wasn't shielded coming in. I could be tracked."

Maggie turns and offers her a small, tired smile.

"No," she says softly. "You couldn't. Looks to me like you need to ask some questions of those closest to you. Someone's got you under a full signal block. That's why I was freaked earlier. You're invisible, hon."

dead ends and corners

Sat in a noodle bar on Plaza slurping the last slippery noodles from a bowl of salty miso, bitter against the bump residue coating his throat, Shock nearly drops the lot as the shriek of an IM temporarily shorts every circuit in his brainpan. Whoever's calling has the loudest chime he's ever heard in his life. It's like an air-raid siren, like a million seagulls screaming blue murder over a shoal of tuna, like the thunder of earth spears rubbing together.

Then again, Shock's in what might be delicately referred to as a fucking state and anything louder than a delicate whisper is guaranteed to work his lobes like jackhammers on asphalt. Choking, he swills the mouthful down with a gulp of Ginger-Apple Tab and accesses.

What the fuck and who the fuck? Nearly made me chuck my lunch on the damn floor. Nearly made me breathe my last over goddamn udon. Not cool. Not. Cool. That's a loud-arse chime you have. Dim it.

S'Johnny. Johnny Sez.

Shock makes a face. Catches sight of it in the window and twists his face harder, gurning at himself. If he were any less mature he'd stick a finger down his throat and make gagging noises.

Am I up?

Yup.

That was quick.

Yeah, well, she had good intel. Johnny sniffs. Through his IM link it sounds like a gale-force wind. Shock winces. Makes a two-finger gun at his lobes BAM as Johnny says, Now uh… this info Mim needs you t'grab, s'got a barcode lock innit, so remember to lock it back up.

Shock gawps at himself in the window. What. The. Fuck. No way. No. Not again. He is not getting dicked again.

Now you hear me clear, Johnny. Shock turns his finger gun into a knife, stabbing the shiny red surface of the noodle bar hard enough to hurt. People stare. He ignores them. Mim didn't say shit about barcodes. This was supposed to be a cruise. Easy money. Fucking sleep walking! He stabs the table extra hard, nearly taking off the end of his finger. And if it's not exactly classified, by the bye, not that I'm interested but I have to ask because what the fuck—what's it doing barcoded?

Hey, you know Mim, honesty isn't exactly her forte, so if you were sucker enough to say yes then I don' give a shit about what you did n' didn't agree to. Besides, I don' think it's top-level barcode.

Shock laughs. No such thing as levels in barcode. Depends on what types of bar they're using. As neither Mim nor you would know one bar-type from another, I'm going to make a wild guess that she has no idea whether or not the damn thing she wants is classified or no. And thus my answer is as follows: get it yourself or get fucked.

There's another wind down his IM. More like a hurricane this time. Shock grinds his teeth. When does a lowlife like Sez get to sigh at him?

Man, dude, bro. Look, I'm gonna do ya a favour. I got some visitors the other day. Uninvited you might say. Go by the names Li n' Ho. You might know 'em? Upshot is they're after knowing who Mim was working with, n' I might've given them your name. Johnny actually sounds sorry, the shitty little coward. You might need this flim to get out of dodge, because they're after killing you n' they don' mess around. This may be the last job you c'n take someone won't immediately rat you out on.

Cardinal rule, Sez, you never give names! Especially not to the fucking Harmonys! And I call bullshit. They've wanted me for ages and haven't looked that hard. What's changed?

Reckon our Mim's neck deep in somethin' as per, cos them crazy Harmonys were all over getting' info about who was cracking this job. Your name made for an interestin' response. Just sayin'.

Hit by the overwhelming desire to lob his noodle bowl through the window, Shock has to sit there breathing it out for a while. This is typical Mim, one hundred percent proof pure malice. He wouldn't be surprised if she'd schemed this whole scenario trying to get him to do a barcode on the cheap, because she sure as hell hasn't paid enough for that. Fifty/fifty his arse. Eight K is probably less than twenty percent. Dicked on flim and Li Harmony back on his tail. What a fucking bargain. Mim's such a bitch she'll get animus poisoning and die one of these days. Can't come too soon.

Shock surveys his options. They make flim rates for the bottom ten percent look generous. He could run now, but the flim he has won't last long enough, and living on nothing is scientifically impossible. You can breathe air for sure, but you can't eat it. That crap is not nourishing. All he can do is take his piss-ant pay with gritted teeth and be a good Haunt; get this done quick, clean and quiet as possible and then get the hell gone.

Fine. Fine. I'll do it. But I better have my flim pronto.

It's a done deal. I'm sendin' you the info n' addy for delivery now. Only use that. It's a P.O. but don't peek for ownership history or you'll be.

Don't threaten me, Sez. Next to Li you're not exactly scary, dig?

Sez sniffs, wounded. IM me back on this line when you're done n' I'll arrange delivery of the flim. Mim said no e-T.

Nope. I want my flim physical.

It will be.

And he's gone, leaving an eerie echo down Shock's connection, disruptive as static down a radio-link. He grimaces and slams it shut. Li's definitely not above hacking Sez's IM and listening in. There's a pool of miso at the bottom of his bowl, sitting there looking all delicious, but Shock's appetite's flatlined. Matter of fact, his whole day's dive-bombed. Nothing for it but to get his sorry self to a Slip shop.

"Sooner you work, sooner you get your flim," he reminds himself, as if he ever needed reminding about the vital correlations between work and money. Hand to mouth is a swift tutor. Imminent murder even more so.

Closest Slip shop is four doors away. Fancy joint called Slip-matic. Slip-matic is a chainstore brand, like the Kendo Noodle House where he's left the dregs of his lunch, and where everything is always a combo of shiny red and puke yellow. In Slip-matic the pods are uniform black; the attendants wear uniforms, and are generally uninformed pretty faces, too dumb for office work. Makes these places the perfect base for a bit of snatch and grab hackage.

Shock pays for nine standards. He's got a barcode to wrestle of unknown classification, which is dandy if you're in the mood for a challenge and a pisser if you're not, and not anything any hack could achieve in under eight standards even if it's lower level. There's no manual interface here, thank fuck, he just jumps in his pod and jacks in, sliding direct into the Slip as Octopus.

The path to Paraderm is quiet but Shock doesn't find it reassuring, there's no paranoid like a hack. Freaked out, he wants to use the nodes but Puss does that thing again, acting autonomous. This time actively leading him astray and squeezing acrobatic coils into Paraderm proper, showing him there's nothing to be nervous of. All is well. Okay then, smartass.

Company grids resemble tube mazes built for smart rodents, or smarter cephalopods, re-imagined in ever more bewildering complication and glowing in various eye-watering hues. Back in control and amazed he lost it to an avi of all things, Shock slinks through with liquid haste, hunting for the storage server in Mim's info packet. She was right about one thing—the server's not classified.

He gets in easy as walking. It's some kind of janitorial server with no connections to the main servers and therefore no need for further VA. Here's a mystery then, because no server of this unclassified nature ever held, nor holds, a classified data packet. So why does this one? He's beginning to suspect the chasing of wild geese here. An amusing skit at the expense of one Shock Pao, idiot supreme. Maybe the beginning of Li's cat-and-mouse game, or some such unpleasantry. Then he sees the barcode, nestling in a small nook halfway up the server, and rage stops him in his tracks.

What in the hell?

Barcodes take their name from the fact they're reminiscent of codes once used on products, with each section of a twelve-digit-long security code represented by four bands of black and white, two of each colour, varying in widths from one to four units to a total of seven. But that's where the resemblance ends. These bars are virtual, and alive. They come in different forms, each with its own challenges, some less so than others. The most complex is the Gordian. Which is what he has here. So far from good it's on another goddamn planet.

The black and white lines coil up and around one another in a nausea-inducing pattern of repetitive movement, like a nest of snakes—and these suckers have venom all right. All manner of nasty surprises lurk in those hallucinatory, shifting coils. If you lack skills, you best not approach this sucker. Death in the Slip is never pretty.

As history would suggest, Gordians have to be cut at exactly the right point, and there's an algorithm in the code that translates to an equation for that location. Which means you have to figure out the code first, and as it works back to front but reads front to back, that's no mean feat. Crack it, reverse it, extract the algorithm, extrapolate the equation and snip.

Now he gets what this information is. Company secrets. An inside job. Hidden here in plain sight to keep out curious eyes, with the expense of a Gordian shackled over it to prevent accidental stumblers from being able to access its contents. And Mim is undercutting. This job is worth thousands more than he's getting. His eight K just shrank from under twenty percent to under five. He's worth so much more, fifty/fifty for reals even in his current condition and with all the trouble at his back—if only he had the pride and wherewithal to tell her where to shove it.

Shock stretches his tentacles, the Octopus equivalent of cracking tension out of a neck. However much he wants to throw the world's biggest hissy fit at Mim, or walk away, preferably both, he's stuck with doing his job, getting his insulting payment of flim and forgetting all about it. That's his life skill, and a good life skill is incapable of being over-utilized.

Shoulda bought fifty units, he mutters to himself, and gets to work, thanking all the quirks of a random system that he ended up in an avi with eight fully malleable limbs and a habit of augmenting his ability to think, so he didn't have to drop unnecessary flim on upgrades. Talk about serendipity.

Still, it takes nearly an hour of playing shuffle with the knot, working fast enough to blur tentacles, to get the code. Somewhere up there, IRL, his body is slicked with sweat, the greasy kind you get in the Slip from nerves, feels like you just bathed in luke-warm stir-fry oil. Shock grimaces, his beak tucking in.

Waking's gonna be a bitch.

With the code worked out, the rest is simple, but only because he aced advanced mathematics and somehow remembers all of it when he's Puss down here. If that wasn't the case... well... Gordians have time restrictions on top of their other tricks, and they tend to count down to explosion. From Slip to IRL the damage from such an explosion is all cerebral. He might get out of Slip, considering this shop has rudimentary safety precautions, but he wouldn't wake up. They'd have to carry him, drooling, to the nearest ICU. Probability of waking there? Maybe three to one, which is not so bad. Probability of waking with his faculties intact? Those are odds he never wants to calculate.

Ten mins later he's got the cut point and the data-packet. Shock regards it with disgust through Puss's square pupils.

Just so we're clear, he snaps at it. I should be getting paid way more for plucking you out, you bastard.

Copying the info into his drive, Shock resets the Gordian and heads out of the server. In about as bad a mood as he can muster, he locates the P.O. at a reef a good distance away, and heads off to deliver. The second he opens the P.O. to upload, something gross and sticky lands in his drive. It's heavy. Slick. And moving. Sliding about like mercury, giving him that odd floaty head you get after drinking one too many on an empty stomach and not the fun one either, the one where you really wish you'd bothered to eat.

What the fuck!

Slamming the package into the P.O., Shock takes a second to scrape at his drive with some anti-virals. They do nothing except make him feel instantly sick, tasting copper, magnesium burn, ashes slicked with grease, which freaks him out good and proper. Tasting in the Slip is so not good—means the whole funny head shit is having a physical effect on his body IRL. He could already have tossed his noodles and be choking his last.

Caught between sickness and panic, he ejects from Slip, leaving Puss where it is, knowing it'll be there when he needs it again no matter what. Finding himself alive and vomit-free is a plus, but Shock's not in the least reassured, shit is badly wrong here in his head. This makes tofu brain look like fun times. Calls in fact for a trip to a drive clinic, a virtual colonic for the head, but joy of joys he hasn't flim for that until Sez IMs and he can acknowledge delivery, so he's going to have to improvise.

Only two ways to do that, good drugs or good tea. Guess which one he hasn't got flim for? Dragging himself out of the pod, he clamps his hands to his belly and makes his way on unsteady feet back onto Plaza into the cool wash of evening, under over-bright lights, on the hunt for a temporary liquid solution to his woes.

Moving lights from shop signs slide across grey concrete like water reflections, dragging shadows behind them.

Plaza's too quiet for a Monday, thinks Ko-Ren, peering out at a night sky bled to deep purple by the bright glare of Shin district.

Somewhere up there floats Tokyo City Hub. If he squints through the sea of neon and street lights, the spotlights on 'scraper roofs, he should be able to see it; a dark shadow sliding through purple night like a sea monster, menacing in its sheer size and breadth. Not tonight though, tonight his eyes are tired. Double shifts to make ends meet mean late nights, early mornings. Costs too much to live these days and he's an old man, getting older every day. One day they'll find him dead in this booth, a smile stuck to his face, kabuki-like, warped and disingenuous.

Old Rin, from the same 'rise Ko-Ren reluctantly calls home, walks on by down the Plaza dragging his wife's ugly dog, shaggy as a bear with scabies, on a thin plastic leash. Rin's wife is long dead and he hates the dog, but always walks it. Half eight every evening, the same route he used to take with her. Maybe he thinks she's waiting down the Plaza somewhere. Maybe he thinks she'll brush the damned dog. Ko-Ren winces, clutching a grumbling stomach. No option but long hours, and he can't leave the booth in case he misses a sale. If he forgets to cook rice for the day, he has to graze on what he sells.

Snagging a candy bar from his gaudy display, he cracks the seal to munch on low cal synth-choc. Bares his teeth, stained shit brown. Synth-choc tastes like mud. Nothing like the old days, but only the rich can afford that. Black-market chocolate costs over a month's profit from this shit-hole on Plaza he likes to call a business, and his old heart, reduced to the puttering rhythm of water on a tin roof, would likely quit working altogether from a sniff of the real deal.

"Filthy junk," he says, wiping his mouth on his sleeve. Tries to chew without tasting.

Noise explodes behind the booth. A clamour of voices, excitable as gulls at the fish market squabbling over scraps of squid. Streeks. These scum come from the Cads and the tangle of massive blocks behind Plaza, the Pod hotels. Three-thousand-feet-high edifices filled with enough claustrophobic coffins to bury the dead of a city; open from eleven P.M. to eight A.M. Between those times, when they're not cooped in classrooms learning trade, Streeks run loose as packs of feral dogs, try to outrun the odds of dying before Graduation. Most don't. He doesn't feel sorry for them, they make their own hell.

They burst around the concrete corner of the booth, bright and noisy. Hands scrabbling in his display, they laugh in his face, throwing hard words like insults in Ko-Chun. Streek slang, a mix of Korean, Chinese and pidgin English spoken in rapid bursts, staccato as machine-gun fire. He doesn't understand a word.

Waves his fist as they run off down the plaza with handfuls of smokes, candy and filmy, unactivated e-zines, crumpled to wads. Neon transforms the splash of dirty rainwater in their wake to startling fireworks and the whole Plaza comes to life, as if to hide them from view, thousands of salarymen and women pouring out of the mono towers. No one stops at the booth, or even stops to look.

"Go fuck yourselves," he mutters, collapsing back amongst tumbled boxes, the bright scatter of candy bars and smoke packets.

Behind constricting ribs his heart's struggling to haul blood, sputter-fading through every beat. He sucks air, desperate as a junkie, willing the pain to dull. No medicare for him. Not some stupid old man too weak to labour, too dull to be a salaryman. Used to be a shop worker, a good job, before he got too old for the floor. They kept him on, allowing him to take shifts in the back, but three years in the warehouses reduced him to a shambling wreck, leaving two choices: the retirement complexes or a booth. He chose the booth. That's like choosing life, for whatever value of life is found in a booth.

Breathing usually works, easy in, easy out, remembering days out on the 'scraper roof gardens following the unconscious flow of taiji. Not today. The inside of his ribs burn like smouldering lantern paper as his heart takes longer and longer to complete each pump. Pain becomes ropes strung through his chest pulled tight, tighter yet, and darkness creeps across his vision like Tokyo City across the night, whispers following in its tracks like gossiping stars. He thinks he's dreaming of heaven, but what angels speak like this?

We'll piggyback, it's on the way out. This voice is sexless, and echoes, as though only a portion of it is yet within him. It makes him quail, terrified of some unspecified burden.

Where's Shock Pao? This other voice is equally sexless, holds the same sensation of withheld mass. It's so eerily similar to the first voice, Ko-Ren is certain this thing, whatever it is, must be speaking to itself. Mad then? Or is he going mad himself?

Near. The signal is loud.

There can be no more mistakes.

Trial and error. Everything is in place now.

That is what Calhoun told us last time.

But I am not Calhoun.

True.

Air's down to vapours now. As his perception warps

out of skew, a vast presence, the burden he anticipated, looms inside Ko-Ren's head, pushing him out to the edges. Spread thin as poor man's butter around the inside of his skull, Ko-Ren understands nothing except that this isn't heaven; it hurts too much. And the voices whisper on.

There. On our left.

They pull his vision to one side as if his eyes, on strings, are only their puppets. He sees a sick-looking young man in a thin neoprene jacket, barely able to walk and clutching at his stomach. Long, wild hair in black and candy-bright green partially obscures eyes so startling blue they register as fake in that so-Korean face. He feels a rush of fear. Wants to call out and warn this young man. But about what? And he's not sure he owns his mouth any more.

So this is our Haunt? One of the voices snaps, flat with disgust. Too loud. Ko-Ren needs to cover his ears, but where are they? Where are his hands? Unhealthy.

Addict. Excellent. It won't matter if we damage him.

True. Calhoun means to cheat us.

Of course he does. What are humans if not treacherous? Look at what was done to us.

Trapped.

Confined.

Reduced.

Not for much longer.

The weight disappears, and darkness drops over Ko-Ren, the night in his booth without the shadow of Tokyo to guide his way. His last thoughts are that he should've gone up there as a young man when he had the chance; no rules in Tokyo, no Psychs, no skill tests, no freaking Cads or complexes. No goddamn booths. Just the curve of the earth endlessly falling beneath, and the stars like beacons overhead.

"Could've been looking down instead of looking up,"

he mutters, and tumbles headlong into silence, a grin
frozen to his face, wide and distorted as a Kabuki mask.

land ship showdown

the sea churns under skies dyed the deep purple of cumulonimbi in a rage. Hard winds from the south throw twenty-foot, foam-topped monster waves against the high sides of the Resurrection. Not high enough yet for overspill, but the clouds promise a worsening of the weather and the wheel crews are out in force, securing every last bolt, making certain the Resurrection can survive a storm sailing at full speed.

The Ark, mere hours behind and gaining at a frightening rate, is a storm of another kind, one they may not survive. The Resurrection holds the size advantage, sure, and she can run at a fair clip on smooth seas too, but these seas are far from smooth. The Ark runs faster on both and despite her size, she's packed with soldiers and supported by a fleet of schooners.

As the night wears on, the sea smashes furious fists around them. Wind howls through the upper decks, sending the ropes swinging madly, forcing the use of clipped lines for travel. On the crow, Petrie keeps an eye on their back, along with the drone, finally aloft, whose ability to fly sound in this sort of weather astounds him.

With those eyes in the sky, able to see through the starless darkness, he spots the Ark and her fleet coming over the horizon and closing fast.

"They're here," he says to Cassius.

"How many schooners?"

"Drone counts forty-two."

"Not so bad. Better than fifty, better than sixty. Ready the guns, Bosun, we fire as soon as they're in range."

Word travels by clicker on ships running dark—IM is signal and they want to keep their location hidden even from scans for as long as possible. It takes the clicker teams a good twenty-five minutes to pass word to each different station around the ship. By this time the Ark's fleet of schooners should be well within range, and yet the Resurrection's drone shows them hanging back, slowing to sail in the wake of the Ark.

Petrie's immediate thought is that they plan to use her as a shield, to come out in force when they're close enough to anticipate and avoid Resurrection's guns. Turning to relay these fears to Cassius, he's drowned out by a percussion of explosions. In surreal slow motion, several portions of the Resurrection's upper deck implode, spewing molten chunks of steel and flaming wood. Three guns on the port side topple grandly into the sea, taking their crew with them. Petrie stares up wildly.

"Drones!" he roars over the noise.

"What about our drone? Is it lost?" Cassius shouts back, straining to see through his 'scope, his face a stark illustration of Petrie's own shock and horror.

Connecting back into the drone's eyes, Petrie finds it engaged in a dogfight with two others. The Ark's drones are damaged from pirate fire and shoddily repaired, but their weapons are working all right.

"No, but it's in serious trouble. Needs help now."

Cassius nods. "Light the night. Get this under control, Bosun."

"Cap'n."

Reaching for his control panel, Petrie lights the ship, aiming spotlights skyward to illuminate the drones circling above as he sends a ship-wide IM.

Concentrate half firepower upward. Two enemy drones to take, red-marked in 'scope. The other half firepower on the Ark and her schooners. Repair teams douse those fires, medics move the injured down below. Work fast and careful, folk.

Returning to his 'scope, Petrie watches the pointed mass of the Ark bearing down upon their stern. His stomach clenches, old fear throttling it in callous hands. There's Daly Pentecost, captain of the Ark, a silhouette in miniature against the lights. He stands as he always does, on a crow taller than Cassius's—because Cassius is not just a leader, he's part of the crew.

Pentecost is his ship's lord and master. His power is in every line of his body, standing straight and unassailable. In the somber air of contemplation his people mistake for wisdom. His cruelty is the kind that hides behind easy smiles, a gentle gaze and a soft voice, but it is the whole core of him. Undeniable. Being its focus is to live in terror.

Seeing him again, even from such a distance, Petrie's thrown back through the years. To the sound of Pentecost's voice. The soft tap of his boots on the deck. The shrinking on his skin as they came closer, knowing what would happen when they stopped. He used to piss himself sometimes, fear overriding shame. How can he face this? There's too much terror. He can't even think.

"You're no boy now." Cassius's voice drops into the ocean of Petrie's fear solid as an anchor. He's never told Cassius all that was done to him, only that he was born there and that he ran. He expects his face may have told some of the rest, has no doubt that it speaks eloquently of his current terror. "You're my bosun, and I need you to lead my crew."

The man listens, but the boy within can't hear. Fear leaks through Petrie like freezing water through a hull breach. For long moments, too long, he simply can't separate man from boy.

Cassius's hand falls on his shoulder.

"Petrie. We don't have time for this. The Resurrection, she's burning."

With great difficulty Petrie moves his gaze from Daly to their upper deck. Firestorms punctuate the hull, the roar of their flames underpinning the bombastic thump of heavy guns firing intermittent bursts into sky and earthy hull. His ship, his home, is under siege, and here he is, lost in the past, in old fears, paralyzed.

Dredging for willpower deep within, Petrie pushes the boy he once was far into the background. With a nod to Cassius, he leaps onto the ropes and, sliding at breakneck speed on zip-wires from crow to crow, heads for the stern, stopping to help put out fires, to carry the wounded, and to aid gunners in securing broken struts and scaffolds.

He yells orders via IM as he goes, reining in the gunner crews to fire in tight formation, and one of the Ark's drones drops at last, hitting the Resurrection amidships, punching a giant hole in the upper deck. Like everything else destroyed today, it'll be swiftly repaired, this ship heals fast under the unceasing hands of its crew.

The other two drones, one belonging to the Ark, and their own, finally broken, fall into the sea, trailing flames, and sending vast waves crashing over the fires on the Resurrection's port side. Strapped in tight, the remaining gunners come out still firing. These folk are tough, fierce.

Coming from a place where no one fought back, it's a constant surprise to be amongst those who refuse to surrender. They give him courage.

Two crows from the stern, with the Ark fewer than three hundred metres away and closing fast, Petrie grabs up a long-range rifle. He knows the Ark's strategy, and he's made certain crews are in place at the stern to counter them. The Ark's bowsprit is reinforced with steel, and barbed. Slammed at speed into other ships it serves as an anchor, a bridge for the Ark's forces to swarm aboard, going after the helpless. With their families captive, a ship's armed forces find good reason to surrender.

Not this time.

The people of the Resurrection are Petrie's family. All these good folk, all these kids, they're never going to live under Pentecost's thumb.

The Ark hits, driving metres of armoured bowsprit into the cliff at her stern. The Resurrection jolts. Petrie holds his forces steady. And as the incoming forces are exposed on the bowsprit, he unleashes their full firepower. He doesn't fire with them; his target is higher, far more difficult to reach.

Pentecost remains on his crow at all times, surrounded during conflict by his personal guard, a trusted team of fifteen men. Getting a clear shot past them will be difficult, so Petrie doesn't aim for Pentecost.

Instead, breathing even and slow, and firing on the out breath, he takes out the personal guard. Does it fast, laid flat like a sniper with the automatic rifle rested easily against his shoulder, aware that even though they won't expect this direct attack, they'll swiftly adapt. Indeed the final five die returning fire, their bullets unerring, taking chunks of wood right next to Petrie's head.

When the last has fallen, Petrie leaps up. From this rear crow it's just over a mile to Pentecost's central tower. He'll have a replacement guard up there in no time, so Petrie grabs up a rappel gun. Made for long distance firing, for scavenging as well as warfare, these can run out up to three miles of thin, high-tensile wire, and they're heavy, so he hefts it on his shoulder to fire, aware that as soon as it's hit, Pentecost will know he's coming.

Clamping on with his automated clip and line, he zips in. Beneath him as he spins out, far above the bow, he watches with a mixture of grim satisfaction and churning nausea as wave after wave of the Ark's troops fall. Still taking heavy fire from Resurrection's guns, the Ark is burning too, and the heat makes him sweat almost as much as his own fear.

Pentecost must be just as hot, but he stands as if he feels nothing, as if none of this is unexpected. The man's confidence cuts deep holes in Petrie's certainty, threatening to tear it apart. As he lands mere metres away from the object of his terror, he wonders if he's made the right choice.

As soon as Pentecost's eyes meet his, he knows he hasn't. He can't beat this man. His only hope was to run.

Why didn't he run?

When Pentecost speaks, it is with deceptive warmth.

"Well look who it is, come to kill me. Young Petrie. It is still Petrie, isn't it? Or did you desert everything?"

Petrie did not expect to be recognized. His limbs are weak, his hands shaking.

His voices shakes, too, as he replies, stunned by his ability to speak when his courage has fled, "Still Petrie. And that's my home you're attacking there. I'm going to stop you."

"This is your home, lad," Pentecost responds, holding his arms wide as if there's no argument to the contrary, as if Petrie's a fool for even thinking otherwise. "Waiting to welcome you with open arms, even after you deserted us. Even after all the good people you've put to death today." He sighs, looking over the destruction of the Ark. Shakes his head, a mournful look falling over his face Petrie can't help but respond to, his gut cramping. "See what you've done, Petrie? Killing children to save children. Which child is more worthy of life?"

Under Pentecost's knowing eyes, Petrie withers. Of course he's wrong. He was always wrong. Always making mistakes. His arms begin to droop, the gun loosening in his hands. Pentecost smiles then, and it hits Petrie like lightning. He remembers that smile. Remembers seeing it on Pentecost's face as he beat Petrie until he could barely move. Barely see.

He looks at his hands. They're so big now. He is. But when he lived on the Ark, he was tiny. A runt. What kind of man beats a skinny runt of a child until he can't move? He looks up at Pentecost again, and it's like seeing him for the first time. He's so small. He begins to lift his gun.

Pentecost laughs.

"Best pull that trigger quick, son," he says. "Got men on the way up. I let you waste time, standing there shivering, practically crapping your pants. The man is like the boy. Pathetic. Weak. Worthless. Do you think you can kill me now? You know I won't kill you. I don't need to. They'll tear you apart as soon as they see you. I told them your name. Deserter. Betrayer. Coward."

Fear is a knot, tying you up into yourself leaving no room for movement. Logically he sees how small Pentecost is now. He accepts that he doesn't need to be afraid, and yet he still is. Petrie takes a few steps back as Pentecost's men appear at the edge of the crow. The rappel clip line is still attached to his wrist.

He's got one chance.

Running backward, he leaps, throws the clip at the wire, bouncing hard as the line takes his weight. Bullets zip past him, far too close. Rippling his clothes. Cutting through the edges of his torso, his thighs. He pays them no attention. Lifting his gun again, he aims carefully as he flies backward, swinging to and fro. Fires.

And Pentecost drops like a stone.

rocks and hard bastards

dizziness strikes on top of nausea as soon as his feet hit tarmac and Shock manages by luck alone to head for the lower end of Plaza, toward the piss-cheap plastic-box franchises with their gaudy 3D-printed furniture, prone to cracking, and tinny piped music.

Concentrating hard on the contact between feet and ground, still holding on to his stomach with both hands, he sticks close to the shop fronts. If he's knocked down in this state, getting up is going to involve throwing up, and throwing up is where he draws the line.

Somewhere over the noise of rushing feet, the entertainments, the hum of lights, he hears Streeks hooting and slurs, "Fucking Monday."

Academy classes finish at nine P.M. sharp today and Plaza hosts a dangerous game of "Avoid the Streeks" till podtime. Avoidance is all there is. No one here will stop to help if they catch you. Turning a blind eye has become a habit for the folk of Foon Gung.

Give them a few years and the ones that don't end up Streek stats will be harmless. WAMOS. Separated and shacked up into whatever unhappy marriage of skill and labour their Psych Eval and test scores condemn them to; jacked in to everyday just like every other suit and sorry arse on the street. But there'll always be Streeks to avoid. Mondays are never safe.

Shock glances back up Plaza, scoping out Streek colours. All he sees is some old fartster in a concrete booth, staring at him and grinning wide enough to break his face. Clearly he's tripping harder than Shock is.

"Weirdo."

He stumbles on, eyes skimming the signs for that demarcation between sort-of cheap and super cheap. Scanning for Wunda-cafes, four different franchises owned by different Corps but all selling the same dubious menu, advertised in plastic food scale models inside plasglass boxes. You might die of food poisoning but you can eat at Wundas for a whole week for under five flim.

He collapses into the first one he finds. Orders a long, cold green tea with caffeine shots and gets his arse in a seat before it falls out from under him. Taking massive swallows to counteract nausea, he accesses his IM to chime Sez the man-whore. When he's done, this number is getting exorcized from his drive. Halle-fuckin-lujah.

Haunt?

Man-whore.

Cute. Real cute. You done?

Done.

Where you want the flim?

Sending you a box now. Make sure it's in opaque packaging and well secured.

Done.

Shock cuts off before Sez can. Draining his tea, he shoves the cup to the centre of the plastic table and makes to leave, aiming for sleep until he can get that flim and sort his drive, furious about the waste. This always happens with Mim. Always something going wrong. Always the shitty lining. His IM chimes just as he vacates his seat. He's not expecting a call. Goes to cut it off dead, but it answers itself, and he hears a voice in the top five of his "never want to hear again" list: Twist Calhoun.

Well, well, look what I've caught.

If Shock could drop stone cold dead right now, even in some imitational fashion like a fucking mongoose, he'd be all over that shit. Won't help though, because he knows he's not going to need a drive clean after all.

You fucking toe tagged me? he yells, his virtual tone as high as if he'd never taken testosterone supps. What the fuck, man!

That I did.

Collapsing back into his seat, Shock's incapable of controlling the shaking in his limbs. It rattles the metal legs against the plastic floor. Sounds like a mass of scuttling insects.

Didn't think you'd waste that sort of flim on me.

Toe tags cost an eye-watering stack of flim to make. Once you're tagged you're a walking corpse to whoever paid, because they can always find you. But they're not supposed to feel like this mass of tarry hell—they're supposed to be all but untraceable in a drive, so you can be tagged and not know it until it's too late. So what the hell kind of tag is this? He'd ask, but Twist might tell him.

Interesting assumption you're making, Twist says, and his amusement is neither amusing nor reassuring. You might want to stop making those.

Okay. So here's a thing I'm not assuming. Mim had a part in this, yeah? Was that even a job?

Fucking goddamn Mim. That girl has it in for him, plain and simple. Why could she not just be happy with napalming his heart?

She comes in useful. And yes, the job was legit. Two birds, one stone, etc.

Am I walking dead here?

Shock does not want to know this either, but he has to ask. Looks with a furtive eye for anyone in his vicinity who might be packing heat. Everyone looks suspicious. Oh, well done, Paranoia, that's super helpful.

Twist laughs. You think I'd pay this much just to kill you? Seriously?

I assumed...

If I wanted you dead, you wouldn't have woken up in Slip-matic. You know that. Your stupidity is embarrassing.

All right. Shock tries to think through the high of panic, the sickness, the liquid swilling of the tag. Finds only one plausible reason.

You need me.

Bravo. First glimmer of your usual perspicacity. I do indeed have use of you.

Use, not need. Nausea becomes a vessel of viscera, sinking toward his feet. He's toe tagged, which means two things: one, he won't be getting paid for this; two, he won't be getting away from Twist any time soon. This could be slavery. It could be slavery then death. He could kill Mim right now.

Reminding the Harmonys he exists is one thing, like setting rabid dogs on your arse. Setting Twist on him though? So much worse. Fucking unforgivable. He'd feel hurt, but he's way beyond that, way beyond rage. He doesn't know what this feeling is, only that if he ever sees Mim again he won't be able to prevent himself from punching her. Which is not like him at all. Shock might think violent thoughts, but he'd never be violent. He knows too well how it feels.

What's the job?

You're going to fetch me something from Hive.

Shock hangs on to his dignity by a narrow margin, swallowing mouthfuls of foul-tasting bile, hot as fresh soup. He's watched the Queens plough through corals like they were gossamer, their bulk filling the Slip from murky depths to fake-beamed heights. Horrifying even from a distance. He never wants to be closer. And entering Hive without their knowledge? Difficult as hell. Even for a Haunt.

Why me?

Twist chuckles. He seems genuinely amused. Why not?

Plenty of Haunts out there. Haunts who haven't displeased you. Feng Ho, Base, Joon Bug, maybe even Aliss or Black. All of them are capable of cracking Hive. Not that they'd do it without this toe tag, which I presume is the point.

Precisely. And yes, there were a number of you capable. Let's just say this job is the result of significant trial and error, and you get to be the lucky Haunt to benefit from that.

A conversation he had weeks ago pops vaguely into Shock's head. Was it weeks? Longer than one anyway. Feels like forever. Ducky Took waffling on about Haunts gone signal dead or some shit and he'd scoffed at it. Full on. Couldn't wrap his tofu brain around any such concept. Fuck. How many Haunts has Twist burnt through exactly?

On the back of that comes a sneaking suspicion that this is the only reason he's still alive. After all, Twist doesn't call off his Cleaners, and that Amiga Tanaka nearly had him. By a freakin' whisper. He'd convinced himself that his escape had been purely Haunt skills. Yeah. Of course it was.

How many did you use up?

All you need to know is that you'll be the last. Rather ironic that you're the only one no one will miss.

That hits Shock where he lives, but he doesn't show it. So. Hive.

Core, actually.

The floor seems to plummet away from beneath his feet. Hive is do-able, though it's stupid to try: Core is impossible. Nothing gets in but Core drones. Nothing else can get in.

Core is not Hive, Twist.

No, it's not. But as I said, you're the lucky recipient of previous attempts. Feeling ill right now?

The crude oil?

That what it feels like?

Worse.

Good. You deserve that. The toe tag comes with a little extra, something not meant for a human. The signal given off by a Core drone.

You put virtware in my drive? Ho-lee hell. No wonder it's fucking with his head. Virtware is code designed to exist amongst code. Nothing like this was ever made to enter a drive, to be inside a human mind. How the fuck did you get that?

I have my sources. But there's a problem.

Problem? Like he needs more problems. He's got nothing but.

The signal is loud enough to leak. You're emitting.

People talk about being rendered speechless. What they mean is that no words are quite adequate to describe what they've witnessed, their emotional response to it. That's where Shock is. Dumbstruck. If he's emitting noise, then he's visible. If he's visible then he's no longer a Haunt. Twist just took the single absolute in Shock's world and tore it down like Jericho. Standing in the wreckage, Shock's system experiences the aftermath of siege. The blood, the ruin, the rape and pillage.

You fucking what? His voice is so thin it sounds more like steam escaping through the cracks in a kettle lid.

Oh don't you worry, Shock, you're okay for now. I've got you blocked, all locked up tight. Unfortunately, the block will be obvious to the Tech-savvy people of my criminal peers, who are just a touch curious about my recent endeavours. Happen they'll be interested in cracking it and tracking you down.

So why don't you just grab me now until I have what I need to do the job?

Shock's gone from ruin to rage, but underneath it? Terror. Nothing but. Rising and rising, electrifying his cells. His hands are frozen, his legs are numb, and his head is a bell, ringing out over and over. He finds himself tipping his head to one side to try to hear Twist's response through the clamour.

I like the idea of you running against the clock. Besides, if you decide to be your usual craven self and try to slip my noose, I'll stop the block and let them run you down; and when they've finished taking you apart, I'll take what's left and make you do it. With that toe tag there's nowhere they could take you I couldn't find you, even if they put a block on you themselves. You have to know how much that pleases me.

Shock's chest shrinks to a tight point. Fucking Mim, shoving him into a dead-end and calling it a way out. When did he get so stupid? He rubs his eyes, trying to ignore how his knuckles come away damp.

Then I have no choice.

That's right. And you are a lucky boy, because if you promise to be good, I'll make an effort to keep protecting you.

An effort...?

I might not be able to save you in the long term, Shock, but I'll keep you alive long enough to deliver.

Fine. Nope, not fine, but clear enough. Clear as a glass to the fucking face.

So what am I getting from Core?

Emblem.

Shock rests his face in shaking palms, suddenly exhausted. Yeah, if there's one thing in Core a megalomaniac like Twist might want to get his greasy fingers on, and waste a fuckton of Haunts to do so, it'd be Emblem. That's the pipe dream right there—control Emblem, control Slip, control everything. The fucking motherlode no one's ever dared to try for because you'd have to be really stupid or really sure.

How in hell does Twist expect Shock to pull this off? Even with all these fancy extras it's a job so complex it's more like a kamikaze mission. He'll be in Hive, vulnerable to the Queens, not just for seconds, but for full minutes' worth of seconds, every ticking one of them a doorway through which disaster could erupt no matter how much he prepares, or how clever he is.

And what if the Queens manage to take Emblem from him? What could they do with it? What couldn't they? The same goes for Emblem in Twist's possession. Either scenario makes Shock's gorge rise. He can't do this. Cannot. Shock didn't even know he had a line, but here it is.

What am I, a fucking wizard? A fucking idiot? You know what the Queens will do with that. What they'll do to me.

Twist laughs at him again. Choice, Shock. Where's yours precisely?

I won't do it.

Then I'll use Joon, and I'll kill you in ways you can't imagine. I'll remake you a fucking girl before I do it. That how you want to die, Shock? I know it's not how you wanted to live. What it comes down to is, one way or another, I'm getting Emblem. You can do it and stay alive, die clean with some fucking dignity. Or you can continue refusing.

Can he refuse? Shock looks down at himself. Tries to imagine what it will be like to have taken away what he worked so hard and suffered so long to make right and understands it will break him into tiny pieces, each one a symphony of pain. He should be brave enough to face that, to do the right thing, but Twist is right. He's craven.

It's not only that he's suffered too much to cope with more, it's that he doesn't—can't—care about anyone else. Numero uno is the only number he gives a shit about. If he doesn't, who will? Besides, if he says no, Joon might say yes. What then? What would his attempted morality mean at that point? Nothing.

I'm going to need some things I can't afford.

Twist doesn't bother crowing. Why would he need to?

You'll get a decent wedge of flim for whatever you need delivered to the same P.O. you gave to Sez. But that's all you're getting. Apart from maybe to live.

How long do I have? You said I'm on the clock here.

About forty-eight hours. If we're lucky.

Forty-eight hours to get enough virtual gear together to crack Hive, sneak into Core and hook Emblem out from under Queen noses. It's not long. And if he survives that? Life sentence? Death? If he'd known he'd fuck up this hard, he'd have dropped out long ago, found any way at all to hang on where he felt happiest. Even sell his arse to whomever the fuck might want it.

At least he'd actually be there, instead of just dreaming about it. He still dreams of Sendai every night. Dreams his happiness is there, waiting for him after all these years, like a pound of diamonds in a security box. He'll never know if he was right. The thought is bright, sudden pain, a burst of it, like raw chilli rubbed in a wound. He wants to curl around it, hold on, as if doing so can numb the agony. Instead, he takes his medicine.

Two days. Got it.

When you have Emblem you'll be able to ditch the signal. It'll degrade once used, so be careful about your entry and exit. Don't want to accidentally alert anything Queen-like, do we now?

Where do I upload Emblem?

In my vault. Nowhere else. You fetch it, you bring it to me. Understood?

Understood.

And Twist's gone, leaving a hole in Shock's head big enough to lose the Gung in, aching and ringing like head trauma. He's so fucking stupid. 0.5%? What exactly does it mean to be in that top half of a percent if he's too dumb to see the obvious? Too idiotic to know when he's being duped, even by the woman who made a hobby out of duping him.

Shock clutches his head. Oh hell but he needs sleep so very badly, needs a serious hit too, something strong. Pity he's only got cheap shit. Pressing as many as he dares into his neck he drags himself off the stool. No time for sleep. Forty-eight hours is all he has and there are things he'll need.

'Scrapers drooling around him in sticky S-driven coils, he staggers down the street, heading for his P.O. to fetch Twist's flim. He feels alienated, the world something happening about a million miles away from him. But he can feel it zooming toward him, relentless, wearing an Oni mask with a saw-toothed grin big enough to gobble him up; and he walks faster and faster, hoping to outdistance it.

mim makes a deal

You sleeping, Sez?"

Back from her Imping vacay as Unity Jo-Charbonneau, Mim closes the door of her apartment and strides through into the bedroom. Beholds Johnny Sez, cuddled up to his pillow, snoring and drooling. Urg. She is not sleeping in that bed until every scrap of linen has been boil-washed. Bodies. So goddamn gross. Why do they leak so much? She lifts a deliberate leg, clad in a sleek, black blader, and kicks him in the head.

"Wake up."

Johnny groans, shoves her away without opening his eyes.

"Shit, Mim," he slurs, "you have appallin' timin'."

"For real? I have appalling timing? Wow, you need to wake up."

She reaches down and grabs his leg, yanking him half out of bed. He tries to pull back, shake her off. Mim hisses and tugs again, hard, until his arse thumps onto the floor.

"Ow. Fuckin' ow, bitch. What, no hello?"

Mim leans down right to his ear.

"Who's been in my house, Sez? Someone's been in my

fucking house who shouldn't have been. And I'm not talking about you, you freeloading little fucking donkey shit."

He rubs his face, still half asleep and obviously on the come down from some serious trippage. He better have used his own money this time or he's going to find himself homeless. Possibly skinless.

"What you sayin'?" He blinks up at her stupidly.

His eyes are bright blue. Almost periwinkle. That's what she liked about him. Never as blue as the first blue eyes to slaughter her. She had to make them bluer in the end to preserve herself, and that was a mess. Mim hates mess. She hates cleaning it up, getting her hands dirty, and you can't cleanse the filth of emotional mess. That's why this time she chose the eyes, and not the boy behind them. She grabs his chin and forces him to look through the archway at the rest of her apartment.

"See that?" she snaps. "Do you see?"

"See what? It's clean. I cleaned."

Mim raises a brow, scanning the room with cold, mirrored eyes.

"That's a whole other story, slim. But your paltry efforts don't hide the fact that people were here who shouldn't have been." She turns back to him, moves her hand from chin to ear and tweaks until he squeaks. "Who were they?"

"Fucking hell, Mim." He yanks his ear out of her pincered fingers. "OW!" He glares at her, all his hurt in those ocean-blues. Good. Hurt she knows. Hurt she can deal with. "Harmonys, okay? It was the Harmonys. And I woulda told you anyway. They want a word."

Mim laughs out loud.

"About time. I've been flirting about as hard as is possible without clueing in Twist."

"What?"

"Not very bright this morning, are we? This thing I

helped Twist with. Everyone's interested in it. I want to find out why and I want in, and Twist doesn't do partnerships. The Harmonys do, if you don't get on the wrong side of Li."

Johnny struggles up from the floor.

"I have no idea what the hell you're talking about."

"Dullard."

She strolls off to the kitchen, bladers thumping the floor. She has this thing about cleaning, except when it comes to boots on feet. Therein lies a trade-off. Worry about dirt from boots, or worry about bare feet or worse, sweat-drenched socks, all over the damned floor? Either way she'd get the hideous twitchies about what might be growing in the cracks of her floor, adhering to the soles of her feet, growing, maybe getting into her blood stream and multiplying—so boots it is.

The compromise balances on one hard clean at the end of a day and various low-level tidies if boots trample more dirt than the mind can handle. That's how she knew uninvited guests had been in her apartment. Sez vacuumed, sure, but he didn't vacuum. Their dirt is everywhere.

Shoving his feet into untied boots because he knows the house rules, Sez traipses after her.

"You're gonna fuck Twist over?"

He's flabbergasted, jaw hanging and everything. He looks as gormless as when he drools in his sleep and Mim looks away before it puts her off the coffee she's brewing, or him, which would be worse.

"Where's the harm? He'd fuck me over in a heartbeat. Less. Besides, I'm done now, and he did not stipulate silence in my contract. Fine print, Sez, you should read it."

Sez grabs a string of twisted blue candy from a jar on Mim's kitchen shelf. If she took a moment to appreciate the themes in her life, her apartment, she might hate herself, which is why Mim never thinks about it. You act and you move on, or you grind to a halt. Mim has no time for baggage. Not even her own.

"He'll have you Cleaned." Sez takes a cavalier bite of the candy and raises a brow at her. "You're not invincible. Not invisible like Shock. You won't escape."

Mim snatches the candy and bites a mouthful from the other end.

"I'll be working with the Harmonys, idiot. They'll protect me."

"Only as long as you're useful."

"I'm always useful."

Li is addicted to coconut cake, which is why the Harmonys hold court at one of Shimli's tiny, secret coffee houses. Apart from them, the place is deserted. Mrs Tan, the coffeehouse proprietor, doesn't seem to care. With her prices, why would she? As Mim strolls in Li waves her cake enthusiastically, spilling crumbs everywhere.

"There you are! Look, Ho, she came."

Ho nods, eyes on his long fingers, busy constructing a purple psy. From the sheer, painstaking concentration on his face, he could be attempting to construct an origami lotus small enough to fit on the head of a pin.

"I see," he murmurs.

Li switches so fast it gives Mim psychological whiplash, shooting Ho a glance that could strip the skin from an elephant and burn it.

"You don't. You don't see. You're not even looking. Brat."

She switches again. Lightning fast. Beams at Mim.

"Sit. Have cake."

"Coffee?" shouts Mrs Tan from behind the prow of her gargantuan service desk, magnificent walnut with marquetry depicting a war between dragons over a glowing ball of wisdom. The whole cafe is decorated the same. It gives Mim migraines.

"Please," Mim yells back. "Triple shots. And don't give me dregs this time, old woman. Last time I was picking grounds out of my teeth for hours."

Mrs Tan throws back her head laughing as she disappears into the kitchen, and Li shakes her head, sharing a conspiratorial glance with Mim.

"That woman," she says. "Wicked. Wants me to whack Yang for her. In good time I might, if I'm feeling playful. Isn't life grand?"

"If you say so," says Mim, taking a forkful of the cake Li generously served her and groaning as she eats. "Dear heaven, that's perfect."

"Usefulness," Li responds, running as ever completely off piste. "If you can be useful, you can get away with a great deal. But if you can be indispensable, oh then my dearest Mim, you can get away with anything."

"Which am I?"

Li considers her for a moment, lips pursed.

"Verging on useful, if you've come here for the reasons I'm assuming."

"This business with Twist," Mim replies, thanking Mrs Tan as she plunks a cup of thick, black coffee at her elbow and another beside Li's plate, taking her empty cup away. "I've been watching his almost profligate use of Haunts and wondering what on earth he's been using them for. Then he asks me to contact my Shocking boy for him, get him to help me on a job so Twist can tag him. Twist obviously wants him for whatever these other Haunts have failed to do, but he sounds confident, which makes me think Shock is his eureka."

"Correct. What pains Ho and I so very much is that

Twist isn't going to share, and we don't like children who won't share their toys."

"And what toy would that be?"

Li drops a cube of sugar in her coffee. Considers the ripples for a long moment, smiling.

"The prize in Twist's Haunt tombola, my dearest little Mimic," she says eventually, "is Emblem."

Sipping slowly at her coffee, Mim searches for signs of amusement in Li's face, or Ho's. Trouble is, both are psychopathic, thus have no facility for real emotion. Expressions on those stone-like countenances appear worse than disingenuous, they inspire real horror: Oh look the spider is trying to smile. Mim licks her lips, worried. How does one anticipate a test when one is sat opposite what are, despite all that human meatiness and blood, automata?

Disadvantage doesn't suit Mim, it makes her itchy. If this is not a joke, then she's into something huge. This could be it, her break into the big time. Her ticket out of Shimli. Mim wants everything, including a penthouse in the Heights, the most exclusive address in Foon Gung. Nothing less will do. She never understood Shock settling for Sendai. The biggest names, the very wealthiest, the WAMOS elite, they don't do the Garden District. It's not expensive enough.

"The Emblem?"

"That's the one."

"But Emblem's in Core. Core's unbreachable."

"It would seem Twist has found a way."

"Why now?"

That's the jackpot question for Mim. Emblem's been a holy grail for as long as it's been in Core, holding in the Queens, holding Slip and Hive together. Until now no one's been stupid enough to try to boost it. After all, who the fuck wants to mess with the Queens in their Hive?

Li looks at Ho, who shrugs.

"An interesting development," she says. "After Kamilla finally succumbed to mortality."

"Oh?"

"Josef Lakatos mysteriously hires Breaker, starts working with him and that J-Hack collective of his, the Movement. We were aware of them buzzing around Fulcrum when Kamilla was alive, but she swatted them rather effectively and rightly so. We found it quite striking that Josef did not follow suit."

"Seriously? Fulcrum hiring in Fails?" This is deeper shit than Mim supposed. Downright meaty shit. Her teeth are tingling.

Ho speaks up, his voice dreamy as he lights his blunt. "That's not the most interesting part." He takes a long, blissful toke. Coughs. "The most interesting part is that Breaker went missing not long after. AWOL. MIA. Poof." Ho blows out a huge stream of velvety smoke and Mim watches it, enchanted.

"Presumed dead?" she asks.

"Uncertain; though a good deal of the Movement went signal dead at about the same time, and the rest have scarpered. Signal dark all around."

"What?" Mim's lost.

Li sips her coffee. Smiles. Knowing. Mim shudders.

"The underground is hidden in plain sight. We know the movers and shakers, all of them, just as they know us. Transparency is important. The Gung is rather flammable with all of us essentially pressed cheek to jowl as we are. When the Movement suffers a mass loss of personnel and the rest go signal dark, even Agen-Z, who does not do hiding, then anyone with half a brain knows things have become desperately interesting."

"What do they know? What's going on?" Ho slurs out,

and then sings off-key, "We want to know."

"But before we can do anything, before any of us can do anything," Li says, her voice soft but filled with enough cold menace to make Mim's feet twitchy for finding the door. "There's Twist. Suddenly in the game and gunning for Emblem no less, going through Haunts like no tomorrow as if he's certain one can actually manage to steal it. We thought at first it was his customary delusions of grandeur, but it quickly became obvious he has information we are not party to."

"Frustrating." Ho, blank faced, spat out like a cherry pit.

Li pats his hand, without looking at him. Eerie, how synchronized they are.

"After the loss of Feng Ho," she continues, "Twist ups his game. And here we arrive back at you and your Shocking boy. We assume Twist's found a way past Core defences—"

"Five percent margin of error either way," Ho interjects through a cloud of smoke.

"—And is sending Shock into Core to steal Emblem."

"Which you want to take from him," says Mim, hanging on to the thread of conversation for dear life.

"Bingo. Ten points to that girl," says Ho, his finger in the air like he's asking for more coffee. It seems he is, because Mrs Tan comes over with a re-fill. "Twist in control of Fulcrum just doesn't have the same ring as Li and Ho Harmony in charge of Fulcrum."

Secretly, in the very back of her thoughts, where she hopes it can't be seen even by the gimlet eye of Li, Mim thinks any of them in charge of Fulcrum is a super-bad idea, but hey she's angling for a life upgrade and as long as it doesn't affect her, they can have whatever the hell they like.

"You want me to get to Shock before he delivers."

"Catch or kill, we don't care, we only need his drive,"

Ho singsongs. Mim really wishes he wouldn't; it's as creepy as one of the mannequins or dolls in those horrendous fucking J-horror movies Sez tries to make her watch.

Li reaches over and places a finger over his mouth.

"My brother is a touch enthusiastic. We may actually need your Shocking boy alive. All you need to do is catch him for us."

"He's not going to respond to my IM again. Not now."

"He won't need to. Whatever Twist's given him to help him get into Core, it's making him noisy. Twist has him blocked at the moment, but we can crack that. We presume your boy will make a move very soon. Given a margin of prep time, and Twist's awareness of our interest in that block, we think no less than a day or two. You know him better than anyone. What shops he'd use for a job like this. Which area he might be in. Yes?"

"Yes."

"So you'll be waiting for when he comes out, and you will catch him. I don't care how. Bullet. Taser. Boomerang. Just take the boy out when he exits Slip and bring him to us, avoiding Twist's people, or anyone else who might be after him. Can you do that?"

Li stares at Mim. It's like being in the sight line of a hungry anaconda.

Mim holds Li's gaze, her mind working so fast it aches. Throwing Shock to the lions is heatless malice, her version of making him live in interesting times as punishment for tangling her so effortlessly around him. For making it impossible to forget how much it hurt to excise him from her life.

She doesn't feel bad about giving him to Twist. Twist won't kill him. He might threaten to, might hurt Shock enough to make him think he's going to die, but Shock's too useful to kill. So he won't. She shies away from other things he might do. That might make her feel guilty, and Mim's not a fan.

Li though, she doesn't care how useful anyone is, despite what she said. Li kills because it makes her happy. And she wants to kill Shock. He outwitted her, no one gets to outwit her and live. Giving him up to Li, therefore, is malice aforethought. It's signing his death sentence. Can she do it?

"I can."

She's not sure if she's lying. But saying it makes it real, whether it's truth or not. Means she has to do it. So there it is, isn't it?

"So you're in?" Li sips her coffee. Offers inquisitive eyes over the brim.

Mim experiences a moment of uncertainty.

"How much?"

Li sends her a closed IM rather than responding verbally. With extreme caution, after hitting it with every sneaky malware and virus-nuke she has, Mim opens it. The amount is staggering and comes half before and half after the job is done. Her uncertainty vanishes. This is it. Her financial passport, the first step toward the Heights, whether she aces this task or not.

Fuck you, Shimli, it was shit knowing you.

"I'm in," she says.

everything's eventual

head throbbing like a rotten tooth, Shock takes the coastal mono around the slummy, cage-apartment blocks of the Alley, one of which he calls home, and the narrow slick of poorly built 'rises spooning Cash Corner. An equally grim collection of slighter larger, less cage-like hellholes. He can't afford those, so he has to bunk in the Alley with the oldsters. Going down in the world. No prizes for what's on the next rung below this. Six feet under. Or it would be, if the Gung buried its dead.

Sat in a window seat, Shock watches the gulls wheeling far below, between the cliffs at the edge of the Gung and the equally steep sides of 'scrapers built along the cliffs with no regard for safety or regulations. Their calls sound like screams, like they're crying for help. He can relate. Everything inside of him is screaming, a whole colony of gulls from pelvis to collarbones, lining his ribcage in messy, shit-shellacked disarray.

Over the cliffs, even further down, a furious sea slams white-capped shoulders into jagged rock, the waves huge to his eyes even from here, hundreds of feet above the ground. For some reason it puts him in mind of the land ships. He can't imagine how he'd bear that proximity. Those massive waves smashing too close for comfort, spewing salty spray into his face. Leaving his clothes, his hair, his skin, stiff with salt. Leaving him beleaguered and bedraggled, and probably suicidal. In which case the ocean would constitute endless temptation. He shudders.

The mono weaves along the coast, in and out of the 'scrapers, blocks and 'risers, for twenty-eight minutes, chased by guillemots and angry pelicans, dogged by gangs of gulls; stalked by the occasional sec-drone. Shock resists the urge to duck down every time. Way to look suspicious. Instead he gazes casually at his boots, allowing his shock of hair to fall over his face. Instant camouflage. He'd like to say that's why he grows it, but he just prefers it this way.

Long hair was the only thing he dug about being a girl. The rest of it he's glad to be rid of, glad too that he managed to get the lot removed before the spectre of periods, tits and hormones rose up to torment him. If he'd ever seen blood in his underwear, or any swelling of his flat chest, he'd have come to a mono platform and taken a dive. There are some things a person can't live with.

The mono screeches to a halt, the noise drowning out the shrieks of the gulls in its wake. Shock takes the elevator down. He doesn't normally, having little trust for these rickety things, all squealing lines and clear, plastic-looking shells giving a 360-degree of the ground too damn far beneath your feet. He's not afraid of heights— he's afraid of losing his life to shonky engineering, so he sighs genuine relief when it touches ground.

This is the IndoChinese quarter, the very outskirts of it. A slum called Pimchi. The only J-Hack collective Shock's had dealings with works out of this district. They're the "Qua.". The Crows. Who descend en masse and leave chaos in their wake. The number of Qua. hospitalized, deceased, arrested or disappeared in the seven years they've been a going concern is sobering. Of the original members, only five remain, surrounded by an ever-shifting, ever-changing murder made up of some 175 Qua. recruits, Fails and non-Fails alike. Out here, no one gives a shit. Not really.

Of those remaining five originals, one is Shock's connection, Heng. Or Well Heng, if you're a close buddy. Anyone not within his inner circle tries to call him that ends up less Well Heng. Shock calls him Aitch, just to be contrary. Heng has a workshop in whatever dingy, well-hidden hole the Qua. call home, but he also has one in the local high-rise shopping mart, for paying customers, which is what Shock intends to be.

Inside the shopping mart, a block-like tangle of shops and stalls, crowded and filled with the hysterical squawk of live poultry, it's like midday in high summer. Humid air clinging stickily to the skin, tempers rising, the deranged buzz of flies courting the food stalls. Although exhausted and in serious pain, Shock takes the stairs, fully aware that stepping into an elevator here is basically asking to be mugged, or worse.

He finds Heng, a slightly overweight, classically handsome Cambodian sat at his monitors, goggles down, deep into a chat with some girl in a pink "YO! Takei!" j-pop band tee, who pops gum more than she talks and radiates boredom toxic as nuclear waste. Trust Heng to go old Tech. The guy knows as much about new Tech as Shock does, maybe more now and then, right on the cutting edge of what's going down in the community, but he's always dabbling in this ancient crap. Who wants to face-to-face on a screen when you can do it all mind-to-mind?

"Girlfriend?" Shock asks, when Heng spots him and dials off.

Heng looks disgusted. "No, jerk. Cousin. She's got some problem at Cad. My mak told me to give her some advice. I'm sure you noticed her high levels of interest."

"The enthusiasm burned."

"Damn right. So what brings you to Pimchi, Shock? Usual shit?"

Shock collapses into a rickety-looking chair next to Heng's desk and nods.

"Usual shit."

"Can you pay?"

Shock grins. He likes Heng. Zero BS.

"I have flim. Enough for what I need."

"And what is it you need?"

"Need a full quota of scums and the code specs for a Hive drone." He winces as he says the latter. Not only is the request stupid, because no one is daft enough to try cracking Hive, it's also probably going to be difficult to find. Shock may end up owing Heng a serious favour or three, if he lives.

Heng heaves forward, staring.

"Hive? You're going in to Hive?" He seems genuinely concerned, which is a thing. Heng doesn't much care for Shock. No one of sense does.

Shock shrugs. "For my health."

"Flim? Or breathing?"

"Make a wild guess."

Heng makes a face. "Ouch. My condolences."

"I'm not dead yet. And I don't intend to be."

"Well, we all have the best intentions..."

"That we do," Shock agrees, liking the direction of this conversation less and less. "Do you have what I need?"

Grabbing a set of keys from in amongst the metric tonne of crap cluttering his desk, Heng gets up, scraping his chair back, making it scream against the floor. Everything's screaming today. It's lucky Shock's not sensitive to signs and portents, or else he might get worried.

"Fifty grenades do?"

"Reckon so."

It only takes ten minutes for Heng to return, which is a surprise. He's got two flash keys, the types that jack directly in. One has those scums; the other holds extensive, beautiful, specs on the Hive drones. Shock can't quite believe his luck. So he doesn't.

"Where the hell you get these?"

Heng screws up his face. J-Hacks have this bullshit code preventing them spilling info that might be damaging to the collective. Fuck knows they get into enough scrapes to make it necessary, but this is important. Twist said trial and error, which basically means dead Haunts. And here Shock comes to his old connection, sort of a mate—if someone who doesn't like you much can be called any such thing—and lo and behold he's got this shit right to hand. Suspicious.

I mean, okay, Shock needed it right to hand, he's got very little time. But he'd expected to wait maybe six hours, a little more, for something this tricky to obtain. Expected Heng to have to go around those with an interest in Hive and cajole or bribe the specs out of them. Yet here it is. How involved is Heng in all this shit? Collectives do work for the Gung's criminal elements but unless he's got Heng seriously wrong, he'd not be an active participant in the wholesale slaughter of Haunts.

"You're not the first Haunt set to cracking Hive recently, okay?" Heng says at last, reluctantly. "I've had at least three here, including Feng Ho, and all of them are dead. The kind of luck I expect to find you with, and here you are. Presumably next."

Guts twanging relief like guitar strings, Shock lets

air into his lungs. Okay, so Heng is still legit, and unless Shock's mistaken he's legit concerned too. Since when did Heng give a shit about what happens to him? Maybe he knows the deal. Maybe that's why.

"What do you know about this, Aitch?"

"Not word one. I keep my eyes and ears closed."

"Any of the others dragging luck as bad as mine?"

"Well of course, but you're the only one had it coming to you. What happened to you, man?" Heng stares at Shock wonderingly, and with a little distaste, like he's some new species of bacteria, glowing in the corner of a dark bathroom. "How'd you end up on the thin end of the wedge with all your fucking skill? I mean, you're in the highest percentile, could've been a major player in the J-Hack community, another fucking Breaker, and you piss it all away. I like you man, genuinely, but you're an idiot."

Heng means what he says, which is another surprise. Shock was sure Heng hated his guts. He doesn't really know how to deal with this. No one cares for him. Why would they? For a moment he's tempted to pretend he has a friend. Unburden himself. Admit that he wanted one thing and he couldn't see anything beyond it—not even his life disappearing down the fucking drain—until it was too late to take it back.

Unable to find the energy to put that into words or the courage to trust another human being with it, Shock simply shrugs, pays for his gear and fucks off. Whatever happens now, this here, this gig, it's his swan song. End of the line. Time to get off in one piece, or crash. His choice, if he has one? He intends to remain intact. Hah. As Heng so eloquently put it: we all have the best intentions.

It's four in the afternoon. Trusting Twist's semi-promise of forty-eight hours about as much as he trusts Twist, Shock wants to be ready to do this in the morning. First thing. If he really pushes himself, he can force another ten hours of consciousness out of his aching head. Will it be long enough?

It'll take as long as it takes to build a Hive worker skin-matrix perfect enough and long-lasting enough to get him in and out. Because the signal is only for Core, everything else is on his skills alone. And he's got to get to Hive first, which means getting through an eye-watering array of VA. He knows what it is, the other Haunts made a record of each level, but knowing is not the same as doing. And they're all dead for a reason.

Way beyond jittery, he goes back to his P.O., which doubles as a locker for anything too valuable to stash in his cage, and fetches his tablet, taking it to a small water park he likes in Ginzo. He stays there until the sun goes down, planning and building, fussing over every detail; buying coffees, sodas and greasy, tasteless udon from the brightly painted booth at the centre of the park.

Night comes, and the biome trees hit maximum light. Their hazy blue-tinted glow is pleasant, peaceful even, but not enough for him to see his complicated specs properly, leaving him unable to work. So he wanders back toward Ginzo proper; sets up again in a twenty-four-hour coffee bar, snacking on bowls of cashews and dried squid and rubbing at aching eyes. It's two A.M. before he's satisfied with his plan, his skin-matrix. He'd prefer to be happy rather than satisfied, but he's too tired, too wired, to continue. His countdown is near enough over. Tomorrow he has to do the job, and nail it. Or that's it.

Desperate to rest, he hurries back to his apartment block. Careens to his cage, his waiting mattress. He falls in fully dressed and drowns in sleep straight away, as if it was waiting for him, deep and encompassing, the ocean in his bed. He dreams of the birds in Sendai. They're singing in cherry blossom trees, but one by one their beaks fall silent and they drop to the earth.

inner spaces and awkward places

Wearing nothing but black market GarGoil panties, Amiga rifles savagely through her cupboards hunting for something that might pass for edible if she turns her head and squints. Muttering under her breath, she slams each door shut as she's done. There aren't many cupboards in her hovel and tearing through them does not feel half as satisfying as it should, so she kicks the bottom doors, and then the table. It slides across the floor, bumping into the sofa, and her washing tips majestically to the floor in picture-perfect slow-mo.

"Shoulda had breakfast at the boys' place, you fucking idiot," she snarls at herself, grabbing clean clothes and chucking them back on the table without folding them. Why bother? They only get creased when she puts them on.

She really should have eaten at the boys' place. She's starved and there's nothing nutritious here, unless plastic plates, dusty glasses and a half empty bottle of flat beer give your stomach a hard-on. They don't do anything for hers. She'd kill for one of Knee Jerk's tamagoyaki. Boy's talented, that's all there is to it. Except she scarpered like the unmitigated moron that she is, and so it's her own damn fault her stomach's starting to sound like a rusty axle.

Honestly she has no idea why she ran for it. She's spent most of the last twenty-four hours waiting for Breaker to get back to her shacked up on their couch, hugging a pillow and checking in on EVaC every ten minutes; getting fed too, which beats this shit. Well, okay, she knows why she ran for it. Deuce came back. From Fen Maa's to be precise, from her swanky fuckin' panky apartment somewhere in Hangoon. Rich bitch with rich folks. Vomit.

How'd Amiga know he was there? Huh, obvious. He was wearing a fucking suit of all things, and he looked good. Enough to make her want to throw up just about every bone in her body. And she needs those. So she grabbed up her things and split, the heavenly scent of tamagoyaki following her like a lost puppy.

"No two ways about it, bitch," she admits, throwing herself on the couch miserably. "Deuce is making you crazy."

It's about the last thing she needs right now. Her head's been a bit like an ocean full of continental shards— hazardous. That's basically why she landed up on the boys' sofa, nurse-maiding. She hates worrying about EVaC, worrying is weakness, but it beats hell out of going on a merry-go-round of thoughts about what she saw down with Maggie and Mollie. The worst thing about the truth is that you can't hide from it, especially not when it's tearing through your goddamn head with giant circular blade jaws.

She rams both hands into the mess of her hair and groans. Shouldn't have thought about it. It's stolen her sleep. All she sees when she closes her eyes are giant engines, their circular jaws working ceaselessly, tearing apart the world. The sound of it is something terrible, and she'd give just about anything to block it out. She's considering breaking out a bump or two to carry that sound, those visions, away on the tide. Except she has to be straight because, if Maggie and her angel are right, Breaker's due to call.

"Fuck me, Amiga girl," she tells herself, as if she didn't already know. "You run at trouble like it's an all-you-can-eat cake buffet."

Knuckles dance staccato beats across the plastic of her hovel. She groans again.

"Whaaaat? Go away, Deuce. I'm cocooning."

"Asking me what and telling me to go away straight after? Sounds more like contrariness than cocooning to me. Can I come in?"

"I only have panties on and I have no inclination to dress up," she yells. "Talk through the fuckin' wall."

"I'm coming in. Either get something on or put up with me trying not to look at your tits."

Amiga grumbles under her breath "Ohhhh fu'fuck'sake, fuckin' difficult bloody bastard."

"I heard that." His voice is near her hatch. She shrieks annoyance, grabbing a top from the floor and dragging it on just as he lands, light-footed, on her table, still wearing the suit pants and the shirt, unbuttoned at the top. Be still her tango-ing heart. Seriously. Cease and desist.

"So, this place is still a mess." He holds out a bento box. There's a cold beer hooked under his thumb too.

"And? So is yours. Those for me?"

"Who else?"

She reaches out and snags them, snatching like a toddler. She can smell what's in the bento already, tamagoyaki. Probably cold, but who gives a shit. Manna, that's what this is. She pops the top of the beer and knocks back half as Deuce takes a seat next to her.

"Sit down, why don't you," comes out snarkier than

she'd intended, almost enough to curdle her beer.

He gives her this long, considering look, and then says softly, "If you didn't want to dump me, you shouldn't have."

The words react on her like wasp stings on allergic flesh. Where's a mental epi-stim when she needs one? Unable to deal, she ignores him instead, placing her beer down on the table with a bit too much force and peeking in her bento. Oh my glob. Not just tamagoyaki. California rolls. Rice and green pepper. Pickled ginger. And a cucumber cut to look like a panda. Knee Jerk is a god. She pulls out the chopsticks and starts shovelling it in before her stomach forces its way out through a nostril and starts without her.

Paying no attention to Deuce is harder than she expected, what with the ridiculous, sonar-like awareness of his presence she has going on. Why is nothing simple? Why does she have to feel bad for feeling bad when he's around and taking it out on him? Oh yeah. Because it's not his fault. Shit. She starts to formulate an apology, but he talks before she can.

"Ignoring me. Nice."

And just like that she's angry again. She shrugs, says through a mouthful of rice and egg, "I had a problem. I'm over it."

He doesn't reply for so long she spares him a glance, and stops mid-chew. He looks upset. A lot upset. And angry. She explains through the mouthful of sushi she's currently experiencing taste-bud orgasm over.

"Look, that was harsh. But really, I ended things for all the right reasons and yeah, I totally regret it, but I wouldn't take it back. This whole snotty bitch thing I have going on, it's my problem. I will get a handle on it. You didn't need a mess like me cluttering up your life."

He crosses his arms and leans back.

"It takes a year for you to admit this and you do it with a mouthful of rice? Really? Gee, Amiga, I guess all I can say is, thanks for making decisions about my life without asking. You didn't think I should have a say?"

Amiga holds a piece of ginger in her chopsticks and nibbles thoughtfully.

"No."

"Wow." He shakes his head. "Maybe I am better off."

"That's what I said."

He leans forward then.

"You hate being alone. You hate being what you are. This family here is the first thing you've had in a long time that means anything to you. And I don't think it's arrogance to say that what we had was part of that. But you cut me away from you without warning or explanation and now you're trying to cut yourself away from the group as a whole too. You're running scared from people who care about you, because... What? Afraid you'll lose us?"

Amiga hasn't cried in forever, not even when she dumped Deuce. Now she wants to cry. There's this pressure, hard enough to hurt her chest, prickling needle-sharp in the corners of her eyes. Amiga takes a moment, because this will not do, however close to the fucking bone he just sliced with that. When she's calm, when she can talk without crying a river all over her food, she puts the bento down.

"I'm not," she says, loving her voice for coming out so calm, and hating her guts for going all Pompeii pre-eruption on her. Shoving emotion down should not feel this dangerous, she's been doing it for years. "I've gone out of the way to help EVaC. That's not holding anyone out. That's not cutting anyone off."

Deuce sighs. "He's unconscious, babe. Don't try and

tell me that doesn't make it easier to care for him, just like his habit of only ever talking bollocks makes it easy for you to remain close to him instead of shutting him out like you have the rest of us."

This is what she loves and hates most about Deuce. He knows her, and she can't make excuses with him, can't improvise emotion or plain lie to his face. Somehow, without her ever having told him a damn thing about what goes on in her singularly fucked-up mind, he's always been able to see it and call it. And he's never wrong. Bastard.

"Maybe. But it's a start. Yes?"

He sighs again, he clearly doesn't agree. "I suppose." He looks at her carefully, and immediately she sees him worry as he picks up her underlying distress like a goddamn mental detector. Why does he have to do that? Why is she so goddamn grateful that he does? "Subject change?"

Ah, that's why. "Please." She picks up the bento again. Her appetite is all but bust but she's damned if she'll stop eating Knee Jerk's divine handiwork. He should be a saint of food or some shit.

"Heard from Breaker yet? Still can't believe he was our connection all along. Incredible." You can tell he's a code nerd, his face has gone rapt, like he's seeing Buddha rising to Nirvana, fingers plucking out a seriously enlightened solo on the most radical axe ever spawned from Banyan wood. She'd vomit, but again... waste of food.

"Yeah, well, he's not exactly fast to RSV..."

A bolt of agony, sharp as a screw, hits her drive. Amiga drops the bento, too busy screaming and clutching her head to lament all that lovely lost food. Pain radiates heavily from her drive as if it's a stone thrown hard into water, her brain meat rippling in ever-increasing circles. From far away, she feels Deuce grab her up and hold her.

She half wishes he'd do that forever, and half wants him to back the fuck off. Then the noise starts; the screech of metals, the hiss of static, and everything else disappears.

Amiga's wrenched out of her head and pulled backward through her own flash, through the tiny link of her IM connection, meant only for recorded thoughts, not part or whole of a consciousness. Cleaner through the eye of a needle. Sucked in and away, like unconsciousness, like sleep, screaming as she goes. The tunnel she's yanked through is long, dark and too tight. It abrades at her. If her mind was skin, it'd be red raw and bleeding, transmitting a symphony of nerve pain. The journey seems to take forever and no time all at once, and she's literally vomited out, still screaming.

Expecting to splash into the eerily real fake water of the Slip, Amiga isn't prepared for violent impact. Her reward is the air knocked clean out of her chest and eye-watering reverberations tingling through every bone in her body. Gasping, she curls into a ball, holding tight to her limbs until the sensation fades away. This is one of those moments she truly wishes that the slipping experience was not directly connected to the nervous system for max reality-field experience. Who the hell wants reality when a dream takes on nightmarish qualities?

When it becomes bearable, she pulls herself up from the ground, taking care with her head. Looks around to see where she is.

J-Net, but not as she knows it.

What the fuck?

Amiga's jacked into J-Net before with Deuce's by-your-leave. It's a slick, bright-lights/big-city deal; fast-paced and hectic. Stands as a spiritual opposite to the Slip's open consumerism, with communication and information the priority. She has the J-Net take on an avi when she's in it, a thick-wheeled, low-slung cater-bike, clumsier than a Slip avi, and inexplicably impersonal.

This time she's in an avi like her own body but angular and cast in ugly shades of steel and black, almost like a robot—she had no idea human-shaped avis were even possible. And this J-Net, it's nothing like it should be. Half collapsed to filthy, grim-faced ruins, and empty of any avi-chles. There's a muted buzz somewhere, like a broken cable dancing insane electric patterns on damp concrete.

Hello? she calls, tentative, feeling like sound is some sort of intrusion. Anybody here?

A shifting, human-shaped black hole, hard to look at directly, steps out of thin air directly in front of her. She nods a wary greeting, because who else could do this but the man whose call she's been waiting for.

Breaker. You're not coming through clear.

Apologies. The reply comes with a rushing delay obscuring the ends, like a lisp. I'm stealing frequency. I can't keep it up for long.

So why bring me to J-Net instead of IMing? This is J-Net, right?

It's a J-Net adjunct destroyed by the Queens. It belonged to my collective, the Movement.

That's a new one, not entirely comforting.

Since when can they get further than Slip before Emblem yanks them back?

A while. And they mean to do far worse.

Stellar. Just freaking stellar. Why is everyone dumping psychological ballast into her brain? It's like she's wearing a sign or some shit. And all this bears precisely zero relevance to her task for Mother Zero.

Whatever. I sleep badly enough. I'm here for a package.

You are Amiga Tanaka, Cleaner for Twist Calhoun. The black hole fades, flickers. Comes back patchy. ...need...help.

Hold the hell on, Batman. I already helped you enough, Fellows. Nice subterfuge there by the bye, but why bother? Your name is way more of a dead cert than Fellows. You know if Twist finds out what I did for you I'm a corpse? Probably worse.

Please... important. Twist... working with Queens.

Amiga's mouth drops open, full-on gorm face. There's no way she heard that right.

He's not that stupid. You're tripping.

...true. The signal fades out entirely, then comes back clear again. This frequency is hard to maintain. I have to borrow heavily. Please hear me out.

Desperation has its own timbre, an unmistakable pitch. It scythes through her, straight into that soft centre she likes to pretend she doesn't have. Fucking hell.

Fine, she snaps. Speak.

There's a Haunt, name of Shock Pao. In less than twelve hours he'll crack Core for Twist and take Emblem.

What? Pao will what? No. No way.

But as she's dismissing the notion a few puzzle pieces snap together in her mind. A distracted boss. Three Haunts dead. Being called off Pao's tail out of the blue when Twist had very much wanted him laid out like a side of salmon. She'd assumed he'd let it go for the time being to nudge other crime lords off the scent, but maybe not. Maybe he called her off Pao because he realized he might need him?

If it's Emblem he's been angling for, then all of this— those dead Haunts and his hot/cold gunning for Pao— starts to make an awful kind of sense. And Breaker thinks Shock will succeed where they failed?

Core can't be cracked. Pao is a dead man.

Shock will succeed, I assure you, and he'll need protection when he does.

From Twist? There's an amusing concept, and an unlikely outcome.

And other crime lords who've been watching Twist with great interest. Please, this is serious.

I get that, I do. But it has nothing to do with me. All I want to do is fetch this package and go before my headache becomes terminal. Look, Breaker, Haunts are smoke, and this one's a full-on weasel. Trust me, if he manages this, he'll poof like a magician's rabbit.

Shock is no longer a Haunt.

What? Explain.

No time. Get to him first, Amiga Tanaka. Protect him. Bring him to the Heights. To me. The Queens have me here, but I can help him, and he will need my help. Breaker flickers out of view. Comes back piecemeal, see-through. You don't want… Emblem… wrong hands… terrible. He's fading away as he speaks, and then he's gone. Kapoof.

Amiga throws her arms up. Oi! Still fucking here! She looks around, seething with rage. How the hell do I get home? She turns in a circle, looking for a link-up, anything. This place is a wasteland. No way in or out she can see. Goddamn it.

She drops to the ground, cross-legged. Waiting. He wants her out there helping him, so he'll find a way. He better do anyway. And if she gets back IRL, what does she do with this whole Emblem boosting business? For reals? If it's the real deal. Twist has indeed been going through Haunts, but that's the only bit she's certain of. The whole idea of a Queenly alliance… the theft of Emblem; she doesn't know enough to verify it.

So what if she assumes this might be true, for the sake of argument? Well then there's one aspect that bothers her more than the rest, something of a bum note in fact— Breaker's insistence on bringing Shock to the Heights.

Why would he do that? The Queens' server is at Heights, and Breaker said they have him there. His exact words. So if this is all true, does that make Breaker a prisoner or a collaborator? Hard to tell. As always, given the choice between trusting and not, Amiga strikes for the latter.

Too dodgy by half, she mutters to herself.

A rushing noise like a mono accelerates toward her. Hits much the same, slamming the package into her drive and throwing her backward, yelling obscenities, into that tunnel. This time there's no screeching noise, only the pain of being squeezed like toothpaste through a too-tight conduit.

When she falls out again, she's still in Deuce's arms, and her mind feels bruised, tattered, raw, like someone's taken a cheese grater to the inside of her cranium. She sees Knee Jerk's turned up whilst she was gone, Vivid too. They're sat either side of Deuce, watching her.

"Hey, why didn't you get everyone around?" she croaks, and realizes her throat is dry enough to crack apart. "Make it a party."

Deuce shakes her. "Hey. Hey. Where'd you go?"

He's got this traumatized look she doesn't like. Oh no buddy, you can't still care. No fucking way. Amiga wrestles her way up out of his arms, paying no attention to the raw hurt on his face. Her beer is where she left it, thank fuck. She downs the other half as if she's been in a desert for a week.

"Breaker called," she says when she's done, lobbing the empty bottle into her sink and wincing at the clatter. She sends Maggie the package and waits for her response, going over and over everything Breaker said, vastly annoyed with him and feeling handled. Still reluctant to believe, she thinks of a way to be sure of at least some of Breaker's claims. She turns to Deuce, who's watching her like she might explode, like he might.

"Gotta question."

"Shoot."

"J-Net. The Queens have been breaking it, yeah?"

He stares at her. "Who the hell told you that?"

"Who do you think? And not just told, shown first-hand. What I want to know is this: could they do more, and have they tried to?"

His face closes off. Security doors slammed tight. Hoo boy. Secretive and more secret. She just loves these reminders about how her job makes her not trustworthy enough, they don't sting at all.

"Deuce, I need to know."

"Yes they could, and yes they have," he says quietly, clearly unhappy with revealing this much. Shit. So here's the clicker.

"Okay, so... would they try to, I dunno, work with a crime lord maybe?"

A look of sheer panic flits across Deuce's face.

"Who? Who are they working with? What did Breaker say, Amiga?"

Amiga lets him hang for a minute, not out of any spite; her head's just gone a little fuzzy around the edges again. Yeah, and here comes that nausea. Breaker she doesn't know and does not trust, especially considering his close proximity to the Queens' server. Deuce she'd trust with her life, like it or not, and she doesn't.

If he thinks it's possible the Queens could access outside help, then she has to accept it. Problem. Because that means it's possible they could actually end up boosting Emblem, and there's no way in hell she can let it end up in Twist's hands. Or anyone else's. Including the Queens'. Do ants even have hands? Who the fuck cares.

"Breaker said that within the next twelve one Shock Pao, idiot Haunt, will steal Emblem for Twist and the Queens."

Deuce looks downright bewildered.

"But...?"

"Yeah. My thoughts exactly, and yet Breaker insists not only is Emblem boost-able now for whatever reason, but Pao's going to do so imminently. So I reckon we need to bypass the "oh my gods" and get straight on to the afterglow, just in case he's not huffing fumes and tripping."

"What does he want us to do?"

"Not us. Me. I've been told to grab Pao before he gets Emblem to Twist and take him to Breaker at the Heights, but I have severe reservations. I think he's safer here for the time being."

"Haunts can't simply be grabbed, not unless you know where they're going to be," Vivid points out helpfully.

"Normally true, Vee, but according to Breaker this one's thoroughly borked his Haunt-fu somehow and become a walking target for every crime lord in the Gung."

"And you want to bring him here?" KJ, worried for his own hide as usual. Honestly, she likes the guy, adores his cooking, but he's such a goddamn liability.

"This is the safest place I know, Knee Jerk. Cool your panties down."

"You just got yanked right out of your head in the safest place you know," Deuce reminds her.

"Breaker had my direct IM, and I've a feeling that whatever line he was using is gone now," she says. Then adds casually, just dropping it in there or out there or whatever, "It's not as if your block works for direct IM."

He shakes his head. He's got no shame, the fucker, none whatsoever.

"Nope. It wouldn't." He reaches out, touches her arm. "What's going on with Breaker, Amiga? Why is he at Heights?"

"The Queens have him there. Not sure why, but as you

rate him I'll assume for your benefit that it's not because he wants to be."

"Shit."

Maggie's response pings into Amiga's IM. She wants to meet now. On a head like this? Terrific. Grabbing a pair of thick green leggings from the table, Amiga yanks them on and stuffs her feet into Bladers. She grabs her bag and smiles at them all hopefully.

"Anyone got a migraine tab? The inside of my head is like a bare arse on melted tarmac. I do not fancy blading in this condition."

Vivid digs in her backpack, chucks her a tab.

"Where you going?"

"I have a date with Maggie concerning our EVaC, and you guys need to get a move on locking this place down just in case we need to. I'm hoping to fuck not."

Amiga glances down at Deuce. He's watching her, those black eyes shuttered. She knows what he's thinking though. She wishes he wouldn't.

"I'll be back this evening," she says.

He nods. "We'll talk then."

"No," she says softly, "we won't." And she jumps onto the table, her hands reaching for the exit hatch.

part two

Journey to the centre of the hive

Shock groans, burrowing his face under the pillow to escape the insistent knock of sunlight on his eyelids. He'd stay there all day if he could, cocooned, but it occurs to him that he's slept and very soundly too from the drool slicked across his cheek, the thick goo of his head. Wasn't there something he needed to do? Some countdown ticking away?

Memory hits like a siren, alarms ringing, adrenal kick on overload, sending him ricocheting upward, his pillow flying into the mesh of his cage with a dull clang. Similar clangs echo through his skull.

"Uuurrrgh." Is all Shock can manage initially as, in accompaniment to waking, the re-fried brain meats sensation of the drone signal asserts itself, alongside weird, sticky, not otherwise specified nausea. A mixture of too hungry and hungover as hell. Shock hopes the block is still working. It all depends on how much of his forty-eight hours he's slept away.

"What's the time?" he slurs out, glaring through his cage at the five other occupants of the room, all sat in their own cages, slurping either tea, bowls of steaming noodles or soup. Could be breakfast, lunch or dinner for all he knows. The smell makes his stomach moan.

Apart from Shock, no one in this room, hell, no one in this building is below the age of ninety, and his roommates are all well over their first century. Mr Yoichi, 153 years old with a squint and a halo of white hair fine as dandelion seeds, points a trembling finger at Shock.

"Use your drive, boy."

"Please, old Uncle, my head is pounding. If I access my drive it may explode. Consider the mess."

Mr Yoichi makes a big deal of reaching back into his cage and fetching this ancient pocket watch he claims was passed down to him from his father, because of course men of his age can't be expected to use a fucking accurate neuro-drive for time.

"It wants twenty minutes to ten."

Shock takes a moment or two to process as it was supposed to be twenty to something a lot earlier. Panic hits like a faceful of concrete, sending him scrambling out of his cage and across to the bathroom.

"You overslept, you fucking idiot," he tells his stupid face in the mirror.

It stares back at him, looking as bad as he feels and pale from sleep. Too much fucking sleep. He can't believe it's almost ten o'clock. Ten o'cock-up.

Racing out into grey skies, he wants to head straight for his Slip shop of choice, but Slipping this deep on an empty stomach is asking for trouble, so he stops off at Some Dim for a steamer of siu bao and a coffee. No, two coffees. Make that three. Frankly he needs to dive head first into the giant coffee urn behind the serving station. Syrupy sleep combined with this hideous signal tar hangs a gloopy weight from various muscle groups, and has him feeling, bizarrely, like a mixture of chewy and snappy toffee, what with the whole panic thing and no bumps to take the edge off.

"Today's going to suck giant balls," he says, tearing apart a bun and trying not to envisage that thick red centre as his own vitals oozing out. There are moments when he's actually thankful for the iron cast to his stomach. Seriously, he could eat Yook Hwe in a slaughterhouse, fresh from the cow.

He takes a final coffee to go in a paper cup so enormous he'd take bets on being able to bathe in it and heads for the mono and Foon Gung's crowded and exclusive centre. By the time he gets off, thin drizzle paints the sky slick and flimsy as old celluloid, bringing a damp chill to the air, into the bones. Feeling as miserable as the day, Shock huddles into his too-thin neoprene jacket, and dodges tight-pressed cars out for blood.

Worried Twist's block is already near to being broken, he's twitching like he's necked a handful of top-notch bumps; skin breaking beats, hair on end, eyes wired, transmitting anxiety on every known frequency. Shock doesn't get the freaks on like this, full body power-up, stage fright, Slip fright, but this job is a different beast, horned and dangerous.

Tucking his hands in his pockets to hide the tremors, he heads for the Slip shop on level twenty-two of the Gangway tower. Located bang smack on the edge of the inner city, Gangway is a shopping mall for the rich and famous and hardly anyone knows of the Slip shop in its belly. The rich have home kiosks or internal uplinks, and they rarely use this place. Yet here it stands.

Shock slopes over to the hydra-haired super-model-in-training at the kiosk.

"Take for how long?" she asks, voice flat as cardboard, and about as interesting.

"Shop limit." he tells her, feeling like he's got this fuck-off huge sign above his head blinking in neon: "UP TO NO GOOD".

Cell #108 is plastic, tacky despite the wealthy ambience, but the room's an abstract study in desertion; so empty it echoes its own sounds for company. Blinking to access his neural jack, Shock leaps in cold, no prep. Like fucking bareback, warm and slick and sexy. He feels the mesh swallowing him whole, flinging him into Puss, into Slip, into the usual early morning traffic; crammed with weekenders bugging the feed.

Puss feels different today. Distant. There's a reluctance to cooperate and Shock has to work hard, spiralling down through teeming crowds in an impatient swirl of tentacles to hit one of the biggest veins. A gusher leading out of public domain toward Hive.

Swept away, he weaves mid-stream, still fighting his reluctant avi and hella frustration, because this is not the time for glitches. He runs a quick scan as he sweeps through the first block of firewalls, role-playing innocuous data. Finds nothing. Puss is simply not wanting to play ball today. What?

Fucking focus, he snaps at it, as if a thing formed of code can talk, or even understand him. I have no choice and I don't need my Tech fucking my day any further.

Puss cooperates almost immediately, as if acquiescing. Its control algorithms mesh fully with his mind, opening it out, giving him full access to that part of his brain seemingly dormant IRL and helping him recall things locked behind walls of hurt and anger. Why is it that trying to forget the things that hurt can obscure so much of you it reduces you to almost nothing? It's like in winning by forgetting, you also lose. Down here, having it all back, it's like having a superpower. All the memory and none of the hurt. Magic. And boy does he need magic right now.

Hiding in data is playtime for a Haunt, even one only still Haunting by virtue of a block, but the next ten levels of VA would be impossible without this Slip superpower of his. Firewall mazes, controlled by ever-changing equations. They look insane, like the grids of roadways at night time stuck on fast-forward, so many colours zipping around, bright as fireflies. It hurts the eyes.

Shock allows the information streams feeding the maze calculators to flow through him and winces. Man, that's some chewy math. Lucky Puss is back up to speed and functioning as it should, because he has no time to stop, solving these beasts on the run; every opening snapping shut on his heels with increasing hunger.

Calculations flowing in a continuous loop through his mind, like when he was a kid and first realized how fucking easy this stuff was for him, Shock skims through the gauntlet in seventeen minutes flat. A personal best. He's about to hit self-congratulation in spades until he groks the fact that there's something very wrong here on the other side. Something he hadn't anticipated.

The info feed is mute.

Trial and error discovered all the obstacles on the way in. But the way out? No one got that far. They got here, floating in this silence like he is. Maybe wondering, like he is, whether they could make it out and unaware that they'd never have to worry about it. Will he? That's one hell of a thought, too large for his mind right now. The weight of it beneath water drives his head inward, throbs like the beginnings of a migraine, and his three Octopus hearts, not quite under his control, pump a frantic rhythm he's afraid will transmit back to the single heart in the chest of his sling-bound body and burst it.

He has no time to calm himself. He's going to need

every last second if there's more of this shit to find. Gotta press on. He'll worry later, if there is a later.

Beyond the maze lies a whole fucking field of his very favourite thing: barcodes. Most are in the top five difficulty: Gordian, Gunner, Boa, Double-Fisher and Figure 8. He scans the field, finding exactly what he'd feared: the short route comes up against a whole row of Gordians so extreme they turn cranial throbbing into pure migraine.

His best bet is to follow a convoluted pattern like the letter S. One or two fairly horrifying Gordians lurk therein, but most are in the next category and an easier target. Plotting the course so he doesn't get lost, Shock dives in. He gives himself thirty minutes just for the challenge, does it in twenty-eight point four, and exits to the last twenty levels of VA thinking if he never has to solve an equation again it'll be too soon.

Up next? The big Daddies. Twenty rows of all-seeing eyes, impossible to cross. This is where the scum grenades he bought from Heng come in. Scums hit, explode and cling like taffy. A touch bio, they throw out sticky tendrils like virus vine, but totally neutral. Clueless Daddies will scrape that shit off their eyes for at least a double score, not realizing they're being punked. By the time they've cleared their peepers, he'll have been in and out despite activating alarms. If he's lucky.

Beyond the Daddies, Hive is the horizon as far as the eyes can see, both up and across. Fulcrum made Slip like the sea, deep and teeming with multifarious life; confusing in its madness, overwhelming in its vastness, so no one ever gets ideas. But Hive, that's a whole different design: cool, logical, absolute function. Mountainous and black, it's a digital fortress that dwarfs the Slip. No eyes, no need for them.

Hive has the Queens, and to get past them requires more guile than gung-ho.

Info moves on the surface in Hive, along speeding lines. Nowhere to hide, no gullies or troughs. Hence his drone-skin matrix. The matrix is flawless, should scan him in and out no sweat, survive to get him through the part he's most afraid of, Core, but it'll last a mere five mins. If he misjudges by so much as a nano-second, the Queens will be after him, and he'll be Puss satay. Game over.

Tingling with nerves, some his, others bizarrely coming from the golden body he's tucked inside, as if fear is transmitting between mind and shell on a loop, Shock rolls out, tentacles lashing forward to slam the scums bang on target. Taffy-thick slick leaches out over the great red eyes of the rows of Daddies and, line-by-line, they switch to clearance mode, their attention temporarily away from him, away from Hive. Moving fast he slips on further, throwing scums as he goes, covering all the eyes in his path.

Clock's ticking now. Eyes in a line unable to see will alert Hive to trouble real soon, less than a minute. Sirens will go off when that happens and that's when his clock starts ticking down quick smart. They'll send out Seekers, viral nukes, and this shit will get real. And here it is, shining like fucking Mecca: the Hive. No time to waste, Shock activates his drone matrix and fast foots over to a speeding golden pathway, diving into a duckling trail of drones heading back to their Queens.

Scans roll over his skin as he passes inside, clocking him as Hive-registered. He tries not to whoop it up. Knowing his skill and practicing it are two different beasts, not always simpatico, and seconds are ticking down too damned fast for comfort. In fact he's only just whizzed past the final checkpoints inside when alert sirens begin howling through the fortress.

They fire him up like napalm. Somewhere out there his flesh suit is sweating fit to drown him. Frantic, Shock seeks out Core, uncertain what to look for as no one's seen it before, and finds a shimmering column at the centre of the mountainous fortress, the shadows of towers within. Seeing it triggers a deep swell of nausea, and the signal from the P.O. rises in his drive, loud as Hive sirens, sweeping thought and coherence away.

Dimly he feels the drones around him lift him up, carry him away to another, faster, line. The sensation of impossible speed is like drunkenness, like standing on the roof of a mono, the world spinning away far below. Core looms through it like sunrise, bright and overwhelming, and a sensation like ropes twangs deep inside, as if trying to tear him inside out. He's aware of pain that isn't his, Puss's beak gaping wide like it's screaming, and then the signal dulls to a sound like tinnitus.

When Shock comes to seconds later, he's marching in a line of drones toward vast pillars like the close-grown trunks of a petrified forest, glowing with intense black light.

Core.

No one knows what's kept in here, besides Emblem. He'll be the first to know outside of the Lakatos family, and maybe one or two of their top Corps and Techs. In any other circumstances, that'd be such a fucking rush. He checks the time. He's lost forty seconds.

Stuffing panic down where it can't frag his processes, Shock sends out his secret weapon, his bio-wires, the reason he's so damned good at this Haunting shit. Unlike nano-wires, they're intelligent, adaptive, and have to be carried in, because they can't be made in Slip. These will work alone to find anything he tells them to, hopefully including a thing he's never seen. Everyone knows what Emblem does, what it is, but there's no telling what it looks like. And he's got three minutes to locate it, crack it, and get the hell out.

These bio-wires are his last. He won't be able to afford to make them again. Armed with Emblem's code-designation, the numeric representation of its design name, engraved into their search algorithms they sift the info-towers swift as thinking. What they find confounds him.

Avis. Only avis. Billions of them. Every avi there is. Finding Emblem amongst them should be easy, considering it's the only thing different, instead it takes one min thirty-two of unbearable tension.

Turns out Emblem is tiny, a red packet-node stamped with the Slip sign, a stylized fish, hidden under layers and layers of crypt. Shock bites down a wild flare of despair. He needs nano-wires now. Lots of them. It's not safe in this environment to have so many, in case the Queens notice, but he makes them anyway—what choice does he have?—and instructs them to decode. Hundreds of thousands of wires working at full speed take a damn near endless forty-three seconds to crack the crypt.

Once done, they separate to two units. One unit unpacks Emblem and brings it to his drive for storage, the other half creates an inert copy giving off the correct signal and recodes every last layer of crypt to hide it.

And that's it, Emblem's secured.

But the relief of having it is short-lived. Dropping into his drive like a deep-sea mine, it's a spiky package several dozen levels more hideous than the Core drone signal. He wants to vomit it up like a belly-load of bad liquor. The pain is unreal, makes him feel woozy, discombobulated.

Bio, he mutters, not sure if the sickness is terror or Emblem. It's fucking bio.

Emblem should not be in a drive. It's going to kill him. How the hell is he going to do this? He'd waste time on serious worry, but he's seconds left before his skin-matrix fails. Gotta crank him some serious skedaddle.

He tacks his arse onto the tail end of a team of drones heading out of Core toward the border of Hive, trying not to look suspect. No easy task. Around their orderly line, speeding along, all hell has broken loose. Alerts are full volume, Seekers out in force. The Hive is alive and searching for a breach.

Fucking come on! he begs, still hoping he'll make it out before his skin fails.

Through the stacks, just ahead, one of the Queens looms from between the outer towers. Large as life. Larger.

Tall as her fortress, she's the same shade of black, but her skin glows with yellow phosphorescence. She's scintillating. Gorgeous. Like gold dust in oil on black marble. Vast feelers prodding at the ground, she moves gracefully toward him. Shock closes his eyes as the line speeds him toward her. She can't see him yet—he's not been scanned, would've felt it. Just coming in his direction, that's all.

Then her shadow falls across him, and he feels her in his mind. She's bright white light, she blinds, engulfs. Her voice is a tidal wave of sound, obliterating thought, drowning the feel of Emblem's hooks.

Shock Pao.

It's not a question. She knows. No scan, no nothing. Just seen straight the fuck through him like this skin's not even there. He scuttles on, half insane fear, half pure insanity, hoping to outrun her, knowing he can't. Her shadow goes on forever. She's in charge here. Hive can be whatever she wills it: a labyrinth, a trap, a coffin.

Do you have it?

Shock can't breathe, which is stupid, no need in here. He's not even real, just a collection of data thinking its way into a preset, pre-paid, supposedly state-registered form that if anything feels like it's more terrified than him. Fear's got his voice in a box.

I see it. Keep it safe. Do not take it to Twist. We no longer require his services.

What the holy fuck? Twist was working for the Queens and now they want to cut him out of the deal? Any chance of surviving this madness shrinks to a pinpoint and pops out of sight.

I can't keep this from Twist! Shock doesn't know if he's speaking to her, or to himself. He'll kill me.

We will deal with Twist. You will deal with us.

The threat is implicit. Also insane. Twist is not to be fucked with, not even by these crazy ant dames. He's not in their Hive, they can't touch him. He can get Shock though, oh yeah he can, and Emblem with him. Then see what that crazy Scots fucker does to their Hive, their home. He'll crush it. Surely they know that. Surely? Shock drops his common sense like a handful of bad trips.

Are you crazy? Twist won't walk away from this like a good dog. He'll take this shit from my head by any means necessary and he will shut you down.

He feels her censure as hellish pain, like every tooth extracted at once, twelve-inch drill bits churning his lobes, a head full of flash bombs. Queenie could crush him without thinking. That she's put so much thought into making him hurt this bad without killing tells him how far he's crossed the line. And a message rides atop the pain.

Shock's her errand boy. He's alive because she needs him to be, no other reason. It's human/ant dynamics reversed and she's wearing big fucking boots. He vibrates apology, sends it out on all frequencies, praying to whatever God they bothered to replace the last with that she's in a forgiving mood.

Bring Emblem to the Heights. Do not delay. You will

be signal loud, and there will be others after you, but they are far behind. Once you are at Heights, you will be safe. We can remove Emblem. Then we will help you run, Shock Pao. We will ensure your survival. Her voice is a tornado in his mind, howling and roaring. Still pissed. So not good.

The exact address, a penthouse number so high even thinking about it gives him vertigo, drives into his flash with diamond-tipped power. Adds several powerful dimensions to the pain already bleeding out in concentric circles from where Emblem squats, leaden, and spiked with unexpected armature. Feels as if it's damn near decapitated him.

Go. We will be waiting, and we will be watching you, Shock Pao.

Her weight, her voice, her shadow, disappear. He opens his eyes. He's outside the Hive, beyond the Daddies, the barcode field and the Firewall maze, at the mouth of the trough running back to Slip. In terms of an expression of absolute power it's as convincing as a bullet to the cranium.

He recalls with a disbelieving laugh what Twist said about choice, incredulous that he assumed that was the worst he could face. What ignorance. Throwing his drone skin aside like so much junk, Shock dashes in to the gusher. Doesn't so much as think back, let alone look. Wakes in the cell a few minutes later, breathing hard, head pounding and aching, body drenched in sweat, nerves jumping like ECT, and wondering what the hell time-bomb he's got hooked in his skull that it gets to hurt this bad.

Back out to drizzle, aiming for casual, Shock's striking out on all levels, freaking hard enough to bust a fit. Freak should be over by now. Adrenalin should have frog-hopped that fucker and be running rings 'round his veins like victory laps. But there're two things in the way.

One: he just got spoken to by a genuine, honest-to-goddamn-hell Hive Queen. Moreover she and her kind are watching him. Watching him. He's stuck in the spotlight. Hell for a Haunt, even one so signal loud he's no longer anything like.

Two: Emblem's toxic, deadly, inside his skull, and he's no option but to carry it where the Queens want it to go. Talk about your human garbage disposal.

Feeling distinctly used and abused, Shock makes for the Heights, thoughts of Twist dimming beneath the need to get this out of his head before it reduces his grey matter to mush. Those hooks are hurting as if they're real, not mental manifestations of security protocol, and he can feel Emblem pulsing in there like a freaking heartbeat.

Thing is, the Heights, that well-protected jut of prime real estate, is over two blocks away, through more people, more traffic, than you could safely cram into the centre of the moon. If Shock blows before he gets there he'll be all over the daily news on every flash in the Gung, as well the soles of several hundred thousand feet. Bodes so far from well it's in a different fucking dimension.

Only option here is to keep moving, and he's got that all sewn up from here to kingdom come. As he enters the inner city, drizzle picks up to the point where it earns the right to be called rain. Looks like drops of mercury in the glaring light of scrolling neon and sulphur-bright street lamps. Silver pools collect across polished concrete, splashing his genuine-as-dammit Beng boots. Clearly today has not reached its optimum shit level and his freak cranks up to DEFCON 1, because the inner ring is a whole different ball game.

Between outer and inner city, it's like the difference between Slip and Hive. Buildings that look big as dammit suddenly dwarf next to gargantuan monuments that rise into the sky like God's own fingers. This here's money territory, claustrophobic and exposed all at once, and surrounded by sec-drones. Luckily they belong to Fulcrum, are controlled by Hive, and therefore should leave him alone, considering the Queens want him at Heights.

Embalmed in pain, Shock stumbles on, foot following foot, eyes fixed like Araldite on the Heights, that neo-gothic pathway to heaven's colon, lit up bright enough to form a neon halo. He tries to ignore that ka-thump ka-thump in his bloated flash, but it's beginning to sound like the drum beat to the end of the goddamn world. Bomb trails arcing over the brain horizon, pretty and all-out deadly as a meteor shower aimed at your window. He could do with dropping a handful of blockers, just to shut out the screaming migraine before it drops him, stone cold, to the sidewalk.

He reels on, clutching his skull. Just gotta keep going until he's home free from this shit but as the crowd surges around him, ka-thump becomes full-on jungle trip-hop track and the missiles, thus far arcing silent and splendid across the cranial horizon, slam into his lobes. The resulting explosion is like a sun going nova in his brain, sound hitting long after light, deafening, then the shock waves, cranial earthquakes, blast reason to oblivion.

It's painless but leaves no room for anything but itself, and Shock pushes on blindly, shoving folk aside, stumbling like a drunkard. Screaming at nothing and nobody. Blood wells, thick and choking, in his nose, drips for a second in globes large as cherry-bombs, then all-out gushes, and he's a walking gore-factory, neoprene jacket streaked with thick, clotted rivulets. They hit the pavement: mini paint-balls dyeing the rain red as gochujang sauce, and not one soul's clocked his condition, walking on oblivious or uncaring. Probably have him down as some loser trip-whore or liver-hound on a one-way journey to flatlines and ash. Oh the irony.

Cranial aftershocks become pain again at last; deep, grinding pain, and somewhere in there, a siren begins to go off, although the blitz has already been and gone, leaving his brainscape flattened and burning. This sound, rippling as it does through raddled nerves on some low, undeniable frequency, unseats whatever control he has over his stomach and he throws up the siu bao he choked down for breakfast in one heave, blood from his nose dripping into the brownish slew like undigested ketchup.

The siren simultaneously builds and quietens until it's less sound than pressure pounding against the inside of his skull and Shock's sure this is the big goodbye. Bread-box implosion. Skull-scattering fireworks. Instead, as pressure reaches max, golden lights burst from his eyes.

The whine snaps off. Snaps everything. His connection to Slip severs clean as flesh under a blade. He feels it go, just like those moments as a child when you walk into a room at night and the lights snap off, leaving you lost in darkness with only the sound of your breath coming faster and faster as fear crawls upward from your toes on spindly legs. Marooned in silence, Shock finally stops moving. He's forgotten how. Every atom is focused on what was lost, what's been broken.

Held in a vacuum, he's captured, hypnotized, by the light beams shining from his eyes, their reflection in the rain-soaked sidewalk. Obviously he's honest to goodness tripping out, or maybe dead. Dead would be good. Shock stares at his face in the muddled mirror of a puddle, astounded. He looks like a degenerate God. Around him, there's a ripple of reaction at last. A murmured crescendo. Sounds like voices. Who's talking to him? He can't answer, his eyes are headlights, and he's frozen inside them.

Threads of brighter gold, like nano-necklaces, trickle down the gold beams, begin to weave together and, from golden threads, before his bomb-blasted, God-bright, dissipated peepers, two shapes begin to form. Avis. His avis. Shark, cruising in circles around his head, coalescing closer to 3D with each circuit. And Puss, ghostly tentacles swirling on the sidewalk as it turns toward his leg and slides up. He can feel it there, against the material of his trousers. Solid. But the material doesn't move.

Dead. He has to be dead. Except he feels them, both of them, right there in his mind. Distinct and present as his own consciousness. Not an illusion as he thought, but real. Real. Sound fades in, the world on its heels, and Shock finds he's not dead. Not dreaming. He's stood in the middle of the street, Puss clinging to his chest, Shark swimming hungry circles between himself and a crowd of people who look as stunned as he feels. Mouths agape, pupils blown wide.

Shock watches the shark, the crowd, not knowing what to think, to say. They're real. They're real. And they're with him, within him, listening in to his every thought.

Then a woman on the edge of the crowd snaps.

Terror ignites in her eyes, blazes across her face. She begins screaming, her bag dropping from her hand, sumptuous grey leather soaking up gore-spattered rain. The impasse breaks with her, people exploding away like flocks of hysterical gulls colliding and screeching, bags flying like feathers. In the mayhem, feeling Shock's spike of panic, Shark powers forward, creating a pathway. Quick on the up-take thanks to their connection—intimate in ways he's still struggling to adjust to—Shock races away from the scene, unable to feel his feet.

He runs until his legs give out, and he staggers to a

wall, gasping for breath. With every attempt for air a tight knot of tears rises in his throat. Slip is gone, its absence absolute as a slammed door. His avis, real and locked out with him, are vulnerable. Helpless. They need him to be together, but he's not, he can't. Everything's wrong, and Emblem's still stuck in his drive, no longer painful but so fucking big and growing now, filling it bit by bit. What will happen when it reaches the edges?

Focused on the Heights before, he's all but forgotten that objective. It flits into his mind now, so tempting, but the thing inside of him that's no longer him but them, Puss and Shark made real, alive, and separate, shies away from heading toward anywhere the Queens might find them with such vehemence he's running in the opposite direction almost before he realizes it.

Shock's hands tangle in his hair, scraping at his skull. In the distance he hears screaming, sec-drone sirens. The wail of security vans. They parallel his internal alarms. Twist is coming. Every fucking crime lord in the Gung will follow. He has to scramble. Find a bolthole, somewhere safe. He has no idea where to go. Tears finally find their way through, coiling hot paths down his cheeks, capturing locks of his hair, dripping onto his chest, through Puss, who clings there like a child.

"What the fuck do I do? Just what the fuck do I do?"

time to call in joon bug

Stumbling to the temporary safety of a refuse-bay, the deep, square cubby designed to conceal huge refuse bins for the recycling plants, Shock huddles in the damp and the darkness. Listens with growing despair to the hubbub boiling in the inner city. The muffled thud of footsteps can be heard nearby as security forces, guided by sec-drones, hunt him down in the maze of service-alleys between 'scrapers.

They come close then veer away, making him light-headed, a potent brew of fear and anxiety. If it gets any worse he'll pass out, and then what will happen? He's got to get the hell away, right now. Find help. How exactly does he do that? He's probably on every screen and feed in the known world, and his avis are unmissable.

Puss is giant, covering his entire torso, its glow of gold as bright IRL as it is in Slip. He has to squint to look at it. Then there's Shark, his Great White. Seventeen feet of muscular gold menace, graceful and deadly, and impossible to hide outside of this bin bay.

Swimming in close proximity, it shows no inclination to escape, content to be near to Shock, but how do you hide that much freaking fish? Where do you take it? How do you move it without people freaking out? He can't leave them. They're both traumatized by their ejection from Slip, their pain tangling with his own, fresh and sharp, but it's not just that. They're him. It'd be like ripping half his head out and throwing it on the pavement.

There's only one solution he can think of. One group of people who know everything about hiding big secret shit. J-Hacks. Only he's got no affiliations to speak of, not with any J-Hack group. Sure he knows members of the Qua, well a member: Heng. He's the sum total of Shock's J-Hack connections. There's no one else he knows. Not well enough to ask a favour like this. An imposition. Heck, he doesn't even know Heng well enough for that.

Oh Shock's fucked himself good, for sure. His futile desperation to return to Sendai promulgated the single-minded belief that he could, that he must, disregard all else. After all, no connections are necessary for a man trying to get home, to find his solitary peace of mind, his escape. In fact, after Mim, he's actively feared companionship; sure that most of the warped, unhealthy and damaging shit between he and Mim must be directly traceable back to his stupidity. Isn't everything?

So what else is there? Who else? Only two, if he stretches the meaning of their shared gifts to the limit. Two Haunts he knows he can talk to about this, if not exactly request assistance. Feng Ho, who's dead. And Joon. Owing her favours has got him into more messes than he cares to mention.

Except, she's all he's got. Because he's not going to Mim. No way.

"That's it then, we go to Joon," he says to Shark, not wondering for a second why it is he's talking to it. It's like talking to himself. It is talking to himself, just less mad...

well, not really. But it understands him either way. Scary as all hell really, considering it has eyes like a sec-drone, dead and flat, but somehow worse, gleaming with this singular, potent hunger.

Puss squeezes his chest with a gentle flexing of its tentacles. Agreement. He nods. Sneaks to the edge of the inlet and peers around. The pounding of feet and sirens are many streets away. There's no guarantee they won't head back toward him, meaning he can't run far. A drone could find him easily too, several drones, especially now they're actively hunting him for the Queens.

Why haven't they clocked his signal? Do they not yet know what to look for? Maybe his being snapped out of Slip hurt the Queens? After all, the lock is now in his head. That's an advantage in cover, but once he's out, he has no protection at all. Shock realizes he's going to have to jack a vehicle. But into what vehicle can he fit a seventeen-foot Great White?

"Limo." Shock states the obvious, with slow-rising horror.

Jacking a limo in broad daylight will be one hell of a feat. He can't put Shark or Puss back into his flash, and even if he could, it's swollen with Emblem. It doesn't hurt now, with no interference he can feel, but it's taking up a lot of available space and growing fast. It's changing in there, too. Changing itself. Changing him. Fuck, he wants to worry about that, have a full-on, high-pitched, melodramatic freak about it, but he has no time to waste on such self-indulgent shit. How times change.

Shock looks again at his avis. In Slip, theoretically, they could have operated as a team, although he had never tested it. Could they not be a team IRL too? Even if he's no longer riding inside them, they're still his, still him, though he couldn't tell whether he is in them, or they are in him, he can feel them more and more the longer they're out. Eventually he thinks they'll be three minds in one.

He peers down at Puss, into the golden, square pupils of its eyes.

"We need to scan for the closest stretch."

There's no indication it's heard, but one of Puss's tentacles slides up to Shock's jack and slips in. A weird sensation, like static, prickling, and a touch itchy, it brings with it a surprise, not pleasant. Puss is female, or identifies as such. What? Why the hell is she she? How the hell?

Shock's way past appalled. Couldn't begin to describe these emotions, but they're old. Septic. Boils he thought lanced when he left female behind. How can Puss be something he isn't? Aren't they one and the same? Impossible that Puss could be this different, this alien from everything he is. His immediate reaction is to reject her, to oust her from him. But the thought is somehow unclean, makes him want to scrape filth from mind and body, so he tries to rationalize, to justify her apparent choice.

Puss is his original, given avi. Perhaps avis are gendered. How else could he be male and she remain female? Following that thought comes another, even less appealing. Are these aspects of him entirely separate personalities, or somehow both? Have they been prisoners, trapped and waiting for his arrival in Slip in order to experience anything like living? Or maybe his arrivals into Slip are the moments they've been trapped most of all, forced to carry him around, suffer his weight within them.

Discomfited by the notion and unable to continue looking into her eyes, Shock looks away, and recoils back against the wall hard enough to bruise his skull. The world's been rendered an apparition, covered in gleaming map lines; buildings overlaid with plans, their specs scrolling beside them. Mere silhouettes in the maze, people register as human-shaped blobs of body-heat signature, and between 'scrapers the roads stretch out as a mass of intersecting blue lines crawling with vehicles of every shape and size. Even cut off as they are from Slip, the detail is extraordinary. Mind-blowing.

Engines float in each vehicle: components clear as day, shining with white and red heat. Chauffeurs and passengers sit inside, wearing a palette of red, yellow and blue. Some Slipping via car-jacks, heads shining silver and gold. Others on IM, trailing conversation. This data should be private, limited to Slip. That it's not is horrifying. And he can see for miles in this way; layer upon layer of buildings and roads, right to the edges of the Gung, where contoured cliffs stand in see-through opposition to an angry, ghostly sea.

"Incredible."

Puss nudges him. The message is clear: Quit stalling. Embarrassed to be caught slacking, he searches for limos parked close by. This being inner city, there are seven such limos. Two easiest to reach. Shock singles out the one furthest from his pursuers. The chauffeur's locked into his flash, chatting away. On a break maybe. Perhaps lunch. Shock sees the IM conversation the same as all the others, streams of data zipping away from the chauffeur's flash. So easy to follow. Anyone could track down who the guy is talking to. Or tap the IM and find them in an instant. Amazing. Terrifying.

Fulcrum can't possibly know about this, or they'd be using it to their advantage, and if Fulcrum has no idea then it's doubtful anyone else does. Mind you, he's the only soul alive with avis out of Slip. Maybe this is the only way to see it. Good thing that, as there's no one in the Gung, criminal or Corp, within whose hands this would not be dangerous as hell. Same goes for Emblem. He can't let the Queens, or Twist, or any other cartel boss, get hold of it. Allow. Fuck that makes him laugh. If he can't hide, if he can't find safety, how the hell will he stop them?

Still connected to Puss, Shock leaves his hiding place and heads for their limo of choice. Plan is, Puss sneaks in and shorts out the chauffeur by jacking into his drive, then unlocks the car for Shock and Shark. His avis are haptic holograms, rendered 3D and corporeal to an extent by linkage with his nervous system, with the extended networks of the Gung's massive infrastructures. They can interact, but are not physically present. Such is the nature of a sensory illusion made tangible.

They make it to the limo without trouble and, right up until the last moment, Shock thinks they've nailed it. Puss goes in, moving with a swiftness and elegance those tentacles and the lack of water would seem to decry, and the chauffeur's out cold within seconds, mid-sentence by the looks. Even if Shock weren't linked to his avis, he'd hear the soft thunk as the doors unlock.

Smiling, he makes to move toward the limo, sending a note of caution to Shark, who's to wait until they're in and the engine's running to swim out to them and get into the back. That's when he hears the sirens, hears the shouts. Eyes wide, he looks left and right, finds teams of security guards closing in fast, crowds of people who should know better following behind them. Above the whirring of sec-drones fills the sky.

"Fuck!"

He pounds it for the car, pulling out the chauffeur and throwing himself into his place, bruising just about every inch of his right side, sec-drones swooping so close they whip his hair about his face. Lucky they aren't firing, or he'd be spray-painting the limo interior various shades of human remains. Or not so lucky, because it means the

Queens are determined to get him where they want him. He straps in and, cracking in through Puss's connection, starts the car, throwing on the ignition too fast, giving himself an insta-headache.

As the engine purrs to life, eliciting an odd echoed purr from Puss, the on-foot contingent of his pursuers reach the car and surround it. The security guards of the inner city don't carry projectile weapons. They have flash stuns, meshes under the skin of their right hands—similar to a Gamer mesh—with the power to send an immobilising signal flare. Like an EMP for humans. Shock's got dampers for that but he won't need them. These limos are everything proof. All his pursuers can do is shout at him.

There's no way he's surrendering. This bunch of idiots can't protect him from Twist and co, and the drones will deliver him direct to the Queens. He peers through the shoving, encircled bodies surrounding the car. Shark's out there in the alley, lurking in the shadows of the refuse inlet, waiting for his signal. The crowd of security officers around the car seem to have begun to notice the shark's not with Shock, they look around nervously, hands raised ready to send waves, as if that can protect them from seventeen feet of hologrammatic fury. Shock smiles.

Hey, Shark, he says. Get in the damn car.

Shark erupts from the alley, its length scintillating in the sun. It's no less terrifying than the footage of Great Whites in the water, or that old celluloid Jaws, and the effect is immediate. Visceral screams of terror. Chaos of bodies running in all directions, falling fast and sudden as bowling pins, scrambling along on all fours, desperate to run from that yawning, blank-eyed horror. And Shark's attack is silent, which somehow makes it all the more horrifying. Bodies flying, spraying blood in gouts from gaping wounds. How the fuck is it doing that and why can't he sense it? Is Shark holding him out?

Shock bangs on the window. C'mon!

He can't believe it. Shark's a hologram. Yet there it is, looming toward the limo, blood dripping from its teeth, lumps of flesh quivering between those vicious, golden shards. Everywhere there's blood. Screaming. Sec-drones fire, but the lasers go straight through Shark and into the sidewalk, exploding angry spurts of dust and chunks of concrete.

Then Shark's in the limo, bringing a warm, meaty stench to turn Shock's stomach, and he's slamming his thoughts down on the accelerator. Sending the limo jack-knifing away so fast it damn near leaps out of the road. Drones follow, firing at the roof, the persistent thud of lasers heavy as hail large as golf balls.

Puss nudges his mind, shows him the city laid out in lines. If this much data is available outside of Slip, they can use it to their advantage. Wipe the limo from the board completely. Shock approves the notion wholeheartedly. She tilts her head, a gesture so human it throws him, and the lines of their limo disappear from the map, taking his heat signature with them.

Boom, and they're gone, wiped from the mass of data feeding everyone's drives at every moment. It's not just the drones who can't see them; anyone who looks at their limo will see it without seeing it. The car simply won't register to them. Haunting again is delicious, albeit makeshift and brief. Now all he has to do is find Joon. She's still a Haunt, of course, and thus invisible in or out of the system, but he has a good idea of where she might be hanging. So he points the limo in that direction, and floors it.

mim and johnny
sez go hunting

Atop the edge of a 'scraper on the outskirts of inner city, Mim teeters on teal bladers, her dark coat flapping in a twenty-knot breeze, eye-to-eye with ravenous gulls teasing the updrafts. Perched there like some fellow carrion eater, bored of scraps and on the hunt for warm mouse meat, she's puffing on a slender purple psy stick and squinting into the middle distance, her whole body radiating disgust. The wind has teeth even at ground level today, and holds the first spitting needles of freezing rain. Considering they've been up here a while, her amusement levels are at an all-time low.

Johnny, casually draped over an air-conditioning duct behind her, calls out, "What you hunting for up there?"

Mim snorts, throws a contemptuous glare over a leather-clad shoulder.

"Are you high?" She spots the thin blue stick in his mouth and raises a brow. No need to ask. Obviously. Fake psy, too. Guh, gross. She takes a big old draw on her own, pointedly, making him flush red. Envy. Green-eyed monster in her blue-eyed waste of space. Serves him right. "Shock flavour," she shouts.

"He has a flavour?"

Sez obviously found the important part.

"Caramel and violets."

"Very specific."

Snitty. Serves him right.

Mim smiles to herself.

"I have a good memory."

She might be smiling, feeling that little dart hit home in Johnny's sudden, pointed silence, but it's true. Shock did smell like that. It's unnerving how extraordinarily clear her recollection is, as though his naked skin is under her nose: warm and covered in a light sheen of sweat, like disco glitter. He fucked like he danced. Dancing with him was her favourite thing once. She never told him that. Never give the enemy ammunition.

Mim scans the inner city again, zooming in, on the hunt for that flash of green hair she knows so well. Not many of her contacts and none of her friends, not even Sez, know that Mim's got a lot more in these eyes of hers than a simple glamour mod. No point having surgery done for the one thing, so Mim had pretty much everything available, including what the surgeon called "sniper-vision". It's so precise she can count the feathers on a pigeon strutting drunkenly down the sidewalk five blocks away.

Her drive connection is wide open too, in hopes of his block being comped so she can sniff out the signal she imagines will smell uniquely like Shock, because she was only half joking about that. That's Mim's secret superpower, or so she likes to call it, stealing the phrase from Shock and his so-called Slip superpowers. She smells signals. Her drive has a form of synaesthesia—a glitch in all honesty, one that's turned out useful—transmuting all signals in her immediate location and any she hunts for into scents.

Sez is like copper, giving her a constant reminder that he's not for keeps, just a transition. An easy stop between Shock and... what? Where exactly does a girl go after cutting off the only S.O. who felt like a limb? It was supposed to be a swift, painless amputation. Intention versus reality; always surprising when they diverge.

She looks at the ground, hundreds of feet below her overhanging bladers, and swallows a smile whole, like bad medicine. Synchronicity. When she met Shock she was perched in a window at Tech, smoking a purple psy, her favourite, for the sharp edges of the buzz, the clarity of the visions. Her bladers were red then. They matched her bodysuit. Used to be her favourite thing to wear.

Who the hell was she then? And who is she now? Hard to tell. She wore those selfsame bladers the other day, to the party. Was that on purpose? Was she trying to remind him for him or for her? Mim carefully examines the motivation, and finds it exactly as she suspected. She grimaces into the bitter wind. Ugh. Humiliating.

"Messy," she mutters around the psy, spewing smoke into an uncaring grey sky, and caramel invades her incipient attack of self-approbation. The faintest whiff. Trailing behind it is the winsome bouquet of shy violets.

Both there, brief and all but intangible, then gone.

Mim tilts her head, throws her connection open even further, the tissue around her drive singing pain. She ignores it. Strains. There. Again. A ghost of scent, little puffs of it, like smoke signals. Fitting for a Haunt. He's still in Slip, just out of Hive most likely, and already broadcasting. Way to go Li and Ho. She realizes she's grinning. Not for her victory, scenting him, or theirs for cracking the block. For his. He did it. The crazy bastard did it. He hit Hive, cracked Core, jacked Emblem. Survived the Queens.

"You crazy cunt," she yells into the wind. "You crazy fucking awesome cunt. Fucking hell but I hate you!" She chucks her psy down between her feet and mutters furiously, "Don't you realize I've got to screw you over again now."

As if in answer, his scent comes back at her, sharp and clear. Like he's standing next to her.

She shouts over her shoulder, "Sez, get a shake on. He's out."

From her belt she unsnaps a mobile rappelling clip. It's a small, matt-black, tear-shaped unit with a folded grapple hook and integral wrist-strap, concealing a long reel of nylon wire strong enough to carry three times her weight. She whips the grapple open and flicks it at the edge, securing it; shoves one hand through the loop and vaults.

Over the side, as the wire reels out, Mim aims her bladers at the wall and braces, whooping as she picks up speed. Sez flies over the edge before she's a fifth of the way down, his blue psy careening past her ear. Bastard.

By the time they hit the floor, side by side, Mim's got a lock on her boy.

"Gangway," she says to Sez, setting off in that direction.

He looks impressed.

"Not far. Good call to wait here."

Mim smiles to herself. Self-satisfied. It doesn't last. Now she's adjusted to having Shock's signal clear in her feed, it's obvious something's very wrong. She's never felt a Haunt before today, only smelt one, but Haunts aren't this different. She has proof. Context. Up there on the roof, catching the first clear shot of his signal, he was normal. The usual bright, strong signal anyone of his Tech level might project. Now he's going bug-eye and fast, scary fast. A mixture of interference and high-pitched feedback from some sort of pressure, gradually mounting.

With every pound of her foot on the sidewalk his signal becomes more scrambled and unstable, almost like her rhythm is compounding it. For a second she wants to stop running, until logic face-punches stupidity, leaving her free to wonder what in holy hell is going on in his drive. Is he about to explode? He's vibrating hard enough. If he blows he takes her ticket out of Shimli with him.

"Shit!"

"What?"

"Shock's in trouble. His signal's gone bug-eye. Massive internal reverb. I think he might blow"

"Emblem?"

"Doubtless."

"What do we do?"

"Find him, shut him down. If he's unconscious his drive will go into sleep mode."

Sez nods and they kick it up a gear, Mim's bladers resounding like bullets. She's listening hard as they run, following Shock as he reels down the street. Until he stops. Locked as she is into his signal, Mim stops dead with him.

Sez clocks it ten metres ahead and spins on his heels. Yells, "What's up?"

"I... don't know."

In her head she feels Shock's pain, his surprise, as it reels down the signal feed. There's so much pressure; his signal's inflating like a balloon, fit to burst. In unintended sympathy, Mim braces, waiting for the explosion.

It never comes.

His signal stills. Calm as water. And begins to unravel. Two small portions reel away, like thread, and rebuild into two alternate signals. Separate but the same.

Not one Shock: three, all interconnected, their signal reverberating between them. Not in ugly feedback blare.

Symphonically. Three melodic lines forming to a song. Got to be Emblem's work again, some sort of fracturing of Shock's personality. Drive D.I.D. So perfect though, not the insane mess she'd expect from this sudden, wanton breakage.

"Mim!"

Mim realizes Sez is shaking her shoulder, calling her name. She goes to shout at him, furious. Stops, seeing his face. He points at the 'scraper screens.

There's Shock, in full HD. Swimming around him is Shark, his self-made killer avi. Seventeen feet of ferocious Great White. There's Puss too, slithering up his leg toward his chest. Avis out of Slip, golden hologrammatic ghosts, as bizarre IRL as a land ship would be in Slip. Unreal. For a moment Mim's convinced it's the psy, rolling out hallucinations inside her eyeballs, then sound explodes in her ears as she stops listening to Shock's feed and focuses on the screen.

People are screaming, shouting, a storm of hysteria with Shock the frozen centre. Finally, he seems to grok the impressive fuckery of his situation, and with Shark punching an escape route through scattering bodies, he runs for it, his face white, those baby blues shoved aside by pupils the size of plates. The camera zooms in, dramatic, making black holes of them and falling inside.

Drone sirens enter the mix, high up, and the screams of the crowds converge into bedlam. Full-on riot. Some trying to go after Shock, most running in any other direction and falling over each other. There's blood on the sidewalk, discarded shoes, a couple of bodies collapsed like puppets, unconscious. Casualties to the chaos.

Mim and Sez share a look, and they're off, Mim tracking Shock like a blood hound. Shock just became a bullseye, and if he's not in their hands soon, he'll be in the wrong hands, and the Harmonys will remove theirs. They burst out onto the street Shock exited a mere five minutes ago, awash with onlookers flooding the scene to rubber-neck now the drama's over.

Above them the screens replay the same scene over and over. Mim pauses to watch, having missed the moment of truth. It's beautiful. He's beautiful. Golden eyes weaving sea creatures into the rain-speckled air like some Tech Freak wizard. She wants to touch them, experience their golden skin crackling like static against her palm. Of course, after she does what she's got to do, he'll never come near her again. But at least she won't be in Shimli.

Teeth bared, she turns from the screens and elbows on through the crowds, shoving aside well-dressed inner-city socialites like ninepins. Nips into the tight maze of alleys between 'scrapers, too far behind Shock for comfort, and there are no short cuts here, no easy way through, even if they rappelled up and used the roofs.

"What direction?" Sez shouts from behind, muffled as he lights another psy.

"None particular. He's freaking out." Bitten out. She's mad at herself for stopping to watch the screens. Time wasted. Fucking stupid.

"Can you feel it?"

Mim nods. His signal's like a beacon to her now. Port in the storm. Clear enough to differentiate between the parts of his new triumvirate signal. Shark keen as a knife blade, dangerous in her mind, its part of the signal has teeth, no surprises there. Puss is complex, a cat's cradle of interweaving lines, a puzzle. She wants to hold it in her hands and play with it. But there's something else in that complex weave. Gobsmacking. It makes her laugh aloud.

"Oh, Shocking boy," she mutters. "What will you do?"

In the midst of Shark and Puss flares her Shocking boy, sulphur-bright and familiar as his face, his skin. His signal is a riot of panic, confusion and fear. He's struggling to adjust. She can't judge. She'd be the same. Avis IRL for fuck's sake. It's something out of an anime V-sim. Crazy. Abandoning the idea of catching him up in this warren of streets, Mim simply keeps track as he veers from one narrow alley to another. He's lost his pursuers for the time being, they're searching all the wrong places.

"Why don't they track his signal?" Sez shouts as the drones come close and fly off, apparently having found no sign.

"Two important facts they're missing," she yells, patient for once with Sez's inability to think laterally. "One, he's a Fail. Unregistered. No ID to find unless they think to look in the Fail records, and they won't. Two, he's a Haunt, and this is the first time he's ever been signal loud. To them his signal's diffuse, spread over a wide area, I only found him because I knew what to look for to pinpoint him. Pretty sure other interested parties will home in soon, but we're in the front of this race. All we need to do is keep following, and catch him when he stops."

It's like Shock's listening in, because the moment she says that, he does. Mim tries to triangulate the easiest route to his position. There isn't one. So she just keeps running. They've got a little time. With all the Slip shops in the Gung to pick from, the others would assume he'd go somewhere like Korea-town. One of the cheaper shops, hidden in the labyrinthine innards of the blocks. Or maybe somewhere in Sakkura's malls. They don't know him like she does.

Shock keeps tabs on every Slip shop in the Gung, including several high-profile outlets in the inner city. Unadvertized. Rarely used. Mim knows they exist because he told her, and her instinct to wait here has given her the advantage. It won't last long, not with Shock on every news feed, every channel, but it's enough she hopes to land their fish and his surprising new companions.

At full speed, Mim veers into the alley where Shock's sheltering, in time to see him disappear out the other side, way in the distance.

"Fuck!"

Should she call out? No, Shock would run faster. Besides, he's gone. All she can do is follow. Then it registers. Where's Puss? Where's Shark? Back in his flash? Recalling the footage from the screens Mim discards that option wholesale. Nothing comes out of your flash that catastrophically only to be so easily forced back in. And his signal is still odd. Out of key. Warped. Pushed out of true by the presence of Emblem. Probably there'd be no room left for avis even if he could put them back. In which case, why is she still running?

Way past the inlet Shock was using as a hidey-hole, Mim slams on the brakes, trying to go from sprint to dead still before she ends up shark bait. Bladers aren't as easy to control as normal boots, and they're categorically not meant for running. She slides, falls hard on her arse, the impact clacking her teeth together. Her bodysuit, slippery enough as it is, skids on the rain. Frantic to stop and hide, Mim slams her hands down, shredding skin, biting out a curse as several fingers pop out of their joints, and slithers to an ugly halt.

"Madre de dios," she breathes, dredging up long forgotten words from her early childhood, when her father's father was still alive and trying to keep something of his heritage present in his grandchildren.

Rising to her feet, she carefully wipes half-denuded palms on her thighs, smearing rain, filth and blood all over them. Her popped fingers hurt like hell, but they're a small price to pay. She turns, gesturing at Sez to stop, stay put.

He's way behind. Sailor boy still isn't up to speed on dry land. The look of confusion the stupid psy-baked donkey rocks at her frantic signalling deepens to horror as sirens wail in the near distance and Shark surges out of the inlet.

Casting a bright golden glow that swallows everything in sight, Shark powers straight at her, its mouth ever widening. Why can't she run? She tries to run, tries so very hard, but her legs don't seem to work. They've quit on her, the skiving fucks. From somewhere beyond Shark's tail, she hears Sez shouting, but she can't work out what he's saying over the roaring in her head. Probably "run" "get the hell out of there" "fucking move" everything she's saying to herself, until it's too late to act any more. Shark's upon her.

Teeth don't hurt as they wrap her from hips to shoulders, yanking her up off the alley floor. There's no pain at all, only sound and strange, disjointed sensation: deep, rumbling crunching noises, a bubbling warmth curdling in her throat, and a tight sensation in her torso and gut, like everything inside is squeezing together. Shark tosses her in the air, high up, her hair fluttering across her cheeks, soft and ticklish. As she falls, she spins, almost elegant, and marvels at its whole, massive golden length passing beneath her. She reaches out to touch it, or at least she thinks she does.

And then she hits the ground.

Mim can't move. Nothing works. Nothing feels. She blinks, but her eyes remain wide, blurred with blood, or mud, or maybe tears. Mim doesn't cry. She never has. Crying is weakness, lack of control. Mim's always been in control, even when she wasn't. Now she's not even in control of her bodily functions.

If she could, she'd laugh at that irony, or maybe she'd cry. She's not sure. There's a smudge of colour against the black, it moves toward her, then veers away, disappearing into darkness. Sez, deserting her. No more or less than she'd do to him. She wants to scream, call out "Don't leave me alone" but nothing works. Nothing feels.

And darkness is everywhere, closing in.

Li's voice, brittle as old bone, crackles into her IM, resonating through her whole head. What a mess. I hate messes. I trusted you not to make a mess, Mim. Such a shame. Her voice cuts out, then comes back, soft with malice. One can enjoy failure a little too much, Mim. Look at all you've lost. Was it worth it, darling?

Then she's gone. Leaving Mim all alone in the dark.

resurrection comes

he Resurrection limps into Foon Gung Harbour on
seventeen of her twenty-four wheels, still smoking,
her ravaged back swarming with crews working double-
time to salvage what they can and assess the cost of
repairs. The Ark is stranded way behind them and Daly
is gone. Petrie's bullet took him out fair and square, right
between the eyes.

After he fell, as word spread, the Ark's people retreated
en masse, a sight to behold, and the Resurrection,
seaworthy despite the damage done to her port side, her
stern and her upper deck, sailed on without a backward
glance. Whatever the Ark does now, however she
survives, is the business of her crew, her citizens.

Their attack failed, so all is forgotten. The people of the
Resurrection tend their wounded and mourn their dead,
and they hold no grudges. Life on the ocean is what it is,
and they live looking forward, to the next storm, the next
salvage, always prepared.

Petrie jumps from the ropes to the rungs of Cassius's
crow. His body is sore from bullet scores and burns, but
his centre is light, calm as the sea, the sky. Filled with a

quiet pride. He didn't stand and fight, but he stood up for the boy within, he avenged him.

Up top, heavily wounded in the fray, Cassius pores over incoming damage reports. He looks at Petrie, shakes his head.

"This is going to take some doing."

"That it is. You okay with my leading the off-shore party for Volk?"

"Only man I'd trust for the job," Cassius replies, then his face grows serious. "Back there, that was something. Proud to have you here, man. I know I've said it before, and likely I'll have reason to say it again, but that's why you're my bosun. Never met a soul more capable of putting himself to one side for the benefit of his crew."

Uneasy with such praise, as usual, Petrie merely smiles, nods. Cassius knows he's not the effusive sort, won't be expecting Petrie to acknowledge any other way. That's why this is his family. People who allow you to be who you are, who'll await your growth and change patiently, aware that everything happens in good time, they're hard to come by. He's never felt happier, and to think he once believed happiness was something that happened to other people. He's glad to be wrong.

"We're ready to go."

"Report back regular. And boot that damned Harbour Marshall in the arse for me, would you? Claiming they have no struts or girders when I see a whole mess of 'em right there in the shipyard." Cassius snorts. "Next that old crook will insist he's got no bolts or cutters. What does he think we are?"

Petrie laughs. "He hopes we're blind, stupid and deep of pocket. I'll gladly kick his arse. I'll wear my biggest boots."

They take one of the schooners captured from the Ark, top-notch salvage, and a team of roughly 250 able men and women, eager to help even in the wake of the battle with the Ark. Petrie expected as much, he knows these people, but even so he's amazed by the sheer number who responded to their call for volunteers. Good folk and good fighters all. He couldn't ask for better.

The harbour's serene, nothing of the storm they encountered on the open sea seems to have made it to the Gung, not even a breath of wind, though the temperature's scary low. Upon landing, Petrie takes a moment to do as promised, although his kick up the backside, as was implicitly understood between he and Cassius, is more of a stern lecture on withholding good materials from paying customers.

That done, he turns to Volk.

"What now, then? Where do we go?"

Volk's not paying attention. Her gaze is focused upward, on the screens placed on scaffolds high above the harbour. There are such screens everywhere in the Gung, showing an endless relay of news, music and shows streamed from hubs where the film and television industries still thrive.

"Volk. Where do we go?"

"City centre. Look. Breaking news." She points to the screens. "The Haunt's already been into Slip."

If Petrie couldn't see it with his own eyes, he wouldn't believe it. Shock's a skinny little Korean with ratty black and candy-green hair, shining gold from his eyes like sunbeams. Unreal. Like one of the shows from the hubs. From those beams two avis build themselves IRL from golden thread, an octopus and a shark. It'd be beautiful if it weren't so freaking bizarre, so unnerving, so evidently wrong.

"What the hell am I seeing?" he asks. "Was this supposed to happen?"

"I'm not sure," Volk says, she's frowning, concentrating

hard. She winces. "Grief, his signal's in a bad way. Emblem's causing havoc in his drive. It won't be contained for long." Her eyes widen. "He's been disconnected from Slip. Cut off completely. That's what we're seeing. That's why we're seeing them. We have to get to him."

Petrie looks at the screens. The footage is on repeat. He watches it right to the end, to the moment Shock runs, a look of terror set deep into his thin face. Faces fall into expression two ways, they either strain the features, appear unnatural, or they fit into pre-existing lines, like a smile or a frown. Fear has been on that face before, enough times to make the fit perfect. That makes Petrie angry. Seeing this boy, his fear, he finds himself concerned about what they've come to do.

"Are you going to use that drug on him?"

Volk offers him a look of sheer disbelief.

"You don't understand. I can't. He's already out. Whatever we do to help, it can't be that. All I can think to do is take him to Breaker. And soon. Before that thing grows outside of his drive."

Petrie stares at her. "Breaker's with the Queens. We can't go to him. He specifically told you to prevent Shock from delivering Emblem."

"I know, and he was right. But Emblem's mutating. Whatever it was in Core, it's not that any more. It needs to be taken out of his drive as soon as possible, especially in light of what it's done to him. He's out, Petrie. Can you imagine how that feels?" The look of horror on her face tells him she can. Maybe through Shock's signal.

He tries to do the same. Fails. "I can't."

"You won't need to imagine if Emblem breaks from his drive. It could do the same to us. Worse maybe, because it's already gone way beyond what it was when he plucked it from Core. I don't know what the hell it is now.

The only person I know who might be capable of halting its progress, getting it out of that drive—"

"Is Breaker," Petrie finishes for her, understanding.

"It's beyond risky, I know, but so is leaving Emblem in there. Emblem's more dangerous than the Queens at this moment, because it's out already and it's changing fast. Growing at a frightening rate. I don't think his drive can hold it for long, they were never meant for something like that. If Breaker can remove it, he might be able to contain it again. Confine it. Might be able to confine the Queens too. It's not much, I know, but it's the only chance we have."

He nods. "Right then. Let's move. We won't be the only ones after him."

"No, not even close. There are dozens of signals converging on him. He's a huge, golden target." She blinks. "And he's gone."

"What?"

"Found a way to hide. Probably stole a vehicle, wiped its signal from Slip."

"So how do we find him?"

"We head for the centre. His signal will pop back up, it'll have to. State of his drive he won't be hiding long, he'll know he has to act fast, find someone to help. When he does, he'll be vulnerable again."

"And we won't be the only ones on his tail."

"No," she says quietly, "so we'll just have to be the ones who catch him."

They hire trucks and cater-bikes at the harbour yard and head off at high speed, Volk locked in to Shock's signal's last location, waiting for it to pop up again. Petric trusts his people to fight, and fight hard, but what chance do they have? Their one ace in the hole, Volk's drug, is useless. Firepower might work against Twist Calhoun, against other criminals also after Emblem, but it won't work against Queens. If the Queens get Emblem, if they get out of Slip, they've got no means of stopping them.

As they drive up out of Harbour District, Petrie keeps eyes on the Resurrection until she's impossible to see. He always expected ship life to come to an end, and probably within his lifetime considering his age. It's not exactly a missable trend that decline in numbers, but at least it was going to be somewhat natural.

He tries to imagine what might happen now: huge Queens striding across the Gung, and into the ocean? What could they do? What couldn't they? He should be angry with Fulcrum, with Kamilla, even with Josef for not pushing his mother hard enough, but there's no point. Done is done. Just gotta hope that they're not all done for.

why bugs have
a bad rap

Foot down, weaving erratically through the highway traffic, Shock negotiates with his inner hysteria. Not only are they cut off from Slip, a state so excruciating they've united against feeling it, but Shock's signal loud and getting louder. At some point even the limo won't be able to conceal that. Panic and need seize his intestines. Goddamit but he needs something for all of this shit. Anything. He'd take a year-old S-series half-melted in a puddle of piss at this point.

"Fuck," he snarls, grinding a fist into his belly, trying to erase the cramping of withdrawal and succeeding only in adding muscular distress.

Puss slides across the passenger seat and settles into his lap, coiled in a nest of her own tentacles. Strange how reassuring that is, how much it helps, despite his continued wariness of her being her. Strange too that the close proximity of Shark's meat-flecked jaws, the churning power of its muscular bulk in the back of the limo, comfort Shock much the same. He's never felt this close to anyone. He finds it disarming. Disconcerting. It's too real.

He wants illusion. The world a dream, soft focus and fleeting, ending whenever he closes his eyes. Wants the option of shutting his eyes and never opening them again. The world is too raw, too loud. It swamps him, drowns him out like a shout in a club, diminishing him even when he's trying to stand tall. Defeats him. Or leads him to defeat himself, who knows?

Breathing in deep, Shock shuts his eyes, sinking into the comfort of Puss on his lap, Shark at his spine, and trying to ignore a thought that wants to march into his head and stage a takeover: How can he protect his avis when he can't even protect himself?

Starting awake, Shock blinks, sleepy and bemused, at the car display. Ninety minutes. Ninety minutes gone. He shoots an accusing glare at Puss, back in the passenger seat but clearly still in control of the car because he sure as hell isn't. Her eyes swivel in a surprising approximation of an exasperated roll. The expression is so unutterably female it spikes his already irritable mood into a full-on strop.

"If I needed to sleep, I'd have asked for it," he snaps.

She turns away. Total cold shoulder. The second she does it, he's sorry for snapping. All the odd moments in Slip make sense to him now. The way Puss made him change course or avoid certain areas, the way his head just works in there. Not a superpower at all. Puss looking after him, as she's trying to even now, way out of her natural habitat.

He did need sleep. The bitch of bruising in his side has muted to a mumble and his head feels better, though that easing is more illusory; Emblem's no less destructive than it was when it tore his avis from Slip and cut them, and him, out cold. Unable to find the words to apologize for being a dick, Shock looks out of the limo and finds they're on the outskirts of Sakkura. She's driven them all the way, plucking the destination straight out of his head.

"Hey, thanks," he says, meaning both this and sleep. Relieved to find a way to say what he couldn't before.

Puss rolls out a tentacle and squeezes his arm. All forgiven. It makes him feel better and he starts to formulate what the hell he's going to say to Joon when they reach her apartment.

He knows she'll be there. Joon's a magpie. When she's settled in, her hovels look like they've been spackled in hippy glitter. Scarves everywhere. Walls painted in crazy, hypnotic patterns. Every piece of furniture mismatched and covered in polka dots and paisley. Primary-coloured chaos. This apartment is yet to be spackled, so she's still there, and she'll be in too.

Daytime is hang time for Joon. She's a night owl, or rather a night sea creature, her avi being a rockfish. Scorpaena. Ugly, scary-looking thing. She hates it, but refuses on principle to buy or build another. She'll have seen the news for sure, the footage of his avis bursting IRL, so he'll leave them in the limo. Still, Emblem is enough of a sparkly for her magpie eyes, and he needs her help. Not to become her newest acquisition, sold to the highest bidder. Why does she have to be his only option?

"Can't catch a fucking break, can I?" he mutters, locked into worry over that feed and exactly how many people are after him right now, how easy he might be to catch all exposed like this. He's only mildly surprised when Shark responds to the unpleasant thought-loop with a pronounced, and spine-wrenching, butt of the head to the back of his seat. Message is clear as the bruise no doubt brewing on his spine: Buck up.

Fair enough. Consider him bucked.

Puss parks up in front of Joon's 'scraper, throwing their exclusion zone a little wider, in case of unwary drivers. Flipping up his hood, Shock checks all is clear and, pausing to calm Shark, who's all manner of jittery about Shock leaving the safe enclosure of the limo, gets out, keeping a wary eye all around.

Dirty red plastic kanji up the side of Joon's building translate to Garden Palace Court. All 'scrapers in Sakkura's arse-end have equally grand names. They've changed hands multiple times, never enduring anything so useful as a re-vamp or name-change, and they're always rammed with tenants. The poor, spikers, the desperate, or people like him and Joon—safe-housing in hellholes to steer clear of unwanted trouble, the sort that often plagues those working for the Gung's criminal element.

Shock avoids the entrance. Walks to the narrow space at the side nearest, riddled with steep metal fire escapes, like spider webs in the cracks. Freezing water drips through the structure from overnight rainfall, and the metal stinks of rust, and the organic filth slimed in the joints. Not mud, not human waste, an accumulation of rot and surface mosses.

Keeping his hands off the filthy rails, he runs up, light-footed. Joon's thankfully not too high, only on the eleventh floor. Shock steals in through the window, makes his way to her door and knocks. The silence tells him that she's in.

"Joon," he calls softly. "It's Shock. Need a favour, por favore."

The door is yanked open, and a large crossbow rammed into his face. Joon's head is somewhere behind it, eyes on stalks, electrocution hair re-dyed slime green. Shock approves. He ducks away from the bolt.

"Ease up, Joon, I'm all cool."

"Cool, not cold," she snaps, jabbing the crossbow back at his face.

He holds up his hands, palm out.

"Cool is enough. I'm off-Slip, bitch. Cut off. No fucker can trace me, and they'll take a while to re-catch my sig after I scarpered so hard and fast." Tension creeps further into his shoulders as he speaks, knotting them to his spine. How long has he really got before he gets tracked? He might have just aped bravado to Joon, but truthfully he's clueless. He needs to get back to the limo ASAP.

"There was a limo on the feeds. Where is it?" she asks, still too wary. Too damned slow. He loses patience.

"Scan, bitch. Just scan. You'll see. Or not."

She sniffs. "Stay put. I will shoot you." Her eyes unfocus a touch. When they focus again, they're not on him. She's in Slip. Lucky bitch has an internal uplink. Expensive doohicky, involving invasive surgery. That's the bit puts him off. She's always scorned his squeamishness, citing the replacement of his vagina with a dick. Joon thinks that's invasion of a far more nail-biting nature. She has no idea. It was fucking heaven. He'd do it again a million times over. And it's one hell of a long way from chopping open your head for the sake of more tech.

After a moment, she snaps back. Nods.

"Neat trick. I assume it's parked outside?"

"It is."

"Best come in then." The crossbow lowers and she jerks it inward, opening the door wide so he can slip through. "So," she says as he passes, casual as a butt dropped onto sofa cushions. "Avis still in there?" He notes she hasn't relinquished the bow, and makes a point to keep space between himself and the door.

"Classified."

This look fleets across her face, sneaky as fuck the

untrustworthy bitch, but to her credit she takes the block on the nose.

"Okay. Business then. What do you need?"

Shock shrugs. Diffident.

"Place to hide. Help getting help. Something. Anything. I mean, for fuck's sake, they do not cover this crap in the manuals."

"Truth. Well, don't know what the hell you thought I could put on the table. Clueless in my first, last, and middle name on this one. You just pulled a trick I never imagined in my wildest fucking trips, and let me tell you I've ridden some crazy goddamn rides." She's full-on impressed.

"You don't have a middle name."

"Do. It's Casey." She throws herself into a chair; spider legs sprawled way out onto the carpet. Still holding the bow though. White knuckles showing a trace. Untrustworthy bitch.

He chokes back a laugh. "Casey?"

"Juniper Casey Shimura."

"Mouthful."

"Nothing on your full handle."

"Fuck off. So, can you point me toward salvation of any stripe, Juniper Casey Shimura?"

"Don't fuckin' push me."

He rolls his eyes.

"Sorry, Joon."

She bites her lips, lifts a shoulder.

"Might... might... just know someone who can help. Might."

"Okay, might. Got it. Who?"

She sighs. "Idiot. Can't name names, can I? Not with a might. But I can take you."

Here comes the suspicion.

"Where?"

"J-Hack underground."

"They've got an underground?"

"Dude," she replies scornfully, "of course they fucking have. You just never dirtied yourself looking for it."

Shock's heart is a pincushion these days. Every needle strikes clean and true, lodges inside. He'd prefer to think she's wrong about the idea of him not dirtying himself, but that's almost exactly how it's been. He's fixated on Sendai above all else. Used it as an excuse to steer clear of any affiliations, to be almost terminally life avoidant. Surely that's some kind of disorder?

"Take me."

"Take you," she says. "Suuuuure. Eaaaasy. Let's just go, hey? Right now!"

"Joon, for serious, I am hardcore in need. If there is any way you can do just that, minus the sarcasm infection, I would be eternally grateful. Might even be persuaded to be in your debt."

She stares at him a long time, scathing, then unwinds from the sofa, tossing the bow onto the cushion.

"Fine. I'll take you. But that's it. Rest is up to you."

It's only then the knot in his shoulders begins to untie. She snags her coat from the bewildering sprawl of branches on a coat tree painted to look like a neon giraffe wearing a medusa wig.

"We'll take the limo," she says.

Joon near his avis? Fuck no.

"Er... not sure it's safe for you." He's giving away intel on avi location, but it can't be helped.

She purses her lips. "Your fucking Shark, amirite?"

"Yup."

She shrugs. "Plan B. You'll come on my bike, the limo stays here."

"Can't it follow?"

"Your Shark can drive?" She's unconvinced.

"No," he replies. "But my Octopus can."

Sakkura's an upright urban wasteland. Miles of jutting 'scrapers slowly rotting against dull grey sky. It rains here as much as it does over Korea-town, drenching everything. Flooding the poorly built bridges strung in ugly shades of dirty concrete between dilapidated blocks.

Shock keeps his head close to Joon's back to avoid the perpetual spill of old rain as she whips past each bridge, the heavy throb of her bike engine coughing too loud in the quiet. It does no good, ice-cold drops of two-day-old rain strike square down the back of his jacket, straight through his thin tee, and onto his spine. Make him shiver uncontrollably.

It begins to rain again. A desultory spatter fast develops into full-on deluge. Joon utters a wind-snatched curse and strangles the throttle. She's got this ancient cater-bike, like the ones they use for avis in J-Net. The engine belches black smoke, and the cat-track tears at the tarmac like scrabbling hands, spraying them both with loose grit. They pass long-toothed factories, disgorging invisible walls of effluent rippled like heat haze against the clouds.

Pass the squats, where buildings so rotten they've been abandoned by paying tenants are repopulated by art collectives, their sides re-imagined to murals. Sculptures cling to corners and ledges like insects from other worlds, other dimensions, their fragile limbs at odds with the laws of physics.

One squat has an old mono carriage rigged against the side, halfway up, painted with a symbol that looks like the bastard offspring of the anarchy sign and a question mark. Anarchy? Shock tries to figure out what it means.

Is it asking if anarchy still exists? He thinks it does, but then again, what's anarchic about this life? Forced to live a certain way because normal society rejects you for your failure to pass a test, to conform.

He remembers the Pysch. Everyone does. Two hours of questions and reactions in a room where your every twitch is minutely recorded and catalogued against you. There's no cheating this test. For those who would not consider themselves anarchists the unexpected betrayal of a rebellious brain must be devastating.

Shock was always aware he'd Fail. He didn't really care. Working with Corps from the age of nine, he saw what their lives were like. The financial freedom disguising suffocating hierarchies and an impenetrable glass ceiling of Psych eval limitations often keeping those with brighter minds in duller jobs, allowing the unlimited advancement of the dull.

He didn't want that, knew that even if he scraped a Pass he'd be one of those bright minds leashed into a harness, held back, held down. It reminded him of being born in the wrong body, restrained by biology. He didn't ditch the tits to strap a desk to his chest. But he didn't want this either. This rootless, dangerous, paycheck-to-paycheck scramble at the mercy of criminals and psychopaths.

Perhaps that's what the symbol means. What's the point of anarchy when the society you live in can shove you into a box no matter how hard you rebel? He can't help but think that's why the system evolved. To contain the uncontainable. Limit the prospects of those with limitless capacity for thought, creativity and analysis. In which case, what the fuck has he been doing skirting the borders?

Simple, complicated, painful answer?

Given a choice, he chose not to choose. He chose Sendai, aware how impossible a dream that was. No Fail has ever lived in Sendai, and no Pass who stayed out of line long enough to be harnessed ever made it there either. It's a non-stance. Says: If I can't win, I won't play ball. But this is not ball, it's life. Look at how badly he's fucked it up.

Shock lifts his head, lets the rain slam into his face, hoping it will wake him on some deep, un-nameable level. Stir whatever spirit, whatever nerve he has remaining. Give him the fight he needs to make it through this. To get rid of Emblem, get off the Gung, and maybe start afresh on a hub, or even a land ship. If it means escape he can get over his fears, can't he?

Besides, he could learn a lot from those peripatetic land ships, moving between continental shards and scavenging scraps of civilization. Utilising the old to build the new. Isn't that how it's always done, the re-building of something broken? If that's so, he can do it too. Scavenge the scraps of himself worth keeping, the Shock he could have been, and rebuild a new Shock on those foundations. A better one.

It's an unusual determination, one he attributes to the continued presence of his avis, whose appropriated limo follows in their wake, silent and sleek. Funny that Shock can see it and Joon can't. Funny how secure that makes him feel, although he's still not entirely comfortable with these constant companions. Never being alone in his own head is quite the state to acclimatize to, and one of his selves being female is even harder. He feels both attached to and alienated from his deepest self.

Joon aims the cater-bike left, and into the long, low darkness of a block tunnel. Carved out through what would be extra apartment space for traffic flow between overpopulated portions of the Gung's provinces it takes them to the territory behind Sakkura, a neighbourhood Shock's entirely unfamiliar with, where slender blocks crowd together like ghoulish onlookers to some gruesome murder—probably his.

Painted a dizzying array of bright colours, they appear at first glance to be uniform, as though built to an architectural formula. Pass that momentary confusion and they reveal an array of unique designs. The only thing these buildings have in common are the eye-watering blocks of colour daubed from foundation to roof, and multitudes of balconies strung with plants and clothes. Some hold wary tenants, peering aggressively out through the rain at the racket of the cater-bike in quiet streets, that throaty bugle of unwelcome noise.

The narrowness of the streets between bright 'scrapers provokes vague recollections of a drunken conversation with Yani, his old study-bud. A year ahead of him at Tech, Yani scraped a Pass on his Pysch and was relegated to work as a courier. That last conversation in some shabby little bar in Shimli was unpleasant.

Yani knocking back straight-up gin with grim dedication, muttering about some crazy plan to jump the system. Go rogue. He'd convinced himself that he could live without ends meeting if he didn't have to meet the expectations of a life lived WAMOS. Shock wonders what the hell ever happened to him. He hopes Yani managed to do better than he has.

The cater-bike wobbles, throwing his shoulder dangerously close to a thick, filthy window on the ground floor of the nearest 'scraper. There's literally no room here, the blocks growing direct from either side of muddy strips of cracked concrete passing for both sidewalk and road. Shock leans forward, instinctive, trying to protect himself from possible harm. Yells into Joon's ear.

"Where are we?"

"Nanking," she shouts back.

Oh. Nanking. Not a place Shock has any desire to be. This grotty back-district is part of Yang's territory. There are no J-Hacks in Nanking. This is an overflow region, a densely populated adjunct to the main districts, scornful of amenities and probably an hour at least from the nearest district with schools, malls and hospitals. A residential hellhole, claustrophobic with misery. Living in such a place himself, Shock can't judge, but neither can he rustle up any good reason for Joon to bring him here.

Yeah, good, that's the pertinent word. Shock's warning sirens, ever slow to react, begin to sound somewhere deep in his overfull skull.

"Why here?"

"Short cut."

Why doesn't he believe her? Shock explores his connection with Puss, trying to get a bead on the limo. Puss is skirting around, hunting for a way back to wherever it is Joon might be going. That's when he knows she's done this on purpose. He could call Shark and Puss now, but they'd have to leave the limo to come to him, and then everyone will know where he is. Where they are.

It occurs to Shock that he's still not awake or aware. How is that? You'd think years of making the wrong decision would have armoured him against it. Not so. Clinging to Joon's jacket, he tries to work out a way he can get out of this. Whatever this is.

The conclusion he reaches does nothing to reassure him. Unless Shark exposes itself by getting out of the limo and coming to Shock's rescue should he need one, then he's fucked, and he's not risking Shark like that. His only hope at this point is that someone else tracking his signal will try to snatch him from Joon. Frying-pan-to-fire kind of hope, the sort that makes your bowels feel frisky, and boy do his feel frisky. He can't try to fight to get away either. The likelihood of that going well is slim to none. He's no fighter. He's a skinny, unfit loser, with a serious dependence on illegal substances.

My name is Shock Pao, he thinks, half amused, half despairing, and I am an addict. And an idiot.

De-throttling, the cater-bike growls, a lion in narrow streets warning other predators away. Joon and Shock dismount, helmet-less, Joon out of sheer reckless bravado, Shock because there was none to wear, and leave the bike cooling in the rain. At this point Shock could probably run. Probably. Joon's a giant by comparison. He runs, those excessive limbs of hers will catch him up in no time.

Puss radiates "keep cool" vibes from wherever she's waiting with the limo, somewhere outside of Nanking. Reminds him that if he doesn't know how to fix what's happened to them, or what this Emblem shit is all about, then who will? Even Twist didn't bank on this. Hell, he didn't even bank on the Queens cutting his arse out of the deal. In other words, they can damage him, but that's all. Shock's survived plenty of damage, he can survive more.

Full of the subtle, puke-inducing panic of the soul walking into certain danger, Shock follows Joon into a 'scraper clashing in peacock blue and orange so bright his eyes try to turn inside out to escape the glare. Through grubby doors, the lobby is grim, the lifts stuck open, revealing stained grey walls and shiny red floors littered with cans and psy butts. None of these buildings have janitors. Poor folk can't afford to fork out for such luxury, and the type of corporate interests who own areas like this don't much care about how their tenants get to and from their accommodations.

They take the stairs, naturally, though these stairs are anything but natural. Eighteen flights of full-on thigh-burning horror, set at a gradient Shock's convinced can't be necessary, not even in a building as anorexic as this. At the apparently correct floor Joon sails through the door with zero indication of having raced up the stair equivalent of a mountain. Shock not so much. He slumps on the wall, fighting for air. Joon's feet clomp back along the corridor. The door slams open. The wall groans. Joon snaps.

"Come on. Pussy."

Shock glares through his hair and manages to squeeze out, "Sexist bitch."

Leaning against the door to keep it open, Joon regards him with bland amusement.

"How? I have one, and you used to. If I want to use my own fucking parts in an insult, I will. You want to stop me, quit being so pathetic."

Straightening up against the pain, Shock staggers past her into the corridor.

"I'm not the pathetic one."

"Oh?"

"You think I don't know what this is?"

Joon laughs. "So run."

"Where? Where can I run? I needed help, Joon, not this shit. But I figure what the fuck, someone at some point is going to catch up with me. Let's see what they think they can do. I don't know what Emblem is now or what to do with it. It's just in here," he taps his head, "taking up all available space."

"Hey." She's unmollified, but the tone is somewhat gentler. "Look, I gotta make a living. I feel for you. Honestly. But I have pre-existing ties with Yang, and I got a good offer. I'm sure you'll be treated well enough. You're the fucking holy grail walking right now."

"I'm comforted. Really." Full sarcasm mode. Yang hates him.

She shrugs. "Be comforted or don't. Your choice."

Third corridor, walking the line. Feels like Death Row. Green Mile. Shock would drag his feet, but delaying the inevitable won't make it go away. Joon's fully aware her reassurance is cold comfort. Yang has no qualms about hurting anyone. Hurt isn't dead after all, and there's a lot he can do with Shock before he can't use him any more.

Besides, there's that whole hating him thing. The Twist debacle, as Shock likes to call it. Twist hires him for a big job. Major flim. Yang comes along at the eleventh hour and bribes Twist's shit away from Shock for even bigger flim—and honestly Shock does not make it that hard, being in full idiot mode.

Twist finds out quick smart what's gone down, sets Amiga on Shock and retaliates against Yang, hard. Beyond all logic Yang blames Shock for this, putting his own price out on Shock's head. Double trouble. Shock's busy counting his fingers, enjoying his toes. He's pretty sure he's going to leave here without some.

Striding ahead, Joon knocks a random-seeming tattoo of knuckles on one of the doors. It opens to reveal Yang's personal guard. The hulks. Goons with no necks and biceps like balloons. They step aside to allow him through, but when he's between them they lunge in and grab his arms, yanking them up and back.

His muscles explode with pain. Shock grunts, gritting his teeth and rising up on his toes to try to relieve the pressure. Somewhere miles away, he senses Puss's upset and Shark thrashing about, desperate to come rescue him.

Easy, easy, he sends down their connection. I'm okay.

Then there's a blade at his throat, and he's not actually sure he is.

"Shock. Here's a surprise. Yet again I find you carrying something for Twist Calhoun that I myself am in dire need of."

Yang.

Sat in the corner. His bulk resided in a grey leather chair that creaks with every movement. Yang was once rikishi. A Yokozuna. Part of the legendary Ineo stable, he was champion for seven years in a row before retiring to become the Chinese District's most feared and revered crime lord.

Yang is his rikishi name, one he chose for himself when he entered training at thirteen. No one knows his real name any more, perhaps not even Yang, and no one outside of China District knows much about him at all beyond public history, and that's exactly how he likes it.

"Is it really necessary to have the hulks restrain me?" Shock's on the wrong side of scared, but the one thing you never do is show your fear. Showing fear to these crime lords is like bleeding in front of a shark.

Yang's brows rise.

"You find this excessive?"

"A little. I'm no threat."

"Your shark is."

Shock chuckles. "I think Joon's seen to that problem."

"She's always had a good grasp of my requirements. It's why I continue to retain her services despite her inability to conduct herself in a manner becoming to her gender."

Out of the corner of his eye, Shock sees Joon's face blush vermilion. No pity. She shopped him, so she can take this BS right on her pert little nose for all he cares. Yang leans back into the plush leather of his chair and grins at Joon's discomfort. He likes to bait. He's akin to Li in that, but she's crueller. No words for her when actions will do more damage. In a way, Shock's glad it was Yang. He's neither as complex nor as devious as Twist or the Harmonys. He's a thug, straight up. No ice.

"How do you propose to get this out of my head then,

Yang?" Shock asks the ten-million-flim question, shifting against the pain in his arms.

Lifting his hands in a supremely careless shrug, Yang replies, "I propose that you'll do it for me, Haunt."

As answers go, Shock could've used that one to prove psychic abilities. He sighs, because he also knows that his response is unlikely to be believed.

"Sorry, man, genuinely. I can't. Dunno know how it's stuck in there, or how to work it, and definitely not how to get it out." He flexes each leg, the calves beginning to ache from standing on tiptoe; strives for time, for something to delay the moment Yang orders him tortured. "I know the Queens wanted me to have it though, they want it bad, and I suspect their drones are looking for it right now. How's your VA?"

Shock's actually not sure what the Queens can do. They're still in Hive and he's walking around with the lock in his head. Until they get hold of it they're stuck inside Slip with no way out, and not his main concern despite their drones and their obvious influence IRL.

It's everyone else he's worried about at the moment. He anticipates maybe another twenty minutes, probably less, before someone else has a fix on this exact building, this very room, and comes after him. He's beginning to feel like a chew toy in a room full of terriers.

"Adequate." Is Yang's response. Terse. Tinged with cold humour. That's when Shock knows Yang is not going to wait. Yang nods at Joon. "Your recompense is in the usual account."

Joon sidles out, sparing Shock an apologetic glance he scorns. She doesn't care. No one does. Not that Shock would in her shoes. It's just business, and as usual Shock's working for the wrong people. He makes no sound as they drag him through that dark hollow into the next room. Shit. It's exactly what he knew it would be. One chair, a ton of plastic, and a woman known only as Pill. And nobody likes taking her medicine. She studies him as he's dragged in, stripped of his jacket and shirt, and secured to the chair.

"Skinny," she states, to no one in particular.

Yang appears in the doorway.

"Make him talk. We need to know about Emblem, how it works."

"Are we in a hurry?"

"No," Yang says, and offers Shock another of those brief, cold smiles, faintly smug. "We're well protected. You can take as long as you like."

Those words might be a blatant lie, and Shock might be fully aware of that, but that doesn't stop his heart from stuttering, slipping, and sinking into his boots.

cavalry on blades

Wearing Deuce's homemade hyper-goggles—multi-functioning J-Net connected smartware—Amiga blades at double-time speed to Sakkura on Shock's heels, fuming at her stupid self. And at Shock, the idiot, who's in serious need of help right now. Lucky for him, he has a cavalry. Unlucky for him, she's running late. But she has a solid plan. Sneak in signal dark, snatch Shock from wherever he is, whether he's willing or not, and whisk him away to Jong Phu.

Deuce is tracking Shock by his signal. He's got her blocked from it, much to her annoyance, convinced she can't do this and handle that. Oh he of little faith. Once they have Shock secure, Deuce says he can hide the signal noise temporarily with some hands-on help from his buds. Then they'll figure out what the hell do to with Shock now he's achieved the impossible.

Amiga fumes a little harder at the thought. Trust that fucking idiot to actually pull this off. Why couldn't he pull his usual stunt and run for it? Jeez you can't even rely on people to be unreliable.

Amiga.

Wobbling like a drunken bird, Amiga manages to stay on the line, stay alive, but her heart damn near gives out, pumping hard enough to pop.

'Sup boss?

I have a runaway I need lassoing.

She was wondering when the shit-tsunami might hit. Stellar.

Wouldn't be anything to do with the images on every vid feed in the Slip, would it?

It would.

Amiga rolls her eyeballs hard enough to braid her optic nerves. Typical. Now she has to try to wriggle out of obligation.

Shock Pao again, Twist? No freaking way. He's a nightmare. He's fucking smoke.

He's got something of mine.

Twist is furious. Serves him right. Doubtless he's tried to double-cross the Queens, a level of stupid she thought only losers like Shock Pao could hit. If only they could crush Twist flat. Oh what she wouldn't give for such an easy way out of her current employment issues.

Again, he's smoke. I'm not a freaking magician.

He's not smoke at the moment, says Twist, grim satisfaction underlying the heavy lashings of aggro in his tone. He's in Sakkura. I'll link you. Heads up, his signal's a bit strange.

She's about to reply when the link-up hits, making her feet stutter again, lose their rhythm. Fuck, no wonder Deuce blocked her from this shit. Shock's signal is like a dropped mic, all high screeching feedback and white noise. Feels like sickness: that shudder in the bones, the nausea in the pit of the belly. Where's anti-bac for the drive when you need it?

Twist's voice slices into her thoughts, Move it, Amiga,

and when you have him, bring him straight to me. I don't like to be kept waiting.

At your home?

Where else? He says it like it's the simplest thing in the world to escort a wanted man to Sendai when the Gung's most vicious bastards are all after him.

Jim Dandy, she snaps as he cuts her off.

Such confidence she'll obey, that it'll even be possible. Ordinarily she'd have to try nonetheless, but there's that tiny matter of this being Emblem and therefore not the sort of delivery she'd ever drop into Twist's hands. All she has left are her principles, withered and ill used, but enough to prevent her from sinking quite that low. Before this moment, refusing Twist was a dangerous enough task. Now? Lethal to her health. To the health of everyone she cares about.

Freaking out hard, Amiga whips along the line. Shock's twenty minutes ahead of her on a small vehicle, possibly a bike, and moving fast toward Sakkura's border. Amiga's got a horrible feeling about that. He should take the outskirts, head for some of Sakkura's safe houses, but he won't. As if to prove her point, his vehicle hits the border, and keeps going. Deuce cannons into her IM, radiating alarm.

Shock's left Sakkura. I thought he'd follow the limits but he went straight through to Nanking. Yang's territory.

I know, Deuce. Something's bugging her about it being Nanking, and not just the whole Yang/Twist super-rivalry thing either.

How?

Twist.

Oh fucking hell. Do you need to drop out of this?

Not. Even. I'm good. He linked me to Shock's signal though, and it's horrendous. You got anything for horrendous?

Fuck's sake, Amiga. Sure. IMing a signal damper and some stronger VA for your drive. The VA will not feel nice, but that's tough shit. Use it. Stay safe.

Not nice. Understatement. The damper works a charm, she can hear Shock without feeling him, but the VA takes over from that discomfort. Sitting like wire wool in the head, poking painful, imaginary loose ends into the soft matter of her brain. Gritting her teeth, Amiga tries to focus only on the movement of her blades, and that's when it hits her. Not a metro. Something worse.

I know why he's in Nanking, she tells Deuce.

Oh?

Joon Bug.

Shock knows Joon Bug?

Well duh. Haunts. Top level. Of course he does.

I thought he didn't mingle.

Not often, which means I'm pretty sure he doesn't know that she's affiliated with Yang, or he wouldn't be with her right now.

Clusterfuck much? Yang won't kill him though. Pretty sure Emblem's not extractable at the moment, especially not from a dead man.

Doesn't matter. Pill works for Yang, remember? I'm twenty minutes behind. She can do things in twenty minutes that will make Shock wish he were dead.

Deuce has no response to that, there's nothing to say, and Amiga has more immediate problems than Shock's predicament. An urgent need to get onto the Nanking lines if she wants to reach him before he's too damaged to move without a stretcher. There's no junction at this point, of course there wouldn't be, that'd be easy, or suspiciously convenient, but there are several places where the Nanking line veers close enough to jump if you're insane, desperate and lacking in sense.

"I'm not," she mutters to herself, through chattering teeth. "Oh hell, I am."

Ignoring the fact that twice is not a habit, even if it's within the space of a week, Amiga puts on a burst of speed as the Nanking line appears in the distance. Just like jumping over to the drone, it's plain stupidity, but she had no time to think about that, and she has no time to think about this. The jump is long, roughly fifty metres, over a drop so high the ground's hidden under cloud, but she doesn't dwell on it. Think without thinking, that's the trick, and it's something Cleaners learn to do early on, or they have very short careers. Amiga's been at this a long-arse time.

Disengaging her magnets at full speed, she leaps, paying little attention to the sudden screaming of a system thrown into panic mode by the loss of solid ground. The line seems too far and she spends the first few seconds convinced that she'll never reach it, convinced that death is the obvious consequence of her actions. Her perspective changes in what seems like a heartbeat. Too far away to right fucking there, solid and unassailable, and she lets out a scream, unprepared. Instinctively, her hands fly up to protect her from impact—and instinct saves her too.

Use bladers enough and controlling them becomes a reflex. Her drive switches the magnets on full strength the moment her legs flip toward the fast approaching line. The magnets attract, pulling her in at triple speed to reconnect. Impact hurts every bone and muscle in her legs; her knees groaning as propulsion and magnetic hold collide, flinging her face first toward the unforgiving strip of solid steel. Wheeling her arms to prevent collision, she hears the angry whine of the next mono shrieking at her rear. Amiga shrieks with it and pushes off against the traction in the soles of her bladers, opting for speed over balance and hoping it works.

It's ugly, n00b graceless, but she finds her stride in a series of awkward full body jerks and shoots off, the headwind rushing before the mono giving her a welcome boost. Unable to look back and check, all she can do is gamble on having enough space to disembark the line when she needs to without being flattened. In her head, amidst the haywire sparking of a brain barely out of crisis, she still has that lock on Shock's scrambled signal: until it disappears.

Deuce!

I know. On it. He's been blocked but it's amateur-hour stuff.

How long until everyone else breaks this and pinpoints his position?

Depends on the quality of their Tech team. Less than thirty mins for sure. There. Back.

The signal comes back so abruptly she hisses. But she knows where they are now. This line won't get her there, and she hasn't time to follow it around and switch to the other circle line, the one winding through Nanking's centre within spitting distance of the very building Shock's inside. After the next three stops, she'll have to get off and run. In bladers. Typical. Amiga snarls into the wind.

"Bastard."

It takes ten excruciating minutes, blasting ahead of the mono on brutal headwinds and aching legs. Judging it to the millisecond, she disengages her bladers and jumps off at the fourth platform, the mono whining to a stop at her back, the pressure of it throwing her forward, blasting her hair around her face. Close. Too close. She takes the shoot down, and hits the sidewalk sprinting, wincing at the sound of bladers on concrete. They really aren't made for this. Not that they'll break. But her ears might. Possibly her ankles too.

Nanking has all the appeal of a crowded mono cabin. The air's cold but thick, and nigh on unbreathable. With all these tiny alleys and pathways squeezed between 'scrapers, she'd have thought wind would find a way through, but it's obviously an unwelcome visitor here. She can relate. Following Shock's signal as fast as she can in these stupid boots, she tries not to think about what he's going through. His signal's so screwed it all sounds like pain, and trying to figure out what's Emblem and what's Pill will only slow her down.

There's no bike outside the building, meaning Joon Bug's gone. No surprises there. Joon's not the type to be around violence unless she's handing it out. Casually strolling past to nip down the side alley, Amiga checks the time. She's taken more than she thought getting here. Shit.

Deuce.

Here. What's up?

I'm by the building. His signal still blocked to the others?

He hesitates, and in that tiny pause she reads the worst before he even says it.

He's been visible on all freqs for over five minutes. You need to move. There's one hell of a crowd headed your way.

"Gee, thanks for the heads up," she mutters, though there was no point telling her till now. It's not like she could have bladed harder, or run faster.

Cramming her hands into her gloves, designed to muffle sound on top of all their other clever tricks, Amiga leaps for the lowest fire-exit balcony. Scales the staircase with swift, economical grace. Outside the correct floor she pauses for a second, using Deuce's goggles to link with every other signal in the building. Yang's got about 150 troops inside, patrolling in pairs. Joy.

She clicks on her dart gun. Damn thing carries barely

any ammo, but it's the easiest way to avoid hand-to-hand combat. If she's injured there's no way she's getting Shock to safety. She's got to get him out of here first anyway, and there's no way out but the way she's come in, which will play havoc with whatever damage Pill's done.

"This is the real world, he'll have to deal if he wants out," she mutters furiously, attaching a small rappelling line to the balcony. She peers over. Once they're down, they can get out the back way, but after that...

Deuce I need a schematic, preferably adaptive. I've got to get Shock back to Jong-Phu through whatever hell is on the way.

I'll see what I can do.

Don't see, just do. Clock's ticking, she snaps.

You know I will. I've got a temp block to put on Shock, too. I won't use it until you're out, because it won't last long or save you from immediate attack, only shield you from prying eyes once you're away. Twenty mins to half hour max. His signal is continuing to ramp up. Be careful, Amiga. His tone is calming, sends waves of guilt washing over her, but there's no time to apologize and he wouldn't need her to, which makes her feel worse.

Amiga breaks in as softly as she climbed. Cleaners have all sorts of skills, and apart from murder, breaking into things is arguably her finest. Expecting to hear Shock screaming or otherwise responding to Pill's work, she's deeply concerned by the silence. Has Pill gone too far already? Moving off down the corridor, primed to act, she hears distant gunfire, followed by shouts from downstairs. That'll be the crowd Deuce mentioned. Oh smart, let everyone know you're on the way in before you arrive. Twist would never stand for it, that's why he's sent her. One Cleaner to do the job of an army.

"I am in such deep shit," she says, flattening herself into

a doorway as guards from all floors thunder down to the lower levels.

Yang won't have left Shock unguarded, which is a problem. Amiga will need to be long gone before they find the bodies. In this situation, with warfare on his doorstep, Yang will avoid alerting others to Shock's escape. He'll send a maximum ten of his people after her, no more, but she hasn't time to dispense with that many, not whilst protecting Shock. Everything depends on speed.

She finds her way to Shock as much by smell as the scrambled wail of his signal: the thick, metal tang of his blood hangs like smog outside the room. Amiga holds the back of her hand up to her nose and scans briefly. Yeah, Yang's favourite heavies are inside. Time to do her job. Bracing, she snaps her foot at the handle, smashing the door open, the noise drowned out by the gunfire and shouting from below.

Yang's heavies run at her, pulling guns from holsters strapped against their ribs. She lifts her arm, downs them with two precise darts, one through each right eye. Pill's directly behind them; serene, swift, and blood spattered, wielding what look like serrated saws for rib separation. With no time for artistry, or darts, Amiga ploughs forward, grabbing both the torturer's arms and driving her forehead into that bland, bloodied face with everything she's got. Fight dirty, fight quick, she learnt that in her first week of Cleaner training.

Pill grunts, staggers, and drops to the floor, shedding her blades like leaves. Amiga assesses the situation. Guards dead, good. Pill out cold, which is a shame. Amiga has a rule: she won't kill the helpless, but she boots Pill in the head for good measure, twice, and goes through to collect Shock. One look at him tells her how hard the next bit is going to be.

"Oh for fuck's sake. You're a mess."

Secured to a chair with plastic ties, he's half naked and drenched in blood; his head drooping onto his chest, tangling dyed hair into red gore. She flicks out a knife and goes to cut him loose, kneeling between his legs. Up close the damage is eye watering. Six missing fingertips, no nails, significant bruising to the torso, arms and neck, and cuts fucking everywhere. Amazing how many times you can cut a body before it gives out.

For a moment she worries about his silence. His chest is rising but he seems unconscious. Then he raises his head slowly to look at her. Above a battered nose, bright blue eyes shine luminous with pain. Good god but those are some eyes. He grins, showing gaps and bloodstained teeth. Awake then. Alert too. Good.

"Amiga Tanaka. Here to finish what you couldn't before?" His voice is thin and cracked. Well shit, she never guessed he might've clocked her that first time she hunted him. What is he, a wizard?

"Not here for that, sport. I'm the cavalry."

He sneers. "Twist's cavalry? Thanks, I'll pass."

"Not Twist. Hornets."

He stares at her, those blue eyes searching her face like spotlights.

"For real?"

"For real. That thing in your head does not belong with anyone like Twist."

"No. No it doesn't."

It's obvious he still doesn't trust her, but he's relaxed a little bit. How the hell do you relax with that much damage shrieking in your nerves?

"I see Pill had fun with you."

"Am I still pretty?"

"Were you ever?"

He coughs out a laugh, and crimson dribbles down his chin. His face is far too pale beneath the mask of blood.

Finishing with the ties, she braces her arms either side of him.

"Are you good to walk?"

He looks at his legs. "She used a hammer, I think."

"Feet or thighs?"

"Thighs."

Amiga examines his legs, digging right in to feel past muscle. No broken bones. He doesn't react either, which is unusual.

"You're fucked up, but they'll work." He seems unconvinced, so she gets good and close. "If you want to get out of here, with the one person who may actually be intent on helping you rather than using you, I'd make an effort to move." Harsh words, but there's no time for sympathy.

"Then fucking help me up." His response is no less harsh, and she sees that he already knew. She didn't expect that.

Shock Pao should be what you find in a dictionary under "waste of space"; jaded and junked up, with a knack for fucking up. She wouldn't have bet a single unit he'd have a whiff of chutzpah, or any of that rarely seen sense they call common, as if calling it such can conjure it forth where it so grievously lacks. Then again, boy's from Korea-town, the rabbit warrens, and was born a girl, so it kinda figures he'd have grown somewhat of a carapace, gathered some street smarts. He should use them more.

"C'mon then." Amiga wraps an arm around his chest, and braces.

He relaxes into the pain as she pulls him up out of the chair, which, again, rather like his non-reaction to her feeling his bones, is the exact opposite to normal. That shouldn't affect her, but it does, so does his silence, and two clicks together with two, making formative trauma. Now she understands why she heard no screaming: he's used to pain like this. Fuck, that's actually a bit heartbreaking. Draping his arm over her shoulders, she supports him as he breathes through the adjustment, clearly fighting the urges his body has to up and quit on him now he's vertical.

"Ready?"

He nods, and helps her help him by trying his best to hold some of his own weight. She admires that. Unfortunately he's fighting a losing battle, and she's forced to haul him to the window and shove him through. He collapses against the balcony, head dangling again, eyes drooping shut. He can't go on, and they've a long way to go. The only way you can help an addict in this predicament is by feeding the addiction. Problematic, and against those withered principles of hers. However, on balance, Amiga finds the evil a necessary one. She snaps out a couple of high-quality bumps, presses them into his neck.

He side-eyes a query.

"I don't normally enable," she says, by way of explanation, "but you're tapping out and we don't have time for it." She ties the rappel line around his chest and groin into a makeshift harness. "This is going to hurt like fuck, but if you make a sound, we'll die."

He offers her those neon blues, filled with pupils wide as deranged grins, and nods assent. Working quickly, she levers him over, and lets go. He doesn't make a sound.

Following him down by hand, dropping gently from balcony to balcony, Amiga carries on worrying nonetheless. That bump high is acting in opposition to a total body shut down from blood loss and trauma. In other words, it will not last.

On the ground, the sound of bullets resonates through

the alley like the throaty hacking of a tramp. Dragging Shock behind the fire escape, she untangles him from the rappel wire.

Deuce pops into her IM. Silent. Just a nod, and the schematic she asked for. It's a long way round, has to be, to avoid the fight escalating out front, but way too long for Shock to make it, and any minute now, any second, someone is going to think to check on Pill and find Shock gone. Amiga spends about ten seconds in full-on, free-fall panic. Then it hits her. She looks up.

"Ever blade-surfed?" she murmurs to Shock, her eyes fixed on the distant ribbon of the metro.

going underground...

hey make it down two alleys and across two streets without Yang's clean-up crew on their heels. Not the kind of luck that lasts. Shock's leaving a clear trail of bright red breadcrumbs too, which can't be helped but makes Amiga downright twitchy. Beyond the second alley, she clocks the mono entrance. It's a few hundred metres up to their left. So damn close.

Half carrying Shock, who's stumbling like a liver-whore, she digs deep and speeds up to a run. Literally seconds from safety, their luck collapses in an entirely unexpected direction. A peppering of bullets hits the 'scraper next to Shock, showering his hair and bloodied chest with grey brick dust. Amiga dodges toward the road, yelling out in fury.

"Are they honest to shit actually shooting at you?"

Unable to believe it, she risks a swift, disbelieving glance over her shoulder, spotting brief flutters of movement in the alley. Another volley of shots strike the sidewalk behind Shock's feet. Okay, so they're not stupid enough to shoot at him, but close is too close and she doesn't give these dingbats much credit. Odds are on one of them missing the mark and hitting Shock by accident or ricochet. That'll be game over.

Gritting her teeth, Amiga hauls Shock to the elevator, trying to anticipate and avoid the bullets pinging all around them. As she waves a hand over the sensor, the firing ceases, replaced by the pounding of feet. She turns to assess the situation. Ten of Yang's troops, out of the alley and catching up fast. Of course it would be ten. Sometimes she could stab shit out of her loudmouth brain and its self-fulfilling prophecies. How's she supposed to fight ten with Shock in her arms? She checks her dart supply. Three.

"Hate to tell you this," she mutters through her teeth, "but we are so screwed."

In answer to unspoken prayers, the elevator doors sigh open. Amen to that. Dragging Shock inside, she shields him with her body as Yang's people, scary close now, pull out their guns and begin firing at her. Priorities straight at last. Joy. If only her long-term luck as a Cleaner could hold out. It doesn't, of course. A bullet ricochets off the metal of the doors as they close, striking clean through her leg and impacting the bulletproof plas-glas with a crack loud enough to hurt her teeth. She staggers, catching herself on the sides as the elevator sets off.

"You okay?" Shock sounds exhausted, his voice a blurry remnant. He's got about ten minutes of good consciousness left. Maybe fifteen if he hangs onto that high like the good little junkie she knows him to be.

Amiga takes a moment to get stable, and examines her wound. Clean shot, no bone impact, but blood is beginning to ooze in a thick stream out of both entry and exit wounds. Fuck. She tears a strip off her tee, tying it around her thigh, tight enough to hurt like hell.

"I'll live. How you holding up?"

"Kinda not..."

She turns to find him slumped against the side, bleeding all over the plas-glas. Not enough tee strips in the world to tourniquet that lot.

"Jeez, dude, you're a fucking state."

"You keep saying it like it's going to change." He lifts his head a fraction as high-pitched whining vibrates into the elevator. Despair clouds the shine of bump high in his eyes. "Mono," he says, though they both know what it is. What it means.

Amiga closes her eyes. What does she do now? She leans to look for Yang's troops. They're on the narrow stairs, running up two at a time. Plans have a way of screwing themselves up when it's least convenient. Lucky she's adaptable. Lucky she's had to be. Funny how it's never felt particularly lucky. Not even now, when it's useful.

"We need to get on that mono. C'mon."

Stepping across to Shock, she pulls him up, her muscles protesting, her leg throbbing bite-sized chunks of raw pain. Designed to self-adjust speed in transit when a mono is approaching, the elevator arrives just as the mono does. There are maybe eight other people waiting. They ignore Amiga and Shock. This is Yang's territory; violence and bloodshed are things that happen. But when Yang's troops hit the last rise of stairs with guns firing, the waiting folk hit the deck, leaving Amiga and Shock fully exposed as the doors slide open.

"Gonna push you again," Amiga says to Shock, dragging him to the mono doors and offering an entirely redundant, "Sorry."

Shoving him into the end carriage, she jumps in behind and wrestles him along by the belt of his trousers. She dumps him behind a pair of seats at the back. The occupants gape at her, and she smiles, places a finger over her mouth as she turns, stance low, to take whoever comes aboard. Six of Yang's troops make it before the doors close. Two of them into their carriage.

The mono lurches out of the station and they barrel straight for her, using the mono's momentum to barge through the crowded aisle, knocking screaming passengers to the floor. One of them: short, stocky, covered in tattoos, fires his gun wildly. Hits a passenger huddled in his seat, using a briefcase as a shield. He jerks and slides to the floor, curled over his case, and the carriage implodes panic, seething out into the next carriage, not realizing or not caring that there are four more of Yang's troops ahead.

Taking advantage of the moment, the other soldier, a woman, makes a beeline for Amiga and tries to shoot her in close quarters. Scooting to the side, Amiga tucks into her personal space, pressing her wrist up against the edge of the woman's armoured vest. One dart under the ribs shreds her heart and she collapses in slow-mo, face still set into a snarl, her second bullet going wide, through the roof, leaving a ragged hole for wind to whistle through. Sounds jaunty. Bizarre.

Grabbing her armoured vest as she falls, Amiga rams the woman backward through the carriage and into her partner. Shouting, he lunges out, his finger trigger-happy as ever. Amiga gets there first, calm and easy. Pops a dart through his neck casual as you please, leaving a gaping hole. He doesn't realize he's dead, and the look on his face as he topples is priceless. Amiga yanks his gun from his hand, kicking him aside to finish dying amongst the seats as two more of Yang's troops enter the carriage.

Ducking down out of sight, she takes them out with the stolen gun. Swift, economic shots to the head. Bullet whiplash. Like the woman and her partner they're dead before they even realize, and now there're only two left, struggling through the mass of passengers to get to her. Going about it possibly the worst way ever, guns out and firing, as if that ever pacified a crowd. Not in Nanking. Not in many places in the Gung to be honest.

"Hang on in there," she mutters to Shock, to the dizziness invading her head. Blood loss is no fun. "Hang the fuck on."

Amiga checks the gun. Four bullets left. It's a piece of crap, though. Disposable. Probably printed. These things aim for shit over anything longer than a few metres, meaning the bullets earlier were indeed meant for her and the shot to her thigh was pure chance. If she wants to take out the other two without further injury to herself, she has to wait for them to come in, and they're taking their time. They've quit firing too, which is interesting. Probably clocked the fact that the others are dead.

She has one dart left. Use it, or save it?

No thought required. One arsehole with a gun is easier to handle than two.

Utilizing Deuce's goggles again, which she may never give back, she cops the sights on a sweet shot and takes out the bigger one, enjoying the reaction of the one left. Honestly, people forget there's a difference between being a general thug and a paid killer. Swift and quiet, she makes her way back to Shock. He's still going, just about. Thank fuck he knows how to hang on to a high.

"Two stops to go," she says, trying to offer a little boost, knowing it's worth nothing with him dying by degrees and all too aware of it. "Your limo waiting?"

He nods. Murmurs, "Shark's angry."

"Will it eat me?"

"Don't know."

"Comforting."

"How many left?"

"One."

"Impressive."

She shrugs. "It's my job."

He laughs, and more blood dribbles out of his mouth, down his chest. If it doesn't stop soon he'll have none left.

"Hell of a job."

"Dude, I'm not the one avis out, carrying hell on a stick in my head and cut half to fuck."

"Tou-fuckin'-che."

He grins at her like a lunatic. She finds herself grinning back. Crap, she genuinely likes the fuck-up. When will she learn? Protecting her own back is a full-time job in itself; she needs to stop collecting other backs to protect. Mind you, stupid and reckless he might be, but the boy has heart, same as her Hornets, and she'd rather have friends like this than friends like Twist. Twist, and people like him, have done nothing but blight her life. Survival is not worth that shit.

Drones gathering, Shock says into her IM, out of nowhere.

"What?" She looks over at him. He's slumped, head back, eyes closed. Not out yet, but no juice left for vox.

Puss says there're loads of them headed for Sakkura. The back end. Aren't your friends there?

Amiga rises a little, wary of Yang's remaining soldier, and looks out.

Can't see anything.

They're almost there, he replies softly.

Her immediate thought pattern bypasses any notion of Queenly interference and strikes a jackpot on the drone they stole, her fears about the collective tracing it to the Hornets. No other thoughts manage to enter her mind after that, they'd have to wade through a rising sea of blind panic and the dead certainty that she's right and they've been busted at the worst possible time. Sod and his law, how very helpful.

Deuce! Get out of there now!

On it, Amiga. We clocked 'em.

Is it the drone we stole?

Goddamn it, Amiga, as if. This is Queens trying for collateral. We need somewhere safe to go, and fast. Somewhere the Haunt will be safe. That block I put on him is all but done. Any ideas?

Helplessness rises, drowning her from inside out. Shit. Where do they go? The only people she can honestly say she trusts at this moment are about to suffer extreme close-up from sec-drone fire. She needs to get everyone to safety. But where's safe? Then it occurs to her she's only recently been somewhere so secret maybe only she and two others know about it.

Mollie's.

More precisely, the server beneath. Shin's an hour and a half away by the shortest route. Can they get there, get safe, before they're caught? They have to try.

Shin District, the B-Movies. There's a square near the BatCave. Fountain. Has a new place called Mollie's. Go there. Find Maggie Joust, tell her Amiga sent you. Take EVaC, likely he will get you in more than my name.

EVaC's already benefitted from Maggie's help—some drug that though it isn't curing him is making him one hell of a lot more comfortable—and he's about to again. Amiga hopes to fuck Maggie doesn't mind.

Done. Just make sure you're...

He's gone. Cut off.

Deuce!

For a moment, nothing.

Then he snaps back. They're firing. We're outta here.

You deal with you, don't worry about us.

And he's gone again before she can reply.

Trying not to think about what's happening at Jong-Phu, she turns her attention to Shock. He's frighteningly pale and quiet. If she gives him a bump now it won't hold him to the limo, no matter how close it is. Best wait. Deal with the situation as it stands. That last soldier of Yang's for instance.

The first of their two stops is approaching. If Amiga were Yang's man, she'd use what'll be a mass passenger exodus to attack. Well fuck that, how about she attacks now and saves him the trouble? If he's dead their chances of making it to the limo increase by a factor of no fucking bullets. Besides, she needs to kill something. Every nerve is screaming.

Slipping out along the seats, ignoring the protest of her damaged thigh, she flips down Deuce's goggles to check for heat signatures. The guy's still hunkered down near the door of the other carriage. If she had any darts left, she could take him out no sweat. But no point dwelling on the impossible, she's going to have to provoke a hand to hand, or a shoot out. Fun. Amiga swiftly checks her leg, just to be sure. Still bleeding. Best not get hit again then. Easy. What she wouldn't give for a bullet-retardant body suit right now.

"Halle-fucking-luyah," she mutters, edging closer to the door, one row of seats at a time.

Her advantage here is that Yang's soldier's got no goggles, no mods, and Deuce has her blocked more thoroughly than Shock. That covers her until she reaches the doors and they slide open, giving away her position. Yang's soldier starts firing immediately, over the top of the seats. Throwing herself forward and down, Amiga rolls in, comes up firing herself.

There's no clean shot, he's got his head tucked down, his torso protected by the seats. So she takes off his hand, two ugly but serviceable shots to the wrist. Limping down the remaining corridor to his hiding place she ignores his screams for mercy. Puts him out of his misery with a single shot. Swift. Cold. Slick. Her job description in words of one syllable.

At the platform, the mono empties out a stream of silent passengers. No one else boards. They all know better. None of Yang's troops are waiting either, but Amiga allows no relief. They could be at the next platform, waiting to ambush them. She checks all remaining guns, taking any with more than one bullet and stashing them in her pack, and fetches Shock, supporting him to the doors.

Their stop is deserted, a fact that does zip all for her confidence. At street level she presses another bump into Shock's neck, praying it won't kill him. As it hits, blowing his pupils wide, Deuce's block wears off and Shock's effed up signal rolls back into her awareness, silent but deadly. She grits her teeth hard against the urge to scream.

"Limo. Now."

Shock inclines his head to the left, throwing a small schematic into her head with the exact spot. Blanking the pain and growing weakness in her thigh, she takes his weight and they set off at a pace more dangerously slow than she's comfortable with, considering he's a beacon for trouble and trouble is not far away.

The limo's parked in a side road, just beyond the border. Damn near faint with relief, or blood loss, Amiga opens the door and heaves Shock inside, wincing as his battered body falls across the seats, spattering blood on the upholstery, the dash and into the footwell. One and a half hours to Shin. There's no way he's surviving that long.

Climbing in carefully after him, she flinches backward as

Shark's nose batters the dividing window in her direction, its vast mouth a golden cavern filled with rows of teeth. There are gobbets of flesh stuck between them, the meat-red outrageous against the purity of Shark's gold. How the fuck is it trapped in there? It's a hologram. She should be meaty human goodness right now, considering this hologram can apparently chow down. Thank fuck she's not. But she cannot, will not, deal with that thrashing all the way to Shin District.

"Sort that fucking beast out," she snaps.

Shock doesn't move, or acknowledge her, but Shark quits battering the window. Amiga nods.

"Right. Get that octopus to hide you in the damn limo and get us the fuck to Shimli."

I can't hide him. He's vibrating beyond a frequency the limo's connection to Slip can cover.

The reply is musical, hums like electricity and static in her mind, making her blink, sit back hard in her seat. Was that Shock? She checks him. Out cold. Her eyes shift to the octopus. Find it watching her. A direct gaze filled with such life, such personality, Amiga all but recoils, because avis aren't fucking real. They're not anything. They're imprints. Golden masks, if that.

I haven't time to muscle past your prejudices, Octopus informs her acidly. We are currently fucked to a monumental degree.

Talking? It's talking? What the...? Amiga blows out. Tries to speak. Fails. Tries again. You er... But... Shock's out of commission... She feels crazy. Yeah, definitely crazy. Talking to an avi. Certifiable.

There's a brief sputtering noise in her IM. Laughter?

If we follow that logic, Octopus replies, then I could not possibly be functioning enough to drive a limo.

That's a point and a half. As Shock said earlier: tou-fuckin'-che.

So you're not Shock then?

We are both Shock and not Shock. We are three iterations of the same person acting as both individuals and a singular, united entity.

Is Emblem doing that?

No.

There's that moment when you drop something when you know it's going to smash into a million pieces all over the floor. You get this pinch in the intestines as you anticipate the noise, the mess, the hours of clean up. So it goes with Amiga's preconceptions. In shattering they make a mess she imagines it will take years to clean up. She should have been braced for this, but even with everything she's learnt over the past few days she's still hanging on to whatever ignorance she can find. Stupid really, Amiga was never going to find her bliss. Not in this lifetime.

So you're...

Alive. Yes.

Is Shark?

Yes, although he's more… instinct than consciousness. He's a tool, I am a gestalt, but we are both still beings. Okay with that? Ready to move on to the fuckage?

Wow, Puss is one acid-tongued, straight-talking SOB. Amiga can dig that.

Yup. Moving on. Fuckage. Go.

All activity at Yang's current HQ mobilized in our direction as soon as the block broke.

Can we outrun them?

No.

Shit. ETA?

Even at top speed, they are currently due to intercept within minutes. Their vehicles are faster.

I have no guns. The ones she took are less than useless in this situation.

This vehicle is bullet proof, even the tyres will withstand barrage, but they will surround us. We are out of options.

Shark?

If Shark is damaged at this moment, Shock will die, he's too weak to cope with the loss. That is why we have remained separate until now; we were maximizing our chances of surviving and therefore maximizing his.

Ah.

As I said, we are fucked to a monumental degree.

Note to self: Puss does not do exaggeration. Good to know. Amiga peers out the side window, spies the shit-ton of cars speeding into view, catching up too quickly. Within range for guns clearly not made with a printer, their windows slide down and they begin to fire. Experiencing that catastrophic elevator crash of the vitals as bullets begin to pepper the road around them, Amiga finds her mind capable of only one single thought: Exactly how long do bullet-proof tyres hold out?

monumentally fucked

As it happens, Amiga doesn't get to answer her question. The bullets cease and four of the cars in pursuit manoeuvre to intimate positions on all sides, their windows gliding upward.

"Oh hell no!"

Amiga scoots back at double speed, hitting the belt button with her foot and taking firm grip of Shock. Just in time. The cars surrounding them move in concert, slamming metal elbows into their front, back and sides. Crunching the limo between them, a car compactor formed of cars. And the noise is excruciating, hits her body the way the sound of Shock's drive agony hits her mind.

She hunkers low in the seat, enduring it all, cradling him her lap. It's all she can do. It's not enough. He's bleeding again, not only from the heavy impacts shaking him around, but from the simple fact of her hands on his skin. She doesn't know what else to do to help him. This has never happened before, this helplessness. Cleaners always have a back-up plan, a way out, that's their job, that's her job. Get it done, get away clean. Where's her clean getaway?

Inside, she's screaming frustration. She wants weapons, some kind of fucking firepower, a way to fight back. There is none. Only the persistent thunder of collision. And blood. Way too much blood. Shock's and hers.

Amiga. You have my Haunt. Why is he not in my possession?

Twist's voice in her IM usually drops a shot of liquid ice into her guts, so Amiga's surprised to find fury bubbling up, hot and ugly. How fucking dare he? She's not some lackey, fulfilling a duty. Following orders won't magically erase the epic shit mountain she's straddling the peak of, enabling her to jolly along to Sendai and casually drop Shock into Twist's lap. Like she would anyway. Even if handing over Emblem were not ninety-nine percent of the problem, she wouldn't give Shock to Twist.

That pulls her up short.

She hasn't had a moment since Breaker yanked her through her IM to contemplate why she made the choice to follow shrivelled principles and protect this boy. Didn't consider where the choice came from, what insane impulse drove it. Because there's nothing sensible about it. In her position what she's doing is a surefire death sentence, more certain than cracking Twist's vault ever was. But she's set. At peace with the outcome. What's changed to make her feel that way? She's not suicidal. She wants to get out of this alive.

Amiga. You know how unwise it is to ignore me.

There's that tone again. Oh and the anger to follow, sharp as indigestion. Closing her eyes, Amiga breathes through it, surprised by how much it hurts. She's so full. There's not one millimetre of her that this anger does not reside in. It's as if by stepping outside of the path she chose, she's opened herself wide to everything she ignored to stay on it, and she's so fucking sick. Sick to death of Twist, of being his hands, of doing his dirty work and never, ever being clean. She's wanted to erase him from her life for the longest time and never had the courage. Now she realizes it wasn't courage she needed, but this anger. This sickening, all-consuming rage.

Deuce once showed Amiga how to burn an IM link out. That's the thing about virtual links. You can eradicate them. They aren't fucking real. Amiga sends the command Deuce taught her to Twist's link. It's probably going to hurt him. Hell, it's probably going to hurt her, but it's okay. It's good. Funny thing about taking a stand that, it might hurt like hell but if it's right, there's no feeling better. She's only just realized that, and now she knows she wants to do it every single day. If she lives to see another.

Twist shouts her name as the link fries. Twist never shouts. It makes her laugh, and she realizes that this is how she's going to die. Laughing. The thought makes her laugh harder. Jeez but she's clearly gone off the wrong side of crazy.

Drones incoming, Puss shouts in warning.

Laughter dying in her throat, Amiga checks the rearview. Dozens of drones bear down on them from between 'scrapers, silver glints in the sky swift and deadly as meteorites. Unexpected tears gather in her chest, hard and fast as gunfire. These could be other drones, of course they could, but her instinct screams otherwise. Tell her what she doesn't want to know: these are the drones that hit Jong-Phu, and now they're here. That means one thing only. Anger drops away, sudden as the ground in an earthquake, leaving her hollow. Light-headed.

She starts to tremble. At the centre of her chest pressure builds, a hard knot of it, burning and burning. Her lungs push in on either side of it, heaving for air. The

Hornets. What the fuck has happened to her family? Is Deuce gone? Can she imagine that? No, it hurts too much. She just burnt her bridges with Twist, and now she's an island, like it or not. She'd forgotten how painful it is to be alone. How it constricts every cell. She can't fucking breathe, can't stand it. For a moment all she wants is for it to end. For a bullet to breach the engine and burn her away. Every last aching cell.

Tyres screech at their rear, cutting sharply through the dull retort of constant gunfire. Wiping wet eyes on her shoulders, one after the other, Amiga tries to see what's happening, but there are too many cars around them, blocking the view, shuffling together. Why are they doing that? A moment ago they were all focused on attacking the limo. How did she not notice they'd stopped? Her game is all over the place.

What's happening? she asks Puss.

Company.

Amiga looks around. Tries to see between cars struggling to spin in close quarters, their gunners still firing. She can't tell the direction of the shots. Are they firing behind, or up? Are the drones after them? They certainly haven't yet fired on the limo, which confirms Deuce's assumption about the attack on Jong-Phu being a calculated move by the Queens. Amiga had assumed with Emblem in Shock's head, the Queens would be trapped. Powerless. Stupid of her. How do people know what trapped means to things like them.

Finally she catches sight of the drones again, firing at something behind the limo and its accompanying vehicular swarm. But they're also falling.

"What?"

She squints to focus. No she wasn't imagining it. Stuttering and then slipping as though their strings have been severed, drones are falling mid-flight. The impacts as they begin to hit the ground reverberate in ripples, making the limo shudder. Even knowing it's not an earthquake Amiga cries out, slams a shaking hand onto the dash, bracing for the worst. Some things are ingrained so deep in the DNA they become part of human nature.

Writhing as it loses power, one drone careens across the sky into another and straight into a 'scraper, taking a huge chunk of the wall, smashing windows as it tears a channel all the way to the sidewalk. There are bodies in there, caught in the collapse; she can see their limbs flailing in the falling rubble. Can she hear them screaming? Not over the traffic and gunfire, no, and yet she hears them loud and clear, instinctually adding voice to violence, knowing too well what it sounds like.

The cars collected about the limo's flanks spin away, leaving huge gaps. She's about to scream at Puss to get them the hell out of here when trucks roar through the chaos of vehicles, blocking them in again. She doesn't know these trucks. Black, featureless, and bristling with gun ports. On two of them, pointing upward from the roof, sit makeshift EMP devices. Who has EMP devices? Twist does. Probably the Harmonys too.

Amiga closes her eyes for a second. There's nothing like finding yourself in even deeper shit when you imagined you were in the deepest shit you could find. Still, she's well beyond panic at this point. Her friends are dead. Shock is basically dead too, considering there's no way she can get him to safety. And now she's dead herself, something she expected to happen sooner rather than later even before this shit tsunami hit. The fact that she's breathing makes no difference. It's semantics. All she wishes for is a weapon. To give these bastards a little pain before they neutralize her. But her pack is in the footwell and her arms around Shock.

One of the trucks pulls alongside, its side door sliding open. Not one to face her end with anything like fear, Amiga turns with a snarl to take it head on, and there's Deuce, grinning at her, a gun rested on his thighs. Next to him is Ravi, waving, his moustaches plastered back against his cheeks.

Amiga! He yells into her IM cheerfully. We know you can see us! Is there any way we can get the Haunt across here? Or should you and I swap places?

She's got no words. None. They're alive. They're alive and they couldn't even send a swift IM to let her know. She could simultaneously shoot and hug the lot of them. Struggling under a metric tonne of relief-rage she weighs up the outcomes, aware Shock's time is all but run out. He can't be moved, but she finds herself reluctant to let go of him. Seems when she picks a side her conscience takes it deadly serious.

She has a swift internal word. If she doesn't let go and allow Ravi to take her place, Shock will die, and what difference will she have made then? What change? Murderer to murderer is not what she had in mind.

You take my place. He won't survive being moved. She turns to Puss. I need you to hold him steady whilst I swap places with my friend. Can you do that and drive?

I'm a haptic hologram IRL. I can't hold him at all.

But... you're holding the wheel. Shark ate people.

No. I'm appearing to for your comfort. And Shark didn't eat people, he mauled them. I am, however, not Shark. He can use nervous systems against people. I cannot. I am not built for offensive manoeuvres.

Fuck. So how do we do this?

Carefully, Puss replies. As if it's obvious.

Amiga nudges the belt button to loose the harness, and

moves Shock over between her and Puss. There's no way to belt him in, so she opts for moving fast, shoving open the door and throwing herself at Deuce, hoping no bullets make it through the Hornet's covering fire. Deuce grabs her out of the air. Her legs hit the side of the truck as he hauls her in and she bites back a scream. She'd all but forgotten her thigh. Ravi claps a hand on her shoulder.

"Closer in," he yells to whoever's driving, and throws his bag across as they veer in toward the limo.

Perching on the edge, he times it perfectly, leaping across the gap. Catching his body on the door he pulls it shut behind him as he ducks inside, his attention already on Shock. If anyone can save that boy, Ravi can. The limo shakes violently under what must be an attempted Shark attack. Amiga's horrified at herself.

"I forgot to warn him about the avis," she gasps.

"He'll be all right," Deuce snaps, and she looks up, wondering what the heck bit his arse. Ah. He's got his hands on her leg, undoing the blood-soaked rag of shirt she used as a tourniquet, his face a potent mixture of worry and rage. "Look at this fucking mess," he says. "Jesus, Amiga, it's gone right through. When were you going to let us know you'd been hit?"

"When were you going to let me know you were alive?" she snaps back.

He glares at her, as if there's no comparison. Fuck that shit, and fuck him. He has no idea. She returns the glare, refusing to wince as he shoves in a foam gun and packs the wound on each side. He pushes her leg away from him.

"If you didn't constantly underestimate us," he says viciously, grabbing something from the bag behind him and half-throwing it into her lap, "you'd have known we'd be coming for you. No matter what."

"Word, girl," Vivid chimes in from one of the gun-slots. "What exactly do you think we are? Hobbyists? We're J-Hacks, sweetie. Nothing about our lives is safe."

Nothing to say to that. It's truth. Amiga's lived with these guys for over two years, but she's not lived with them. Thanks to her involvement with Twist they've had to hold her out of most of what they do, for their own safety. Helping with the drone was one of the few times she's been able to join in. It's not like they didn't give her the chance to choose who to work with right from the beginning. They did. Deuce did. She chose wrong, let her fear talk for her, let old habits prevail.

Thing is, she's always been convinced that this couldn't last, so she went out of her way to prove it. Probably too late to fix that now really, but having quite literally burnt her bridges with Twist, and happily so, it's good to know the last thing she does will be alongside them. A fitting end. One she probably doesn't deserve, which makes it all the more precious.

Amiga looks down at her lap. The object Deuce threw is a compact silver oblong edged in black. Her new crossbow. Well holy hallelujah! It's a beautiful thing. Lethal. Fires titanium bolts from tight-packed, 200-capacity clips; single, multiple, arrayed or targeted. There's no clip in the bow, so she rifles in the bag, hoping to fuck Janosz remembered to include them. He does not disappoint. A quick count comes to thirty clips. That's a fuckload of ammo.

Flipping the bow open with her thumb, she slams in one clip, shoves two in her belt and takes up position at an unmanned slot; finally able to scope the trouble brewing at their rear with intent and boy does it feel orgasmic. Part of her, the part that still sort of belongs to her life as a Cleaner, tries to use this. Tell her that killing is all she's good for, all she is. Maybe for the first time ever,

Amiga ignores it. Killing does not have to make you a killer. That's a choice you make, and she's been making the wrong one all along.

The gang troops behind are all muddled in together, an occurrence so rare she almost gives it a minute of silence. She recognizes members of Yang's troops, the Grey Cartel, and the Dengway Mafia amongst the rabble. No more or less than she expected. None of Twist's people are present, and none of the Harmonys' either, which means they're hanging back, waiting for the right moment to attack. She'd do the same for sure; use the competition as the front line. Let them take all the fire. Wait until ammo and energy is low, then hit hard and fast with everything you've got.

Taking her time, judging each shot, Amiga cherry-picks familiar faces, people she definitely doesn't want at her back if they're heading into yet more danger. Done dealing with them, she takes a moment to reach up and pull off the goggles, handing them to Deuce, glad to have gotten them back to him. That he's alive to give them to. Her intention to keep them has evaporated under those things. Probably she'd never have kept them anyway. Probably.

"You stole my goggles?"

"Borrowed."

He sighs. "Right. Borrowed."

"Figured you could use them back now."

He shakes his head in disbelief, turning back to his post. Has he run out of patience with her at last? She's been coasting on the certainty it'll never happen when he's only human, and she's pushed him further than anyone she knows. Even now, long after dumping him, when he's in a new relationship he should be able to focus on, she's pushed and prodded at his limits. Fuck. He must hate her.

Deep down, she thought she wanted that. Thought it would be easier. It's not. Heart in her throat, Amiga concentrates on firing, but with each hit her throat tightens, threatening tears, the very last thing she needs.

Taking heavy fire, they move onto a main district freeway. They're more open here, more vulnerable to attack from side roads and junctions. Amiga tries to keep eyes both behind and ahead, but it's impossible, and seemingly out of nowhere, tyres shrieking, dozens of new vehicles slam into them.

Two of the Hornet's trucks career out of control, falling behind and crashing through the trail of cars at their rear. Explosions like chain reactions follow in their wake. At the wheel, Raid, a Hornet Amiga barely knows, fights to keep their truck under control and stop it from running into the limo, where Ravi's still trying to save Shock.

With nothing to hold onto, KJ is thrown away from his console at the second impact. He hits the side of the truck and falls into Vivid's lap, out cold. The only other truck with EMP capability is now a fireball and the drones, realizing the threat is gone, swoop in and begin peppering them with laser fire from above.

Hanging on to the slot next to hers for stability, Amiga fires back at them, clinical shots aimed straight at their ocular processes. Bullets won't damage the reinforced carapaces much but her crossbow bolts slam right through minute eye-screens, tearing out huge chunks of vital hardware as they exit. She takes out eight drones in swift succession and, as they spiral out of control, the rest fall back. Smart tech indeed. Or else the Queens have called them off.

Take that, you bitches, she thinks, hoping they hear it somehow.

Their earlier pursuers have fallen back too, though

they're still firing intermittently. Mostly they're waiting. What do they know that she doesn't? Amiga runs a swift visual check on the remaining Hornet trucks. They're riddled with bullet scars and dents from impacts, and five out of seven bear long melted runnels from drone laser fire. At least two of them are running on tyres trying to self-heal significant hits, and the newcomers are herding in close, keeping the Hornet formation tight.

She can't see who these newcomers are, all of their trucks are as dark as these, with blackened glass, and no one's firing. That worries her, especially with the others hanging back. Unbidden, the thought occurs that the Hornets had to carry EVaC out of Jong-Phu. Where is he now? Is he in one of those fireballs behind them? There are members of the Hornets she's never met, and losing them before she's had the chance is bad enough. Losing him though...

"Tell me EVaC isn't in the middle of this," she shouts over at Deuce, her heart actually aching.

"Of course he's fucking not. We sent him in another direction, with some of the n00bs. He's almost at Shin, almost safe. How the fuck we gonna get there?"

Helpless, she shakes her head.

"Don't know. Any word from Ravi on Shock?"

"None. Reckon he's too busy for updates."

"Sorry about this," she blurts out. "It's my fault. Should've kept you all out of it."

"Don't be fucking stupid," he snaps. "You're family, Amiga. If I found out you got yourself into this kind of shit and didn't ask for our help, I'd come kill you my fucking self."

"You could try," her smart mouth whips out before she can catch it, and he smiles. Properly.

Jeez but it's good to see him smile like that so soon

after she thought she'd lost the right. Funny how happy his death threat made her as well. Probably down to the fact he doesn't mean a word of it. These Hornets of hers are tough as hell, but they're not killers. They're the only people she knows who wouldn't kill her without blinking. There's safety in that. A safety she thought she didn't want, because it felt too raw, too personal, too intimate. She was kidding herself. She not only wants it, she needs it. Knew it as soon as she thought she'd lost them.

The end of the freeway looms, the road narrowing to two lanes. Metal screams as the surrounding echelon slams inward in concert, and they go into a sideways skid, belching black smoke as they burn rubber on the road. Vivid, busy supporting the unconscious KJ loses hold of her firing slot and Amiga grabs for her jacket before she's thrown against the other side of the truck.

Across from her, Deuce skids on his arse, legs akimbo, into the front seats, wrapping his arms around the back of the passenger seat as Raid and the other drivers swerve madly to steer clear of the limo. This is what was planned, crash the Hornets, single out the limo.

Get the hell out of here! Amiga screams at Puss as the trucks slide on, colliding with each other to keep out of the limo's way.

"Raid!" she yells, her right hand aching as she hangs on to the nearest slot, pulled by the doubled weight of Vivid and KJ. "Don't let any of those fuckers past!"

"Done," he shouts back not even thinking to argue. All the Hornets know what's at stake here, but their unthinking commitment to help some guy they've never met and probably only heard bad things about still impresses her. He starts to turn the wheel. Yells wildly instead, "Brace!"

Amiga cranes to see the nearest Hornet truck bearing

down on them at speed, one of the enemy trucks practically welded to its rear. The crash deafens, metal against metal, metal scraping along tarmac. Sparks shoot upward like fireworks, and the side door wrenches away with a hideous screech of torn hinges, dragged under the truck as it skids.

Another truck slams in on that side, flipping them from one extreme to another. Jolted by the impact, Deuce loses his grip on the seats and slides across the floor of the truck. Both hands occupied and utterly helpless to prevent it, Amiga watches him flip out onto the road through billowing smoke as the trucks slam together and come to a screeching halt.

A scream tears out of her, raking her throat,"Deuce!"

Making sure Vivid is secure; Amiga struggles upward out of the wreckage. Aching all over from the impact, and clumsy with only the one leg working properly, she turns to help Vivid with KJ, but Raid shoves her away.

"Go! I've got this."

She nods thanks and scrambles awkwardly back up on to the truck, stuck on its side in a tangle of others. Scanning desperately for Deuce through the smoke, she spots him lying off to the side of the road. There's blood, a small pool of it, and his arm's twisted behind him at an unnatural angle.

"No."

Dropping to the road, Amiga limps toward him, her entire body numb, remote. All she can see is Deuce, but she can't focus on him properly. Can't see him. Is he breathing? Why isn't he breathing? Please let him be breathing. She tries to move faster, her injured leg leaden, alight with pain. Swearing, she drags it through every step, determined to reach him.

Remotely, she registers the sound of a door opening,

the click of heels on tarmac, and someone steps into view, one arm out, pointed at Deuce. She focuses on the hand, bewildered. There's a gun. There's a gun pointed at Deuce. Alarm floods her system. Rage. She can't get to Deuce in time, but she can kill the fucker threatening him.

"Amiga."

Focused on getting to the gun, she stumbles as the voice registers, and stops.

"Twist?"

She looks up and it's him. Standing there with a gun pointed at Deuce. His gaze is pitiless. Disappointed.

"Would it really be this easy to punish you? Hmmm? Have you gone soft, Amiga, as well as stupid?"

"Try me," she snarls.

He looks her over, those cold eyes of his calculating, missing nothing.

"Forgotten something?"

"Don't need a weapon to kill you."

"You'd have to get to me first. Let's see how fast you can run."

He fires the gun.

Amiga yells, incoherent, and lurches for her boss, knowing that, if Deuce was alive, Twist's just changed that for the worst. She cannot bear it. Doesn't want to look at Deuce, literally could not stand to see him lying there, his head blown apart, but she can't stop herself, and she looks anyway. That's when she knows that Twist is being especially cruel. The first bullet struck the lower leg, midway along the calf. Twist laughs softly.

"Come on then, Amiga, run," he says.

Sobbing, Amiga tries to run as he fires again, hitting the knee. She's screaming as the third shot fires, impacting Deuce's thigh. That's when all hell breaks loose. The roar of heavy engines fills the air and several large trucks burst through Twist's cavalcade, punching a hole in his circle of vans. Behind them follow what seems like a hundred cater-bikes, whipping through and spewing bullets at Twist's troops.

From the look of their clothes, their weather-beaten faces, these newcomers to the fray are land-ship folk, far from the ocean. One of the truck drivers, an ugly bald man, aims at Twist, punching the gun from his hand with precise shots that tear off two fingers and a chunk of palm. Amiga dives, hoping to take her ex-boss off-guard, but he's already running back to his truck, calling a retreat, and she full-lengths the tarmac, feeling it grind into every inch of her.

Sprawled out like a spider, squashed and bleeding, Amiga tries to get up. Her leg refuses to cooperate. She yells fury at it and crawls toward Deuce instead. His leg is a wreck, there's so much blood. And she still can't tell if he's breathing. Can hardly breathe herself as she reaches him and fumbles for his pulse with desperate fingers.

There's a moment in which everything stops. The background falls away. Sound roars into the distance, swallowed by silence. Breath halts, suspended as the heart in its sling of muscle, paused and awaiting the responding thud of another heart. That pulse of life. The reassurance required to continue beating.

Her fingers are cold against his neck, numb. She's caught in the moment for what feels like a lifetime, waiting, just waiting, and hoping to feel something, anything. Fearing there's nothing to feel, that his heart is done with beating, and hers will be too.

The first flutter is indifferent. Almost not a pulse at all. The second the same. But they're there, one faint flutter after another and the world roars back in. She's surrounded by strangers, pulling her away. She screams, lashes out, but there's Vivid, shouting in her face, the sound of the words delayed, like thunder after lightning.

"They're here to help! They're helping! Let them help him!"

slipping irl and breathing problems

Consciousness calls close by, loud and insistent as the klaxon of a vehicle reversing, and behind it, like fifty tons of truck behind a klaxon, waits pain. He's not afraid of pain. Not usually. But this pain is special, unavoidably personal. Not remotely physical. He's not sure he's strong enough to face it unmedicated. He's not had to since he was nine years old, bar a few slim-in-the-pocket moments he'd rather forget, and some recent times he's had carved into his skin. Now he's been stranded in his head without means to distance himself, stripped of the ability to use his coping mechanisms.

Some bastard's gone and cleaned his system out, left it scrubbed brand new, de-scaled, everything shining in hundred megawatt beams, clean enough to see your face in. Some people don't fucking want to see their own face. Some people dirty the mirror on purpose. Or smash it to pieces. That's a personal choice, and no one but the person involved has the right to gainsay it. There are, however, substances called "cold cures", used to do that very thing. Most often without permission.

Cold cures are used to purify WAMOS who don't deal

with addiction as the system expects them to. They travel through the body hoovering up whatever sordid crap the addict's drugs of choice lay down amongst the wetware to ensure continued reliance upon them. Once they're done, cold cures have eliminated every single impulse left behind, including the mental impulse.

What makes the cold cure so effective is what it does to that impulse. Ring-fencing it. Locking it away. Reducing it to a shout echoing in a box, going nowhere. That's all Shock's addiction is now, and he doesn't want to wake up. He's afraid of the pain.

Fear or no, his choices have dwindled to one, and he gradually rises through levels of consciousness, surrounded by the din of memories he's silenced too long, all fighting for dominance. The result is overload. White noise so loud it becomes deafening, cancelling itself out, leaving only agony behind, and Shock surfaces fast, like breaking out of deep water, his ears ringing, lungs crying for air.

Finds himself laid out in the front seat of the limo, stuck inside a body riddled with pain from the damage done by Pill, a head full of bad memories all determined to be heard at once, and perhaps worst of all, the awful weight of Emblem, ever growing. Using one against the other, Shock breathes in the scream of amputated fingers and cracked bone, the cringe of cut flesh and hollowed gums, the moan of muscles bruised all the way to the bone; breathes out everything else. It won't stay suppressed for long though, and the thought terrifies him.

Puss slithers into his lap, sliding her tentacles around his neck and, once again, her presence eases the clamour of his mind. He's still not at ease with the fact of her, despite their powerful connection, always present and growing stronger, but he's glad she's here. Glad of Shark, too, floating behind the glass screen, the wall of his furious hunger something to lean against. They make him feel like he could be safe, sane. Whole. Funny that he had to be split into three to feel like he's capable of coming together.

A face looms into view. Pimp-styled black hair flopping majestically over energetic brown eyes. Can't be more than twenty-two this guy, but looks like a character from the Mahabharata, complete with giant handlebar moustache.

"Name's Ravi," he says in a musical voice that doesn't come close to matching his appearance. "Sawbones to the Hornets. Also put you back together. How do you feel?"

Ah, so this is the bastard with the cold cure.

"Like hell," Shock rasps through a throat so dry he could grow cacti in it. "Too clean."

Ravi appears unmoved by his anger.

"Yeah, man. You were one sorry mess. Don't think there was an organ in your body your little habit hadn't fucked with. All good now though." He places a hand on Shock's shoulder, enough pressure to mean business. "Gonna have to deal with the shit you were avoiding. I have no apology for that. Can't have an addict hauling Emblem around in his bonce. We need you focused. Cruel to be kind etc. etc."

"Without the bumps," Shock says, opting for the same level of honesty, "I'm pretty much fucking useless."

"Matter of opinion, man, and I don't share it," the sawbones says, maintaining that hideous level of cheer. "We're almost to Shin. Left my friends behind in some serious shit for you y'know."

Shock immediately feels guilty. Responsible. Fuck, but that's the worst feeling ever. Why didn't anyone ever tell him?

"Sorry."

Ravi nods. "Just do me a favour and stay still. You're nowhere near good to go physically. I ran out of C-Gen early on. Ended up gluing most of you back together. Have no idea how long it'll hold if you get feisty and, frankly, you haven't enough blood left to safely lose any more."

"Oh."

"Yeah. You can thank your golden friends here for keeping you with us long enough for me to stick you back together. That fucking Shark, though, tried to eat me until Puss told him to back the fuck off."

"He's very protective."

Ravi raises a brow. "That what you call it? You know, most people deal with their anger instead of making seventeen-foot-long killing machines."

Shock wants to laugh but it hurts too much, so he smiles instead. Thinks about those friends Ravi left behind, how it is Ravi came to be in the limo with him instead of Amiga. He wonders if Amiga counts as a friend to this guy. Cleaners don't have friends. They're like him. Solitary. Unburdened. They have to be. She seemed different though. Less frosty, more like a human being. Odd quirk for a Cleaner. He wonders if it was new. She didn't seem to know what to do with it. With herself. Only looked certain when she was killing.

"Amiga a friend of yours?"

"Yup."

"Really?"

"No shit. Amiga's good people." Ravi's checking the side mirrors as he talks, his face tight with concern.

"I'm sure they made it out safe," Shock offers, not sure why he's trying to reassure the guy, but needing to anyway.

Ravi nods absently, smiles much the same.

"Yeah. Yeah they probably did."

Uneasy silence grows between them. Shock doesn't like it. Unsure of how to break the silence, he looks out of the window, and blinks as it jumps away from him, receding down a black tunnel. Before he can react, his mind leaps after it like it's base jumping, parachute-less, into an abyss; gung-ho and knife-edged.

He thinks he's moving forward until he passes what can only be the complex knot of Emblem, this massive byzantine cluster of code enmeshed within him and shifting amongst itself. Growing incrementally with every movement, a tumour out of control. Unchecked. Uncheckable. It makes a noise like the distant roaring of monstrous wheels and then it's behind him, and he's squeezed through a too-narrow link and dropped onto a sheer white floor, lit from below and warm against his skin.

Dazed, and beyond confusion into disorientation, he peers up through the tangles of his hair. It's gold. Blinking, he stares down at his arms, his torso, his knees against the white wood. Gold. All gold. How the hell?

"You're out of Slip, so it took me a while to fix a way to talk to you."

Real voice? How?

The voice belongs to a thing. A converging of shadows, blurred and continually changing. Form melting into form. It looks nothing like a person but it's not the Queens. Nowhere near big enough. Who the fuck, or what the fuck is it? More importantly, what the fuck is this? He's never Slipped this way. Never knew it was possible.

"This is not J-Net," he says.

"Correct. We're IMing face-to-face, well your face to my distortion-algorithm. It's a little... different, with you out."

Shock gets up from the floor. There's no pain. Of course, this body is only a representation. He can control it. He finds he wants the pain though, and so he lets it back in, gritting the remaining teeth in his mouth as nerves flood his body and mind with pain alarms. That's better.

He breathes out slow, checking his surroundings. Interesting. A huge room with a circular wall of windows, filled with slender glass tables and white leather couches shaped like conch shells. The only colour in the room comes from a firepit in the centre, flickering with holographic green flames. He's never been to this place, but he's seen similar to it in pictures, on adverts in plush Corp room vid-feeds.

"This is the Heights."

"Yes. I tried to form a makeshift J-Net, but in the end it was easier to bring you here as an avi. You're Slipping IRL. Never been done and likely won't ever be again."

Shock offers a moment's silence for that feat, couldn't prevent himself if he tried. He's a Hack and he knows Hacking history when he's making it. Three times in one day, too. Gotta be a record. He also knows a fucking full-on genius when in the presence of one.

"Breaker, right?"

"Right."

"Why am I here? Why are you?"

The shifting shadow briefly looks human, before fading back to an amorphous shade.

"I underestimated the Queens. I didn't realize what they were, and now I'm stuck. Look, they're distracted at the moment, playing shoot 'em up games with those drones, but I don't have long. They need you here, and I know you want to stay away, normally you'd be right to do that, but not now. You need to come. It's important."

"I don't think so."

Whatever Shock does now, it will not include taking Emblem anywhere near the Queens. He's not brave, just tired of being used, and those Queens, they'll use him; use Emblem to use everyone. No way he's being party to that. No way. He's a loser and an idiot, not a fucking arsehole.

"You don't understand. We need Emblem out of your head..."

"Out of my head?" Shock's just seen Emblem. That's a

whole different thing to feeling it. Everything he thought about it and worse was confirmed in that moment. "You can't get it out of my head. It's hooked in. Stuck solid. I'm pretty much a dead man walking." And as he says it, he accepts it. Nothing else he can do. He thinks about Amiga and her friends. Guilt is one hell of a bitch. "A lot of people are risking their lives for me today. Pointlessly as it happens. Kinda done with that level of suckage."

Breaker's avi billows, thins out, and ripples back.

"I'm not talking about saving you, I have no idea if that's possible, but as long as Emblem is contained in your drive, I can take it out, and we need to. It was never supposed to do any of this; it was supposed to become a deadlock. Permanent. Trap the Queens in Hive for good."

"It's bio-ware. You can't predict bio-ware responses out of their virtual environment. Any idiot knows that." And any idiot knows the courier always gets fried in these situations. Thing is, if it had fucking worked, Shock's not sure he'd have minded.

"Nonetheless we tried. We had no option, you understand? The Queens were not about to stop trying for Emblem and they had help. We didn't have time to ponder consequences. All we can do now is try and limit the damage, and if we leave Emblem in your drive, using your biology to evolve, the result could be catastrophic."

Well okay, that's on the level, it's too much fucking horror to be otherwise. What Breaker's asking though, that's not. Makes a shot in the dark look like a safe bet.

"What if removing it from my head doesn't stop it? What if by coming there I end up handing it to them? Make a bad situation worse."

"Refusing to come won't stop them. They want out and they don't care what gets destroyed in the process. You can face them and fight them, or sit around waiting for them to destroy everyone around you until their drones can pluck you up—if Emblem doesn't leak before then."

"You haven't answered my first question."

"I don't know if removing it will stop it, or just kill you. I'm not certain I can stop the process, but I have to try. You have to let me try. Doing nothing is simply not an option. You're a smart kid, do me a favour and extrapolate the possible outcomes of what that thing in your head could do left to its own devices."

Shock extrapolates. The results scare the crap out of him. If he hadn't been cold cured he'd run far and fast, straight into the arms of a butt-load of drugs. But what would that solve? Emblem would evolve or the Queens would escape, and it'd be his fault. He couldn't live with that. Not even gorked off his skull.

The Gung's thrived on misery for too long, on people being punished for daring to have their own minds. He can listen to his fear and end up aiding and abetting the replacement of that horror with one far worse, or he can turn and fight. Try and put a stop to it all. Maybe find a reason to like himself, to be able to look in a mirror and not feel sickened by the stinking mess staring back at him.

"Fine. I'll come. Even if I have to come alone."

"You won't need to. Help is coming. Be quick, Shock Pao. Time is ru..."

Breaker's gone. Snapped away like elastic. Only an echo remains, an emanation of pain. From the direction in which he disappeared, something massive shifts. A shadow of a limb, Queen-sized.

Quick as he can, Shock reaches back to his connection with Puss and Shark and lets them pull him out, burning the path between himself and Breaker as he goes so he can't be followed. He wakes to find Ravi bent over him, giving CPR, his moustaches tickling Shock's cheeks.

Shock half pushes him away, trying to catch breath that keeps running away from him, jumping rebelliously out of his lungs as soon as he's hauled it in. He blinks stupidly at Ravi, who looks exhausted.

"How long?" he forces out between breaths.

Ravi's mouth hits a straight line. Serious as all shit.

"A while, man," he says without any of his former cheer.

"Ah."

"We're here, by the way. Arrived during my mega session of trying to keep you alive. What the fuck happened?"

Shock huffs out a laugh. His lungs are finally beginning to cooperate. He wants to hug them. Not being able to breathe sucks arse.

"Got pulled away unexpectedly."

"Well that just explains everything." Ravi shakes his head, obviously irritated with Shock. "Whatever. You can explain later, and by that I mean you will. Now I know I told you not to move, but we're sitting ducks and I don't know who's still after us, or how quick they can get here."

"What about your friends? Amiga?"

Ravi makes a "dunno" face.

"Sent an SOS flare via IM when you tapped out, but I haven't heard from them. Have to assume they're not coming."

Shock's not really surprised by how much that upsets him. No one should die on his behalf. Even with Emblem in his head, he's not worth any sort of sacrifice. If he hadn't already decided to go to the Heights somehow, and help Breaker to end this, he'd go just for them, for the sacrifice they may have made. Puss tightens her grip on his torso. She's there with him. So is Shark.

It makes all the difference.

when a plan comes together

Shin District is scary quiet. Apocalypse quiet. Not many DethRok folk traipse the squares during daylight hours, it's not the done thing. Vampire hair; vampire rules. Shock's never been much for DethRok but he can dig the lifestyle. He prefers the night too. Deserted streets and darkness. No chance of running into anyone you might know. No chance of running into anyone. That there is bliss. Probably the only bliss he'll ever get now he's been scrubbed squeaky clean.

The club Ravi says they have to get into, Mollie's, seems deserted too as they make slow progress across the square, Shock clinging to Ravi, Puss clinging to Shock and Shark cruising behind, on alert for trouble. Shock wonders what the fuck they must look like. Thank fuck no one's around to see. He's been the centre of attention enough today; he can do without another moment in the spotlight.

At Mollie's Ravi peers up, trying to see in through shaded porthole windows.

"Don't think Amiga was expecting this," he mutters, and bashes on the door.

They wait as the sound evaporates.

Two minutes.

Three.

Five.

Ravi's getting anxious, scanning the square. Still empty as far as the eyes can see, but they're both expecting trouble and Shark's circling with intent, rippling the air with savage tail flicks.

Ravi knocks again. This time, seconds after the sound dies, they hear heels clacking across woodwork, the whir of electronic locks, and the door cracks open.

"Maggie Joust?" Ravi asks the shadowed figure hiding behind.

Leaning in to the light and revealing huge green eyes in a face made for jaunty make-up, the woman nods, smiles. Putting a finger on her lips, she hurries them in, fussing like a mother, albeit a mother attired like a grease-punk mermaid, all sooty grey, spiked fabrics and shimmering metal scales on trousers so tight it looks like she's wearing an oil-slick. Sexy. Unfazed by the golden octopus on Shock's chest, she doesn't seem to mind Shark either, pointing him imperiously into a corner so she can close the door without standing near his jaws.

"Sorry to be so long," she says as soon as the door closes and locks. "I was downstairs."

"Downstairs?" Ravi looks around, frowning confusion.

Maggie smiles. "Later. For now let's get this Haunt of yours settled before he comes apart at the seams. He looks a trifle roughly patched."

Shock's installed somewhat shambolically on a frilled candy-striped chaise with feet so ornate he's concerned they're more for show than holding up furniture. Catching his sideways glances at them, Maggie pats his head reassuringly.

"Don't worry about the chaise," she says with a wink.

"It's made for action."

"This a cathouse then?"

A thoroughly filthy grin takes ownership of her face.

"Not by license, no. Nor by intent. But after two A.M., when everybody is fully lubricated, they tend to lubricate each another."

"Sounds like my kinda place," Ravi says.

"Indeed. Not yours though, is it?" she says to Shock knowingly.

"I don't really have a kind of place," he says, speaking before he can stop himself yet again. He's not normally so candid with strangers. This woman is obviously some kind of wizard. Freaking out, he zips it, then feels angry when she looks all knowing again and, giving him another pat on the head, goes to fetch Ravi some better medical equipment "to cement the Haunt together a little more firmly".

"I like her," says Ravi, watching her arse leave the room.

"You're not her type," Shock replies, trying not to laugh.

"No. And it's a damn shame, man," Ravi responds with a grin.

Armed with good quality C-Gen from Maggie's med-kit, Ravi carefully peels apart and re-seals every cut and slice he glued. It's like being back with Pill, and without Puss by his side, a coiled comfort about arm and neck, Shock couldn't cope. Proper clean is about as bad as he imagined it might be, and worse than clean, worse than re-living Pill's fun clean, is being this aware of Emblem, acutely in tune with the interactions it has with his drive. It's getting to be all he can think about, mingling uneasily alongside how far away the Heights are and how in hell he's going to get there.

Ravi's almost done with the C-Gen retouch torture when there's a knock at the door. Maggie runs over, her delight a sign written in ten-foot-high neon. She ushers in a skinny, weird-looking woman, grabbing her into a tight hug. There might even be tears. Behind them, an absolute shit-ton of people stream into the room, some carrying injured or dead bodies. Cue insta-anxiety overload. Shock's simultaneously claustrophobic and panic-stricken, on the verge of hyperventilation. Shit but he forgot how bad it is to be around people unmedicated. Then Amiga's face is in his, nose to goddamn nose, and he feels okay. What? That's new.

"Hey, Haunt. Looking better."

He snorts. "Your sawbones here scrubbed my brain clean. Better is not currently a word in my vox. Have to say you're looking rough as fuck."

She plucks ruefully at the foam poking out of the wound on her thigh.

"Yeah. You should see my ex."

"Shut up, Amiga." Comes from the chaise next to his.

Shock cranes his head. Ex is a half-Asian giant and a walking K-Rock ad, made serious by dark-matter eyes. Ex is also shot half to fuck, bullet holes ranged up his left leg, and there's some serious grazing on face and arms, one of which is in a printed splint. Shock would commiserate, but he's currently a human colander carrying apocalyptic code in his skull, so figures he gets to be the sorry bastard here. The guy nods, equal to equal. Hack then. Figures.

"Deuce."

Shock nods back. "Shock." It doesn't need saying, Deuce is wise to who he is, but there are ways to do things amongst hacks, and Shock isn't about to drop his manners. These guys just saved his life.

"Shock?" The weird-looking woman Maggie hugged, who's been engaged in an intense whispered conference with Maggie and some massive bald guy with muscles on his muscles and the most goddamn ugly mug Shock's ever seen, turns to stare at him. Fuck but her eyes are creepy. She turns to Maggie. "That's the Haunt? His hair wasn't red."

"That's blood, and I'm right fucking here, by the way." he snaps, just about done with being invisible, even with this many people in the room.

She grabs a chair and drags it over, making a state of the floor, and his ears. Sits right in front of him, as close as Amiga was, but Amiga she is not. Personal space much. And every fucker in the room is staring right at him now. Too many eyes. Man he thought he was through with invisible but this visible shit is worse than being flayed alive, and he knows how that feels. Sort of. He wants to get up and run the fuck out, but his legs feel like used cotton buds, so he sucks it up and gives the woman invading his personal space the attention she's obviously gunning for.

"Yes?"

"Volk," she replies, staring at him intently.

He's about to complain, then realizes she's not actually looking at him. More like through him. He takes a closer look at her eyes. Yup. Mods. She's basically a human computer, chock-full of extras, which makes sense of the weirdness and the freaky eyes, and she's currently scrutinizing the inside of his skull. Oh the sights she's seeing. It's Hiroshima in there.

"Well," she says after a moment, "the inside matches the outside." She exchanges a look with Maggie, one of those deep-ass worried looks parents get about kids going out to do seriously questionable acts of drunken stupidity. The kind never aimed at him before. Another first. "We have to take him to the Heights, to Breaker. Right now."

The sound of a gun cocking punctuates Volk's last

sentence. Then it's pressed against Volk's nose.

"Oh no you fucking don't. He's not going anywhere." Amiga, soft spoken and deadly. "He's been through enough. Right now we protect him here until Deuce there can figure out a way to get that crap out of his skull."

Shock can count on his missing fingers-tips the amount of people who've ever stood up for him, so this is a first too. The clincher is she's not doing it out of duty. She's doing it because she genuinely gives a shit. How the hell did he manage to deserve having her in his corner? It doesn't seem fair. Fair or not though, he's going to take it. You don't say no to that sort of luck.

"You spoke to Breaker?" he asks Volk.

Volk's gaze, casually rested on the gun at her nose, rises to his face.

"No," she says. Her voice is calm. Even. Nope, she's not even a little bit freaked out. Talk about fried. "But I know he's being held at the Heights and I know he's the only chance we've got to get that out of your head."

"The Queens are there," says Amiga, her gun unwavering. "Shock can't go."

"I can," Shock says.

She stares at him.

"Why? What earthly reason would persuade you to go to them?"

"I spoke to Breaker, which was fun." He gives her the full benefit of his sarcasm, but it's unnecessary, looks like she knows.

"Been there. So what did he say?"

"Emblem is fucking dangerous. When it grows beyond my drive, and that's soon, we are well and truly screwed. He has no idea if getting it out will stop it, but he needs to try. So I have to go to Heights. I told him I'd go."

"Hold on," says Deuce. "I'm missing something.

Emblem in a neural drive is bad news, yes, but for that drive in particular. What exactly did Breaker do to it?"

"Altered the code. It was supposed to deadlock the Queens into Hive. Prevent them from ever being able to escape. Clearly it failed."

"No shit. I thought he was a genius."

"Ditto," Shock says. "Guess even geniuses fuck up."

"Word. It definitely needs to come out."

"I hate arriving in the middle of conversations," Amiga says, and it's clear she's really not kidding. "Could you explain, in layman's terms, why the fuck Emblem is now a threat to all of us? I thought this was a simple DL and safekeep."

"You know it's bioware?" Shock says.

"Yeah, I know that."

"Well, so are we. Inside me, it's like it's drowning in new info. To put it bluntly, it's evolving, growing. Once it grows beyond my drive, into my brain, it'll take over. Then it could do anything. Destroy Slip and everything in it. Or tear all the locks off, freeing the Queens. Maybe lock us in forever. Who knows? But we can't risk letting it happen, considering the wealth of bad scenarios. Breaker can try and stop it, but it has to be out of my drive, and it has to be before Emblem leaks beyond. Once that happens, there's no way to get to it—or stop it."

"Hold on now," Amiga says. "If Emblem's filling your drive, how will Breaker get it out?"

"He'll have to take my drive out, link to it direct for an extraction."

"But that'll kill you."

"Could do, yeah."

Amiga sort of quietly implodes with fury at that point. It's impressive. And viral. Within seconds the whole room has erupted into argument, some for, some against, neatly divided between the pirates and the Hornets. Everyone has a fucking opinion one way or another. Thing is, there's only one person carrying Emblem in their skull. One person who gets to choose what happens to it, and to him.

"I want to go," Shock says, all but shouting, and then talking too loudly into too heavy silence. "I promised I would, and if we get there too late, or he can't do what he thinks he can, then I'll destroy my drive with a fucking bullet myself. Or you can."

He throws that one at Amiga, because she can do it if he can't. And she would. She'd probably do it now if he asked, but he won't. Emblem is their only hope against the Queens. If she destroys his drive, destroys Emblem, then that option is gone forever and so are the locks on Hive. Breaker won't have time to write anything like this again. A bullet is only for the worst-case scenario.

Amiga tilts her head, fixing him with an inscrutable gaze. "That so?"

It's like she's asking a question based on what he's thinking rather than what he's said. Probably she's seen straight through him. Amiga's sharp, a human flensing knife. She's what was made of her, and so is he. And both of them want to change it. That's why they're here. He knows she'll understand.

"If this is fixable, I need to try and fix it, whatever it costs me. I'm done being a fuck-up, okay? I'm done."

She smiles just a little, goes to talk, but Volk totally screws the moment. Woman's got all the subtlety of a land ship ploughing into rocks.

"That's decided then," she says, giving him this look like he's gone and surprised her. Pleasantly so. Probably she thought they'd have to drag him kicking and screaming, or lie to him to get him there. A day ago they would have.

"And if the Queens get it?" Amiga asks, bristling with tension, or temper. Considering her gun's still tickling

Volk's nose, Shock votes for the latter. "If the fucking Harmonys are waiting for him to go to the Heights, and they get it? What then?"

The ugly man speaks up then. He's got the sort of voice you can lean on, thick and rough as rock.

"If he needs protection, he's got it. He's not doing this alone."

"Who the fuck are you that I should trust you?" snarls Amiga.

"Someone who wants to help," he says, with a shrug. "Who knows the value of chance. I presume, not being short of intelligence, you dig all the chance that brought you here?"

Amiga shrugs one shoulder. "Sure."

"Well, I'm a pragmatist. I say maybe things happen for a reason, maybe they don't, but when you reach a point where you can take chance and turn it into intent, you don't walk away. You act."

Amiga lowers her gun.

"That's a philosophy I can align with," she says quietly. "But we are not in a position to act recklessly. Twist's still out there. You know, the guy who was casually shooting up my friend just to fuck with me? And a few missing fingers won't stop him any more than they've stopped this Haunt. Twist will regroup and come back harder. So will the rest. And then we have the Harmonys, who I can assure you are beyond lunatic. We cannot casually step out and wander on up to the Heights. That shit is doomed to failure. That shit ends in cremations all round."

"Not arguing with that," he says. "Any ideas? Because staying here ain't gonna fly either."

Sniffing, Amiga directs a considering gaze down at the floor of all things.

"Gotta be a way to get to that engine," she says to Maggie.

Maggie shakes her head. "I've never found one. And who even knows if the damn thing works. Probably best if it doesn't."

"We have to try. It's our only way out of here without attracting attention."

"Er... engine?" asks Shock, stealing the words right out of everyone else's mouths by the looks. He's not usually the first to speak up, but he's burning through a lot of firsts today. One more won't hurt.

"Earth Engine," Amiga replies. "Long story. Horror. Worst kind. But maybe we can change the genre..."

In a haze of dismay thick as early morning smog, Shock stands by the window of the server, staring out at the Earth Engine. The sight of it, the unequivocal reality, festers in the brain meats like a bad trip. He's heard the breaking of the world was not an accident; that sort of rumour has its own life, refuses to be laid to rest even when large corporate interest seeks to quash it. It's not something Shock dwelt on, having no real relevance to his life, or so he thought.

It should help that everyone stood here in this server, looking out at the engine, feels just as destabilized. It doesn't. Shock has no doubt that no one here is at ease with this, not one soul is feeling any comfort, not even those who would have staked their lives on this truth. But they're not standing here holding yet another thing that could destroy everything in their heads. Not standing here feeling guilt and responsibility and absolute terror. How could he have let it happen? How can he stop it?

Serene on her web of glowing tubes, Mother Zero watches them watch the engine. He can feel her eyes on him, mini-suns warming his spine. He wants to talk to her direct, ask her to help him understand what he needs to do, because he doesn't know, even though he's chosen to do it. Life has never been this complicated. He knows how to run, to hide, to escape. That's all he knows. He hasn't the first clue about standing and fighting.

"How do we get to it?" Volk. Impatient. Sounds comfortable on her. This is a woman who suffers on the wrong end of the patience spectrum.

Maggie shakes her head.

"I don't know. I've never known. But Amiga's right, there has to be a way in and out to the station. It's obvious the server was built from out there."

Shock looks down at Puss, curled around his chest, seemingly content.

Show me the layout, he says. Like you did before. Maybe we'll see the way down.

Puss slides a tentacle into his jack. This time he's braced for the grid, the underlying reality of his world, but the sheer wealth of information leaking through the interface still takes him by surprise. Through the server walls he sees the station, the Engine, and the innards of the beast, a blueprint with instructions scrolling like rain down a window, trickling droplets of information.

Fuck, this machine is not a metal carcass; it's still vibrant, vibrating. Alive in the way machines sometimes are when idle, that sinister static energy warning of great power held in check. Beyond it lies a network of tunnels, delineated in bright shades of green, red and blue. They span the city, more vast than even his wildest imaginings could have conjured and—this is the biggest surprise, though it shouldn't have been—they lead to other stations, other servers, other engines. So many of them across the Gung's breadth.

Is this where they rested when the world was broken? More likely they were left here once the network of servers was finished. Perhaps as a backup plan. A means to start afresh from nothing if the Gung didn't pan out, though why you'd rid the earth of its last land standing, he does not know.

Well this is unexpected, Puss says.

She's music in his mind, a background symphony, and he realizes he's always heard it, heard her. No more so than now. He's been ignoring her, still refusing to accept a world wherein part of him can still somehow be female. Doing the same to her, in fact, that was done to him over and over, making cracks that have never healed. And for the second time with her, he feels like a selfish shit. Worse. Because he knows how it feels to be rejected. Why can't he be better? Why can't he just accept her?

I'm sorry. I'm trying. It's just hard. I don't understand.

She squeezes his midriff ever so gently. I know. Amiga was quite correct by the way. Bad company will be with us in approximately ten minutes. Twist and his troops are moving fast. The drones follow them. Soon this server will be the only safe place at Mollie's. Until they find it...

Oh shit.

"Can Mother be moved?" he asks Maggie.

Taken aback, Maggie blinks.

"Yes, she can. Easily."

Still seeing through Puss's eyes, Shock limps to a place in the server wall that, to any eyes but theirs, seems the same as all the rest. A combination of code sent to an intricate lock hidden in the cracks causes the whole section to uncouple and swing back, revealing a staircase spiralling down toward the platform—rails automatically rising from some hidden enclosure to make safe the descent.

Amiga strides over and looks down.

"How the hell...?"

"Avi vision."

She turns, frowning, so he points to his head, to the tentacle snaked beneath his hair.

"Oh that's good."

He smiles. "I know."

Volk shoves her way through the crowd.

"Let's go."

"Wait," says Amiga. "That engine. Is it the only one?" Volk makes to protest, but Amiga steps in front her. "I need to know. If we manage to contain Emblem and the Queens, we're essentially bringing down the Corp monopoly. There'll be a vacuum. A vacuum is a dangerous thing, and there are too many bad people who'd try to fill it. Something needs to be done about that."

With a sigh, Volk relents.

"Fine, but speak fast, Emblem will not be contained for much longer."

"Fully compos of that, Volk, it's in my fucking head," Shock tells her. Then says to Amiga, "There are dozens of engines abandoned under the Gung. Three of them on route to the Heights."

"They all work?"

"Yeah."

"What about the network?"

"Goes everywhere. All across the Gung."

"So we could attack the cartels from below? Take their HQs whilst they're preoccupied," says Amiga.

Shock's astounded, and a touch embarrassed. He hadn't thought to do something like that. But then, he's no Cleaner, just a loser with a scrubbed-out drug habit.

"That's fucking audacious. I love it. You planning to take out Twist?"

She looks tempted, but shakes her head.

"I'll be with you. You're going to need all the help you can get."

"I've got Volk and the big guy."

"Petrie. My name is Petrie," snaps the big guy, looking like an infuriated bald bear. "And he'll have a strong team from my ship behind him. He'll be fine." Amiga still seems unsure, and Petrie asks her, "You're Twist's Cleaner, right?"

"I am."

"Then no one knows better than you what he is, or where to hit him hardest. Or would you prefer to keep him around? Pretty sure he'll finish what he started on your friend there if you don't deal with him. I have long experience of men like that. They never forget, and they never forgive."

Amiga bites her lip, torn, the conflict visible on her face, in her eyes. As is the moment she relents.

"We need five teams, one for each major player, and we can't fuck up. We need to come out of this looking all powerful, so none of the minor-league players dares to act."

"We're with you for Twist," Deuce says, hobbling over between Ravi and Vivid.

"No way. You're fucked, Deuce. Shot to fuck in fact. You can't fight." Amiga's expression is this strange combo of anxiety and rage. Shock would bet a serious amount of flim that she has no idea her feelings for Deuce are written all over her face. She'd probably rip it off.

"No," Deuce replies, smiling viciously. "But I can hack. What argument you got against that, Amiga?"

She has precisely zero, and things happen way too quickly after that. Between them, Amiga and Petrie split their 220 battered survivors into five teams plus a tiny group composed of EVaC, Maggie, Mother Zero and anyone too injured to fight. This done, they all leave the server, locking it behind them, and trail down to the platform, into the Engine.

It starts with ease, filling the tunnel with a feral roar,

and they're off into darkness, into the earth, and none of them talk about what they're really thinking: how utterly weird it is to be given no option but to use something that destroyed their world in order to try to save it.

The first of the three stations between Shin District and the Heights takes almost no time at all to reach, and two teams leave together, heading for other stations to pick up other engines. Amiga comes over to Shock before she leaves and slides a gun into the pocket of the blazer Maggie scared up to keep him warm.

"For the moment it goes wrong, if it does," she says to him. "And if you can't, if Breaker's wrecked your head or anything goes wrong, I have Petrie's fucking word he'll do right by you."

"Thanks, Amiga."

"No sweat, Haunt. If I don't see you again, I'm glad I didn't Clean you. I'm glad I got to save you instead. You're okay."

He smiles at that. "You're not too bad yourself."

The engine moves on. Only one more stop before the Heights. Volk and Petrie huddle with their people, discussing tactics for the incursion. Shock sits there like a third freaking wheel, feeling all kinds of useless. He looks around the engine, trying to distract himself and ends up staring at the business end, where one of the land-ship folk stands monitoring the automatic systems. It's old tech all right, but the computers are bloody powerful. He smiles. Here's where he can help.

Hey, Puss, fancy doing a bit of lock picking?

You quite literally read my mind.

Cracking the engine's complex tech systems, they use them to get into Heights systems, stopping to stare, dumbfounded, at the amount of VA crammed into its networks. This security is mind-boggling, and they have to somehow clear a path into Heights and up as high as where Breaker's being kept, somewhere on the top three floors. Getting to him will be even harder, but that can wait.

An hour later, the final and most vulnerable group leaves, heading for a safe house offered by Volk. Done with the initial picking of Heights locks and sporting the accompanying headache breaking so much VA so quickly provides, Shock watches out of the windows as they load up EVaC and Mother into another Engine. Mother looks up, seemingly aware of his gaze. Her pale-yellow eyes, soft as primroses, pin him in place. Deceptive shade that. It's not soft at all when you're caught in its grip, but neon bright as her tattoos.

I don't know what to do, he sends tentatively and, to his surprise, she responds.

No one does. Just do what you can.

The effort it takes a Patient Zero to speak without the interference of virad jingles is immense, and means her words strike their target clean. From the satisfaction in her smile, he knows this is what she intended. She wanted to help. How has he never known people like this before? How has he never known people could be like this? He smiles back, raising his hand to wave goodbye. Maggie waves for her, which makes him smile a little more. There's so much between those two, it's a beautiful thing to witness.

It occurs to him that, in these past forty-eight hours, he's smiled more, and more genuinely, than he has for years. And here he is, in the deepest shit he's ever encountered, heading for certain death with missing fingertips, missing teeth, broken ribs, and half his skin C-genned together. Happiness is clearly unpredictable. Or else he's just a complete fucking weirdo. Either seems good.

When they reach Heights, Shark's waiting for them, swimming elliptic shapes around the bay. There's no server here, only an elevator. Petrie comes to stand beside Shock. He looks stressed, Shock can't really blame him. He's not exactly relaxed down here himself. Every now and then it occurs that they are under fucking ground and his head goes blank, shivery at the edges. Under any other circumstances, Shock would be hella anxious to leave.

"Can you get us in? Volk was sure you could," the big guy says, reaching out to run a hand over the elevator doors as if he might be able to get them in via sheer will power. This guy would probably try.

"I already have." Shock leans to press the elevator call button. "We've got access to one of the staff shoots and codes to lock access to the rest. Breaker is on one of the topmost floors, not the highest but definitely a penthouse. There's no way I can get in through the front door, but I can crack staff access with Puss's assistance."

The elevator doors slide open but Shock holds them up a moment longer.

"There are residential shoots, and I didn't have time to get locks for those, so be prepared for guards. And I'm with Amiga on the Harmonys. Li's an Archeologist. If she's been looking for me, chances are she'll have picked up Breaker's communication and come straight here. There's no way to be ready for the Harmonys, just try and stay alive."

"Sure thing." Petrie inclines his head at Shark, who's still circling the station. "You not bringing the killing machine? We could use it."

"Not at the moment. If Puss or I are injured, our connection to him will help us hang on long enough to do what needs to be done. If he got injured too…"

Petrie nods. "Got it. But you understand we're at your back? We'll get you in and out alive."

"Even so. Just in case," says Shock, with a smile.

Tough as this guy is, Shock's a realist. This is a one-

way trip. He knew that before he started, and he's okay
with it. Really. He's okay.

good company and a good day to die

Watching artificial lights flash past in darkness, Amiga thinks back to the day everything changed. The day she met Deuce. She'd been in the dark for so long she didn't even recognize it as darkness. It was life. Survival. Bunking in the same Shimli apartment she had in Tech, an absolute shit-hole she hardly ever saw. Avoiding sleep had become her religion. At that point she didn't recognize why. She barely recognized her face in a mirror. Amiga the Cleaner wasn't anyone she knew. Still isn't.

She met Deuce after buying takeaway shrimp pad thai from some nothing little noodle bar in Sakkura. Half a street away she bit into the shrimp and realized it was that disgusting reconstituted protein shit they try to pass for shrimp if they think you're a bit dumb. It was that assumption more than the substitute itself that drove her rage, her decision to go back and rip the shit out of the poor sap behind the till. We share our hurt, oh boy do we ever.

Deuce was ordering chilli beef ramen when she bust back in, all snarls and vicious fury, bringing with her fear that infected everyone in the shop. Except him. He smiled at her. She caught his eye, that smile, and the rage drained away. Left her standing there, hollowed out. She doesn't even remember leaving, only that he followed her, noodle-less, and invited her for a coffee. She still has no idea why she said yes. Still has no regrets. But meeting him was like a light switched on unexpectedly, illuminating grime on the walls, damp and mildew, cockroaches huddled in the cracks, chittering.

Horrified to find herself amongst such filth, Amiga ran from it. She moved in with the Hornets, and began to do things that felt like living rather than dying. And she slept, curled up in the warmth of his body. Real, refreshing sleep. For a while, she felt almost free, like she could actually breathe instead of trying to suck air in a vacuum. She can't pinpoint the moment it stopped working. But it did. Cracks had formed somewhere inside, and she sank into them: lost herself again.

That's when she dumped Deuce.

She did it without warning, via IM, lacking the courage to say it to his face. She has no idea how he's forgiven her for that, but he has. And the Hornets... She expected them to close ranks around him, ask her to leave. Instead, they remained her friends, her family, no questions asked. She's pretty sure the Hornets have been the saving of her, even if the lesson's taken a while to sink in.

It's only recently that the lights inside her have begun to flicker on again, unexpectedly, focusing with painful brightness on the parts of her life that still interface directly with death. There's a darkness there, so profound it terrifies her, and all the rage, all the annoyance she directs at life, at Deuce, at circumstance, is redirected from that darkness, her frustrating reliance upon it. She wanted to find the courage to do what's right, but she's been too afraid that she's incapable of doing anything right. Anything healthy.

Some actions have greater consequences than others. Her recent actions with Twist almost lost her Deuce. Nothing makes that okay, and all her bad choices led to that moment, seeing him lying there, sure he wasn't breathing. It can't happen again. What she's going to do today has to constitute a full stop. After this, if she survives, she'll have to find another way to live.

"This is the last time," she says to herself.

"For what?"

Deuce.

She realizes he's been watching her. He does that. It'd be creepy if she didn't find it so fucking reassuring.

"Killing. I don't want to do it any more. After today, I'm not going to."

"What if you need to?"

"Need is different," she says quietly. "Need is to defend or protect. What I meant was, after today, I'm not a Cleaner any more. I fucking quit."

Deuce smiles at her, just like the first time. If only she knew what that smile meant, she's never seen him show it to anyone else.

"'Bout fucking time," he says, serious, not even a little bit of heat in it. "Let's go hand in your notice."

From a large bag at his feet he pulls out a bulky semi-automatic and begins a series of efficient, practiced checks. Handing it along, he pulls out another gun and starts again, until everyone has a gun. Including him.

"Uh... thought you were staying in the engine? Thought maybe Ravi and KJ should stay behind too."

He offers her a very real, very pissed starring role in his line of sight. Ouch. She prefers the smile.

"Why?"

Riding her fury and terrified for him, for Ravi and KJ, Amiga gets aggro, communes with her inner bitch.

"You're physically fucked, KJ's melon's all fracked up and Ravi's the fucking doc. We need him to prevent us from dying, not to die himself. Not. Much. Use."

"Gee, thanks, Amiga." Ravi.

Just about reining in her frustration, Amiga snaps, "You know what I mean, Ravi. Surely?"

"No," Deuce tells her. "No, he doesn't. He just sees your problem. Your fucking ever present problem."

"And what in fuck would that be, Deuce?"

Deuce leans over the gun on his lap.

"Your problem, Amiga, is that you only see people in terms of yourself, and we all fail to match up, whether we could or not. I get it. I get the difference between what you do and what we've done. But you need to quit underestimating us. We've earned it."

Amiga runs out of words to argue with. Deuce is right, as usual. The Hornets saved her and Shock both today, she owes them some fucking credit whether she likes it or not. And oh man does she ever hate it, not because they're useless; because she can't control anything that happens today, and she needs to if their lives are at stake as well as her own. Sighing, she straps her crossbow into a chest harness.

"Just be careful, okay? This is Twist's territory. His people are everywhere and I'm number one on their Cleaning list right now. I won't be able to watch any back but mine no matter how much I want to."

Vivid throws her a smile, and a candy bar, brightly wrapped.

"We know it, shug. And if we all survive today, you can buy us all a fucking beer to apologize for insulting the shit out of us right there. Jeez but you are hard motherfuckin' work."

"Preach it, Vee," KJ calls out, toasting her with his candy bar.

*

The Sendai Station elevator comes out in the back of a rather swish apartment block a ten-minute walk from Denenchofu Plaza. Needless to say, they get some looks, which they ignore. Deuce steals a cater-bike as soon as they're street-level and leaves with Raid to go crack security.

They'd tried to crack the Engine for that, but the damn thing was too complex, despite being old as all hell and Deuce had to give up, muttering something about needing to borrow Shock's fucking avi to get anything done. The rest of the group, forty-three including Amiga, take a circuitous route to Central Gardens to give Deuce and Raid time to crack them a way in.

Almost to the plaza, Amiga, keeping point, shoves out an arm to stop everyone.

"What is it?" Vivid asks quietly, moving forward to stand beside her.

Amiga points to the cadre of vans parked, haphazard, in the roadway before the plaza, not usually used for such a thing, but these vehicles were in a hurry.

"Twist. He came home."

Vivid nods. "Good."

"Good? Really?"

"Yeah, bitch, of course good! Now you get to kill him." The last is said as if it's a thick slice of chocolate cake Vivid can't wait to sink teeth into.

Oh. Point. And wow Vivid's more vicious than Amiga took her for. Probably this is what Deuce meant. She does underestimate them. Vivid's no Cleaner, but her nasty streak is definitely more developed than Amiga's. And it looks like she owns that shit, a huge grin plastered across her face as she contemplates mass crime-lord minion massacre.

Vivid pats her on the back, and gestures the rest of the Hornets out into a semi-circle. They're all low and gun ready, professional as hell to Amiga's critical gaze. Have they done this before?

"We've done this before," Vivid murmurs, as if reading Amiga's mind. "Not with someone like Twist, granted, but it's a fact guys like him don't always send in the Cleaners. Sometimes they hire a bunch like us to go in and take out the competition. It pays better than hacking, so we've never yet turned it down."

"You've helped guys like Twist stay on top?"

"Just like you have, shug. Devil you know, innit?"

Point two to Vivid. She's on a winning streak, or else Amiga's been an ignorant bitch. Unattractive as it might be, she's pretty sure the latter is closest to the truth.

Vivid indicates for Amiga to follow her into the plaza and, without question, she does. They haven't underestimated Twist; she can feel the tension throughout the group, the hyper-awareness. The Hornets know what they're doing, and it's about time she started working with them, instead of for herself. Frankly, after all she's learnt about the sheer depth of her dumb-assery, she no longer wants to be self-employed.

They reach the complex and slip around to the maintenance entrances at the side, where they wait until Deuce and Raid coast up on the bike. Deuce chucks a bag to Vivid. She hands out passkeys to all the Hornets and they go in two by two, not bothering to make it seem random, and head for the shoots. Deuce takes his goggles off and holds them out to Amiga. She tries to refuse, but he drapes them around her right wrist and takes her hands in his. IMs her direct, so she can't ignore him.

There're forty-five of us, over one hundred of them. I've been careful, left as minimal a trail as I can, but he'll be onto the breach before we get to him. He'll be ready. I'm staying down in the building control-centre with Raid, we have some surprises planned. Be prepared. You'll know when to strike, and you'll need these. Okay?

His hands are warm. Feeling them on hers she understands just how cold she's been without them. Without him. Too late now to change that, but she can show him how much she trusts him.

Okay.

He smiles, lets go of her hands and coasts the bike away, back toward the control building nestled in the trees behind the plaza. Takes half of her with him, as he always has. How long is it she's been denying that? Too long. Pulling the goggles onto her head, she nods to Vivid and they enter the building, make their way to the shoots. This will be the first time Amiga's ever taken them. Kinda fitting when this is the last time she's ever coming here.

When Amiga and Vivid reach Twist's house, gunfire is already raging between the Hornets and Twist's troops. Taking shelter behind the rock garden to join the gunfight, Amiga IMs Vivid.

I need to get inside. Deuce has something planned. You guys stay out here. Reckon he's going to light the competition.

Vivid nods. Sounds like Deuce. She pauses, then sucks in her top lip before blurting abruptly, He's single, y'know. Broke up with Fen Maa weeks ago.

Amiga stops firing. Stares.

"What?"

Vivid's eyes shoot wide.

"Hey, IM, bitch," she mutters, and adds, Just thought you should know, because fuck knows he's not going to get around to telling you. You guys make stubborn look downright cooperative.

Well shit. There's a thing Amiga does not know what to do with. Packing it away for the moment, deep down, where it can't affect the decisions she makes today, Amiga continues firing, sticking to her gun for now rather than the crossbow and waiting for whatever it is Deuce and Raid have planned. It's taking a long time.

Minutes go by. Losses begin to pile up on both sides. Most on Twist's, but he's got more to lose. Six minutes passes like an hour. Two more Hornets go down, no time to check whether injured or dead, six more of Twist's troops. Then the building hums all over. And the lights go out.

Snapping the goggles over her eyes, Amiga hits night vision and heads for the house, skirting around the troops hunkered in the garden. Geo's at the front door, his entire bulk taking it up. Damn. She has no desire to kill him, he's no fighter. But where's choice when you need it?

Lifting her wrist, Amiga takes him out quick with a dart to the head. She jumps lightly over his body and runs through to the back room, toward three heat signatures, the only ones in the house. Outside, the lights come back up like Christmas. Every roof light pointed at Twist's, lighting the competition, and judging by the gunfire, the shouts cut off midway, the Hornets are already taking them out.

There'll be no lights in here. No sudden exposure and blinding. Surprise is the only weapon available, and Amiga uses it well, firing her crossbow several times into Twist's heat signature as she enters the back room. He goes down hard, vibrating the wooden floor, and the Guns are on her before she can react, swords cutting at her arms, her torso.

They get in several good slices before she spins out of their way, firing as she goes. Her bolts take out the knees of one, rattle across the torso of the other and they hit the floor, one after the other; all of it in absolute silence.

Seeing her sister fall, Gun Two's mouth gapes in soundless horror. She scrambles across the floor, dragging her legs behind her. Grabs Gun One's hand and starts making shapes with it, trying to speak, but her sister's hand just falls open every time and Gun Two curls over it, her shoulders heaving.

Amiga's shocked to find herself choking back tears. Not helpful. Gun Two won't cry for long, she'll get up and kill Amiga. Emotion won't change that. Tomorrow she can feel all of this, feel as sick and tired and inhuman as she likes; today, right now, she hasn't time. Amiga lifts the crossbow and takes out Gun Two with a clean shot to the head that makes her feel unclean.

Before Gun One stops breathing, Amiga's checking herself over through blurring eyes. The cut in her side is deepest, her fingers slipping into slick flesh, sending a shot of pain darting between belly and knees. Warm blood soaks her shirt, seeps down her trousers. Weigh it up, Amiga. How much more blood can you lose? Not much. Holding her side with her injured arm she goes to make sure Twist is down for good. He's lying face to the floor. Wincing, she shoves him back over with her foot. Finds herself staring at a stranger.

"What?"

The light comes on, blinding her. Swearing, she flings off the goggles.

From behind her, Twist says, "Soft as well as stupid. Tears for my Guns? Really? They're tools. Like you were."

Amiga daren't turn. Can't bear to witness the look on his face. And here she thought collective blood loss was her biggest obstacle to remaining alive. Wow, how wrong can you be? She hears him cocking his gun, deliberately slow. He's going to enjoy this.

"I'm not going to enjoy this." Liar. "It's too fucking

easy. I'm not a fan of easy. It feels like cheating."

As he talks, Amiga closes her eyes and turns the crossbow, careful not to give away movement. This might kill her, it might not. Who cares? Either way she's pretty much a goner. Unlike Twist, she doesn't hesitate, doesn't speak, she just pulls the fucking trigger as many times as she can before her hand stops working. It's painless going in, hurts like hell on the way out, but she's smiling as she hears the thuds of bolts striking flesh. Hears Twist's "Oh" of surprise. They fall together, hit the floor like a heartbeat, bah-dump. Last thing she thinks about before the darkness comes is what Vivid said about Deuce.

Funny how late is always too late.

the towering infernal

Out of the station elevator, Shock leads the pirates to the shoot he cracked with Puss, a dull grey capsule almost too small to hold them all. It rises smoothly, eating up the floors to reach the 498th in minutes and without that peculiar belly sensation of too-fast movement. Shock turns to Petrie before the doors open.

"I've isolated control from the mainframe," he murmurs. "But that's no guarantee they won't wrestle it back. Do not rely on this as an escape route once they're alerted to our presence."

Petrie nods tersely. "That's a given."

They burst from the shoot in small groups, scattering to cover and ready to fire, but no one's there. The whole stone terrace, and the long atrium beyond, studded with islands of trees and ornate pots, drowns in oppressive, ringing silence. None of the usual piped music is playing, and the mechanical birds found in these wealthy buildings are either deactivated or gone. The unexpected emptiness has every alarm in Shock's slow-to-react skull blaring.

"Too fuckin' quiet," Petrie says, gesturing his teams out ahead to the right and left of the terrace, close to the walls. "Don't think we're here first." Keeping Shock just behind him, he moves to the left, asking over his shoulder, "These Harmonys, we've heard rumours, but they really that crazy?"

"Oh yeah. Completely off the rez."

"Fuck."

"You got that right."

Petrie flashes a hand signal and everyone peels out in swift formation into the atrium, using the islands of trees as cover. It'd be perfect if their footsteps didn't ring on the polished stone floor, giving away their position. Still, gunfire takes them off guard, crude in the silence, coming from troops concealed behind the islands up ahead.

The heavy hail of bullets penetrates the foliage with ease, laying out seven of their fifty-strong party in under ten seconds, spattering white stone and bright foliage in Rorschach patterns of blood and gore. Petrie barks out an order to take deeper cover and begins to return fire, dragging Shock behind one of the bulbous plant pots against the wall.

Careening in behind Petrie's broad back, Shock succumbs to dizziness. His head cramps. Pulses like a flash migraine. Seems to disintegrate at the core, becoming heavy, molten—threatening eruption. His body responds with fever, a cold sweat sluicing his skin. He was expecting this, but not so soon. Surely it's too soon, no matter how dire Volk's prognosis was?

He looks for Volk. She's on the other side of the corridor, automatic weapon in hand and laying down fire. If he calls her, they'll know where to shoot. He needs Breaker. Right now. Puss takes the initiative, tapping in to the building's systems and scouting this floor and the two above, looking for anything that feels like Breaker's signal. Finds faint traces in a penthouse on the floor above.

Shock leans in close to Petrie. Murmurs, "I need to go. My drive's not going to hold. Puss found Breaker on the floor above. Going to backtrack and make my way there."

"Go. We'll keep them occupied."

Puss clinging to his torso as he clings to the wall, Shock retreats to the terraced area, closing his eyes to scoot around each pot on the way, sure a stray bullet will end him before Emblem does, almost welcoming the idea. He calls the shoot. Could be locked by now, could be he's stuck here, but it isn't and he's not. He steps in, unsteady on his feet and the shoot moves off, gunfire fading to a distant patter like rain. Soothing. He misses it when it fades away altogether, leaving him alone in silence. Puss tightens her grip on his chest.

We'll be okay.

I hope so, he says, but he remains unconvinced. Puss is reliant upon him, clever as she is, and he's not strong. He's never been strong. He has no idea how he's still standing. Odds were against it from day one.

There's no terraced area on the 499th floor, only a large, echoing lobby with a single feature. A biome tree, leafless and massive, its roots and branches contained beneath glass and stretching all the way out to the walls. There's something melancholy about it, stranded up here so far from earth and sunlight, so far from where it belongs. It shouldn't be alive, trapped in all this steel and glass. That it is feels like an affront.

The centre of the trunk is hollowed out into a walkway, and through it Shock sees the short, cul-de-sac corridor containing the staff entrances to each penthouse, double doors with a scan pad for the passkey. The penthouse with traces of Breaker's signal lies to the left, but he has no passkey to get in. Puss, who's been scanning them, puts his mind at ease.

They're not on the mainframe.

Really?

Jumping into her scan, he offers fleeting thanks to the code jockeys responsible. Whoever they were, they've assumed that with all the layers of Heights VA surrounding them the software and systems for these doors need not be overly complex. They're not stupid simple, but Shock and Puss together are a formidable force. It takes minutes for them to smash past, and then they're in, stepping from polished stone to that echoing white wood floor he remembers from his meeting with Breaker. He tries not to give in to relief. There are only traces here; Breaker himself may be long gone.

Taking the gun from his pocket, Shock closes the door behind him, soft as he can. Fuck but he loathes firearms. He knows the mechanics of shooting, but he's a crap shot. Seems hacking and coding skills requiring excellent hand/eye coord don't necessarily translate IRL. His don't anyway. Puss connects to his jack, and they scan the penthouse for body heat. Find one faint signature in the foremost room, the one he recalls from his meeting with Breaker, with the window curved around the outside edge. The lounge. Someone, possibly Breaker, is sat on one of the large white sofas. Such a thin sliver of heat. Breaker's either not much bigger than Shock, or he's dying and losing body heat fast.

"Fuck."

Shock makes his way through the enormous penthouse as fast as he can. Not fast at all considering the state of him. He's physically wrecked, hurting in every cell, and then there's Emblem, on the verge of implosion. He can feel it moving in there. Rolling from side to side like mercury in a jar, bringing a sensation of liquid sickness to his gut that yaws dizzily with every movement. He's staggering by the time he reaches the lounge. Making his way to the sofa, he sees the back of Breaker's head. Statue-still. Gingerly, he reaches out and pokes his shoulder with the gun.

"Breaker?"

The slight figure damn near elevates out of the sofa, reversing at speed into the window, hands raised, eyes so wide the pupils look like islands in the white. Shock's first thought, after "Fuck, I hope the window holds" is "Scarecrow". Breaker's taller than Shock, though not by much, and skeletally thin.

Splayed against the window he appears somehow pinched in, as if cringing, and far too tense, his entire frame shaking so hard he looks like he might fly apart. His face is all bones, the eyes already huge within that hollowed wasteland. Oddly, the clothes are all wrong. Corp gear. Grubby and threadbare from what looks like continuous wear, but expensive. Haute couture even.

"Breaker?" Shock asks again, more gently.

The hollowed head shakes frantically.

"Lakatos. Josef." His voice is cracked. Trembling. "You can't be here. You shouldn't. Why are you here? He promised me he'd keep you away."

This is Josef Lakatos? This is the owner of Fulcrum? Somehow Shock had imagined him taller, more like a movie villain, Dracula in a hundred-thousand-flim suit maybe. At least the clothes make sense now, but nothing else adds up. What's with the state of him? And why is he here? Word was Kamilla moved to one of the wealthier hubs decades ago. She certainly had no need to stay, Fulcrum could be run from anywhere. Shock would love answers, really, but Emblem won't wait for that and Breaker is not in this room. Shock and Puss scan again, briefly, for Breaker's signal. Still there. Faint, fading traces of it. They aren't anywhere else. He has to be here.

"Where the fuck is Breaker?" Shock demands, too scared to be kind, despite Josef's horrific, enervated state. "He was here. I know he was."

Josef nods, shaking so hard his features are blurring.

"Was. Gone. They took him."

Shock circles the sofa on unsteady legs.

"Who? Where?"

Josef points toward the far exit.

"My floor."

"There's a shoot?"

Josef nods. "Internal."

"Protected?"

"No. Only I use it."

Gathering energy from a body determined to quit on him, Shock makes his way out. Somewhere behind him, he hears Josef say something desperate, pleading, but he hasn't time to stop and listen, his time is almost up.

It takes forever to get through the lounge. The shoot is just outside, rising in the middle of a circular hallway between the rooms of the penthouse. It's a glass shoot, and for a moment he thinks the capsule is missing, then he sees it, glass against glass, and waves the door open to step in. This shoot is warm inside. Hums as if singing. He finds he's humming along, his counter-melody an endless moan, low and miserable. The sickness in his gut is spreading to his bones, and his head pounds and pounds, a hot weight thudding into the top of his spine.

The shoot opens into another hall surrounded by rooms. Where should he go? Breaker could be anywhere here.

Puss slides her tentacles into his jack, carefully, wary of Emblem and they peer through the walls, seeking out a heat signature. There's something twisted back over one of the sofas in the room behind, a puddle of cooling heat around it that can only be one thing. Poised above, like some ravenous bird about to pluck out an eye, curls a wiry, voluptuous shape.

Li Harmony.

Ho's by the window, watching her as he always does, the soft glow of his ever-present psy stick apparent in one elegant hand.

In his desperation to find Breaker, Shock had forgotten them. Thought they'd be with their troops. Foolishness. The Harmonys are never predictable. And here they are, with him. Fear dumps adrenaline across Shock's entire system, a toxic amount, shuddering in his bones, torquing his belly and guts into a single throbbing entity of aching nausea. Spinning back to the door, he tries to get back into the shoot, only to find it gone. His mind disconnects, the weight and heat of Emblem combining with fear to steal comprehension. Puss squeezes his midriff.

Calm, she advises. Remain calm. Inevitability has its own median. Find it.

Shock manages a small nod. He waves for the shoot. It doesn't respond, so he turns toward the room opposite the Harmonys' position and tries to run, only his legs are too wobbly, his body too tired, too ravaged by whatever finale Emblem's dreaming up. The most he can manage is a hitching walk, nowhere near fast enough.

He realizes he's listening, waiting for their feet to follow him. Tries not to think about that cooling shape. Has to be Breaker. Gone. And his only chance to be rid of Emblem gone with him.

And Shock realizes he's not ready to die. He's been holding on to hope for dear life, and now it's gone. Everything's lost, and Li Harmony this close to him is the culmination of a thousand nightmares.

He's halfway through the opposite room, a gallery

of sorts, filled with erotic art formed from bold swirls of hypnotic colour, when he hears them after him. They're not running. He doesn't need to look to see that. On these wooden floors he can hear the resonant clack of Li's strutting and Ho's strolling as if they're a drumbeat tapped out on his skull, counting down the seconds.

"Do stop, Shock," Li says. She's still a way behind but she doesn't bother shouting. The high, vaulted ceilings of these rooms carry sound perfectly.

"Fuck off," he replies, more forcefully than he meant to, putting up a middle finger missing its top joint.

He'd forgotten until now how many of them Pill cut off. It makes him giggle. Li will have to go a long way to beat Pill. She doesn't like being outdone. He laughs harder at the thought, hearing Li's disapproving tut somewhere behind him. Fuck, why is this making him laugh? It's so not funny. Ah, he's fucking terrified. That makes sense. Inappropriate humour are us.

Seconds click down to zero. Ground zero. A hand touches his shoulder, fingers like hooks digging in. Pulling him backward until Li's mouth is at his ear, her soft breath caressing his lobe.

"Did you miss me, baby?"

"Not even," he says, cursing his inner cocky bastard even as he forces Puss to slither down and away, to get clear. Puss goes reluctantly, radiating fury Li probably can't sense.

Spinning him around to face her, Li drives him backward into the wall, right up against a painting depicting some sort of bacchanalian orgy between swirling rainbow figures. As if eager to recreate the scene, she crowds in close. Too close. Body to body. Grinding his broken ribs against each other. Snapping him into that too-clear space pain can invoke. Strange thoughts can strike in those moments—he thinks about how you couldn't slide a blade between them right now without cutting them both, and how much she'd like that. It makes him shudder.

Cold and flat, her eyes stare into his, almost as deep as Volk's, but without any of that distance. She's got nothing in her, so how is it she can be this intimate? Her eyes practically caressing the insides of his skull. Curious. Seeking.

"Where is it in there?" she murmurs. "Right now I'm wondering do I want it more than I want to kill you? I don't know." She sighs. "What do I want, Ho?"

Ho blows out a long stream of smoke. Considers the question with utmost solemnity. He's not Li's shadow. He's her reflection. That's where their likeness rests. Twins with different faces, identical hearts and minds. Cold, dead and little more.

"You expressed a definite interest in killing him. But you wanted to fuck him first," he responds in the end, speaking with careful slowness, each word a morsel.

Imagine a half-circle crack in the ground, that has more personality than Li Harmony's smile.

"So I did," she says, and tilts her head to look down at his body against hers. "You're gay, aren't you, despite the packaging? The package. A girl that likes girls, wearing a boy suit. Cute."

Hatred coils like heat from his bones, steals sense from his head, and he reacts, snarling into her face, her stupid, waxy, fake, fucking blank face, "I'm not a fucking girl."

"Oh really? But you like fucking them. Like your little Mim." She fixes a faux-concerned look to her face. It sits there like it's been painted on plastic. Gross. "Hey, did you know your Shark ate her? Fun fact of the day. Well, I found it funny." She leans in and sniffs his eyes, as if expecting him to cry.

He can't cry. Not for Mim. Not any more. If Shark ate her then she was after him. If Li knows it, then Mim was after him for Li. No prize for guessing what she was after doing. She didn't deserve to die, not really, but he deserved better than her. Or maybe he didn't. Maybe they deserved better than each other.

Disappointed by his lack of response, Li whispers in his ear, "Did you ever pretend you still had your pussy when you fucked her?"

Using his whole torso, Shock shoves her back. It hurts so fucking much, but goddamn it feels good. He snarls into her face, "I was never a girl. Understand? Sometimes, the body lies. Like yours does."

"Mine?"

"Yeah. You look like a human being."

Her face smooths out like oil.

"Very clever. Now I think I just want to kill you. But I really, really want to hurt you first."

She turns her head to look at Puss. He sees nothing in her eyes but Puss's reflection, and he wants to scream at Puss to flee. Disappear. Go back to Shark down there in the station. Anywhere but here. Why is he so scared for Puss? She's a hologram. Li can't touch her. Li blinks in slow motion, the movement cutting off his view of Puss in her eyes.

"Guess what I made?" she asks him.

"I don't know, and I don't care."

She turns her head to look at Ho and they share this little laugh. It makes Shock's skin crawl.

"Oh, you will," she murmurs to Shock, leaning right in to his ear, her body crushing his into the wall again, bringing that awful clarity back.

He doesn't want it. Wants to be anywhere else but here with her body pressed into his, making him nauseous.

She raises one hand. There's a thin mesh on it, with plain metal circles facing outwards on the fingertips and palm. Oh so gently, in a movement of over-familiar sensuality, she slides it round his neck, under his hair, until her hand rests where his jack lies, over the part of his brain holding his neural drive. Li pulls back from his ear so they're face-to-face, close enough for him to smell her breath. Sweet mint. If she kisses him, he'll throw up.

"Boom," she whispers.

White light flashes across his whole vision, flares through his body; forked lightning arcing from nerve cluster to nerve cluster, lighting his body from head to toe. Instant agony. In his mind he hears Puss: screaming. Puss is a haptic hologram; she's connected to his drive, his nervous system, and Li's flooding it with pain, disruption. What she's hoping to do he doesn't know. Can't know. His whole body is aflame with pain, his mind's bursting with it. Overloading. Too much sensation at once. He flickers between consciousness and unconsciousness, trying to find peace in oblivion, but he can't switch off. Whatever Li's made it it's overriding his body's impulse to shut down.

In his drive, bloated and massive, molten with its own incredible heat, Emblem picks up the impulses as it throbs and rolls within him. Begins to vibrate in tune. The sensations grow and intermingle; pain becomes light, vibration becomes thunder, and behind Shock's eyes, blinded by white pain, by black flickers of unconsciousness, the complex knot of Emblem swells, straining the very limits of his drive, and bursts out, exploding across his mind, that heat lapping into every corner, burning everything in its path.

Lost in nerve-agony, and deafened by the screams of his avi, Shock experiences the pyrotechnics from far above himself, watching almost incuriously as the tidal wave sweeps across his brain. It steals pain, then thought, then screams, then Shock himself. Sweeping him away momentarily until the tide turns, sweeping him back in. And like the sea engulfing the spaces between rocks at the cliff's edge, he re-fills his own mind, but it's no longer just him. It's Emblem. He and Emblem mixing together. One in the other. No tangles, no knots, no seams. He's still here, still him, but pain free and different.

He looks at Li, who has yet to realize something's wrong. His body's still shaking, responding to the effect of her continued attack on his nervous system, but he's outside of it, and inside of her, seeing directly into her like Puss vision. He can see into her drive. Beyond it. View her other self, floating in Slip, waiting for her. Golden and vile that other self is. A huge distortion of flesh, tentacles and teeth, holding all the hunger she hides; such polluted, grotesque hunger he feels violated to witness it. Yet even as he recoils he sees the link between Li and her avi self. Invisible until now, but always there.

Casually, he realizes he can cut it.

So he does.

Li snaps away from him, screeching, a high noise without form. Tears mindlessly at her head. The thing on her hand makes her body jerk like a marionette, and blood begins leaking down her neck, onto her shirt, mingling with a stain that can only be from Breaker. She spins away down the corridor. Disappears into the room beyond, that dreadful animalistic screech punctuated by the crash of objects smashing to the floor. Ho lowers his psy, staring after her with empty eyes. For a second or two it looks like he might smile, but he takes off at a run, calling her name. He sounds like a child.

Shock tries to move. His body's still scrambled by Li's glove, by the sudden explosion of Emblem and the subsequent info-overload. Nothing's working properly; whatever synergy enabled him to look into Li is gone for the moment. He can't even panic, his senses and reactions short-circuited. Fused out. He can hear though, and the sound from the room beyond resounds loud as trucks colliding, breaking the standoff between his senses. But it's too late. There's Ho, at the end of the gallery, body rested languidly against the wall.

"She flew," he says, careless, emotionless, leaving Shock wondering what he's done. "She always flew. Now she's flown away. Such a pretty picture."

Shock has no idea what to say. Anything could provoke Ho, and he's one of the few people who's never dismissed Ho. He might have bought that drugged-up demeanour wholesale if he weren't an addict himself. Being is knowing. He's always known Ho's addiction was a front. Ho can give or take those expensive psy he constantly sucks on. He's been hiding behind them, aware of Li's need to take centre stage and clearly too smart to let her kill him easily.

Ho pushes away from the wall. Walks toward Shock.

"So, what do I do with you?"

He tosses the psy to one side as he comes, discarding his high just as casually. Does nothing touch this guy? 'Course not. There's nothing to touch. Shock's not a fighter. He has the gun but his body's not together enough to use it. So he does what he should have done with Li and perhaps a few times before.

He calls Shark.

Shock feels the surge of movement as Shark explodes through 400-odd floors, bursting up through the gallery between them just as Ho removes a thin filleting knife from his jacket. Seventeen feet of enraged golden predator plough into him teeth first. With a toss of the head, Shark flips Ho up against the ceiling. Hot blood spatters down, chased by gobbets of flesh as Shark drives into Ho's body, shaking its head.

Horrified by the level of his violence, the depth of his rage, Shock tries to stop Shark, but Shark ignores his pleas. The predator has waited, as it was asked, and now it won't wait, will not listen. It has its own anger to appease, Shock's anger. Hidden too long and now finally unleashed. When it's done, Shark swims serenely away down the gallery, radiating satisfaction, leaving Ho to drop to the floor, a rag of flesh in a sharp suit. Hands shaking, Shock wipes his face with the bottom of his tee, too numb to feel, too scrambled to process. Unsure of whether to laugh or cry.

Puss slides up his leg, onto his torso, gently, careful not to disturb rib bones still broken and now moving again thanks to Li Harmony.

Is it over? he asks her. Because he really doesn't know.

"Run." The voice is weak. Broken. Pleading. "I told you to run. Why didn't you run? They're coming. You brought Emblem too close, and they're coming for it. I can't hold them any more. I'm so sorry."

Shock turns. Behind him stands Josef, holding himself against the wall with one arm, his body drooping, heaving with exhaustion. Josef looks up, and in his eyes golden lights swirl. Particles gather. "Run," he whispers. "Now."

change is underrated

darkness is like the deep sea. There's no comfort in that thick swell around you, pulling you under, only panic gripping the limbs, the heart, the guts, and squeezing hard. Amiga's never been near the sea, but she dreams of drowning. Doesn't everyone? Now she's not dreaming. She's drowning in darkness, in liquid cold filling her chest, dragging at her limbs.

The urge to sleep, to let go, is overwhelming, but there's no coming back from that, and Amiga's beyond terrified of the finality in it. She's not ready for this. Not ready to give up, to let it all end. Frantic she clings on to awareness, fights the drag of a body convinced it's too damaged to continue, weakened by blood loss and become so terribly heavy. Too heavy to hold onto.

The thought of losing her grip galvanizes her. She's screaming inside as she claws back consciousness, determined to find light, find air, to beat her body. They are at war and she refuses to surrender. With ferocious intent, she fights the darkness, that oh-so-tempting desire to rest, to sleep; and in the darkness peeks a glimmer of light.

Closer and closer it comes. Brighter and brighter. And

then pain hits. So much fucking pain. Her chest burns, her lungs, her throat. Air rasps like wires, every one abrading, and she's pulling at them, trying to tear them out. Hands grab at hers, holding them away, but the air, it hurts.

"Amiga!"

The voice hits from a distance. And again, closer. "Amiga!"

"Amiga!"

Closer still. The rasp in her throat worsens for a second. It rises, choking her, then disappears. It's bliss. Fucking amazing.

"Amiga!"

She starts awake into the middle of a coughing fit, her lungs on fire. There's a shadow hovering above her. She grabs for it. Blinking frantically she tries to clear her vision. In blurry flashes a face comes into view. Moustachioed. Brown eyes alight with concern.

"Ravi?" Dear heaven talking hurts.

"Right here, girl. Right here. Fuck but you had me scared."

It's Ravi. Definitely Ravi. His gloves drenched in gore, a gun full of C-Gen gripped in his hand.

He turns and calls out, "She's awake!"

Footsteps to her side. Vivid appears in her peripheral vision, an odd look on her face.

"Hey. Hey there. Wow, you're fucking crazy, you know that? You popped a lung. Clean smashed it through with almost a dozen fucking darts. Ravi's taken an age to patch and re-inflate it. Had to intubate you and everything. Scary arse shit, bitch. How you feeling?"

"Like I've been chewed up and spat out."

Amiga tries to move, to sit up. Ravi slaps a hand on her forehead.

"Still, dammit. Almost done." He leans down and finishes putting her thigh back together. It hurts like hell. "There. Good as new. Sort of. Well, not really. But you're alive."

"Thanks for that, Ravi," she mutters.

"Well, you know, I do my best. Even when idiots consider it necessary to fire crossbow bolts through their own torso. What the fuck were you thinking?"

"He had a gun pointed at my back."

Ravi makes a considering face.

"'Spose that could be a reason. But you know anatomy. Coulda been a tad more careful."

"Er... not long to think."

He sniffs. "Excuses. Next time use those seconds to rustle up a better angle, eh? Don't like having to patch my friends up. Don't like having to bring them back from the fucking dead. It harshes my fucking shine." He grabs her arm, not allowing her time to respond. "Come on. Up. Let's see if my handiwork is handy enough."

Trying not to feel the guilt sloshing about in her system, because she could have aimed a little better if she weren't being all self-pity machine and shit, Amiga allows him to yank her up from the floor. Immediately, she throws up in spectacular fashion, the violent heaves sending flashes of pain like static electricity across her chest and down her side. Ravi holds on to her, keeping her steady, letting her rest against him as what seems like an entire week's worth of food ejects itself from her stomach.

"There we go. Let it all out," he says, rubbing her back. "Had to pump you full of a few unpleasant drugs to keep you stable whilst I worked. Best they're out, for sure."

"Fucking bastard," she chokes out.

"Fucking idiot," he replies cheerfully. "All done?"

She hangs down, waiting out a few last heaves. Enduring them. Nothing else comes up, so she wipes her mouth and straightens in careful increments, wary of setting herself off again. Asks the important question first.

"Where's Twist?"

Ravi turns her. "There."

Twist's splayed out on the floor in a pool of blood, arms akimbo, and she's pleased to see how well her bolts got him. Just below the heart. Judging by the amount of blood they tore right through the pulmonary. In which case the neat bullet hole in the cranium could be seen as overkill. Ah, there's the reason for that look on Vivid's face. She raises a brow at Vivid.

"Double-tap, Vee? Really?"

"Better to be sure," Vivid replies.

"I can dig that. Grab one of those swords from the Guns there, would you?" Amiga asks her.

"Ooh, souvenir?" asks Vivid, doing just that.

"If you like. First I want you to cut off his head."

Vivid places a hand on her heart.

"You spoil me. Genuinely."

"You ladies are fucking nuts," Ravi says, shaking his head in amazement. "I adore you."

Couple of hard strikes later, interrupted by a reel of cursing, Vivid has the head.

"That was harder than I thought."

"Vertebrae," Amiga says, ever practical. "Never underestimate them."

"Logged and internalized for future ref." Vivid grabs the head by the hair and lifts it. "Where's this going?"

"Vault."

Understanding without having to ask what Amiga wants, Vivid hands her the head and takes her other side to help Ravi lead her to the vault. Deuce is in there on the computers, unravelling Twist's network and anything else he can sabotage. He raises a brow at Amiga, who's got Twist's head rammed under her bad arm. She doesn't buy his insouciance for a second, he's pale as his mother right now, fear hanging in his eyes like unshed tears.

"His head? Really, Amiga? Overkill." He sounds as shaky as he looks. Sounds like he wants to say something else. It can wait.

Amiga untangles from Ravi and Vivid, allows her body to find its equilibrium, and limps to the tanks, lifting the lid from Nero's. She wants to say something meaningful, instead she finds herself rambling.

"I'm sorry about your eyes," she says to him. "And your ears. And your tongue. And... well, actually, I'm kinda sorry about everything. I was having a bad day. It wasn't your fault. Anyway, I brought you some company as an apology of sorts. I think you'll grok the joke."

She plops Twist's head in and replaces the lid. Turns to find Vivid, Ravi and Deuce staring at her.

"What?"

"That was... interesting," says Deuce, trying not to laugh.

"Yeah... well... I felt bad okay?"

He smiles, and it's that smile again. Her smile.

"Fair enough. I'm about done here. Twist's clearly very done. What shall we do next?"

"How are the other teams doing?"

"Efficient. Make us look bad almost."

Taking a break from staring at him before her eyes melt, Amiga struggles to think of what to do. There's a lot she wants to say to Deuce, and from the look in his eyes, oh that look, she can see there's one hell of a lot he wants to say to her.

Jeez, it really can wait. Today has been hella long, and she's feeling all kinds of fucking raw, in body and mind. Besides, she's taken on a new role, one she intends to be as honest as possible in after somehow surviving killing herself. And there's a half-broken ex-Haunt who might be in need of practical help from a half-broken ex-Cleaner.

"Let's go help Shock," she says. "He might be grateful of some back-up."

She looks at Deuce to gauge his reaction, and is relieved to find he's still smiling at her. Except there's something different. Something wrong. In the black depths of his poker-chip eyes, golden lights are swirling.

so what happens
in the end

reality ripples around Shock. He was in the self-same position as Josef only this morning. Gold erupting from his eyes. Something coming through IRL that was never meant for it. Was it this morning? Aeons have passed. Whole lifetimes flashing by on fast forward. At this moment, two feet planted on the ground means nothing. His truth was in another universe where time stood still for years, paused in Sendai. Now he's running ahead of time, feet on fire, mind reeling. Gold lacing through each and every thought he owns.

Does he own his thoughts? Surely he must share them? He's not one but three. Three minds in one. Three minds where there was only one this morning. Or was there? What is the truth?

And how many Queens? Six. Six behemoths against one Shock, one Puss, one Shark.

Still fighting for a truth that fits this moment, just as he's still fighting for a truth that fits his own and all the moments he's encountered since, Shock turns from the gold gathering in Josef's eyes. Walks down the gallery one shaking step at a time, feeling surreal, like a puppet in his own body, unsure who's driving, who's making the decisions. Because this is impossible. You can't run from the impossible. The Queens can't come through Josef. How could they? They're not avis. They're made for Hive. That's where they belong. And yet, gold light fills the gallery. They are coming. Truth has changed. It's changing faster than time these days.

And there's another truth he's trying to grasp. Could the Queens wield the same power out of Hive as they do within it? Surely they'll be reduced out here? Vulnerable maybe. Shock wants to convince himself of it, but Shark disagrees. It's agitated, harrying. Turning every now and then to make sure Shock's following and fear grows through Shock's uncertainty like golden light, obscuring all else.

Shark's a tool, a tool made from Shock, the hungry, angry parts of himself he's suppressed for far too long. Shark can't speak like Puss, and yet it's emanating tension, unease, more eloquent than any language could express. Puss, who can speak, is strangely silent, grips Shock's torso tighter and tighter as the golden glow blooms to dawn-bright intensity.

What? he asks her. What is it?

Get out. Get out, please, she replies, and tries to hide in him. So she can't see.

What the hell? Shock moves faster, trying to run, driven by their fear. As afraid for them as they appear to be for him, for each other. Beyond the gallery, another lounge. Huge. Filled with antique furniture broken beyond repair by Li's manic whirl through the room.

And there's Ho's actions, right there. The tinted sliding windows along the room's right side are pushed wide, their frames bent out of skew. Wind whistles in from the balcony, icy cold. Li flew all right, but not without help.

Was she aware of Ho's treachery? Shock hopes so. There's no justice in her being allowed to die oblivious. That's too kind for one such as her. Shivering, he makes his way to the windows and looks out, his hair blowing madly around his face.

Curling away from the balcony is the outside corridor to the residential shoot. He can use it to get away. He laughs. Crazy thought that: away. In Hive the Queens are easily as tall as Heights, perhaps even taller. If they appear IRL as his avis have, they'll be the same, and if there's reason to fear them there'll be nowhere he can run. Better to turn and fight. But how do you fight hologrammatic colossi who control every sec-drone in the Gung? What do you fight them with?

Giving in to his instinct, he hurries out along the balcony, and makes for the shoot.

We need to crack the res shoot, he says to Puss.

I'll try. There are layers of VA. They come from the entrance, not the staff quarters.

Shock leaves her to it, still too fried to help. If only Emblem were doing what it did with Li, then he could jack into Slip, help Puss bypass all the VA. But Emblem's dormant. He can feel it there, right through him, almost like an avi, with little to distinguish Emblem from self; only its code is visibly different, a delicate filigree sewn through him, into him. Carefully he prods at it, trying to make it respond. Nothing. Perhaps he damaged it somehow by cutting Li's connection to her avi? Just because you can do a thing, doesn't mean that you should. Doesn't mean that it's safe.

Battling against the wind, Shock makes it to the outer walkway. Made entirely from glass, it's like walking on air, floating. How he wishes he could float away. Behind him, Josef lets out one half-choking scream, and gold light explodes through the whole penthouse, followed by the most enormous legs, still weaving into existence.

Here come the Queens.

Those legs pass the corridor, lighting up Shock's face, and keep going, no sign of a body yet to follow. Only when they've almost touched the ground does he see the first head emerging, feelers waving, eyes fixed on him. He feels them. Like weights. Like in Hive. And he knows.

"Ah shit," he says, and shifts up a gear to a shambling run he won't be able to maintain.

Her head moves close to the glass, compound side eyes reflecting multiple Shocks, wild-haired and wide-eyed, terror written all over his skin. She's in his head, too. Small at first, as if unsure of her power, her size outside of Hive, and then vast, confident, overwhelming. Fuck but if he thought Emblem was huge, she smashes that delusion, steamrolling into his mind and crushing it beneath her weight.

Shock Pao, she says, and her voice deafens him, roaring like a hurricane through his brain. Did you not think we knew you would try to run? Did you not think we would have means to bring you back to us? Amuse us. Try again. Try and run.

Shock has no intention of remaining. He stumbles on toward the end of the walkway. Weighed down by the Queen's monstrous presence, Emblem stirs. Wakes. And in those moments of waking, it throws her from his mind, some shadow of its old function temporarily come to life. She exits laughing, as if Emblem is a flea batting at her face. She's right. This eviction is no more than a gesture. Emblem can't keep her out, it's not what it was; not just a lock any more.

Freed from the burden of her, Emblem finishes what it began before he used it to destroy Li; altering his perception, making him a living uplink forever both inside and outside of Slip. He's running along a glass walkway, which is also a schematic, whilst floating inside of Slip, surrounded by millions of avis. The avis see him too. Curious, they stop to stare, and he realizes that he's golden there, just as Breaker made him before. An anomalous human-shaped fish.

Puss is beside him, serene and graceful, and Shark too, back in their ocean at last, and their delight radiates. They've been trapped far away from the familiar, and vulnerable. Now they're like he is, half IRL and half in Slip—stronger than ever before. But they're not strong enough, not dangerous enough. He warns them against attacking the Queens and makes for the shoot.

Through his new perception—the underlying patterns he used to only see with Puss's help augmented by his reconnection to Slip—he can see in a glance how to crack his way in. So simple. Layers of VA undone with a single thought. Why can't everything be like this? He steps in, amazed that even through this information overload and the chaos of Slip he knows where to put his feet.

Looking out across inner city as the shoot begins to travel downward, he finally sees the other Queens, all five of them, striding across the Gung. They dwarf everything, casting endless shadows between 'scrapers, over rooftops. Around them flit hundreds of drones, flashes of silvery light. He looks up again, wary of losing the sixth—or is she the first?—even though she's too big to lose. She's still watching him; he feels her interest as profoundly as if she were still inside his mind.

This close to her, with Emblem alive within him, he can finally see what she is. Avi after all. Josef's avi. But not always his. Running through her in streams, the taste of Kamilla, never entirely forgotten. Stronger than Josef, more able, until she got sick. Until they made her sick, and now Josef too. And before them? Not avi at all. Intelligence. Pure calculation built from code and so strong, so full of intent they were afraid of it, tried to lasso it with human thought, human intent. And all it did was give her different ways to think. Different ways to outthink them. Are the other Queens like her? Like this?

He turns his attention back to them and finds them the same, but lesser. Later models, designed to corral her, and incapable of doing so. She made them part of her gestalt. Fine filaments link them all together, linking them to Josef's Queen and, through her, to Josef. Parasites piggybacking his drive. He's been trying to hold them back. Relying on Emblem to keep them in check, hoping it would hold until they could find a way to make it stronger, whilst suffering the pressure of them inside him.

And how long did Kamilla hold them back before him? Unthinkable that this struggle has gone on in such secrecy, that they've managed to keep it between them. Then again, it's easy to make people believe what you want them to when you have access to their minds through something like Slip. How many times will they have subtly rewritten the truth that way?

The Queen bends down, watching him travel in the shoot, suffocating him with her presence. He wants nothing more than to be wherever she can't touch him. The hunger in her gaze horrifies him.

Shock!

Petrie. Shock nearly drops to the floor, relief stealing what little strength he has. Tries to keep himself from showing elation, so the Queen can't pick up on it. Is Volk there?

Yeah, we lost maybe half of our people though.

Damn, I'm sorry.

Part and parcel. We're on the top floor with Josef. He's on the way out. Says the Queens are beyond his control anyway. What do we do? How can we help you?

How can they help him? He wracks his brain, trying and failing to come up with any solutions.

I don't know.

Volk interrupts with her usual impatience, and something else. Something he's never heard from her. Excitement.

Shock, the Queens are avis. Well, the Alpha is, sort of, and the others resonate that way through her.

Yeah, I know. How'd you guess?

Josef told me. I have an idea.

The shoot reaches ground level. Shock looks out onto a chaotic mass of people trying to run from things so giant there's literally no way outrun them. Trying to escape drones intent upon killing everything in their path. There's blood everywhere, on everyone, people falling down in the street, their avis falling in Slip all around him, some writhing as if fighting death with everything they have, others unfurling to bytes as they go. A confetti of gold.

He sends Shark after the drones, to turn them off, smiles viciously as they too begin to drop from the sky, silver amongst the gold. There are too many for Shark to deal with alone, but it won't tire. It'll keep on until they're all gone. The Queens will remain though, and he already knows they have no good intentions for the Gung.

Tell me.

I brought a weapon with me. A drug called Disconnect. You can guess what it does, the effect it would have. I was going to use it on you. Make sure the Queens could never reach Emblem.

This is news. Not so long ago it would have been enough to end his part in this endeavour, no matter how important. But he understands now. He'd do the same.

What can you do?

Isolate the Queens inside their server, like a giant flash drive.

They're connected to Josef. Will you use it on him?

On his drive. If I embed it in the section dedicated to Core, with all its separate VA protocols, I can make a prison for them, disconnect them from everything. Then we shut down Core, and they're gone.

Core is the centre of Slip, Volk. Know what they put there? Our avis. All their information. Shut Core down, and you shut down all the avis.

Silence.

Shit. What can we do? It needs to be Core. It can't be Hive. Shutting Hive would be catastrophic. Everything would go dark: Gung, hubs, land ships. The world as we know it: gone.

Shock looks around again, at all the people running. At Slip, avis falling gracefully to the seabed. Avis and drives are intertwined. Core might hold all the data for avis, but avis originate from the drive, inextricably linked to each one. Shock contains Emblem, and Emblem freed his avis from Slip. They're linked only to him now, reintegrated. Three into one. What if he could do that for everyone?

I could bring the avis out of Slip, all of them.

Silence.

You can do that? Something like awe in her voice.

Emblem can, I think.

You think?

If it can't, we're screwed huh? Go. Do what you need to.

Okay. She pauses. Shock, when I start to do this, I think they'll come for you. Try to force their way in. Don't let them. If they manage to take over from your avis, then I'll have to use your drive for this, and I will not hesitate, because they cannot stay out, they cannot control us. Understand?

Shock closes his eyes. Yeah. I understand.

IRL he limps to the courtyard, between glistening sculptures, and with Puss in Slip he travels to Core, amazed at how easy it is now, the VA parting before him as if he's a god. He tries to figure out how to recreate what happened to him without quite knowing how Emblem did it. Working blind. Struggling against Emblem until he realizes Emblem is the part of him that knows how to do this. So he leaves it to that part of himself, concentrating on keeping the physical self out of drone fire, hidden from anyone in the crowd who might have followed him to Heights.

Turns out he's not so great at hiding now he's no longer a Haunt. Yang yells his name. Concealed behind sculptures, behind cars, behind anything solid enough to protect them, are his troops, firing at drones alongside the Dengway Mafia and the Grey Cartel, brought together by fear and circumstance. Yang yells again, and they cease firing. Turn their guns on Shock.

"Where can you go?" Yang calls out as Shock continues walking. "You're ours."

Shock doesn't slow. Doesn't even acknowledge them. They won't shoot him, he's too valuable, and Emblem's almost done.

Any. Second. Now.

"Come along, Shock, have some dignity," Yang calls out, almost friendly. He thinks he's won. They all do. In a way they have. They just don't know it yet.

Emblem sighs in his body, in his cells. Not a sound of satisfaction. This sigh is like something once sealed tight finally opening, that breath of release when the locks are breached and the doors swing wide. A lock becomes a key. So much more than Breaker and Josef meant for Emblem to become. Shock stops to watch, seeing in the activity of Slip how breath has paused. None of the avis around him seem to know what to do. The door is open, and they don't understand that they're free.

The exodus begins unexpectedly, with a woman hiding in the shadow of liquid-metal sculptures trapped in plas-glass, her arms clasped to her chest like armour. Her eyes tune out. Go blank. She grabs her head, fingers tensed into her skull. Broken-throated screams erupt from her like vomit and in the depths of her eyes, gold lights begin to swirl, particles to form, bursting like rays of sunlight to illuminate the sculptures, turn liquid metal into liquid light.

From her, it's a knock-on effect. Human dominoes. Hands rise to skulls, eyes burst golden beams like search lights across the sky and, from here to the city limits and beyond, in the hubs and on the land ships, avis weave themselves into being. Millions upon millions of avis threading from Slip to RL. Disappearing from one place to the other like sand through the neck of an hourglass, glistening as they go. Fucking hell but it's beautiful. Shock's arrested by the sight. Stolen. Unable to move as street becomes Slip. Becomes oceanarium. Alive with golden sea life.

Eels dart between legs; ponderous dugongs graze the traffic; schools of tuna dance between streetlights; dolphins dive across the roofs of cars; seals frolic, chasing each other through the air. Everywhere Shock looks are hammerheads, squid, narwhals, lionfish, sunfish, anglerfish, every manner of marine life, real or imagined, from the tiniest shrimp to the impossibly huge pod of great golden humpbacks gliding down the centre of the Strand, silent and majestic as ocean liners. They open their mouths and mournful song echoes from glass and steel. Life is everywhere, glistening even without sunlight. Transforming the street, the city, the world, into a goldmine no one can touch.

Momentarily confused by the chaos, the escape of the

avis, the drones ceased fire. Now they begin again, pushed by the Queens to destroy this rich centre of the Gung. But other avis, looking from Slip through human eyes, have already seen what Shark's been doing, and they join him in their hundreds, their thousands, taking down every drone they touch. Emptying the sky, transforming silver flashes to soaring flocks of gold.

Breathing in deep, Shock begins to limp forward again, aware there's nowhere he can go to hide, but determined not to be caught waiting. Yang runs toward him, lifting his gun, his face full of the same delirium, the same confusion Shock remembers from when his avis first came out of Slip. Only this morning. Still only this morning. How far he's come.

Yang's avi is a moray eel, poking out from under his arm; its face belligerent even in repose. Resting bitch face. Figures.

"Stop," Yang demands, his gun trembling. "What've you done?"

"Saved you," Shock says, still walking. "We have to stop the Queens. We're going to lock them in Core, shut it down. Your avi was in there. You want it in there when that happens? Tell me you could survive it. Go on. Lie to me."

Yang can't seem to find words. His first instinct will be to lie, and there's no way to do it. No words to find that will fit a lie that works. Shock watches as realization follows intent across Yang's face. As his arm, catching up with thought as the body often does—in slow motion, a beat behind—lowers toward the ground.

"Go," he says. "Get the hell out of here."

It happens then, right in front of Yang. The Queens fall on Shock's mind. Dig in, huge and irresistible; their hunger so potent he vomits blood. He falls to the ground on hands and knees, his brain under siege. For the second time he hears Puss scream, feels Shark thrashing in pain as the Queens try to tear them loose, to destroy them, and Shock's screaming too. Pure agony. Screaming, retching, and fighting with everything he's got to hold his drive shut, keep them out. Screaming internally at Emblem to hold him together, to lock him tight.

If the Queens get in, if even one of them gains a foothold, he'll lose his avis, himself, and in this moment, understanding that, he finally begins to comprehend how little of himself he knew. How much of him was hidden in them. How much he let them hide from him, because he couldn't bear to see it. Whole reams of self locked safely within them and about to be ripped away. He wants to see it, to learn himself, to learn to live with himself. It's not too late. It can't be.

Volk yells into his mind. Hold on, Shock! Just hold on in there. I'm going as fast as I can.

He could tell her he's trying. He is. But the Queens are too strong. He can't fight them like this. Has to find another way, a way to be equal to them somehow. An advantage. He can only think of one, and it fills him with as much dismay as hope. Shock looks into Slip for that thing Li left behind when she died. The Kraken. He finds it where it was, coiled up tight, and all as huge, all as revolting.

He picks up the strand of connection he broke, and links it to his drive. It's vile to touch even when no longer active, sending ice through every vein, every neurone. Li was all kinds of wrong, and her thoughts, her impulses infect this mass of suckered flesh all through, their corruption a stench he can't ignore. Bracing himself, he reawakens it, puking again as the filth of it flows through him.

Awake, aware, alive once more, and barely under his control, the Kraken explodes from Shock's eyes in soaring leaps of gold, sending Yang and the men around him running. Hungry, eager to destroy, it tries to break loose, go where it wants, to anything smaller, anything weaker, Puss and Shark included. Shock hauls it back, his mind creaking under the strain as he corrals to his control, driving it upward toward the Queens. As it rises, its tentacles fill the sky: huge fleshy gold appendages covered in suckers the size of craters. It's a city hub of coiled and urgent flesh on the hunt.

Eager to hurt whatever it can, denied easy pickings, the Kraken launches at Josef's Queen, the first, the strongest, flowing through the air to latch onto her body, tangle around her huge limbs. Her silence is terrifying, denotes a fierce will, a determination outstripping even the very size of her. She tries to hold on to the Heights, but the Kraken is too strong, and she topples. Anticipating impact, Shock can only stare, stunned, as she and the Kraken hit the ground together, two gargantua locked into warfare that affects only themselves, each other. It doesn't seem possible.

The Kraken tears at her with relish, pulling one of her legs clean off. Then another. As they break loose, their golden threads untangle, dispersing into the air like mist. Snapping its beak forward, it gouges out one of her eyes, tears off a feeler. She's keening now. Her voice shaking the air as her body could not shake the ground. Shock's unable to think, to see. Everything is her pain, her agony, her outrage. It reaches out, distracts the other Queens from trying to crack his drive.

They rush to her side, grabbing the Kraken's tentacles with their incisors. Obscuring even that great tentacled bulk with their vast bodies, they rip chunks from its thrashing limbs, its golden head. Shock's never felt pain like it. Attaching it to him, he's linked it to his neural system, and the agony prostrates him. He thinks he might have pissed himself.

And the Queens are winning, the Kraken dying, dissipating into mist. In a few seconds it'll be gone for good, and if Shock doesn't break the connection, let it go, it'll take him with it. By the time he remembers, he's too weak, can already feel himself fading away. Puss tries to help but she's too weak herself, too hurt by the Queens.

Shock. I have them.

Volk's voice barely registers. Shock's staring at the remnants of the Kraken, watching as his last moments fade into fragments of mist and dissipate. Too broken to fight. Too lost to care. It's Shark that saves him, saves Puss, powering in from nowhere to savage the fine thread between Shock and the Kraken, rending it apart as the final pieces of that creature dissolve. With nothing to distract them, and aware of Volk's meddling now, the Queens turn on Shock as one, ploughing their minds into his.

Helpless in the wake of their attack on the Kraken, the harm it caused him, Shock has no means to resist. No will to hold against theirs. They hit like a hurricane, tearing his mind apart, tearing Shark's connection from him as if it were nothing. As if it were meaningless. Shark's swimming toward him, desperately trying to reach him when the connection goes. It stutters mid-air, flailing, and mandibles close around it, shattering it to motes of gold. Crying out, Shock reaches for Shark, for everything that's gone with it, atomized into thin air. The grief is immeasurable. All-consuming.

He holds on to Puss for dear life, knowing she's next and then he'll be nothing, an empty slave, the Queens' plaything, but it never happens. They're gone. Their weight out of his mind, leaving it too light, light enough to float away, their bodies no longer devouring the skyline, leaving nothing but vast 'scrapers to dominate in their stead, crowding out his vision.

Shock hears the Queens screaming fury. Is it them? He can't tell if the sound is real or imagined as, through Emblem, he watches Core sputter and go dark. Cease to exist. There's still Slip, everywhere, as far as his eye can see, further, and the life outside of Slip, but at the centre... only darkness. It has swallowed them whole. Swallowed him.

Laying his head on the ground, Shock's too grief-stricken to cry. The darkness within is all but absolute; the part that was once Shark now lies dead. Empty. He's a fractal, core reflecting core reflecting emptiness into infinity. How will he bear it? He can't. If Puss weren't here, her tentacles laid across his back, her head rested on his, he'd die right now. Just let go. It would be so simple.

Shock!

Volk. He can hardly speak, even via IM.

Are you okay?

Stupid question.

Shark, he says, then his throat strangles. Paralyzes. He can't say it. Can't speak any more. What use are words? What use is he?

I'm so sorry, she says. She means it. It doesn't help. Hold on, we'll be there in a minute. We're coming. Just hold on.

Nothing she says registers. Shock wants to lie on the ground forever. Be absorbed into it. Disappear. Atomize like Shark and join it wherever it's gone. But the gold gleam of Puss's head, so close to his, illuminates his lids; turns them into cathedral windows, flooding light and colour into echoing emptiness.

He stares at the red tracing of capillaries, all of them connected, and realizes he's not the only one who's lost someone. He's not the only one hurting. Puss is broken too. Hurt by Li, by the Queens, by Shark's loss. Hurt by his removal in grief. More vulnerable than ever, even though she's partially back in Slip. Pushing himself up, Shock gets to his feet. His body is battered, his mind worse, but he can move. He can find them a place to go. He's good at hiding. Or at least, he used to be.

Come on, he says, and waits for her to slide up his leg to her favourite spot on his torso. It doesn't feel like she's clinging to him any more. It feels like they're clinging to one another.

Curling an arm beneath her, around the sharp flinch of broken ribs, he limps off down a street that looks more like an ocean. Floating at last, but all wrong, like seaweed on the tide, directionless and heartbroken. He thinks of Sendai. Hallucinogenic oblivion. Birds singing in the trees. What was that dream he had of them falling silent one by one and dropping to the earth? That Shock, that dream of Sendai, has fallen silent at last. Dropped to the earth.

Feeling helpless, utterly hopeless, Shock looks down at Puss. She needs somewhere to go, and there's nowhere for him to take her. There hasn't been anywhere for the longest time, only the idea of somewhere. Ideas are ephemeral. Easily lost. And his was lost to him long before he realized it. All he's left with is this feeling, a hollowing combination of humiliation and profound shame over time lost, life wasted and potential squandered. But, as always, there's no way to articulate any of this to anyone. Not even to her. So he keeps on walking.

Puss tightens her tentacles on his chest, enough to grind his broken ribs together.

Wait, she says.

What for? he asks, still moving.

Our friends are coming for us. Not just Volk and Petrie. Amiga will come too.

The urgency in her voice, the plea, stops him in his tracks. You want to wait?

I don't think alone will work. You tried it for a long time, and it wasn't good. I'd like to try something different.

This was not what he expected to hear. Everything's changed so much. Before today he was Shock alone, hanging on by virtue of chemicals and delusions. Then he was Shock, Puss and Shark. Now just Shock and Puss, someone who is and is not him, with different ideas, different needs. Needs it would seem he has to give the same consideration he gives his own, regardless of the fact that he doesn't know how to cope with her difference. The thought is terrifying as much as it is liberating.

I'm scared.

I'm not.

Then can we be you today? Shock's trying to be flippant but it comes out more seriously than he'd intended, unnerving him.

Puss slides a little further up his chest to look him directly in the eyes.

We're me every day from now on, she says. We're you and me. We're us.

You're not me. He wants to take it back as soon as it pops out, but it's true.

Because I'm female, right? her tone is acidic, and filled with hurt. Did you ever stop to consider that I'm not male? That you might therefore be alien to me?

Guilt keeps on coming today, and never feels any less awful. The thought hadn't even occurred to try to see himself from her viewpoint. And it's no excuse for him to say he only knew she had one this morning. Here he is, apparently wanting to protect her, and he hasn't even paid her the common courtesy of trying to know her beyond the abstract concept of Puss, and all because she comes with a different personal pronoun. Talk about being an arsehole. He just won the prize.

Am I never going to stop feeling like an absolute shit around you?

Not if you continue to be one.

Sorry. The word is inadequate, but he says it nonetheless.

Don't apologize to me again, we've been there and it changed nothing. Tell me.

It's a demand, not a request and, in the wake of guilt, takes him off-guard. He's answering before he realizes the words are out, when it's too late to take them back.

How can you be female? It's like a betrayal. I feel like people will think I could have made a different choice, when I couldn't have.

To his endless surprise, she doesn't hate him. Instead he gets that tiny squeeze of reassurance.

I know, and you have to trust me when I say my choice does nothing to trivialize yours. I was created from you when you were barely formed. Parts of us overlap, and parts developed separately, yours IRL, mine in Slip. We are different. Now I have a question for you. Fairly important.

What?

You asked if we could be me today. You didn't want to mean it but you did, because you're scared of change. What scares you more, Shock? The difference between us, or going back to how you were?

Well that's easy. Or rather, it's not. It's just that he's been reduced to only one possible answer.

I can't go back.

Then you need to stop holding me out. We can't do this without each other. You aren't strong enough, and neither am I. Not even Shark was that strong.

I know.

So stop it, stop holding yourself back from me. I promise the only difference will be that this gets easier to cope with.

Shock's still not sure about that, but there was a question he had whilst walking away from the gold gathering in Josef's eyes. How much of himself does he control? It would seem he has his answer: everything. Puss can't force him to accept her, to begin to take the final emotional steps toward full integration. It's up to him. He has absolute autonomy to heal or to hurt them both. His is the key turned in the lock.

And so he unlocks it.

So what happens in the end?

An ex-Haunt and his Puss sit on a seat by a fountain waiting for their friends, holding on tight to one another. The sea is everywhere, within and without, endless and wide open. And on the avenue crowds of shell-shocked people sit side by side on blood-soaked ground, staring upward.

Watching their avis dance.

about the author

en Warom lives in the West Midlands with her three children, innumerable cats, a very friendly corn snake, and far, far too many books. She haunts Twitter as @RenWarom, and can be found on her YouTube channel, talking about mental health issues and, of course, books.

acknowledgments

My thanks go out to my agent, Jennifer Udden, without whom none of this would be possible. I'm also endlessly grateful to the team at Titan Books for championing my work, especially my patient and exacting editor, Cath Trechman.

I want to send out a huge 'you rock' to Colin Barnes, who beta read the heck out of this and gave great feedback as usual. And to Stephen Godden, sadly no longer with us. The best friend, finest writer, and most incisive beta reader a lady could wish for. Miss you, buddy. I'd also like to thank the rest of what was once the Writerlot crew for keeping me writing when I was about to give up, I count Writerlot's four years as some of the most fun writing I've ever had. Finally I need to thank my children, whose mother invariably has her nose in a book, whether she's reading or writing it. I'm sorry, kids, and we're totally going to leave the house this weekend, I promise. I just have to finish this one last paragraph...

virology

ren warom

Core is dark and Slip is everywhere, vital to everything that happens in the world and outside of anyone's control. Avis float the skies and their arrival will trigger a tide of rebellion against the system in Foon Gung.

The key is Shock Pao: within him lies the means to control Slip. Control Slip, control the world. Shock was a Haunt once, impossible to find, but he isn't anymore, and he's running out of places to hide…

praise for escapology

"A deeply immersive and thrilling trip into a terrifying future. I loved this book!"
Emma Newman, author *of Planetfall*

AVAILABLE JUNE 2017

For more fantastic fiction, author events, exclusive excerpts,
competitions, limited editions and more

VISIT OUR WEBSITE

titanbooks.com

LIKE US ON FACEBOOK

facebook.com/titanbooks

FOLLOW US ON TWITTER

@TitanBooks

EMAIL US

readerfeedback@titanemail.com